Praise for Secret Sister

"Secret Sister is compulsively readable. I defy anyone not to race through the pages to find out what happens to Cathy and Nick -- and Nick and Roxanne!"
 —*Patricia Gaffney*, New York Times Best Selling author of *The Saving Graces*

"Lovers of women's fiction have a new must-read! Secret Sister by Emelle Gamble has it all...romance, drama and suspense... I could not put it down."
 —*Beth Harbison*, New York Times Best Selling author of *Chose The Wrong Guy, Gave Him The Wrong Finger* and *Shoe Addicts Anonymous*

SECRET SISTER

EMELLE GAMBLE

SOUL MATE PUBLISHING
New York

SECRET SISTER

Copyright©2013

EMELLE GAMBLE

Cover Design by Ramona Lockwood

This book is a work of fiction. The names, characters, places, and incidents are the products of the author's imagination or are used fictitiously. Any resemblance to actual events, business establishments, locales, or persons, living or dead, is entirely coincidental.

All rights reserved. No part of this publication may be reproduced, stored in a retrieval system, or transmitted in any form or by any means (electronic, mechanical, photocopying, recording, or otherwise) without the priority written permission of both the copyright owner and the publisher. The only exception is brief quotations in printed reviews.

The scanning, uploading, and distribution of this book via the Internet or via any other means without the permission of the publisher is illegal and punishable by law. Please purchase only authorized electronic editions, and do not participate in or encourage electronic piracy of copyrighted materials.

Your support of the author's rights is appreciated.

Published in the United States of America by
Soul Mate Publishing
P.O. Box 24
Macedon, New York, 14502

ISBN: 978-1-61935-455-5
eBook ISBN: 978-1-61935-251-3

www.SoulMatePublishing.com

The publisher does not have any control over and does not assume any responsibility for author or third-party websites or their content.

For Allen Nuccio, my prince,

who always has my back,

and my heart.

For Olivia Rose Nuccio,

daughter and friend,

whose faith and support comfort my every day.

And for Philip,

who is in all ways my truest love.

Acknowledgements

With love and thanks to ….

The *Lifesavers* (Mary Blayney, Elaine Fox, Lavinia Kent, and Yvonne Pinney), critique group *extraordinaire*, dearest friends who helped me keep my head up and never let me down.

Char Chaffin, acquisition editor, whose efforts and constant encouragement made this book stronger, and this writer forever grateful.

Chapter 1

Saturday, July 9, 10:30 a.m.
Cathy and Roxanne

It was sunny and mild the July morning Roxanne and I headed up the state highway into the Verdugo Hills. But the Santa Anas were blowing in from the desert, and those aptly called *devil winds* rocked our car with gusts of heat and dust that caused tiny sparks of electricity to snap against my fingertips every time I touched my hair.

I looked forward to the Santa Anas each summer because they cleared every trace of smog from the vast L.A. basin and left the air sparkling. But that day they were weeks early and their intensity increased a sense of foreboding I'd awakened with.

I squeezed my hands together and glanced at the woman sitting next to me, for she was the true reason for my uneasiness.

My best friend and I should have been relaxed and chatty, but we hadn't been either lately. There was tension between us. She was distracted and distressed by calamity in her personal life and I felt at a loss to help.

Roxanne had recently broken up with the guy she'd been seeing for years, and her mood alarmed me. She had barely said a word at the front door when she picked me up, and nothing at all since we'd been in the car.

Slowly I turned my head from side to side, trying to ease the knot of anxiety in my neck. I reached up to massage my shoulder but the seatbelt held me snugly, so I undid it. The lock made a sharp click as it released.

"What's wrong?" Roxanne asked.

"Nothing." I spoke quietly. "Just a kink. I must have slept weird."

She snorted and shifted gears and the road rose higher in front of us.

I noticed then that she wasn't wearing lipstick. Roxanne always wore lipstick, a shade called *Dangerous When Red*. For her to have left the house without makeup of any kind was one more sign she wasn't in a good place. Though even without it, Roxanne was gorgeous.

I stared out the windshield and thought about how wrong the cliché was that drop-dead beauty guaranteed happiness. If it did, Roxanne would have been delirious from birth. She was so stunning that people stared at her wherever she went. Men and women and kids. Even animals liked her.

Wasp-waisted but voluptuously curvy, she had dark hair and chocolate brown eyes and possessed a laugh described in our high school yearbook as 'midnight sexy with whipped cream on top.' While that teenage compliment was hormone-fueled and extravagant, I had actually seen men stop in their tracks when they heard her laugh, noses in the air like bloodhounds intent on tracking her down.

I joked once that the only body parts of mine that were better looking than hers were my hands and feet. Roxanne laughed and gave me a hug, but we both knew it was true.

Our physical inequality could have made me envy or resent Roxanne, but I didn't. I'd loved her since she befriended me in seventh grade, and had never regretted it. Yes, she was ridiculously good looking, but she was also the most loyal friend a girl ever had.

I wondered if I should just ask her what I could do to help. Roxanne seemed oblivious to everything but what was going on inside her head. Whatever that was.

"What time is it?" she asked suddenly.

I glanced at my watch. "Ten-thirty. What time is your appointment?"

"Now."

"We'll be there in five minutes. Seth will wait."

She gripped the steering wheel tighter. "Hell with it. I'd rather go shopping this morning. It will do me more good than sitting in a doctor's office." Roxanne hit the brakes and steered toward the edge of the road.

"Wait a minute," I replied. "What are you doing?"

She brought the car to a full stop. "Can you dig out my cell and call Seth? Tell him I have to reschedule. His number is in my contacts."

"For heaven's sake, Roxanne! We're almost there. You can't cancel now."

"Yes, I can. I don't need to see him anyway. It won't help."

"You don't know that. And Seth will charge you for canceling. And you'll have to wait a month to get another appointment." I crossed my arms. "And by the way, I changed my plans with Nick because you asked me to come all the way out here with you today. Remember?"

"I know. You and hubby and 'date-day Saturday.'" She grabbed her sunglasses from the visor and stuck them on. "Sorry, but you'll have tonight, like you have every night with Nick. But today I get to buy you lunch. And some new jeans." She looked down at my legs. "What are you wearing anyway, Wranglers?"

"I love these jeans."

"Why?"

"What's wrong with them?"

"Nothing if you're forty and the mother of two." She craned her neck to see behind us and turned the steering wheel hard.

I clutched my stomach and felt a small bulge under my

tee shirt. I wasn't fat, but my jeans were too tight, though that wasn't the reason Roxanne had commented on them.

"Okay, my jeans are kind of frumpy. But you're trying to change the subject, which is that you've been a wreck for weeks. Don't you think it's time to get serious and get help for what's bugging you?" I put my hand on her shoulder.

She shrugged it off.

"Come on, Rox. You're suffering, but you always say Seth helps when you're feeling depressed. So go see him."

The car idled rough and another wave of devil winds rattled the windows.

Rox turned to me. "I'm not depressed, Cathy, I'm broken-hearted. Which is a normal way to feel considering I've lost the only man I ever really loved, isn't it?"

I lowered my voice. "No one thinks you're not normal."

"Then I don't need to see a shrink, do I?"

"I don't know what you need." I pointed toward the road. "But Dr. Seth might. He's that way. Let's go."

Rox sighed, but straightened out the wheel and stepped on the gas. The car fishtailed in the gravel along the road before jumping back up to speed.

"So you do think I need a shrink?" Her voice was flat.

"Seth isn't a shrink." He wasn't. He was a psychologist who used a holistic approach with his patients. Meditation. Exercise. Therapy for the mind, body, and soul.

"Okay, but all he wants to do is talk. I'm sick of myself. Too sick of myself to rehash everything I feel bad about."

"Then let him talk. He likes to talk. That's been my experience."

She stared straight ahead. "There's really no point. I know what's wrong. I want Michael. I want to get married and live happily ever after. Like you. I can't see how Seth can help with this, unless he knows someone who will pull a gun on Michael and order him to marry me or die."

This remark upped my nervousness. Roxanne's humor was usually wry, not morbid. "Well, if marriage is what you want, then you should consider changing your taste in men."

"My taste in men is fine. Michael is perfect for me; it's just that I'm not enough for him. If I were, he would have asked me to marry him by now." A sob caught in her throat. "I don't seem to be enough for any man."

"Come on, that's bull, and you know it. Before Michael, three different men asked you to marry them."

"None of them were Michael."

"No, they weren't. But hasn't Michael always said he didn't want to get married? Didn't you tell me Seth said you're picking the wrong man, out of the hundreds willing to date you, to punish yourself for something? You need to work with Seth and find out why you keep doing that."

"Oh, screw Seth! I'm sick of shrinks. My mom. Him. All five of them before Seth. Everybody has problems, I know. I just want the normal ones. The ones normal people solve. I could handle those. It's all these other flaws I have that get me down."

A warning flickered in my brain. For all her physical beauty, Roxanne was self-conscious about being treated for mental illness early in her life. She'd been diagnosed as bipolar before she was a teenager.

I wondered if Roxanne had gone off her medications. If so, the situation was serious. Roxanne had attempted to commit suicide twice in the past sixteen years. Both times after she'd stopped taking her antidepressants.

I rubbed my palms against my knees. "Look, don't get mad at me for asking, Rox, but have you been taking your meds?"

She snapped on the radio and filled the air with the Rolling Stones, who were in the midst of reminding us that we can't always get what we want.

I turned the music off. "Come on, talk to me, okay?"

Roxanne turned it back on and upped the volume.

I should have reacted with the anger I felt, but I didn't, because Roxanne was crying. And Roxanne rarely cries. I could count on one hand the times she's cried in my presence since we've been friends. Instead, I pinched the back of my hand to stay calm.

Seth was a few minutes away. All I had to do was get her there and hopefully he could stop this meltdown before it happened.

Ahead of us the road narrowed. "Don't judge all men by Michael," I yelled over Jagger. "That guy's an asshole."

He was. My mind flashed on one particularly uncomfortable 'Michael' memory. He hit on me at last year's New Year's Eve party. Nick was sleeping like a baby under the dining room table, and Roxanne was drunk, dancing like a madwoman outside on the patio with our friend, Bradley.

Michael walked up behind me and whispered, "Happy New Year's, Cathy." When I turned he kissed me on the lips, open-mouthed, his hands on my ass before I could register an objection. The image of a quick, hard toss in the bedroom we were standing next to had roiled through my mind like a shot of tequila, which I'd had way, way too much of.

For a second I had considered Michael on me. *In me.* I felt a physical jolt of lust as surprising as it was real. Then the party sounds shifted back into my brain, reminding me of who I was.

I put my hands against his chest and pushed. "Michael, don't be an asshole."

"You're begging for it, babe." He took my hand and pressed it on the bulge in his jeans. "Give me twenty minutes in the dark and you'll be a new woman." He pulled me into the bedroom and shut the door behind us.

"You're crazy!" I reached around to grab the doorknob but he held the door closed. "Michael, get out of my way. Roxanne's right outside, for Christ's sake."

"So?"

"So open the door."

"Is that the only reason, Cathy? Because you're friends with Roxanne?"

"You're insane. And I'm very married. Remember?" I waved my left hand, my tiny diamond glittering. "You know Nick and I don't play around."

"I don't know that." He kissed me again.

I slapped his face.

He didn't seem to feel it. "Tell yourself the truth at least. You want me and you know it." He grinned and walked out.

Now, I yelled, "Michael *really* is an asshole." I heard more disgust than anger in my voice.

"Okay. Don't rub it in." Roxanne snapped off the music.

"I'm not. I'm just trying to get through to you."

"Yes, you are rubbing it in. You always compare how Michael treats me to how Nick treats you."

"If I do, it's only to remind you that you don't have to settle for someone who cheats."

My words were tactless, but I didn't care. Michael had cheated on her for years. "Nick doesn't lie to me. I trust him, which is the most important part of a relationship. We don't have a perfect marriage, and you know that as well as anyone, but we get stronger together every day because we're true to each other. You deserve that kind of relationship, Rox. You deserve to be happy."

"No I don't." Roxanne cried harder.

When she cries she isn't beautiful. She looks like a sick kid, all swollen and blotchy. I put my hand on her arm and squeezed. "Come on now, don't cry. He's not worth it."

She sobbed louder and made the last turn toward Seth's office, veering onto Arroyo Crest.

"You'll feel better if you work through this with Seth," I continued. "You'll get your confidence back and enjoy the rest of the summer. Why don't you come stay at the house for a few days again, like you did last November? We'll watch *That Seventies Show*. Or *I Dream of Jeannie*. 'Nic at Night,' here we come."

"My life is more like *Night of the Living Dead*. Maybe someone needs to shoot me in the head and put me out of my misery." She didn't sound as if she was joking.

"Since when are you watching crap like that?"

"I love horror. Always have."

"You do not. You like American classics. *Casablanca. The Thin Man.* You've watched those twenty times with me."

"Tastes change. You don't know everything about me, Cathy."

"Really? Well, whatever you want to watch, I'm game. We'll sit on the sofa all night and be scared silly and Nick can make us blueberry waffles for dinner."

"I hate waffles."

"That I know is a lie. You love waffles. Last time you stayed at my place, you and Nick were up in the middle of the night eating them cold. Remember?"

Roxanne made a strangling sound.

I lifted my hand to pat her arm again but stopped midair when I noticed the speedometer. It registered 66 mph. In a 25 mph zone.

I pointed to the dashboard. "Hey, slow down. Even you won't be able to talk yourself out of a ticket going this fast."

"I'm the one driving the car," Roxanne yelled. "And why would you care if I got a ticket? Because it would take time out of your weekend? Do you actually care about *me* at all anymore? All you talk about is Nick, Nick, Nick. Who is so perfect. Who you spend *all* your spare time with. Don't pretend to care about me or my problems when you don't."

Her words cut deeply. While I hadn't made as much time for her as I used to, she was still a huge part of my life.

But maybe there had been too much talk about Nick. I suddenly felt terrible, realizing how smug I must seem. "Rox,

I don't pretend anything with you. I never have. You're my dearest friend, and you know that. Haven't you always said we're as close as secret sisters? Nothing's changed."

"I say a lot of things. And so do you. Just stop lecturing me, Cathy. And don't think you know everything. You don't. Not about men. Not about me."

"I never said I know everything."

"You act like you do!"

I sighed and crossed my arms. Somehow my caring about her was turning into a discussion of how I was letting her down. We said nothing for a few moments.

Roxanne wiped at her eyes and sniffled, then poked my arm. "New topic. So, do you like this blouse? It's new. Thirty percent off at Nordstrom's." There was regret in her voice.

The top was red-and-white striped silk, with a simple ruffle at the neckline. She looked like Jennifer Lopez's prettier, younger sister.

"It's gorgeous. Like you. How does that feel, anyway? Being more beautiful than any other woman in the room?"

Roxanne's voice was edgy with bitterness. "Trust me, dear friend, it's not often fun to be me, no matter how I look."

"I wish I were you, Lupeyloo," I said softly.

Roxanne tilted her chin up, surprised by my words, and I caught the shadow of a smile.

This dumb little verse was a line from a school play we'd both seen in middle school, a story about nerdy twelve-year olds who always want to be someone else. In the script, someone got leukemia or a flesh-eating disease or something, and the kids realize they were special just as they were. The play was hokey, but both of us had remembered the line to great laughter in high school. And we'd said it to one another a hundred times over the years.

Mostly me to her.

Rox tossed her sunglasses into the backseat. "I can't

remember the last time you said that to me, Cathy. You wouldn't really want to be me for a second. Would you?"

"I always want to be you. Look at you. Angelina Jolie would want to be you if she was sitting here."

"Don't lie. You never judge people by how they look, but how they treat other people. So fair and kind." Her voice was dreamy, but not particularly happy. "That's why everyone loves you. That's why Nick loves you. Why he's there to watch over you. Believe me, Cathy, it's *me* who would love to be *you*. I really would."

I had never heard such yearning in her voice. "You'll find the *right* man someday, Rox." *A man like Nick.* I kept that thought to myself.

"If I can't have Michael, I'm done with men. All men."

"Don't be crazy." Which was a dumb thing to say. I bit my lip.

"I wish I were you, Lupeyloo." Roxanne laughed then, but it sounded more like a gasp, or a cry.

I turned my eyes back to the road, thinking I should offer to come in with her to talk to Dr. Seth today, if Rox wanted me to. Maybe that would help. We'd done this in the past, given the doc an inside and outside view of Roxanne's aching heart. I opened my mouth to suggest it, but didn't get the words out.

Because that's when I saw the truck.

It was coming directly at us, forty yards ahead. Way, *way* too close. It veered to the middle of the road, as if the driver didn't see us.

I inhaled to scream and grabbed Roxanne's arm, remembering only then that my seatbelt was unfastened.

Roxanne cried out, "Oh my God!"

I thought, *Nick . . .*

She didn't swerve or brake and the truck struck us head-on. The noise of the impact was crueler than I ever imagined a sound could be. The windshield split with the sound of ten tons of ice falling on pavement, the horn blared, the airbags burst with an explosion that burned my eyes and smacked me as senseless as my stepfather did the time he broke my cheekbone.

I smelled gasoline and rubber and hot steel.

The car skidded and flipped sideways and slammed into the granite mountain beside the road. I was thrown through jagged glass and pain poured over me like napalm.

My arm was wrenched behind me as the asphalt flayed skin and meat off my body and I skidded like a human Dunlop, finally cracking my forehead against a curb. As I lay there, a dizzy, faraway feeling like I remembered from the dentist's office enveloped me.

My ears bled and my teeth were in pieces. I couldn't swallow. Or breathe. I sank into blackness, one hundred, ninety-nine . . .

And I floated upward. Below me, the blue Chevy lay on its side. I saw my body on the ground nearby, sprawled and unmoving.

My arm—*my arm?*—rested several yards away in a flood of red running down the middle of the street.

Suddenly, a dark-haired woman grasped my shirt and pulled me closer to the sky. *Don't look down.* She didn't speak aloud but I heard her anyway.

Higher I rose, into fog and blue stars as chimes and flutes pinged around me. A whoosh of air carried me toward the opening of a tunnel.

I was so cold.

The woman whispered, "Cathy, don't be scared. I need to tell you something."

My mother died when I was nine. I couldn't remember exactly what she looked like, but this woman could be her.

"No. Leave me alone, I'm not going!"

"You have to listen. I'm going away." Her voice was so loud. "But I want to do something for you."

"Don't touch me." I flailed wildly to push her away. But I had no arm.

The woman laced her fingers in my hair. Her face had turned away from me but I knew she was crying. I could hear her thinking. She wanted to make things right. Beg my forgiveness for not telling me her secret.

The light at the opening of the tunnel got bright, too bright to look at, too bright to bear.

I wish I were you, Lupeyloo.

The words were a chant, a lullaby. A dirge.

I felt so cold. Dead cold.

Then, I felt nothing.

Chapter 2

Saturday, July 9, 3 p.m.
Nick

When I got to the hospital, I abandoned my car in front of the emergency room entrance and ran to the door. I dropped my keys, picked them up and then dropped them a second time.

I tripped trying to grab them with my shaking hands.

"Fuck!" I yelled as I banged my knees against the asphalt and my elbow on the curb. But the pain of the fall didn't register. I didn't feel anything but the presence of fear.

I thought I had experienced fear before in my life, but I had not. I'd lived with apprehension and embarrassment; I've worried about the ordinary slings and arrows of life, had personal failings drive me to despair.

I have worried I would never rise above, or move beyond, moral weaknesses, especially when I was drinking.

But I had never really experienced fear until now.

Fear, with a capital 'F,' is the real thing. He's a vicious, merciless prick that knocks you on your ass and shrieks that he can, and will, take everything from you, forever. He's a hurricane that pummels you and all you can do is hold on and try to wait him out, praying he will go away.

But Fear doesn't go away that easy. Fear hooked into me the moment I got that cliché of a phone call, and paralysis of brain and nerve endings was my only defense to Fear's presence.

You see, my wife is my life. Poetically corny, but true as a mother's kiss. And I was told in that ridiculous call, curtly, that the woman I have been devoted to for years, first as a geeky high school jerk, lately as a man exultantly secure in knowing that I'd somehow, *Thank God*, married the right woman, was 'seriously injured in a car accident and I needed to come right away.'

But Fear didn't repeat the words 'seriously injured.' Fear told me she was dead.

Dead. *Cathy was dead.*

Inside the hospital, I stared without blinking at the police officer who murmured, "I'm so sorry, your wife is dead."

Fear was right.

I stood silently when the nurse standing beside the cop pressed her condolences to my sleeve.

"How can she be dead?" I wrestled my arm away from her and wanted to slug the cop.

He saw this in my face and his voice changed. "I'm sorry, Mr. Chance." He told me Cathy had been pronounced at the scene. He told me the EMTs had used the Jaws of Life to pry her friend from the car.

Jaws of Life? Seriously injured?

Motherfuckers.

I may have said this aloud.

"Come with me, Mr. Chance." The nurse's voice was practiced. "I'll take you to your wife."

"It's not my wife," I shouted.

The nurse hurried off. I followed, feeling neither blood nor bone in my moving body. A dull whooshing filled my ears when I entered the room where Cathy, my Cathy, lay. She was on a metal table, covered with white sheets, like in a TV show. Her blonde hair hung off the edge, full of debris, dried blood, dirt. She was wearing one of her favorite turquoise earrings, the ones I'd bought for her in New Mexico last Christmas.

When she saw them, Cathy had said, "Oh, we can't

afford those." And we couldn't, but she wanted them so I bought them for her.

She enjoys presents more than anyone I've ever met. Wrapped and bowed and served up with a flourish, or tucked into her hand, or handed over by a sales clerk, she loves them. When she was a little kid she'd never had presents after her mother died. So I make sure she always has bunches of them.

Tears stung my eyes like ashes. I rubbed them, my hands cold.

The nurse whispered, "It's shocking, I know. Would you like me to stay?"

"No, no, I don't need you," I mumbled.

The hospital people said Cathy had lost a limb. Her arm. 'Lost a limb,' like she was a goddamned lemon tree. But someone must have reattached it, for the shape of both of her arms was visible under the blanket. I had the thought I should check, lift up the sheet and be sure they'd attached it to her, so she wouldn't lose it, because . . .

Because she would need it?

I made a noise like a dry heave.

"What can I do?" the nurse asked.

"Go away."

"I'll leave you alone then." She touched my sleeve and made her escape.

Leaving me. Alone.

Fear left, too. He'd done his job.

The noise in my ears got louder as I moved closer to Cathy. She had some dried blood on her neck. Her chin was scratched, her cheeks pitted from their contact with the road. Her eyelashes threw a shadow on her skin, which was not the right color.

I touched her cold face. Cathy seemed pressed into the table as if held by massive magnets, her body sculpted like stone under the thin hospital sheets.

I stepped back. "Cathy." Tears burned my face and I regained some feeling in my arms, which tingled as blood returned to my veins.

"Cathy, don't be dead," I pleaded.

But she didn't answer me.

An hour later in the hospital waiting room, Cathy's friends from work showed up first, then my mom and sister, then our friend Bradley Chandler.

Cathy hadn't spoken to anyone in her family for twelve years, and I didn't know how to find them. 'Them' included a great-aunt on her mother's side, and the stepfather, not that he was really family. Besides, I think he was dead.

Bradley said he would try to locate someone. He's a human GPS who can find anyone on the planet if you give him a name to work with. He hugged me before he walked away in search of some quiet workspace, a laptop folded under his muscular right arm.

Cathy's friend, Vera Apodaca, the secretary at the school where Cathy taught, was crying like a kid lost at the zoo. The principal of St. Anne's, a black woman who had never seemed to like me, was hugging Vera and wiping her own eyes with a pink tissue. A man, whom I numbly recognized as Freddy, Vera's husband, walked over to the little group of mourners and joined in, his big face sad, his shoulders sagging.

Freddy and I had almost come to blows at last year's school Christmas party. He was an arrogant and dishonest son of a bitch, but my reasons for wanting to cold cock him didn't matter anymore.

Our eyes met and I turned away. They were obviously talking about me, but I couldn't make myself get up and cross the waiting room to speak to them. I sat with my mom and sister while they called people on my sister's cell phone.

I heard my mom say, "They said she died instantly. She was thrown from the car."

I put my head in my hands and squeezed my eyes closed as tight as I could, before opening them again. I saw funny bright lights and starburst-type spots, but it made the noise decrease a little in my ears. I suddenly remembered I used to do this in high school, in Algebra II, when I didn't have a clue about the homework. The behavior usually got me called on as soon as I looked up.

I looked up.

"How are you doing, Nick?" the principal asked. She stood in front of me.

"Okay, Mrs. Cordell, thank you." I got to my feet and extended my hand.

"Call me Althea, hon." She grabbed me around the shoulders and pulled me against her bony chest. She was tall, about six feet, and thin as beef jerky. I nearly knocked foreheads with her.

"Thanks for coming here, Althea. How did you hear about the accident?" Though she still held onto me, I took a step back to give us both room to breathe.

"Roxanne's mother called. She told us about Cathy. It's such a shock." Althea Cordell crossed herself and tears welled in her small eyes. "I'll never know why God takes such sweet angels from us. But in his wisdom we cannot question. Only celebrate." She rested her head on my shoulder and patted my back furiously. "Have you seen Roxanne?"

"No." The scent of stale popcorn, probably from the cafeteria, reached my nose. I cleared my throat, feeling like throwing up. "She's in a coma."

"Yes, yes," Althea mumbled. Her tears splashed across her brown skin. "They won't let anyone in to see her. Freddy checked. But the doctors are hopeful she'll wake up. They're watching for brain swelling. That's what they worry about."

Her voice dropped. "And mental impairment. They worry about that. She wasn't breathing when they pulled her from the car, but she started again once they did CPR." Althea dabbed at her eyes. "She's been blessed by above."

I couldn't answer. I had heard all those details about my wife's friend from one of the staff. Gently I led the principal over and introduced her to my mother. They fell into each other's arms and moved back to where the secretary was unleashing a fresh bout of tears against her husband's chest.

He looked at me but I turned away and focused on my sister, Zoë. She was staring at me.

"Was Roxanne driving the car?" my little sister asked.

"Yes."

"Is she going to die?"

"No. The doctors say she has a severe concussion, but she should pull through."

Zoë raised one eyebrow. She was seventeen and had always been an odd duck of a kid. People never knew what to make of her. Zoë is grouchy. And a little spooky. A few months back she told me she heard things in the night and saw things in people other people couldn't see.

I told her she was a fruitcake and to stop watching old Demi Moore movies with Cathy and lay off the pot. But I think Zoë does have a sixth sense about things, about people. My parents adopted her when she was five months old, and I was twelve. I remember when I first looked at her, she stared at me like she was deciding if I could measure up to brother material.

When I said, "Hello sweet baby," she smiled and the sun came out forever. We've loved each other since that second.

"I hope she dies," Zoë whispered.

Her words jolted me. "No, you don't. Don't say that."

"Yes, I do. I hate Roxanne."

"Zoë."

"I love Cathy." Zoë licked her chapped lips. She stared down at the magazine. "Why wasn't she wearing her seat belt? She always wears her seat belt."

Zoë was right.

"I don't know." Tears burned my eyes and I felt like screaming.

"I don't think she's really dead."

"She is, Zoë. I just saw her."

"Maybe if I saw her, I could believe it, too."

"I don't want you to see her." I squeezed her shoulder. "She wouldn't want you to see her like she looks now."

"Right! Like you know what she wants now." Her voice shook. "We have to have her cremated. She always said she never wanted to be buried. She's claustrophobic. You remember that, right?"

I shuddered. *Burn Cathy?* The room began to spin. "I haven't made any plans yet."

"Please don't put her in a box." Zoë's voice was a low wail. "In fact, we better go to the morgue right now. If they've put her in one of those goddamned drawers, we've got to get her out. That will freak her to be in a drawer."

My mother and the principal were staring at us.

"Come on with me." I took Zoë by the hand and led her out of the waiting room and into the hall. There was a popcorn cart parked outside the cafeteria. A few greasy bits lay inside the glass compartment, oily streaks on the glass, paintings of huge, maniacal clowns cavorting on the side panels. I fought to not throw up and hurried Zoë away from the cart and past the cafeteria entrance and out the back exit of the hospital.

It was light outside. For a moment we both stood looking up at the blue sky in surprise. I blinked and walked toward my car. It was where I had left it, in the middle of the emergency entrance driveway. Across the way, a uniformed cop was standing by his police cruiser, watching us. I couldn't see his eyes behind his shades, but I felt like he was holding off giving me a ticket, sensing a catastrophe he didn't want to get involved with.

We got in my car and I started the engine and then looked at my sister. Her face seemed painted on, white and motionless.

"Where to, Zoë?" I put the car into gear, but my fingers were numb on the steering wheel.

She shook her head and flipped the radio on, filling the car with the sounds of NPR's newscast.

Cathy is a news hound. She knows everything about politics, junk factoids about actors, the latest about sports, especially golf. She loved Tiger Woods, was crushed when he crashed his life and lost his family and the world's respect. But she forgave him. Pretty much before anyone else did.

We're going to see him play in a tournament next month in San Diego.

No. We're not.

My hands ached and I flexed my fingers, which were starting to go numb. I didn't know what to do next.

Zoë switched to an oldie station. The Beatles were singing about a girl who was going away because she had a ticket to ride.

I started to cry then. My mouth hung open and the contents of my nose ran down my chin; my chest heaved with gut sobs. The car slowed to about ten miles an hour.

Zoë snapped off the radio. "Nick, pull over and let me drive."

She didn't have her driver's license. But I pulled over in the middle of the street. My little sister ran around the car and motioned me to move. She settled in next to me and handed me a tissue and kissed me on the head like she was my mother.

A horn sounded behind us. Zoë flipped the finger at

the guy who honked as she barreled out of the parking lot, heading for the McDonald's near our house.

My house with Cathy.

There was a long takeout line. We got in it.

"I need something to drink," Zoë said.

"Okay."

Fear breathed on my neck. He was back. He is eight feet tall and his eyes are blood red and he has a forked tongue and he said in a raspy voice that he was moving in for a while.

I knew then that this day wasn't a bad dream.

I'd lost her. I'd lost Cathy. I should have stopped this from happening.

I could have. I'd asked her to stay home with me, suggested we go back to bed and make love and then I would take her out to lunch. Mexican. She loves Mexican food. I asked her not to go out with Roxanne, but she said she had to, that it was really important.

I shuddered and pushed thoughts of Roxanne away.

If I had been a better husband, I would have insisted she choose me over her friend. It would have shifted the reality of the last hours. Cathy would be home with me. Fixing dinner. Smiling at me over a glass of wine.

With that thought, my body started to shake. I knew it was absurd to think I could have made Cathy do anything she didn't want to do. She never did anything unless she wanted to. When we were sixteen and first in love, I'd begged her to come live with my family and get away from her drunk son-of-a-bitch stepfather.

But she wouldn't. She said she had to stay and take care of her new kitten, her first pet. She said she had promised the cat she would never let anything bad happen to it. "It needs me," she'd said. And my mother was allergic to cats. Cathy had giggled about that, how we'd have my mother sneezing all day and night if we tried to hide the cat in my room.

I shut my eyes and tried to remember the sound of Cathy's laugh.

I couldn't.

"She can't be dead," I sobbed.

Zoë sat beside me, rhythmically hitting her forehead against the steering wheel. She pulled up to the takeout window, but didn't order. Instead, she floored the car and we headed back out onto the road.

Chapter 3

Monday, July 18, 1 p.m.
Roxanne's Hospital Room

When I 'woke up'—strange words to use after being unconscious for what was surely days, not hours—I felt remarkably lucid. Which is to say, I opened my eyes and saw and understood that I was in a hospital bed, there were nurses working in the area outside my glassed-in room, and I was hooked to an I.V. and some other kind of machine.

I didn't know the story of how I got here, but assumed it was bad. I remembered hearing, somewhere, that I had been in a terrible car accident, but I was blank to any other details.

For instance, I didn't know my name.

I examined the contents of my brain and started a list of unknown things. Where was I? No clue. What day was it? I looked outside and saw blue sky. Zero. I was blank to the most basic of information.

My chest tightened and a roar began in my head. *Don't panic*. I gulped air, blinked; fought to stay awake.

I had to pee and tried to call out for help, but the only sound I made was a gasp. Then I peed, and realized I was hooked up to a catheter. I closed my eyes and sighed. I remembered when I was four years old, a million years ago, my mother telling me it was okay that I'd wet the bed. She would wash the sheets. No big deal.

"Roxanne? Roxanne, are you awake?"

The voice was insistent but unfamiliar. I felt the pressure of a strange hand on my arm, opened my eyes, and looked into the face of a black woman, dressed as a doctor, standing beside the hospital bed.

"Hi," I said. It sounded like, "aaah." My vocal cords were not functioning very well.

The woman's expression changed from surprised to all business. She put her hand on my face, flashed a light at my eyes and, when I blinked, she nodded. "How do you feel?"

Like I've been hit by a truck. I cleared my throat. She must really be a doctor. Good, because my head hurt so bad I thought I would faint from the pain. I groaned and shut my eyes.

"Why?" I asked. The noise I made came out like, "gaaa."

"Roxanne. Roxanne Ruiz. Do you know where you are?"

I didn't recognize that name. In my brain I saw a face. A kind face, smiling. A great looking guy with strong arms and blue eyes.

I had no idea who he was.

"Aahhh," I said, this time louder, then moaned in surrender.

The doctor patted my shoulder. "Rest, my dear. Don't try to talk. I'll be right back. Your mother is here."

That's not possible.

I told myself to sleep.

When I woke up the second time, I hurt in more places than I have ever hurt in my life. I groaned and only then noticed there were people in my hospital room.

A middle-aged woman with red hair and glasses, an older lady with a gray pixie cut wearing a sweatshirt that said, "Palm Springs is for Lovers," and a very hot, dark-haired guy with his arms crossed over his chest sat in a cluster of chairs opposite my bed. The man's eyes were closed, as if he were napping. The red-haired woman was staring at me; the older lady was reading the *Los Angeles Times.*

As soon as she realized I was awake, the redhead bolted toward my bed. "Oh, my God! Roxanne's awake! Oh my God, someone get the doctor!"

At her words the older woman joined her by my bedside, tears streaming down her powdered skin. The commotion woke up the guy, who stood and grasped the metal bars at the end of my bed.

"Hey doll, how are you feeling?" he asked.

I stared back at the three expectant faces and felt absolutely nothing. I did not recognize them, any of them, in any way.

"I'm sorry." My voice was all rasps and dry phlegm. I wanted to add, 'Would you all please go away,' because I suddenly realized I wasn't wearing panties under the flimsy little hospital gown. Entertaining strangers without panties felt very precarious.

"Poor baby, don't be sorry. It isn't your fault. Oh God, I'm so glad you had your seat belt on. It saved your life." The redhead started to cry, too, and grasped my shoulder as she collapsed against the bedside. The older woman patted her on the back and beamed at me. She started to laugh and cry at the same time. "She's awake, Michael. She's going to be fine. Roxanne is okay!"

"Are you okay, Roxanne? Do you remember what happened? The accident?" The guy called Michael smiled as he asked these questions, but there was doubt in his face. Doubt and something else. Guilt.

Guilt? What the heck was that all about? Did *he* cause me to be in the hospital?

I didn't understand any of this. And I really didn't want to. I pulled the blanket tight against me and closed my eyes. I didn't have enough energy to be polite. Or curious. I wondered briefly if that was how I have always been.

"Roxanne, do you remember the accident?" the older woman said.

"I don't," I whispered. "I don't remember anything."

Even with my eyes closed, I felt their shock in waves rolling toward me. They knew what I meant. I didn't remember anything or anyone. I didn't remember them.

I wet my lips and wished the doctor would return and make them all leave. They seemed nice. Caring. But whoever they were, whatever the story with this 'Roxanne' they cared so much about, it was too hard to deal with right now. I felt a flash of panic.

I longed for sleep and squeezed my eyes tight, as if I were a child.

"How are we doing in here?" a voice asked.

"Dr. Badu," the redhead said. "Roxanne is awake. But I don't think she recognizes us! You said when she came out of the coma she would be okay. She is going to be okay, isn't she?"

I relaxed. *Dr. Badu, right, that's her name*. The pretty doctor. Dr. Badu, it said on the tag on her white doctor's coat. *I like her.* I kept my eyes closed. Surely the good doctor would make them all leave if I kept my eyes closed.

"How are you doing?" Dr. Badu asked close to my ear.

My lids fluttered open. She looked into my eyes as if trying to see my thoughts.

Dr. Badu patted my arm and said in a firm voice, "Okay, everyone. We need to clear out and let Roxanne get some rest. Mrs. Haverty, Mrs. Haverty, Michael, why don't we talk in my office."

Mrs. Haverty and Mrs. Haverty? Both the women visiting were named Mrs. Haverty? This was hilarious. I started to chortle; my throat swelled and a huge, rough laugh burst out of my mouth.

I kept laughing, which was painful, and struggled to breathe. What was wrong with the world? I had no clue who I was, despite all these people calling me 'Roxanne,' and yet there were two women in my room who had the same name. Was my name Mrs. Haverty, too? That would be hysterical! I covered my mouth and rolled over on my side, wincing in the midst of my giggles as the needle in my IV pinched my vein.

"What's wrong with her?" the man asked. He sounded nervous.

"This is a common reaction to the drugs she's been given. And to the stress she's been under," Dr. Badu replied. "She's been unconscious for most of the last several days. It's going to take a while for her to get her emotions under control."

I laughed louder and felt like I would explode. My body screamed in pain, but I couldn't stop. I gasped, choking on my laughter.

"Can't you give her something for this?" Michael asked. "She sounds psycho."

"Michael, please!" the redhead chided. "Roxanne uses humor to diffuse things when she's tense. Surely you remember that." She turned to the doctor. "So this is a good sign, right, Dr. Badu?"

"Come on, everyone, let's leave her alone now. Follow me," the doctor ordered in a stern voice.

One of the Mrs. Havertys squeezed my foot. "I'll be back later, honey."

Great. We'll have a meeting of the Mrs. Haverty Club. Hysterical laughter started again and I felt like I might gag.

The group shuffled out. After a few more belly laughs, I rolled onto my back and tried to get a grip. *Start remembering something useful. Like your name. Because surely it isn't something as fussy as 'Roxanne.'*

Moments later, I took a breath and looked down at my body. It was good. Nice breasts, flat stomach. I touched my hair. It felt like someone else's hair, very coarse. I noted my hands. They looked competent but were kind of wide and mannish. There was a mirror on the table beside the bed.

I picked it up. A stranger blinked back at me. Brown

eyes. Sharp nose. Full lips. Pretty. Actually, beautiful. Wow, this was a surprise. Though the image was no one I knew.

Nausea roiled through my stomach. I put the mirror in the drawer and slammed it shut.

A nurse stuck her head in the door. "Everything okay?"

"Peachy." My voice didn't sound like it belonged to a very nice person.

Wonderful. I'm beautiful and bitchy. Whoever I am, I'm a cliché. My heart raced and one of the monitors started to blip. I willed myself to be calmer.

What was this mental blankness? What had happened to me, whoever the hell I was? Amnesia? Giggles welled up again and I took several deep breaths. This wasn't funny. It was terrifying.

I'd heard about amnesia, read books about it, seen *The Bourne Identity* while Matt Damon bounced around the world not knowing what name his mother had given him. But I'd never known a real person with this affliction.

For a moment the terror receded and it felt kind of cool and exciting. Whatever my life had been, maybe I could now have a new one, like a movie.

Only the movie *was* my life, and no one had shown me the script. What if it was a horror flick?

Panic, tamped down for a few moments, galloped up my spine and I no longer felt like laughing. I felt like running. "What am I supposed to do now?" I asked the empty room. My voice sounded crazy.

Great. Pretty and bitchy and what had that dark-haired man said? 'Psycho?' I sighed and peed into the little bag. And started to cry.

I awoke and fell back to sleep several more times, had a bath in bed, had my hair washed in bed, and found that it was impossible to stand on my own two feet, which seemed odd since they were chunky and looked like they could hold up a piano.

The young nurse who helped me do all these bed tasks told me not to worry about my lack of strength. "If you don't walk for just three days you start to lose body mass and muscle. After a week, most people can't even take a few steps. You've been out nine days. But you'll get there!"

She was cheerful and cute, but she wanted to talk more than I did. I nodded in a noncommittal way.

"So, can I get you anything else?" Her tag said her name was 'Carin.'

"Ice cream?" I asked.

"I'll check," Carin said, her bright smile beaming.

A few moments later Dr. Badu came in my room, accompanied by a short, dark-skinned man with a cultured British accent.

"Hello, I'm Dr. Patel," he said with a nod.

"Dr. Patel is a psychiatric resident. He specializes in head trauma injuries," Dr. Badu explained. "He would like to do a preliminary assessment with you before we make any recommendations about treatment."

She was watching me, measuring my response in some 'doctor way' I couldn't work out.

"I can't walk."

"No, you can walk, Roxanne," Dr. Badu assured. "Your muscles are just weak from spending so long in bed. We had you strapped to a trauma board for two days. And you were heavily sedated once we were certain you had no brain injuries. We didn't know for sure if you had spinal damage. But you are going to be fine. All you have is two cracked ribs. And stitches in your legs. You're very fortunate to have no permanent injuries."

My fingers found the heavy tape on the left side of my ribcage. I was aware of bandages on my legs, my knees, and something on my rear end.

"I have something on my bottom," I said.

Dr. Badu nodded, as if I'd given the right answer to a geography question. "Yes, yes. A burn. From the accident. On your right buttock cheek."

I chuckled, felt hysteria returning; covered my mouth. Dr. Patel narrowed his eyes and stroked his chin as he looked at Dr. Badu. For several moments no one said anything.

Laughing at the words 'right buttock cheek' must be a symptom of something bad.

"The burn is healing nicely," Dr. Badu offered. "The dressing needs to stay on a while longer. And you may need some plastic surgery. But you'll be good as new very soon."

I cleared my throat. "Then what?"

More silence.

"You'll go home. Your mother thinks you should stay with her, but that will be totally up to you."

I pictured 'home.' No image came to mind at first, and then I visualized a large white house. With pillars and huge oaks, full of weeping Spanish moss. I realized it was "Tara," from *Gone with the Wind*. I met Dr. Patel's dark eyes.

Since I doubted I lived in a Pre-Civil War colonial, I moved on. "What about work? What do I do, by the way?"

Dr. Badu looked happy at this question. "You're a teacher. Third grade. But it's still summer, so you've got a little time to do nothing but take care of yourself."

"Do you remember who you are?" Dr. Patel asked, all serious face and penetrating stare. "Do you remember the car accident?"

I shook my head and began to cry, though I did not feel sad. By that I mean, no pang over a specific image, thought, recollection or memory ran through my mind or heart, causing despair. Crying was a reflex, unhooked from emotion.

Dr. Badu murmured something to Dr. Patel I couldn't

make out. "I'll be back in the morning," he said. "We'll start your interview then. Rest now, Roxanne."

The two doctors left my room. I was glad they were gone. I didn't want to do an "interview" now, or ever, for that matter. What the hell did all this mean anyway? They were going to interview me, and if I really had amnesia, would they keep me in the hospital until I remembered enough? What was enough?

What if I never remembered anything?

My heartbeat sped up and the machine beeped. I squinted through the glass wall and saw Carin listening intently to some kind of instructions Dr. Badu was giving her.

Suddenly I thought of an old, black-and-white television show on the Nickelodeon channel. *Hogan's Heroes*, about POWs in a funny concentration camp. I might not recall my own life, but I was sure I could repeat verbatim episodes of this TV show. Even though I found myself thinking I hated the concept. Black humor notwithstanding, there was simply nothing funny about the Nazis with the possible exception of their marching style. 'Goose-stepping,' it was called. A giggle tickled my throat.

I was straying. *Okay, concentrate. So, does my memory of 'Hogan's Heroes' mean I'm German? Or a soldier?*

I fought against the return of hysteria. I love apple strudel. I wished I had one. But I couldn't remember anything about who I was. Not a name, age, not the teaching thing, not the name 'Roxanne.' I sat up straighter in bed and pictured Michael, the hot guy from earlier. My body didn't react when I thought of him. I imagined having sex with him, but I didn't know what he might look like naked. Had we slept together?

I needed information. Especially certain information, such as how one cured amnesia. Because I urgently wanted to remember everything. Anything.

The image of that other man I had thought of earlier shimmered in my mind like a mirage. I couldn't see his face, only his back and shoulders. He was lying in bed, facing away from me, and I longed to touch those broad, smooth shoulders. I looked at my hand. No ring. So, could I be married? *Not sure*.

But I knew I liked apple strudel. Laughter rolled out from me in waves. Oh, God.

Do I believe in God?

I squirmed and put my hand over my mouth and after a moment, my laughter stopped. I listened to the quiet room, and the noisy hospital outside. I heard metal carts and footfalls and people talking. Lots of them. And voices over loudspeakers. And chiming elevators.

I was hot, yet shivered. My hands shook uncontrollably and I stuck them under the covers. I began to wonder if I was dreaming. Or if I was not real. Maybe I was on television.

I stared hard at the corridor where I could see Carin working behind the counter. I didn't see any cameras. I closed my eyes.

"I've got your ice cream," Carin announced from the doorway.

I opened my eyes. "Goody."

Carin tilted her chin at that remark, like a hen sensing a fox lurking nearby. She settled herself beside my bed, unwrapped the ice cream, fussed with napkins and utensils, and watched while I ate. She chatted about her brother, Jacey, who was graduating from med school next month, and about how proud everyone in the family was of him.

I kept picturing her with the *Hogan's Heroes* men. Someone named "Klink." A stupid bad guy. And a nice black guy. And "Hogan" himself, all smirky cute.

I switched off the TV show in my brain and concentrated on gulping bites of ice cream as I planned my next move.

Dabbing at my mouth with a napkin, I met Carin's gaze with what I hoped was a sane expression. "Can I ask you a couple of things, Carin?"

"Sure." Her blue eyes widened. "Anything."

"Did someone die in the car accident I was in?"

Neither of us knew where this question came from, but I hid my surprise better than she did.

Her mouth fell wide open, as if hinged at her chin. "Oh."

"Is that a yes?"

She jumped to her feet. Her arm hit the dinner tray across my bed, sending stuff careening in the air. Ice cream, tissues, a brush and my carton of apple juice went flying. Carin scrambled to pick things up, apologizing.

I kept my eyes on her. "Who was it, Carin? Who died in the accident?"

"I'm not supposed to talk to you about that." Carin clutched the ice cream trash against her nurse's uniform, which had teddy bears and crescent moons patterned on it.

"Why not?"

"Why don't I go get Dr. Badu?"

I grabbed her wrist and squeezed. "Did I kill someone? Is that what's going on here? Who did I kill?"

Dr. Badu appeared at the door like a genie. "Carin, why don't you clean up this stuff and leave Roxanne and me alone for a few minutes."

I let Carin go. I felt like I was going to vomit. And then I did. The nurse grabbed for the pink vomit catcher, and managed to get some of it in the plastic container. She wiped my mouth with a wet washcloth.

"I hope you feel better, honey." She hurried out, streaks of vanilla ice cream gunk and vomit across her uniform, water in her eyes.

I felt horrible then, about everything. Especially about Carin. And the guys in *Hogan's Heroes*.

I started to chortle again, much to my own and Dr. Badu's alarm. When I looked at her I imagined a green-tinged aura around her.

"So, who did I kill?" I demanded.

I was sure Dr. Badu was going to say 'your mother,' or 'three orphan babies,' or 'a dozen nuns,' but instead she gave me a steadying look.

She clasped my hand. "A week ago last Saturday you were driving a car. A truck struck you head-on, from across the median. The driver was drunk. He was not injured badly. He's in jail. Your friend, Cathy Chance, was sitting beside you in the front seat."

Roaring filled my head, as if I was being swallowed by the ocean. *Chance. Cathy. Cathy Chance.* The names pinged against my brain, but bounced off. "Where were we going?"

Dr. Badu thought for a second. "Lunch. And a doctor's appointment of some kind, I think your family said."

My head and heart pounded in unison. I lay back on the pillows. Grief stabbed in my stomach as I considered how upset, how frightened, the people who were in my room earlier must have been. Worrying about me. And this Cathy person. "Who were the people in here earlier? The women?"

"One is your mother, Betty Haverty. The other is your grandmother, Ruth. Ruth is Betty's mother."

"My mother has a different name than I do?"

"Yes, I guess so."

"But my name is Ruiz?"

"Yes. Your mother said she and your father were divorced when you were an infant."

"Where's Ruiz? My father?"

"I don't know," Dr. Badu replied. She watched me for a few moments. "The man who was with them is Michael Cimino. He's your friend."

I frowned. "Boyfriend?"

"I'm not sure. I think he may be an ex-boyfriend. Your mother said something to that effect."

"That woman is not my mother." The words jumped out of my mouth.

"You don't remember her?" Dr. Badu cocked her head to the side.

Panic returned, swelling into a bubble that enveloped me. My tongue stuck to my teeth. "No, no I don't. The guy, Michael, is very good-looking."

"Yes, I'd say he is."

"But I don't like him much."

She nodded. "That may be why he's an 'ex.'"

I blinked away more tears and felt sadness, though I didn't know why, and then fear.

"Is Cathy, is my friend, is she okay?"

"No. I'm sorry."

I knew she was going to say that, but I trembled with shock at her words. The greenish tint I'd imagined surrounding Dr. Badu darkened to lavender, like a light bulb about to burn out. I saw rainbows in the space around her. I spoke louder, but I couldn't hear my own voice clearly. "What's wrong with her?"

"She's dead, Roxanne. I'm very sorry. But Cathy Chance was killed in the accident. She wasn't wearing her seatbelt."

I stared out the window as the room around me disappeared. Far away I heard a siren, felt the wind hot and dusty in my face, saw clouds and blue sky. But not a pretty one, not a summer sky above the beach. It was a sky above a forest fire. Dark and sooty clouds, full of ash, the blue a frantic pool of heat.

I panted, struggling to stay conscious. "She's not dead," I said. "She's not dead."

"I'm sorry, but she is," Dr. Badu said gently. "She was pronounced dead at the scene."

The roar in my brain overwhelmed all other sound and the room started a lazy spin. I broke into a sweat and pushed the blankets and sheets away; tried to stand.

But I collapsed on the cold floor and vomited again, a lot of fluid. My throat felt scalded as the injury to my ribs moved front and center in the pain parade. I could hardly move. Dr. Badu was on the floor beside me, holding me by the shoulders. Another person in a uniform came in to help.

My skull hurt so bad I thought it would crack open like a raw egg.

Dr. Badu ordered the nurse to put something in my IV bag, a sedative and something for nausea. She explained the drugs I'd been taking were causing the vomiting and the head pain.

She was wrong about that. I thought it was something else, something more ominous.

I thought I was dying.

Dr. Badu and the nurse helped me back into bed. She wrote several things on my medical chart and asked if I had been hallucinating.

"A little."

"A little?"

"Uh huh."

She crossed her arms. "What did you see?"

"POWs from an old TV show. Outside in the corridor, flirting with Carin." I shifted my eyes toward the exit.

The doctor's eyes crinkled at the corners. "Carin's pretty professional. I don't think she flirts with anyone. If you told her that, I'm sure she'd think it was funny."

I turned away and willed myself to go unconscious and fell into blackness dark and deep as a well.

Hours later, my eyes flew open and I sat up to ask Dr. Badu a question that seemed very significant, but of course she was gone. And, of course, I couldn't remember the question.

I was alone and it was night. The hospital noises had subsided, except for the elevator. It seemed to ping every ten seconds or so, as if the Invisible Man was pranking the staff.

I lay there and replayed the last conversation I had with my doctor. *Your friend died in the accident.*

I looked around. There was a different nurse, not Carin, sitting at the desk outside. The air was free of rainbows. Somewhere a radio was on and Gotye was mourning somebody he used to know.

My mouth tasted sour, but I was too weak to ring the buzzer by my bed, or to pour myself any water.

Cathy. Cathy Chance was dead. At the scene.

Though I didn't remember her, I closed my eyes and sobbed myself to sleep.

Chapter 4

Thursday, July 21, 10:30 a.m.
Dr. Patel's Office

"Roxanne, if you'll wait here, Dr. Patel will be with you as soon as he's off the phone."

I smiled at the secretary and took a seat in the empty waiting alcove outside Dr. Patel's office, my third appointment with the psychiatrist in the last three days.

Our first meeting was short and established that I did not remember anything about my identity, where I lived, or the accident.

The second confirmed that, although I didn't know my name or my past, I seemed to know stuff about class scheduling, elementary school lesson plans and art, particularly the French Impressionist painters. Which seemed to prove to everyone that I was, indeed, Roxanne Ruiz, and that I would soon remember this fact.

Today's visit was to discuss a discharge treatment plan. The officials in the hospital were ready to let me go out into the world, even though I could remember nothing about my place in it. I kept fighting the urge to say to the hospital staff, "Are you guys crazy?" But frankly, what were they going to do with someone like me?

"Roxanne, you're looking very well. Not so pale." Dr. Patel glanced at me appraisingly.

I was finding the way men looked at me unsettling. The doctors and interns and Michael Cimino all had open admiration in their expressions. And sometimes, expectation.

It unnerved me, as if I were a specimen of something on display. I wondered if this had bothered me before the accident.

"How are your ribs?" he asked.

I touched them gingerly. "Good. Not too sore."

He motioned toward the chair opposite his desk. "Please have a seat."

I sat and folded my hands in my lap. My skin felt dry. So did my eyes. I blinked and smiled. "How's it going?"

Dr. Patel met my glance, his face impassive. "Very well. So, tell me, how is it going for you today?"

"Good. You know, okay. Like I've been in a crack-up."

Dr. Patel blinked, and a giggle vibrated in the bottom of my throat. Saying 'like a crack-up' sounded sarcastic. "I still don't remember anything, if that's what you're asking," I blurted out.

He nodded.

I waited. Somewhere behind me in his tiny, cluttered space, a clock ticked. I thought this was out of character for a psychiatrist's office. As was the clutter. I'd seen plenty of shrinks' offices on TV and the one thing they had in common was tidiness. Probably based on some therapeutic notion of 'uncluttered space, uncluttered mind.'

Dr. Patel cleared his throat. "I ran into your mother this morning. I didn't realize she is a psychologist."

"Neither did I."

"Excuse me?"

I crossed my legs. "Sorry, I was making a joke. I meant I've learned in the past couple of days that Betty Haverty is a psychologist. She told me."

"How's that going?"

"What?"

"Your talks with Betty."

"I'm not sure what you mean."

"She's your mother. Mother-daughter relationships can be challenging."

I raised my eyebrows. "She's fine."

"Is Betty pressuring you to remember?"

I thought of the redhead. She was nice, very bright, if a little cold. She struck me as someone who was unhappy at having to alter the course of her life because of something that happened to her daughter. She acted impatient about my insistence that I couldn't remember my past, almost as if she suspected I was doing it to spite her. However, I saw no reason to share this opinion with Patel.

For some reason, I didn't trust Dr. Patel as one should trust a therapist. He seemed to be looking for some reason to keep me in the hospital, and while I was nervous about being released, I was more afraid he wouldn't. I wanted to be alone, go somewhere quiet and work out what to do.

My plan, made slowly over the last two days, was to go home, visit where I worked and talk to people, see my friend Cathy's husband, Nick, and ask him questions.

I put that thought on hold. I couldn't imagine what I would say to Nick. Every time I considered it, my brain froze.

How can I comfort a man I don't know, about a woman I don't remember?

"Roxanne?" Dr. Patel was staring hard. "Are you okay?"

"Yes. Yes. And no, I wouldn't say Betty is pressuring me in any way. I'm sure she's just worried I may never remember."

"Why would that worry her?"

"Because she doesn't want to lose her daughter."

"I don't understand what you mean. You survived the accident. It was Cathy who was lost."

I laced my fingers together. "If a person doesn't remember the past, doesn't remember a relationship, then it's gone."

"I see."

"You do?" I asked. "So you agree with me?"

The clock ticked four beats. "Are you worried you won't ever remember, Roxanne?"

"Not worried. Impatient, maybe. Anxious."

"Do you think you're depressed?" he asked gently.

"No."

"You were depressed, according to your doctors, before the accident. It would be understandable, normal really, if you were still suffering from this illness. The chemical imbalance that existed in your brain before the accident is still likely to exist, even if your memories are repressed."

Betty Haverty had told me about my previous treatment for depression. Currently I was taking nothing but antibiotics and pain meds, and I was feeling much more lucid than the day I woke up from the coma. But, how would I ever know if I was this thing called 'depressed?'

What did depressed feel like? Sad? Angry? "Do I act depressed?"

"Do you feel depressed?"

"No. I feel confused, and worried. But not sad, or lethargic, or manic. Maybe the car accident fixed my chemical imbalance. From what I've heard, I was thrown around a lot, like being in a blender. Maybe my chemicals are now in the *right* balance."

"You're very witty."

Patel didn't mean 'witty.' I'm sure he meant 'sarcastic.'

He wrote something on his pad. "Let's move on, Roxanne. I told you the prognosis is that your memory will return fairly soon. The concussion was severe, but there is no sign of intracranial bleeding, and the swelling has gone down significantly. Your procedural memory is fully intact, and we expect your declarative memory to restore itself. But you've suffered a great trauma, and it will take time."

His calm voice did little to take the edge off the tension that had built over our last exchange. "Procedural is how to do things, right?" I asked.

"Correct. Tie your shoes. Drive a car. Use the DVD player."

"I might be in trouble there. I tried to use the one in my room when Betty brought me a DVD, but I couldn't figure it out. She had to help me."

"A DVD?"

"Of graduation from college. Pepperdine University. Betty thought seeing it might bring back some of the personal, 'declarative' you call them, memories."

"How'd it go?" He kept his eyes on me.

"It didn't work."

He nodded and wrote something again. I felt like I was failing a test I hadn't been warned to study for. "You said my condition is called retrograde amnesia. That I've lost my memory from right before the accident. But I read some articles on the internet last night that say this type of amnesia usually blots out a period of time of a person's memory, like a few months. But I don't remember *anything* about Roxanne Ruiz. Why can't I remember anything, such as my childhood, that happened before the car accident?"

Patel shrugged. "Head trauma commonly is accompanied by sudden and even persistent memory loss of varying degrees. Yours is unusual, as you've discovered. But not unknown. The combination of striking the right temple, the fearfulness of the accident, the loss of your friend, these are all exacerbating circumstances. I expect the symptoms to disappear when the swelling goes away."

"And then what? I wake up and remember everything? Everyone?" My heart raced. "Will I remember the actual accident?"

"Possibly. But you may not ever recall that day, or even those few weeks of your life."

"Is that my brain's way of protecting me from the truth that I'm responsible for someone's death?"

His eyes were serious. "Do you think you are responsible for your friend's death, Roxanne?"

"I was driving the car."

"Yes, you were. But a drunk driver was behind the wheel of the truck that caused the incident."

I wanted to slap him for saying 'incident' to describe a woman's death. "Well, I feel responsible."

"Your friend wasn't wearing her seatbelt."

"She didn't deserve to die because of it."

Patel took a deep breath. "Did Dr. Badu mention that the police want to talk with you?"

"Yes. But she told them I don't remember anything. She didn't think they'd want to talk to me at all."

"She's wrong. They need to hear from you, that you don't remember anything. A detective, Henry Morales, called today and asked when they could talk with you. If you like, I can ask him to interview you here in my office. Maybe sometime in the next week or so?"

Something in his voice made me tense. "Why would I meet them here, Dr. Patel?"

"So I would be available to explain that the drugs you were taking for depression should not have impaired your driving skills. And that your toxicology reports actually show only traces of them. So there's no reason to question your ability to drive."

"Are you saying the police would put me at fault in the accident? Because of my medication?"

"No one has said that to me, Roxanne. But I'm concerned they might think you had the accident because you *weren't* taking your medication. As I confirmed, the toxicology report shows trace amounts. It's my opinion you hadn't been taking your meds for a week or longer."

After a moment, I realized what he was implying. "So I wasn't taking my medication. Which means the police could think I caused the accident because I wasn't treating my depression?"

"You have a history of serious depression. And yes, you weren't taking your medication as prescribed." Dr. Patel leaned forward. "That shows a lack of caring for yourself. And your mother said you had recently broken off a long-term relationship with your boyfriend. I don't want the police to run away with those facts and imagine they mean something that they don't."

"Like what? Like the accident was a suicide attempt?"

He seemed impressed I'd made the connection. "Very good. But there are no facts to lead the police, or anyone else, to believe that. At my request, your mother searched your house and found no note. And I spoke to your psychiatrist, and to Dr. Seth, your psychologist. Neither indicated to me that a suicide attempt was something they were anticipating."

I felt dizzy. It was clear Dr. Patel had considered the possibility that I attempted suicide by car accident. Enough of a possibility that he'd taken aggressive steps to rule it out. I put my hands to my cheeks, feeling embarrassed and ashamed. *Could I have done such a thing?*

I stood. "I don't need you to talk to the police with me. I don't remember the accident, and that's all I can tell them."

"I see." He waved his hand at the chair. "Please sit down again, Roxanne. I've obviously upset you. That wasn't my intent."

"I wouldn't hurt someone I loved, Dr. Patel. I might not remember the details of my life, but no one would hurt their best friend if they had decided to kill themselves in a car crash. Right? Have you ever heard of such a thing?"

"It would be unusual. Generally this scenario only plays out with mothers or fathers killing their children to keep them from the other parent."

His look remained steady. But 'unusual' didn't mean 'unheard of.' I crossed my arms. "So what, in your opinion, is the bottom line about my current mental state?"

"Please sit. Then we'll discuss it."

I perched on the edge of the chair, the frame nipping at my bruised bottom.

Patel seemed visibly rattled. "Well, let me first say you have perfect semantic recall about your profession as a teacher, as well as prospective memory about events in the future, such as you mentioned you know school starts on September 2 this year. It's your episodic memory about a particular time, or place or person, such as your sixteenth birthday party, or your college graduation that you are missing. But I am confident this is a temporary condition."

"I'm glad you're confident."

"You're not?"

"Why would I be? I feel like a freak." I squeezed my arms against my breasts, which I had decided were ridiculously large for someone my size. The curves of my body were still as unfamiliar to me as my past. "It's a terrible feeling, not to remember anyone."

"I'm sure it is." Dr. Patel nodded. "Have you heard from your friends?"

"A few. A woman named Jen called. And a man named Bradley. Some guy named Freddy, a tennis coach, called to say 'get well.' And Michael Cimino has been around every day."

"How is that going?"

"What do you mean?"

"He was your boyfriend for years, I understand. Do you feel anything for him when you see him?"

"Anything? You mean sexual?"

"Anything that would remind you of a personal history with the man."

"No." But that wasn't totally true. Michael was very compelling. Sexy and glib, the sound of his voice touched something in me. I'd kept him at arm's length, however. "He's trying hard to be nice. But he's nervous. I think he thinks I'm crazy."

"Why do you say that?"

"He stares at me as if he doesn't believe someone could get amnesia and not remember him." I cleared my throat, aware of the damnation in that observation. "I mean, he seems baffled by my condition. Maybe he thinks I crashed the car on purpose, too."

"No one thinks that, Roxanne."

"Except the police?"

"Don't obsess about what the police might think. I'm sure their need to talk to you is routine."

I sighed. I wished Patel hadn't brought up the cops at all. Until he had, I had cast myself as the complete victim in this situation. The thought that I might be viewed as the culprit was horrifying. "Michael seems intent on being in my life again. But I'm not ready."

"Anyone else been in touch?"

"Ruth. Betty's mom. And a nice lady named Althea Cornell. She's principal where . . ."

Patel waited.

I was going to say, 'where *we* taught school,' but when the words formed inside my head they felt alarming. So, I stopped. I wasn't sure, but the 'we' seemed loosely linked to something familiar, almost like the beginning of a thought, or even a memory. Of me and someone else.

"May I have some water?"

"Yes, of course." Dr. Patel reached around to his desk for a plastic bottle and handed it to me.

I drank half of it. The ticking of the clock seemed louder. "So, when can I leave the hospital?"

Dr. Patel leaned back in his chair. "Do you think you're ready to leave?"

"Yes."

"You'll move in with your mother?"

"No. I told Betty I want to go to Roxanne's apartment and live."

"You mean y*our* apartment?"

"Right." I exhaled. "Sorry. It's easier for me to refer to 'Roxanne' in the third person. Right now I'm like an invisible woman, trying to get to know Roxanne a little before I take her on completely."

"Sounds like a good coping mechanism."

"Thank you. So, I can go? Dr. Badu says Saturday morning, if you agree."

Dr. Patel stared as if he could see straight through my flesh to my spinal cord. "Do you have a plan for how you're going to integrate the amnesia into your life?"

"No. Is there a handbook?"

Dr. Patel frowned. I reached across the small desk and touched his arm. "Sorry. I am acting like a smart ass. I'm freaked out by what you said about the police."

"Don't worry about the police, Roxanne. I only brought it up so you wouldn't feel ambushed when they called. I've seen detectives go off on tangents when they hear someone was on medication and has an accident. I wanted you to have backup to handle the technical questions, if you need it. But don't worry."

"Okay. I won't worry." I smiled at him, wondering if he knew I was lying. I hoped he didn't. I wanted him to like me. I felt alone, and incompetent. "Sorry again for being difficult. I've been told I make sarcastic comments when I'm nervous. I have thought about what I am going to do when I leave the hospital. I'm going to look at everything in the apartment, get people to talk to me about the past. Go see Cathy Chance's family. I'm sure they can tell me about her, and I'll hopefully remember something soon."

"Do you think they'll be willing to help you?"

"I don't know. I hope so. Everyone says Cathy and Roxanne were best friends. Really, really close. I hope they don't blame me. I don't mean blame me, like I crashed on purpose. But their person is still dead."

He pulled out an appointment card and started writing. "I'll need to meet with you at least once a week here at my office, possibly twice a week, for a couple of months."

I got up and dropped the water bottle, which rolled under Dr. Patel's desk. "Sorry. Sure. Whatever you think."

The psychiatrist swiveled his chair, grabbed the bottle and handed it back to me.

I was breathing too fast, as if I were about to take part in a jailbreak. "Thank you, Dr. Patel. For everything."

"You are welcome, Roxanne." He squeezed my arm, his fingers lingering for what felt like a moment too long. "I'll see you next Monday. Make sure you rest. And call me if you have any pain, blurred vision, nausea or dizziness." He stood and opened the door for me.

I sprinted back to the hospital elevator. I wanted to go to bed and then to sleep so it would be tomorrow.

Like a child at Christmas. Wanting to sleep so Santa would come.

I pressed the button on the elevator pad, the door slid open and I stepped inside. I needed to find my past. To have a future, you had to have a past.

Right now I was *tabula rasa,* at least as far as I was concerned. Everyone else might have a history with the woman whose features they saw when they looked at me, but for me, life was a book I hadn't yet read, and all things were possible.

Including the fact I might have tried to kill myself?

No. Not that. I might not know much, but I knew in my bones that was not possible. I loved life. This thought buoyed me as I hurried into my hospital room and collapsed into bed.

"Roxanne, are you asleep?"

I fought my way out of sleep and lifted my head off the hospital pillow to meet Michael Cimino's stare. He was standing at the end of my bed. I wondered for how long.

"What do you want?"

"Hey, there she is. How goes the memory? Remember anything yet?" He sat beside me. "Remember *me* yet?"

"What are you doing here?" I asked.

This probably wasn't the reception he had expected. He folded his arms as his eyes roamed over my body. I was wearing a soft gray sweat suit Betty had brought me, but I felt unclothed under Michael's stare.

"I wanted to see how my lady was doing." His grin widened. "It's nice, being alone with you. It's been too long."

I scooted into a sitting position. "I wish I could remember, but I don't."

"I know this has all been hard for you, Rox, but I want you to know I'm here for you." He leaned closer. "I don't know what Betty told you about me, about us, but all I have to say is we're good together, babe. Real good."

"But we weren't together, before the accident?"

"No. We weren't. That's a fact. But I told you when we broke up that we'd be back together eventually. And I meant it. Just like I mean it now."

I swallowed. "Look, I'm in no position to make any kind of plans."

"Hey, I know. I'm not pressuring you. You're banged up and having a tough time with stuff. But when you're feeling yourself again, I want you to know I'm going to be here for you." Michael put his fingers on his lips and then brushed them against mine. "So that's all I'm doing here, okay? Letting you know what I've been thinking, without your mom or granny or the doctors watching and putting their two cents in. Okay?" He stood and shoved his hands in his pockets.

I looked into his green eyes and felt a hum of lust creep up the center of my body. I smelled the spicy fragrance of his aftershave. Michael Cimino was one hot guy, though my body was reacting to him separately from my brain. Because, despite my physical yearning, a voice inside my head whispered one small word while he talked.

Liar.

"Thanks, Michael. For coming by. I hope in the next few days we can meet and talk over some things. Maybe you'd be willing to help me fill in some of the blank spots, help me to remember myself. My life."

"Sure thing. You call, I'm there." He took my chin in his hand and kissed me. His lips were gentle but demanding. "Get some sleep, beautiful. As soon as you're back in the apartment, you call me. We've got some catching up to do."

He winked and sauntered out the door. He seemed much happier than I'd seen him the past few days, as if some burden had been lifted from his shoulders.

I lay back and closed my eyes.

Who can you trust? When you don't know the facts, the past, and the cold, hard history of shared experience with someone, you have to go on instinct. Was mine any good?

Exhausted, I willed myself to sleep, wondering right before I dropped off if Michael would tell me things about myself I might not want to hear.

Chapter 5

Friday, July 25, 8 a.m.
Nick's House

"Zoë, get up, it's time for work and you're late."

"Go away, Nick," my sister mumbled without moving.

"Zoë, now. You're going to get fired if you're late again."

Nothing. She didn't even twitch. I walked out of her bedroom and down the hallway into the kitchen. Outside it was raining, strange for Sierra Monte in mid-summer. Like most of Southern California, we got about three inches of rain in our "rainy season." Which wasn't July.

I looked at the calendar. July 25th.

Cathy had been dead for two weeks and two days. I wondered if I would ever stop measuring time by the date she died. I collapsed onto the hard bench beside the kitchen table and poured my second cup of coffee. It was already eight. When Cathy was here, I was at work early, usually by seven.

Not anymore. Since Zoë had come to stay here with me three days after the memorial service, convinced I needed to have someone around because she didn't think I was doing well, I'd been late to work every day.

I protested to Zoë and my mom when they showed up—unannounced—with Zoë's things, that I didn't need anyone moving in. The two of them glanced around the house and noted unwashed dishes and un-vacuumed floors, so I gave in, mostly because I'm worried about Zoë.

Since Cathy died, my sister has gone into a nosedive, even by teenager standards. She's lost ten pounds and cut off her hair and dyed it blonde, like Cathy's. Then she had her arm tattooed with Cathy's name.

Mom said Zoë was also smoking pot every night, and that she had threatened Zoë with putting her into an in-patient program. So I told Zoë it was okay to move in as long as she got herself to school in the fall and kept her part-time job for the rest of the summer. And gave up the weed.

She was holding up her end about how I expected. So far I'd only smelled pot two or three times, but she'd been late to work every day she'd been here. The coffee shop where she worked was giving her a break because of Cathy, but it was going to catch up with her. I was lucky to get Zoë out the door by eight-thirty and then to my own desk by nine-fifteen.

But I would be lying if I said it wasn't good, having my sister here. When I came home from work, there was someone to pretend for, someone who made it not okay to go lie on my bed and stare at the ceiling, curse the gods, cry like a baby.

She made me feel like I wasn't alone in the world. The people I worked with had been also been great, but the pats on the back, and unguarded looks of compassion were wearing me out.

"What time is it?" Zoë's fuzzy slippers slapped their way through the kitchen. Clumsily she slammed a ceramic cup onto the counter and sloshed coffee all over her hand, swore and repeated, "What time is it, Nick? I don't have my contacts in."

I glanced at the clock. "It's ten after eight."

More swearing. "Why didn't you wake me up?" She ran for the bathroom, spilling coffee on the floor.

I stared at the Spanish terra cotta tile, hand cut, Cathy's last extravagance. I wanted linoleum, sturdy and boring, but she talked me into the tile. The guy who installed it, Enrique, had a crush on Cathy, I think. One she didn't seem aware of. One I didn't worry over, since Enrique is about seventy. Very courtly. We also had him patch a spot on our roof while he was here. The kitchen job took about four weeks, two longer than he'd estimated.

Since I'd known her, a lot of men had crushes on Cathy. Mostly old guys who saw the sparkle, the fight, the love of life in her. Older guys who'd been around and knew what mattered, what kept a man home and warm and happy at night. It was what Cathy had in spades.

Tears fell, and I didn't wipe them away. I walked across the cool tile floor and put my cup in the sink. The phone on the kitchen wall rang softly but I ignored it. I didn't like talking on the phone anymore. Nothing could be as bad as the call I'd received that day. But still . . .

Down the hallway Zoë was banging things around in the bathroom. She'd be ready to leave in a few minutes. Fine with me. I'd go through the motions; what else could I do?

"Did you eat breakfast?" Zoë asked behind me.

Busy rinsing out my cup, I hadn't heard her. She walked sneaky as a cat. I turned and nearly tripped over her. "I had coffee. Why don't you have a granola bar or something?"

"I'm not hungry."

Her face was all bones and shadows. "You're too skinny. Eat something. We need to leave."

"*You* need to eat. *You're* too skinny." She grabbed the belt on my pants. "Look, the incredible shrinking man."

"I eat. And I haven't lost a ton of weight like some people I know. Now go get your shoes and backpack." I pointed toward her room.

She reached behind me and snagged an orange from the basket; nimbly peeled it. "Who was on the phone?"

"I don't know."

She pushed an orange slice into her mouth and regarded me. "You turning into a hermit, Nick?"

"I never answer the phone if it rings before eight."

"Since when?" Zoë rolled her eyes as she walked over and looked at the caller ID. She frowned and pressed the playback.

I had the volume almost at zero so I didn't have to hear people when they left me a message. I felt guilty not answering, but there wasn't anyone I wanted to talk to. Except for a dead woman.

I hadn't even taken calls from Bradley. He'd always had dinner with Cathy and me on Monday nights. He taught a tech class at Sierra Monte Community College, up the street, and Cathy had insisted he come eat with us so we could talk. She loved Bradley. And he loved her, always confided in her about his love life, his 'latest and datest' as he called them.

He'd stopped by to comfort me the first Monday after Cathy died, but showed up shit-faced drunk while I listened to his sobbing about Cathy and felt like killing myself. Bradley never made it to class that night; I never made it to bed. But it allowed both of us to take a little off the top of our grief, at least for one night. I hadn't seen him since.

Zoë finally figured out the volume was off on the answering machine and played it again. A man's voice picked up mid-sentence. ". . . we can discuss the settlement for your wife's death. Again, please call my office at your earliest convenience. Mrs. Haverty would like to schedule this for four p.m. today, if that's possible." The man rattled off his name and address and phone number.

"Turn it off," I demanded.

Zoë flicked the button. "There's another message. Don't you want to hear it, too?"

"No." I looked outside at the two lemon trees next to my patio, aware Zoë was staring at me.

"I'll go with you, if you want."

"I'm not going."

She laid her hand on my sleeve. "You need to settle the insurance thing, Nick. This is the third message from this guy. They'll keep calling you back."

"I'm not taking any money for Cathy." My eyes ached as if they were dry sockets and my pulse pounded in my ears. "Betty Haverty and Roxanne and their goddamned insurance man can screw themselves. They don't have enough money to compensate anyone for anything." I stopped talking and put the table between us. I gripped the back of a chair.

Zoë sat and placed the uneaten half of orange on the table. She crossed her arms over her chest. For the first time in her life, she reminded me of our mother. "I think you need to call Roxanne."

"What?" I nearly shouted.

Zoë nodded at the phone. "The caller ID shows she called twice yesterday afternoon. From her house."

"I'm not calling her."

Zoë raised her left eyebrow, just like Mom. "She was Cathy's best friend, Nick. You're going to have to talk to her sooner or later."

"I've got nothing to say to Roxanne."

"Cathy would be pissed off at you, bro."

"You don't know what you're talking about, so stay out of this."

Zoë's eyes filled with tears and she started to rock herself. "Sorry."

"That bitch killed her."

"Don't do that," she replied. "I was mad at Roxanne, too. I wanted her to die, remember? But the cops say the accident wasn't her fault. There was nothing she could do." Zoë reached out for me. "The asshole truck driver was drunk. It was an accident, Nick."

I forced myself not to pick up the chair and hurl it through the French doors. "Go get your stuff. Right now, Zoë. I can't keep being late to work. I'm going to lose my fucking job." I walked out the kitchen screen door.

"I thought I was going to lose *my* fucking job," Zoë hollered behind me.

"You are! Me, too. We're both going to be out on the street on our asses."

I walked across to the patio door and stared again at the lemon trees. Cathy planted them when we moved here, six years ago. They were big for where she put them. The roots were too near the patio, and the fragrance of the blossoms made it impossible to enjoy sitting outside because of the bees. We'd talked about moving them a few weeks ago.

Before she died.

Aunt Pitty, Cathy's ancient cat, jumped arthritically from the back fence and limped toward the house. I called her. She stopped at the edge of the cement and looked at me and then ran around the side of the house. She grieved for Cathy, and had refused to come inside. For two weeks and two days.

"You okay?" Zoë stepped outside. "Nick? Are you all right?"

I tossed her the keys. "I'm fine. Go warm up the car. I'll be out in a minute."

She caught them and disappeared.

After a moment, I went back inside and punched the replay on the answering machine, and heard Cathy's voice. "See you," she said. My eyes burned; it must be an old message I had not erased. I walked out of the kitchen. I'd heard enough for one day.

"And you're wrong about Roxanne being Cathy's best friend, Zoë!" I yelled to the empty house. "I'm her best friend."

And she was mine. Always was. Always would be.

Chapter 6

Saturday, July 23, 11 a.m.
Roxanne's Apartment

"There are several messages on your answering machine, Roxanne." Betty Haverty smiled. "By the way, did Dr. Patel mention the police want to talk to you about the accident?"

"Yes. He did."

"It's only a formality. I'll be glad to come with you when you go in to talk to them."

"I don't remember anything. So I don't have anything to tell them. Don't worry about the cops. I'm not."

Betty nodded. "I'm not worried." She looked worried.

I glanced at the phone, annoyed she had listened to my messages at all. Which was dumb. Of course she listened to them. Wouldn't anybody's mother listen to messages if their daughter were in the hospital? According to Patel, Betty also looked for a suicide note. I was pissed she hadn't mentioned that.

Just let it go.

I put down my suitcase and packages and looked around me. 19 Lake Street, Apartment 'M,' the home of Roxanne Ruiz for the past three years, felt somehow familiar after just a few minutes. Not familiar as if I remembered living here. But familiar because I seemed to know where the towels and toilet paper were kept, and that the second burner on the stove didn't work right, and that I bet you could hear voices from the parking lot at three a.m. if you didn't close the window before you went to bed.

It was a nice, two-bedroom apartment, with some quality furniture: a floral patterned sofa, two upholstered chairs and some lovely antiques. There were flourishing plants and old ceramic vases and fine artwork whose subject was mostly rainy night scenes or still-life prints of French and American Impressionists.

It was also obsessively neat and organized.

As I walked around exploring, I found canned goods in the cupboard lined up alphabetically, the same as the books in the bookshelves and the CDs and DVDs in the entertainment center. The underwear drawers in the bedroom dresser looked like department store display cases in an upscale neighborhood. Nighties in one, bras in another, panties in neat stacks, divided by hip huggers, bikinis and thongs. I picked up a black lacy thong and thought there was no way I would ever wear such a thing.

The closets looked similar; blouses, jeans, dresses and jackets, all in their own groups. Cleaning supplies from short bottles to tall, towels and sheets by color, by set, bundled and tied with satin ribbon.

It gave me pause, this emphasis on neatness. *Roxanne digs control.* A good way to conquer inner fear? Beat it down with organized attack.

Had I read that somewhere?

Even the shoes, mostly flats and sandals, were in neat rows, with color-coordinated purses resting in little plastic boxes above the shoe shelf, next to folded and bagged sweaters on the top shelf of the closet.

I peeked in at them and turned to Betty, who was hovering nearby. "What a neat freak!"

"I can't claim any credit for the obsessive neatness of the place. You've always been like this." Betty glanced around the bedroom with disdain. "After you were seven years old, I never cleaned your room. You were much more fastidious than I was about the house. Remember?"

She stared at me and I knew she was hoping that at any moment I'd exclaim, 'Oh, Mother, I remember everything,' and run into her arms and let her get back to her own life and her own worries.

Instead I murmured, "Sorry, no."

The two of us continued our small chores. Betty put away groceries we'd grabbed on the way from the hospital, and emptied the clean dishes from the dishwasher. I walked around asking random questions I hoped she would answer without too much baggage attached.

"Your checkbook and mail are on the desk in the bedroom. And your straw bag. I think your set of keys is in there," she said.

I picked up the purse, which had a huge gash in the side, probably from the accident. I smelled it, but all I could pick up was the whiff of cinnamon gum. No smoke. No gasoline or blood and guts.

Nervously I pulled out the wallet, a red 'Kate Spade,' and flipped through it. Ninety-two dollars in cash. Some change, no pennies, in the coin section. A receipt for a dress from Nordstrom's. A driver's license (listing my weight as one-ten, which was surely wrong), social security card, two credit cards, an appointment card for Behavior Therapy Center. Dr. Seth was noted as the doctor.

The appointment was for 10:30 a.m. on July 9, the day of the accident. Over two weeks ago.

I wondered about Dr. Seth. Patel mentioned he knew him professionally. Betty had not brought him up by name, but she had told me a couple of doctors were treating me before the accident. We had picked up a pain medication at the market, but I'd refused her suggestion to refill my antidepressant.

She wasn't happy about that, but avoided causing a scene. Since I didn't feel depressed, other than not knowing a *single thing about my life*, I didn't see the logic of taking meds until I clearly needed them. Which proved I was either completely sane or deeply neurotic, but that was still open for discussion.

At the bottom of the duffle Betty had brought to the hospital, I found the plastic bag the hospital clerk had given me when we checked out. It had a gold signet ring with RLR on it, and a turquoise and silver earring that was found at the accident scene.

I closed my hand around the jewelry and stuffed it in my pocket, not wanting to ask Betty about them. I hugged my arms around my chest. The room smelled musty, like old candles and dust. I pulled back the drapes and opened the windows, then collapsed on the bed. It was very, very firm.

I like soft beds.

I rolled over on my back and looked around. Quality stuff in here, too; not too girly. Tasteful. A comfortable leather chair and ottoman that looked about fifty years old stood beside a small trunk across from the bed. A serious looking halogen light and a stack of novels on top of the trunk indicated a lot of reading took place there. I checked out the books, but saw nothing I wanted to skim through.

There was a huge fichus in the corner, in a terra cotta planter, and a good print of a Van Gogh painting over the bed. A swarm of purple, sinewy irises were huddled in a large gang, menacing a slender white flower cowering on the far left side of the canvas.

I knew it was called 'Irises,' and I knew Van Gogh painted it at the asylum at *Saint Paul-de-Mausole,* the year before his death. I knew it was said he thought by painting it that he would keep himself from going insane. To my eyes, it hadn't helped. The masterpiece was a depiction of vulnerability on the verge of surrender.

I thought it should have been titled, 'Massacre in the Garden,' and smiled. Did my opinion mean I was depressed?

My brain started to flood with images of paintings. When it came to the Impressionists, I knew I'd always liked Renoir. That splash of red to lift the spirits. So romantic, if a little sentimental. But my greatest love was Claude Monet. Outdoor scenes, as painted by God. I looked around the bedroom, but did not see any of his work on the wall.

As I shut my eyes, a painting bloomed in my brain. Was this a memory of a specific occurrence, or a random, masquerading thought? I concentrated on the details of the image. A stone bridge, warm dappled light on a dirt path leading to an unseen river, a woman and a child moving away from the viewer. They'd missed their chance to follow the glorious sunlight beckoning them to turn off the sidewalk and slide their toes in the water. In my mind, I saw the picture hanging somewhere I liked to be, on a papered wall with crown molding. Near a window with a lace curtain.

Where is this?

Did this place exist outside my imagination? Sudden tears flooded my eyes. Would I ever remember?

"Would you like something to eat?" Betty asked loudly from the doorway.

I kept my face averted. "No, I'm good. I'm thinking a nap might be the ticket."

"Do you want me to stay a couple of days? It'll be no problem. I've slept on your sofa many times before."

Oh, really?

There was a lot of drama there, but I wasn't up to diving into it now. This whole 'spending time with Betty Haverty' was uncomfortable. I didn't want to hurt the woman, but I truly didn't want to find out who I was from her. I wanted to *remember.*

I faced her. "Dr. Patel thinks I need to spend time alone, resting, getting familiar with things. I wouldn't want to put you out."

"Jesus, Roxanne, I'm your mother. It wouldn't be putting me out in the least!" She sat at the foot of the bed. She had a picture album in her hands. "I brought this from home. I was going to show it to you at the hospital, but Dr. Patel said to wait a bit. I thought you might like to have some faces to go with the names I've been talking about."

"Thanks." My heart raced. I sat up and took the photos from her and listened as she narrated snaps of Cathy and Nick Chance, school and work friends, pictures of me with Michael, several from my childhood with Betty and her mother, Ruth.

There was one in particular she wanted me to look at. "You were five years old, Roxanne, the first time I took you to see Santa." The photo showed a beautiful child, curly headed and chubby, with candy cane smeared all over her face. Santa's beard was stuck to the child's candied cheek. Santa looked resigned, the little dark-haired girl frightened.

"I always loved that one," Betty said. For a moment she looked far away and, for the first time since I'd known her in my current state of abbreviated memory, happy.

The photo session went on for several minutes. These pictures unsettled me. Opinions buzzed in my brain. And I was absolutely certain that I had never sat on a Santa's lap.

The only photos that didn't make me feel panicky were images of Cathy Chance, always a glint of fun in her eyes, freckled, blue-eyed, smiling and cute. I didn't remember her. But something inside missed her, or rather, wished she were around so I could talk to her, ask her what to do.

She looked like the kind of girl you could depend on. She looked calm.

We'd been friends for a long time, Betty had told me. Since middle school. And the pictures showed proof of a real friendship, gawky girls hugging each other, self-conscious teenagers in tiny skirts and crop tops, standing side by side, though Cathy towered above the other school kids from the earliest snaps.

Betty had masses of pictures of the friends in their graduation robes at high school and college celebrations, and one at what must have been Cathy's wedding. She looked gorgeous that day, short white dress and long legs, sparkling eyes and blonde hair, like a princess.

Surprising both of us, a question popped out of my mouth. "Can you tell me about the memorial service?"

"Cathy's?"

I nodded.

"It was very moving," Betty began. "It was held at Everlast Cemetery in Sierra Monte. All your fellow teachers from school were there, and a lot of the kids and their parents. And her husband and his family. His sister Zoë, who seems a little peculiar. I think she's adopted. Anyway, she doesn't look at all like him. I think she's still in high school. She started crying and yelling at the end of the service that she didn't want Cathy's ashes to be buried."

My mouth went dry. "What about Cathy's parents?"

"They're gone. Her mother died when she was in grade school. The father left when she was an infant. The stepfather hasn't been around for years."

"What happened to Cathy's father?"

Betty pursed her lips. Just then she looked old, and tired. Maybe even ill?

"Heart attack, I understand. He was so young. A tragedy, to leave young children behind."

"Were you friends with Cathy's mother?"

Betty paused for a couple of moments. "Yes, I knew her. When you and Cathy were in third grade, before you started hanging out together, we were on a PTA committee."

"What was she like?"

"Nice enough. She took me aside one night and asked

me if I knew an attorney. To handle her will. She was dying of ovarian cancer."

"How horrible for Cathy," I whispered. "Did you send flowers from me?"

"Yes. From all of us. A huge spray. Roses and lilies. And we sent food over to the house. Nick's mother stayed with him for a few days and organized the reception afterward."

"How was that?" I flashed on an image of a Spanish-styled house, with a shady back patio. I didn't know if it was real. *It might be.*

"I didn't go. Grandma Ruth did. She took the food."

"You should have gone. We both should have gone."

"Don't be ridiculous. You were in and out of a coma! I couldn't leave you alone at the hospital. Nick and his family understood that."

"Really? I think it was a terrible mistake to have missed the service."

"Please, Roxanne. It wasn't possible."

"It might not have been easy, but it was possible." Tears filled my eyes. "I hope you realize Cathy's family surely blames me for all this. I bet they hate me."

"Of course they don't hate you. You were Cathy's best friend. You helped her a million times during the years. They know how close you two were. It's because of you she finished college at all. You helped her with her studies, her papers. She wasn't a very good student."

Betty looked down at her hands. "No one blames you for what happened that day, Roxanne."

I thought of the police. I wondered if the detectives had talked to Cathy's husband, Nick. What would he think if the police told him the accident that killed his wife wasn't an accident?

"I think they do blame me. I haven't heard a word from Nick. Not a card or a visit, or even a call. Has he called you? Asked about me?"

"No. But I'm sure you'll hear from him eventually. Give him some time. Nick's a sensitive guy. Kind of weak, I've always thought, but he's in mourning, Roxanne. And, well, he's been an alcoholic for years. It's under control now, but he's taking Cathy's death very hard."

Me, too. It would have sounded insane to say out loud. That I missed someone I didn't remember.

I glanced through the album. One photo showed Nick staring at Cathy at their wedding reception, his face full of awe, as if he was astonished at his good fortune.

Has any one ever looked at me like that?

I slammed the album closed and handed it back to Betty. "Thanks for bringing this. But you can take it home with you. I've had enough for today."

"Of course." Betty tucked it into her bag. "You've been through so much. We've all been so worried. Are you sure you don't want me to stay a couple of days?"

"Dr. Badu said I was okay to live on my own."

She held up one hand. "Fine. I left my numbers on the bulletin board in the kitchen. In case you need anything. So, I'll be going. There's plenty to eat. The chicken and the quiche we just bought. I also brought over that rice and cheese casserole you like with broccoli. It's in the freezer."

I hate broccoli. "Thank you. That was nice of you."

"For God's sake, stop thanking me! I'm your mother!"

I'd hurt her feelings. *Shit.* "You can stay if you want, Betty, but I'm okay."

She flinched when I called her 'Betty.' She hadn't made an issue of me doing this, but I saw it rankled her the first time I referred to her that way in the hospital.

"Take a nap, Roxanne. And remember, Dr. Patel said absolutely no booze. That pain medication interacts badly with alcohol of any kind."

"Right." I pulled the afghan hanging on a quilt rack beside the bed over me. The afghan smelled nice, like it had dried in the sunshine. It was soft and well worn. I wondered who had made it. Betty?

No, Ruth. 'Granny.' I was sure of this, though such info didn't come from memory, but logic. Betty wasn't the type to knit. I pressed on the bed pillow, which was nice, down-filled, without the crackly plastic liners like those damn things in the hospital.

"Thanks again for everything. I'll call you tomorrow," I said to Betty, who was holding her bag against her chest like a life preserver.

"Okay." Her eyes glistened. "Don't forget."

"Me? Forget? Now that's not a very tactful thing to say."

"Sorry. That was idiotic." She smiled. "You're sure you're okay?"

"I am. And I mean that. You've been great. Really helpful."

She walked away. A moment later I heard her fiddling with the locks, and the front door closed.

I sighed. My ribs ached and my stomach growled. But I wanted to sleep. I stared at the Van Gogh above the bed and shuddered.

That thing had to go. I got up and lifted it off the hook and put it in the closet. Then I went back to bed and buried my head in the pillows. My knees were stiff, the scabs itched. I needed to recharge. Tomorrow was a better day to get started on resuming life.

I glanced at the bedside table that held an antique clock with little roses painted on it and two framed pictures. These were the only two photographs in the whole place. One was of Michael Cimino, no shirt, lounging on his back on a beach chair. He was tan and seemed to be daring whoever took the picture to come closer.

A shiver of appreciation walked down my back. I picked up the second frame. It was a photo of three people at the beach. Roxanne, Cathy, and Nick. We were all smiling and appeared slightly drunk.

I looked at his face. He was handsome. Blonde streaks and hair that was too long. A kind smile. His tanned arms draped over Cathy's, a trio of comrades, not a care in the world.

On the back was the inscription, *"Our little triangle, June 19, 2006,"* in perfect penmanship.

I shut my eyes. *Nick, I'm so, so sorry. Please forgive me.*

Before I fell asleep, I remembered someone . . . a blind man . . . explaining that forgiveness couldn't be asked for. It had to be freely given, when the wronged party was ready, or it meant nothing.

When will you be ready, Nick? When will I?

Chapter 7

Monday, July 25, 9:30 a.m.
Roxanne's Apartment

I stood in front of the full-length mirror hanging on the back of the bathroom door and stared at the naked body that was still so new to me. My legs were nice, if maybe a little skinny. My ass didn't sag but could be a bit more generous. Men like generous rear-ends, right? My breasts were great. Big and firm and bouncy, with small pink nipples.

Flat stomach. Tiny waist. Curvy hips. I had a bikini wax.
You're kidding. Hot wax, there? My face suddenly burned with embarrassment. My body was so unfamiliar, I felt like I was at a peep show.

I sighed and pulled on a robe. *This is all too weird.*

The cell phone lying on the counter rang. The display announced it was 'BJ Chandler.' With an unfamiliar number. Not that any phone numbers were familiar.

"Hello?" The voice speaking was husky and male. "Roxanne! Hi! This is Bradley. Bradley Chandler. Your friend?"

I knew the name 'Bradley.' Betty showed me some pictures in the hospital. Gay, Betty had added, and a dear friend. Computer geek.

"Hi, Bradley." Facts about him fell like dominos inside my brain. I'd been avoiding phone conversations since I was released from the hospital. Not that I felt unfriendly; in fact, I was lonely. But I still struggled with figuring out what I could say to someone I didn't remember.

"How are you feeling?" His voice was hopeful. "How are the ribs doing, and everything physical?"

"Good. I'm good." In his photo he was handsome; strong jaw, wide eyes, thick, dark spiky hair. Very well groomed. "How are you, Bradley? I know who you are because I've been told a little about you, and I saw your photo, but I'm sorry, I still don't remember anything from before the accident. About my friends, I mean."

"No? That's rough, girl. What do the doctors say?"

I sat on the sofa, heartened by his voice. He had an easy, interested manner; I heard no pretense there. "They say, 'Be patient. Rest. Get on with your life.' I say, 'What life' or 'Whose life?' But they don't seem to get my drift."

Silence in my ear. *Am I saying too much, revealing too much? Maybe Bradley isn't actually a close friend.*

"Morons," Bradley finally replied. "Most doctors can only deal with hard, cold facts. I remember the surgeon who operated on my mom for breast cancer saying, 'You're lucky you're healing so well. That's a nice, neat scar.' I thought Mom would slug him."

"She should have." I bit my lip. "How is your mom, Bradley?"

Silence.

"She died six years ago, Rox. Poor kid, you really don't remember anything?"

"I'm so sorry. I'm a freak show."

He chuckled. "Don't worry, little freak. It'll all come back to you. Although, since I turned thirty, I hardly remember anything myself."

We laughed together, and it felt so good it hurt.

"You sound normal to me, Roxanne. Tell me what's going on with you. Do you have a nurse? Are you feeding yourself?"

"Yeah, I can do the basics. But no nurse. Just me here at the apartment. I remember things other than my life, like all the basics of cooking, cleaning, driving. I know who is president, and who isn't, but I can't recall my personal history. With anyone."

"Hard to know who to trust then, eh?"

My heart leapt. At last, someone understood how crazy things were. "Yes. I have to take everyone at face value. Then try to read their reaction and fill in what state my relationship with them might have been. Before, before everything went black."

"You be careful, girl. The men you know will all try to pass themselves off as your current lover. Look out for that tennis coach. I remember you saying he's a pussy hound."

I didn't know who Bradley was referring to, but I thought of Michael Cimino and our encounter in the hospital. I apparently knew a lot of pussy hounds. "Thanks. I'll keep that in mind."

"I'll help you," Bradley said. "I can tell you what I know about your sex life, and you can take it from there."

"Great. Thanks." My face reddened, my brain wondering what exactly I had told Bradley.

"I can be your seeing eye diary. You told me everything, girlfriend. All the gory details." His voice was sweet, not leering, and he seemed to care about me. My neck and shoulders relaxed for the first time since I'd left the hospital.

"Thanks. I'm going to need some help from my friends sorting things out. But don't feel too sorry for me. Life is okay."

"I don't feel sorry for you, Rox. You're a fighter. Always have been. And a bit of a party girl, so fun will come back, too, don't worry your gorgeous head there." Bradley cleared his throat. "Look, I hate talking to you on the phone. Can I buy you dinner? If you're up to going out. Can you drink?"

"Ah, sure." Betty's admonition not to drink floated in and out of my head. "I'm dying for a glass of wine."

"Great. Red wine is one of my basic food groups. Let's go to Simone's."

"Sure. But what is that?"

"Oh. Christ, jeez. It's a great little joint you and I and Cathy," Bradley's voice caught, "you and I and friends have gone to a million times. It's right around the corner from your apartment. Are you up for it?"

"Tonight?"

"I'd love to tonight, but I have to teach a class. How about tomorrow night? I'll fill you in on anything you want to know about *everyone*. I know when you lost your virginity, and to who. I can tell you volumes about what's been going on for the past few years. Maybe it will jar something in your brain and help you remember stuff. Like I owe you fifty dollars."

"What do you owe me fifty dollars for?"

"A wedding present. For this bitch named Quillan neither of us like at all but we had to go to the wedding because Nick works for her, so we did and ate too many canapés and guzzled her champagne."

"So we're not very nice people, then?" I grinned.

"Oh, we're very nice. Cathy was a Girl Scout, and you're not much different. I, on the other hand, am a bit of a slut, but that's why I get invited everywhere." There was a short beat of silence. "You don't mind me mentioning Cathy, do you?"

"No. Of course not. But just so you know, I don't remember her either, Bradley. Or Nick. I know I've lost something, though. My best friend."

Bradley's tone grew more serious. "The heart remembers, Rox. You'll get your past back, and when you do, you will mourn. And it'll be hard. You and Cathy were closer than most sisters I know. But look, let's not talk about sad things. You rest, then make yourself beautiful, which for you means breathe, and I'll see you tomorrow."

"Thanks, Bradley. I'll see you then. But, where exactly is the restaurant?"

"Like I said, it's close, but why don't I pick you up?"

"Great. What time?"

"Seven sharp. Wear anything. Be comfy. It's not a fussy place. And plan for a long night. We've got some catching up to do, girlfriend!"

I laughed out loud. Bradley was upbeat and comforting and it was a joy to feel uncomplicated affection directed toward me. *The heart remembers,* he had said. I laid my hand on my chest and prayed this would prove true.

"I'll see you then, Bradley. At seven. Thanks a lot."

Glancing around the living room, things seemed brighter, as if the sunshine pouring in the windows had increased. This was a good idea, going out with a friend.

But suddenly I wondered how much I could trust Bradley. Who was to say if what he had heard from others, including me, was the *truth*? Was I a naturally cynical person? Maybe fear was making me doubt everyone.

I ran through the texts and missed calls display on the phone. Michael Cimino had called about a dozen times during the four days I'd been home. He'd left texts and messages offering to get together, although his tone was much more suggestive.

He called me 'baby' on one message. "I miss you, baby. I need to see you."

He'd also called the landline. I hadn't answered when I'd heard his voice on the answering machine, which I was using to screen calls. I didn't know why I was avoiding Michael. If we were ex-lovers, he might be able to help me retrieve some of my lost 'narrative memories' that Dr. Patel referred to. I could call and have him come over, ask him about the history of our relationship. He'd said he would help when he visited me in the hospital.

Maybe he could illustrate the high points. My face flushed at the explicit picture flashing through my mind. *Him, naked.*

I shook my head. Maybe the medication they gave me in the hospital was still affecting me and I was hallucinating again. Although the image of Michael Cimino's washboard abs and well-endowed manhood seemed shockingly real. But was it a fantasy or memory? I didn't know.

It would be interesting to hear what Bradley had to say about Michael tomorrow.

I went into the bedroom and got dressed. As I pulled a shirt over my head, the sight of my hands stopped me short. Nothing about this body was familiar, these hands most of all. They weren't bad hands; smooth, except for a couple of scabs from the car accident, with short, rounded nails that looked nice and healthy.

Carin, the nurse in the hospital, had offered to paint them for me. I declined because I didn't like painted nails. She nodded and helped me remove the chipped red polish I was wearing at the time, and I wondered if she thought I had stubby fingers.

She didn't say so, but I bet we were both thinking it.
God, I'm vain.

I threw myself onto the hard mattress. I wondered if I liked myself before the accident, because I was finding myself to be short-tempered and hard to get along with, proved by my constant avoidance of Betty Haverty, whose phone calls I was also not returning.

Having an 'ex' boyfriend who was sure I was willing to sleep with him didn't reflect very well on me, either. At least I had what sounded like a great friend named Bradley. *Too bad he's gay.*

I wondered about Cathy Chance and Bradley. They were good friends, too. His affection for her had been plain in his voice.

What would he say if the cops asked him if he thought it likely I'd deliberately caused a fatal car accident? They hadn't contacted me yet. I was hoping they wouldn't, ever.

"Stop!" I got up and brushed my hair hard, wishing it was longer, and without another glance in the mirror, went back and made the bed.

The blank space above, where the Van Gogh print had hung, reminded me I needed to buy a new picture. I thought again of my favorite Monet, and suddenly remembered it was called *The Bridge at Bougival*.

Where was it? At the L.A. County Art Museum? The Met in New York? No. But I knew I'd seen a print of it lately, on a wall in a cool room.

I finished the bed and stepped into white sandals. Things were starting to look a little disorganized in the closet. The apartment as a whole felt more lived in.

There was a stack of newspapers by the couch, and fresh flowers in every room. A box of school supplies and teaching materials overflowed on the kitchen table. I had spent the last couple of days thumbing through lesson plans on "Our Community," and fractions, and teacher's manuals on vocabulary lists. Even a date book from the last school year with entries like "Frog & Toad Party," or "Dinosaurs Alive Presentations."

These were the only things in the apartment I'd felt an emotional connection with. They seemed familiar, something I had touched and cared about. When I was reviewing a 'year-end summary' and report card list, I heard echoes of children's voices, school bells ringing in corridors that throbbed with sneaker-shod footsteps and chattering wonder.

Althea Cordell, the principal where I taught, had called early and asked me to come in today to go over plans for the next school year. When I suggested my amnesia would keep me from teaching, she disagreed.

"But how can I teach if I don't remember my past interactions with these kids?"

"You remember how to teach," Althea Cornell had replied. "You need to jump back in. Anyone who has been through college can follow a lesson plan. Besides, good teachers are a blessing. I can't afford to lose two."

Tears had filled my eyes at her oblique reference to Cathy Chance. "I appreciate your support. But do you think the kids will accept me if I can't remember them?"

"They will. I find children accept life a lot easier than adults. And I've always felt it best to accentuate the positive."

"Aren't you worried there may be parents who don't want me at school?"

"Not worried one whit. Anybody got any worries, I'll tell them the truth. You might not remember someone's name, or even your own, but you remember how to teach. They've read those two articles in the local paper about the accident and that you have some medical issues. But no one has suggested to me you not return until you're completely recovered."

"Are you sure, Miss Cordell?"

"Get your pretty self in here, Roxanne. It's time to get back on the horse. Besides, I need to give you some information about the new school year."

So, I picked up my purse and headed out. To work. And tomorrow night I had a date with Bradley. A friend! Things were definitely progressing.

I glanced at the photo of Roxanne, Cathy and Nick and smiled, then marched to the front door. *Ready or not, here I come.*

Minutes later, my bravado and my spirits ebbed. I was okay driving, but frankly, it made me nervous. I stared at the rental car for a few moments before I got in, buckled up, and managed to nose it out of the parking lot.

I couldn't remember the accident, but I felt shaky every time I got into a car. I kept thinking how awful it must have been. I rubbed my ribcage and stared straight ahead. My hands were sweating.

Althea had given me directions from the apartment to the school, and once on the street, I didn't feel completely lost. It was familiar in that logical 'but-I-have-no-personal-memory-of-it' way that life had become since I'd awakened in the hospital.

A huge grocery/drug store/Starbucks shopping center at the corner of Howard and Route 28 seemed right, as did the neat rows of older houses, the gas station advertising a sale on tires, and a row of fast food restaurants. I turned left off the main road and drove up to St. Anne's Episcopal School, on Gainsborough Road.

The elementary school sat on a couple of acres of prime residential real estate in the heart of Sierra Monte. With the blazing blue sky and rolling foothills as a backdrop, St. Anne was gracious and rustic, at home in the Southern California landscape of stucco, terra cotta tile and palm trees. Though much smaller, it looked like a mission with its quaint bell tower and wooden casement windows and trim.

A lush bougainvillea, scarlet and green against the dusty walls, made me smile as I walked from the car. I stopped and touched the flowers, like tissue paper jewels, with dry, prickly branches. The parking lots surrounding the school complex were empty in the middle of August. The grass was worn in most places, its summertime brown spilling onto the sidewalk. A billboard in front of the property was blank except for black letters, which read, "School Starts September 2! Have a Nice Summer!"

I hiked my purse strap over my shoulder and headed for the front office. I didn't remember where it was, but followed the footpath up the stairs to the logical place it would be. Through the black, wrought-iron gates, through the glass-paneled door with 'Principal' painted in small letters, I entered a bright room with a worn wooden counter, a waiting area with a scruffy couch and three student chairs.

A young woman was seated at the reception desk outside Althea Cordell's office; 'Vera Apodoca,' according to her nameplate. She was short and heavy-set, with beautiful teeth and wavy dark hair.

Her eyes filled the second she saw me. "Roxanne! Oh my gosh!" A tear rolled down her cheek as she came around the counter to give me a gentle hug. "It's so good to see you."

"Thank you." It was awkward. Everyone was a stranger with a blank slate, though they had a shared history with me only they remembered. An odd sensation, not knowing if someone was friend or foe.

I smiled. "This is a beautiful office. Sunny and warm. I bet the kids don't even mind getting sent up here."

"Oh, no one likes being sent up here. Ms. Cordell can be scary, but she's always fair." Vera searched my face. "How are you feeling? You look fantastic. As usual."

"Thanks."

"We went to the hospital, me and Freddy. And called. But we never heard back from you." She sounded wounded.

"I'm sorry. I'm slow in getting back to everyone. Who is Freddy?"

"My husband. And he won't be pleased to hear you don't remember him." She sounded sarcastic. "You know men. He's your tennis coach. He's been concerned about you. He said to tell you he'll fit you back into his schedule as soon as you're ready."

Tennis coach, huh? A man named Freddy had left a couple of messages I hadn't answered since I couldn't be less interested in playing tennis. "Thank you. And please thank Freddy for me."

"I will." She took a deep breath. "I'm going to miss Cathy so much. I'm sure you are, too. You were best friends,

I know, but she was so wonderful to everyone." She pressed her hands over her stomach. "She helped me so much these past couple of years, I just can't believe she won't be here ever again."

I patted her arm, but dropped my hand when I realized it was Cathy who was Vera's friend, not me.

"Her memorial service was beautiful. All the kids were there. And parents. The choir sang "Ave Maria." It made everyone cry." Vera dabbed at her eyes. "I know you would have been touched if you could have seen it."

"I wish I had been well enough to be there."

"I know you were too ill to attend. And I'm sorry to bring up such an unhappy event. But do you . . ." Vera glanced at the closed door to Althea's office.

"Remember? Sorry, no. Nothing yet." I smiled and my face hurt with the effort. "But don't worry. I'm betting I will soon."

"It's so amazing. You died, didn't you? And came back. Do you remember *anything*?" She brought the small crucifix hanging on a chain around her neck to her lips.

She was being ghoulish, but hey, I *had* died, according to what Dr. Badu had told me. Had stopped breathing. I could understand anyone being curious, and terrified, about this. Especially a practicing Catholic.

"No, Vera. I don't remember anything before the hospital. Weird, huh?"

Vera seemed to be mentally making the sign of the cross to ward off the notion of death, or of me. I thought of a TV show about zombies, and how you had to shoot them in the head to kill them. "Well, tell your husband I said hi. And I guess I'll go see Ms. Cornell. Is she in?"

"Roxanne!" Althea Cornell's voice boomed out and Vera and I glanced toward her, me with a sense of relief.

"Hi. I made it."

"So you did. No problem with my directions? Did you need them?"

"No. I mean, no, no problem. I did need them." I nodded at the secretary. "I was just telling Vera I don't remember anything. She's been filling me in."

Althea gave Vera a stern look and the woman scurried to her desk. "Come on with me, Roxanne." Althea took my arm. "Let's go see your new classroom."

"New?"

"Yes, we repainted it this summer, and moved you over to the east side of the building. I've put you in Room 14, with the big windows."

I felt Vera's eyes on me. For some reason I was sure she was already on the phone, telling someone about her first sighting of the 'back–from-the-dead' teacher.

Althea chatted about a new janitor, increased enrollment, the first scheduled assembly as we walked. I felt buoyant yet disconnected, as if I watched myself from above instead of beside the principal.

The hallway was dark and a bit stuffy, due to the air conditioning being cut back during the summer months. But it was wide and clean, the linoleum gleaming and the bulletin boards lining the walls freshly painted and ready for new displays.

We passed the auditorium and I caught sight of several rows of metal chairs, bolted to the ground, like a movie theatre. Room 14 was right around the corner from the theatre, and it did, indeed, have big windows. Floor to ceiling, they looked out on a courtyard that held a fountain rimmed with cement benches. The fountain had been drained and the orange, white, and green tiles lining the cistern were dry. But inside my head I heard the bubble and gurgle of silky blue water and the splash of children's hands, giggles of conspiracy filling the air over their delight at playing in a forbidden area.

A startling noise, a pop loud as a gunshot, brought me back to the here and now. The noise was from the principal snapping on the classroom's overhead lights. "Let's shed some light on the subject," she announced.

I made a mental note to not jump when I flipped on the switch in front of the kids.

The room was great; four unit areas for reading, painting, tables instead of desks, and a teacher's desk beside a bookcase. I ran my hand across the rows of stories, the Cam Jansen mysteries, Maurice Sendek's lovely monsters, *The Magic School Bus* and *Mr. Popper's Penguins*. I also noted a whole series of books on Impressionist painters that introduced the young kids to the fabulous concepts of pointillism, color and revolution.

All books I loved. *All books I remember*!

"So, what do you think, Roxanne?" Althea asked. She leaned against the green board, her dark eyes watchful.

"It's great to be here. It's the first place I've felt I belonged since I woke up in the hospital."

"Do you think you'll have much problem with lesson plans?"

"No." I told her about my efforts the past couple of days at home.

"Well then, that's settled. I'll expect you the first day." She pointed to a pile of plastic crates beside the teacher's desk. "I had Vera pull everything out of your old desk and bookcases. Do you want help sorting through this stuff or putting it away?"

"No, thanks. What I'd like is to stay a bit and go through it myself. If you don't mind." I looked at Althea, hoping she wouldn't be slighted.

"Not at all. Good idea. No telling what these scraps of papers and files might bring back, Roxanne." She glanced at her watch. "I've got an eleven o'clock meeting with a new student and their parents, so I need to head back to the office. How about I come back in an hour or so? We can go get lunch."

"That would be great." I was grateful for her understanding and the fact that she didn't seem to want anything *personal* from me. My lack of memory didn't matter to her; she needed a teacher. And she seemed more than willing to trust that I was up to the job.

It was a relief after Michael Cimino and Betty Haverty.

For the next several minutes I went through the crates and moved and organized folders full of teaching materials so I could transfer them to the desk. The printing on the folder tabs was bold and block-faced, as if done by a serious seven-year-old. I took several new folders and labeled them, annoyed I couldn't replicate the writing style on the others.

I looked through the books, enjoying this task immensely. I knew I could quote aloud from many of the stories. There were several dictionaries and a complete, unused set of vocabulary workbooks. I went back to the last plastic bin to hunt for scissors, and came across a strange little container.

It was the size of a small box of cigars, and covered with green cloth. Someone had appliquéd a forest scene of felt figures onto the cloth. Two big owls sat in the middle of the scene. One had a bubble drawn in felt marker over its head that said, '$10 Please.'

Inside there was a stack of small bills, held together with a paperclip. Written across the bottom of the box, in the same block-lettered writing on all my folders, were the words, 'Shut-up!' followed by a series of names and dates.

Cathy-Jan3-$10. Cathy-Jan31-$10. Cathy-Feb13-$10.

My hands shook. I had no idea what this meant, but it must have been some kind of game between Cathy Chance and Roxanne.

Cathy and me.

I closed the box and stared out the window at the fountain. An image unfolded of a school auditorium stage filled with children dressed in strange animal-like costumes. "Lupeyloo, Lupeyloo, don't be a fool, just be you," they sang.

A door opened behind me and I gave a little yelp of surprise, turning to find a teenager staring at me.

"Sorry," she said quickly.

As I watched, her expression changed from apology to something that looked, shockingly, like hate. "Roxanne." The girl's voice was flat and oh, so angry.

"Hi." I extended my right hand.

The girl stared at me, blinked, and then looked at my outstretched hand as if it were a snake. "I didn't know you were going to be at school today," she said.

"Yes. First visit since . . ." Words failed me. I sat at the desk. This girl knew me, but I had no clue who she was. She was skinny, with an edgy haircut, bleached blonde, and blue painted fingernails. She wore baggy shorts and a crop top. Her nose was pierced, as was her naval, and a new tattoo was raised and scabby on her right arm.

"Since the accident?" the girl said.

"Yes. Since the accident."

She looked away. She carried a satchel with some folders, much like the ones I was going through. The writing on the top folder looked like mine. Was this a staff member?

God, she's so young.

"I'm sorry, I'm not sure if you've heard, but I was injured badly in an accident, and I don't exactly remember everything very well. People's names, in particular. So forgive me, but who are you?"

The girl's eyes narrowed. "Zoë. Zoë Chance. I'm Nick's sister."

I felt like I took a blow to the chest. "Zoë? You're Cathy's, Cathy's . . ."

"Sister-in-law." Zoë watched as I collapsed back against the desk chair.

"How are you, Zoë? How is Nick?" My voice broke and I laced my fingers together and pushed them into my lap.

"Nick's bad. As bad as it gets. He walks around like the fucking living dead, if you want to know the truth. But then, how else would he be?"

Tears burned my eyes. I thought of saying the words, 'I'm sorry,' but I knew if I tried, I would choke. And Zoë Chance did not look like she wanted to hear them from me, anyway. She was in the grip of her own rage and grief.

And who could blame her?

Zoë stared out the window at the fountain for several moments. "You're moving into this room?"

"Yes."

"Cathy always wanted this room. She said it was the best one in the whole school."

I was again struck mute. So, I killed her sister-in-law, and got her classroom. Pretty cut and dried as another good reason for her hatred.

Zoë glanced at my face, then to the desk. She stared at the box with the money in it. "Do you remember that?"

"No. No, I don't."

There was anguish in Zoë's dark eyes. Without thinking, I went to her and hugged her hard, my tears falling on the pale skin of her arm. "I am so sorry, Zoë. Please tell Nick I am so sorry about the accident. I can't explain what I mean by this, and forgive me for saying it, but I don't even remember Cathy. It's so unfair that she's gone and I'm not. I'm so, so sorry. And I miss her, too."

She went rigid in my embrace but I didn't let her go. I couldn't. After a few seconds, Zoë dropped the canvas bag of files and leaned her head on my shoulder. She gasped and started to cry, making noises like a hurt animal, deep, guttural sounds of loss, sounds almost too hard to bear.

Through my own tears I saw that her new tattoo was one word. *Cathy.*

Zoë caught her breath and stepped away. "I've got to go." She picked up her bag and walked out of the room. The door closed and I stared after her, drained, as the numbness I'd felt in the hospital returned.

I picked up a crate of files, threw in the box with the money and hurried from the room. Despite knowing it was coming, I flinched when I shut off the light. The noise was horrible. Like metal striking metal. Like a car hitting a truck.

My head pounded and my legs shook. I needed to get back to the apartment and into bed. I wanted to sleep and not be awake. Not think of what now ran through my mind, for while I was hugging Zoë I had a vision, one so clear it was surely a memory. It was of the man I'd had thoughts of before.

This time he lay on his side, shirtless, in bed. His wide, strong shoulders were tan and close enough to touch. I could smell him, sweet and soapy and sexy.

The man was Nick Chance, Zoë's brother. *Cathy's husband.*

Why had such an intimate image of Nick Chance taken over my brain? It made no sense. My past was on the verge of coming back to me. And I realized that it might not be full of the memories I had been told to expect.

But one thing was clear. I needed to talk to Nick.

I hurried out to the car, threw the stuff inside, and pulled out of the parking lot, finding it hard to see through my tears but determined to get as far away from this place as I could.

Chapter 8

Monday, July 25, 4:20 p.m.
Nick at Golden State Insurance Office

I shot my sister a questioning look and she nodded, so I picked up a pen and signed the papers releasing Roxanne Ruiz's car insurance company and Betty Haverty's homeowner insurance company, the same conglomerate, from any further claims due to the death of my wife.

There was a case pending against the truck driver, but I had little stomach for a prosecution that would award me 'probably over a million dollars.' So the lawyer had said.

"Payable over ten thousand years," Zoë had added.

This, from the asshole drunk who had no job, no home, no insurance, no nothing. He was going to prison, probably for more than ten years according to the district attorney, for killing her.

It wasn't enough. But it was enough to stop me from thinking about tracking him to where he lived and killing *him*.

I handed the pen back to Steven Schribner, the attorney handling this claim, and wondered how I would feel about the truck driver in ten years. I couldn't imagine ten years. Hard as I tried, I could barely see the end of the day. Not even tomorrow.

"Thank you, Mr. Chance. And if you'd initial this last document, we're done. Your check is in the envelope." He offered me the pen again and I glanced over to where Zoë sat watching. I took it and scribbled my name. Schribner, a portly, white haired gent who smelled like cigarettes, handed me the envelope.

While he worked his way through a few more papers, I gave the envelope to Zoë, as if it would burn my hand if I held onto it too long. She stuck it quickly in her backpack. It was for $263,111; a two hundred thousand-dollar death benefit, the rest for hospital bills, emergency services and burial costs.

Zoë and I were lower middle class kids. We'd never touched this kind of dough, and I could see she was as unsettled as I was to have that kind of money in our possession.

When Cathy and I bought our house, we'd taken a cashier's check for $22,104 to the closing. It was every cent that we had saved for six years, plus an eighteen hundred-dollar advance from our Visa card. When we refinanced a couple years ago to build the patio, put in a new bathroom and the kitchen floor, we'd been given a check for $25,050.

Cathy said, "Wow, we're rich!"

Being handed a check that was ten times Cathy's 'rich' money was one more unreal moment in the surreal past few weeks. Others included having to decide what to bury my wife in.

"The blue dress is nice, it always flattered her," my mother had offered. Five minutes after telling my mom to pick whatever she thought, I answered the front bell and had to tell the Girl Scout mom who was dropping off Cathy's cookie order that Cathy was dead.

"Dead?" The woman's cheeks flushed as worry clouded her eyes. "I'm so sorry. Do you still want the cookies?"

"One last thing, Mr. Chance," the attorney said as Zoë and I headed for the door.

"Yes?"

"Dr. Haverty would like to speak to you for a moment, if you don't mind."

Zoë inhaled loudly.

"What about?" I asked.

"I think she wants to express her condolences. She said she didn't get the opportunity to speak to you at your wife's service."

"I don't remember anything about that." Which was true.

His watery blue eyes looked sympathetic. "I'm sure you don't. My wife died last year. We were married thirty-eight years. I can't recall anything about the day we buried her. I know what you're feeling, Nick. But I also know Dr. Haverty. She's a fine woman. I'm sure she'll keep it brief."

"Nick?" Zoë said.

I realized I had been staring for a longer time than was socially acceptable. Betty Haverty. Okay. I'd met her on a handful of occasions over the years; Cathy's graduation, a wedding, and once at Roxanne's during the holidays. She had seemed nice enough. Maybe a little superior. Cathy didn't think she was a very supportive mother.

"Okay," I said. "When?"

"Now," Mr. Schribner replied. "She's waiting across the hall. Why don't I show her in and leave you folks alone for a couple of minutes? Take all the time you need."

Zoë sank onto the leather sofa. Her eyes were huge. I returned to the chair. We looked at one another.

"You going to be all right?" she asked.

I nodded and heard her stomach growl. Before I could ask if she'd eaten anything at all today, the door opened.

Betty Haverty walked in and promptly burst into tears.

Great. Why the hell was she crying? What was I supposed to say to her?

The attorney handed Betty a box of Kleenex and left. She sat next to Zoë on the couch and seemed to compose herself.

"I'm so sorry for your loss, Nick." She squeezed Zoë's knee. "And yours too, Zoë. How are you doing?"

Zoë clutched her backpack and smiled like a ghost. "Fine."

"Good. You look lovely." She nodded at me. "I wanted to let you know, Nick, that Roxanne is home now. She was released a few days ago. She's doing much better, and getting ready to go back to teaching, if you can believe that. Althea Cornell, the principal—"

"I know who Althea is," I interrupted. "I've known her for years."

"Of course you do, Nick. I'm sorry." Betty turned to Zoë. "Althea told me you spoke with Roxanne today when you went to pick up some of Cathy's things."

Zoë nodded. "Her lunch cooler. Ms. Cordell said Cathy's lunch cooler was in the teacher's room. And some files and stuff. While I was there, I saw Roxanne."

I was shocked.

"Well." Betty folded her hands in her lap. "I wanted the opportunity to tell you in person how sorry I am about Cathy's death, Nick. And I want you to know if there is anything I can do, or Roxanne can do, please let us know."

I nodded again, unable to talk.

Betty stood, and I struggled to my feet to get the door for her. Shockingly, she hugged me. I had known the woman for twenty years and I was pretty sure it was the first time we'd ever hugged. I remembered that even at my wedding, she shook hands with Cathy and kissed her cheek, and smiled at me in the reception line.

'The cold fish,' Cathy used to call her.

Betty's eyes glistened. "I know Roxanne would like to meet with you, Nick."

"With me?"

"Yes. I think it would help you both move past this. Whenever you're ready." She faced me squarely. "I have a couple of books in my car I'd like to give you. They deal with the stages of grief people commonly experience with the sudden loss of a loved one. I've used them in my practice for years, and I've received a lot of feedback from people about how helpful they are. You know, it's very healing sometimes to realize that others have felt the same pain you are experiencing. And that it's okay to grieve, be disbelieving, even angry. It's all part of the process."

Like a bobble head, I moved my skull up and down. I heard that rushing water noise in my ears, the same as in the hospital the day Cathy died.

I didn't want to see Roxanne. Not now. Not ever again. As for moving past the loss of my wife . . . I balled my fingers into fists.

Betty squeezed my arm. "It would also be helpful, Nick, and Zoë as well, to get some counseling. Grief counseling is a very specialized art. I can give you the name of some of my colleagues, if you want. To help you move on."

"I don't want to move on, Betty," I blurted out. "If anything, I want to move back in time. To July 9. I want to go back to that day and pull Roxanne's head out of her ass and tell her to grow up and stop dragging my wife around like a fucking security blanket. If she didn't care about her own life, fine, but she should have been careful not to kill my wife!"

Betty Haverty went white, her arms rigid at her side.

Zoë clutched her backpack. "Nick, don't . . ."

"So tell Roxanne I don't care to meet with her." My voice got louder. "And tell her that when she can remember her life, to remember that Cathy was the best person she ever knew, and the best goddamned friend she ever had. And that she's lost that friend now because she's a careless, selfish, boneheaded bitch who never thinks about anyone but herself."

I brushed past Betty and grabbed Zoë by the arm and pulled her off the creaking leather couch.

Zoë seemed to hover beside me, weightless, a mute Tinkerbell as I stormed through the hallway. I didn't hear her footsteps beside me, but I could hear Betty crying and Steven Schribner call my name as we took the stairs to our car.

I knew I was acting like an asshole. I knew Cathy would be disappointed in my behavior, and that Zoë was probably convinced her brother had tripped right off the deep end.

But I didn't turn back. Call it the *'don't give a fuck whose feelings you hurt'* phase of grieving. Because I didn't.

Chapter 9

Monday, July 25, 6 p.m.
Roxanne's Apartment

Exhausted, my hands shook so badly I could hardly slot the key in the front lock. I'd gotten lost leaving St. Anne's after seeing Zoë Chance, and drove into the Angeles National Forest; pulled off into a scenic overlook. But I didn't watch the scenery, I sat and cried. Finally, I got my sense of direction back and followed the GPS voice back to the apartment.

The confrontation with Zoë had rocked my equilibrium. These past few days I had lulled myself into thinking everyone would react to me as Althea and Michael and Bradley had, with sympathy and support. I had counted on goodwill from people, assuming they would only want the best for me.

As if Roxanne Ruiz is the center of the universe. What a foolish person I am.

Though I had worried about people's reaction to my role in the accident that caused a woman's death, I had not expected to be confronted with criticism, as with Vera Apodoca's comments about the memorial service, or Zoë's naked pain and anger.

Hadn't Mick Jagger explained a person couldn't always get what they wanted? *Duh.*

I hurried in and closed the door, dropping my school bag on the floor. It promptly tipped over and the '$10 Please' box tumbled out, spilling its contents. I picked up the money and threw it and the box back into the bag, then opened the closet, tossed the bag inside, and slammed the door.

It was hell to not remember. I should remember, and feel shame or outrage, or loss or anger or whatever it was I would feel if I could recall my emotional attachment to the people whose lives had been wrecked. If I didn't ever remember, how would these people who had suffered such a loss ever get past it?

How would I?

The tea I made remained untouched in front of me while I sat on the sofa and stared at the cell phone. I needed to call Nick Chance. These past hours convinced me I had to talk to him sooner rather than later, touch base with him, hear his voice.

I lifted the phone. But what would I say other than the obvious? 'I'm sorry about the accident.' I practiced aloud, and sounded lame. Like a zombie, and an insincere one at that.

A glance at the clock told me Nick would probably be home from work by now. I picked up the cell again and punched in his number; let it ring, the tension in my throat intense. When his voicemail came on, I got a shock and slammed down the receiver.

Nick hadn't changed the message since Cathy's death.

Her voice *was* familiar and hearing it brought fresh tears to my eyes. After a few minutes I took a sip of my tepid tea, then got up and stomped into the bedroom, disrobed, and buried myself under the covers. But I couldn't sleep.

After what seemed like days but was actually less than two hours of staring at the ceiling, tossing, turning and trying unsuccessfully to relax, I rolled out of bed and went back to the phone. I had decided, under those non-comforting covers, what I would say. *"Nick, may I come by and talk to you?"* Simple and honest. No trying to 'read him' or save myself from hurt. That was it.

Betty said he was a kind, easygoing guy. He wouldn't turn down a personal request like this. My hands perspired. In my ear, the sound of his phone ringing was clear and measured, like a heartbeat.

Three rings. Four rings. Five rings. Then her voice. "Hi, this is Nick and Cathy. Leave us a message. Bye now."

My eyes ached. *God, this is hard.* "Nick, may I come and talk to you?" I said in a rush. Then I heard a beep.

Had I spoken too quickly? I dropped the phone and slumped back into the sofa and closed my eyes, fighting nausea and a sensation of weightlessness.

From somewhere outside I heard chimes, clear, melodic wind chimes. I listened hard to pinpoint the source of the sound, but now that I was paying attention, the sound disappeared. I rubbed my eyes, swollen with tears or sadness or fatigue. I didn't know which emotion was predominant, though they all held their hands up as I called roll.

And I was exhausted. At least I might now be able to sleep. I snuggled against the cushion but right before I dropped off I realized I had not said my name in my message.

I wondered if Nick would recognize my voice.

I dreamed.

It was raining and I slipped and fell and hurt myself very badly. My arm was broken and my head was bleeding. I was in a hospital, though it looked like my classroom at St. Anne's. A few feet away, a young, blonde-haired girl with long legs and perfect oval eyes was sitting on a student chair across from me, staring.

There was a lemon tree in a pot next to her. I could smell the lemons.

"What happened to you?" I asked her.

"My stepfather hit me," she replied.

"That's horrible." The right side of her face was swollen, black and blue. "Did you call the police?" I asked.

She shook her head and placed a red snow cone against her injured face. As sweet, red liquid dripped down her cheek, a gray cat with yellow eyes rubbed against her legs, but she ignored it.

"There's someone at the door," the girl whispered.

I reached out to pet the cat. There was a crash and I woke up and saw the teacup on the floor. And someone was knocking on the door.

For a moment I had no idea where I was. Then I remembered. *Roxanne's apartment.*

I got up stiffly and walked to the door; peered out the peephole. Michael Cimino was outside. I ran my hand through my hair and looked at my watch; it glowed 9:25. I opened the door, leaving the security chain in place.

"Hi," I said through the slim opening.

"Hey, beautiful." Michael was dressed in jeans and a white tee shirt, a beat up leather jacket under one arm. He held a small paper bag and his dark hair was wet from a shower. He took a step back and met my eyes. "Can I come in?"

I shouldn't have opened the door. "Ah, I was asleep, Michael."

"Little early, isn't it, babe?"

"No, not really. I'm still recovering, remember? You should call before you come over."

He crossed his arms over his broad chest. "Yeah, I did. Several times. You don't answer, and you don't call back. But I need to talk to you, Roxanne. It's important."

"I still don't remember anything. I can't remember you. Or us."

He nodded. "That's okay, babe. I remember 'us' enough for two. Why don't you relax and let me come inside for a few minutes and I'll bring you up to speed. I'm not going to hurt you."

I knew I shouldn't let him in. It wasn't that I was afraid of Michael Cimino; I just didn't want to be alone with him. His kiss in the hospital room loomed in my mind.

"I know that," I said.

"Good. So, let me in. We'll talk."

He made 'talk' sound like something intimate. "Okay, for a couple of minutes," I said sternly.

"Sure. I'll leave whenever you say, Miss Ruiz." His green eyes glowed as he held the paper bag aloft. "But I brought you some ice cream we need to eat first. Your favorite."

"Lemon sorbet?" I said without thinking.

"Whoa! Lemon sorbet? What kind of sissy ice cream is that? Your favorite is 'Cherry Garcia,' same as mine. You really don't remember anything if you've forgotten that." He took a step closer.

"Hang on." I shut the door, undid the security chain, and let him in.

"No lights? What were you doing in here?" Michael asked.

I snapped on the lamp beside the front door. "I was sleeping. I told you."

He gave me a head to toe appraisal, for the first time treated to my appearance, which featured faded sweatpants, baggy tee shirt and no make-up.

"I'll get some bowls for the ice cream." He put the brown sack on the coffee table and disappeared into the kitchen. I took that opportunity to duck into the bathroom. I locked the door while I washed my face, brushed my hair and, as a nod toward civility, rolled on some red lipstick. The face in the mirror looked presentable. Actually, it looked beautiful, but I didn't feel beautiful. I felt pissed off, like I wanted to throttle the truth out of someone.

When I returned to the living room, Michael was sitting on the sofa. He had put on music, Norah Jones singing about not understanding why she didn't go see her lover, and had dished up two huge bowls of ice cream. I smelled the chocolate when I sat at the opposite end of the sofa and my stomach did another little flip.

Do I like cherry vanilla ice cream with chocolate chunks? Yes. Yes, I do.

We ate in silence, the music dreamy around us. "So, how you doing, babe?" Michael set his bowl on the table and leaned back into the pillows. "Tell the truth."

I took a last bite and placed my bowl next to his. "Pretty good." I eased as far from Michael as I could get. "All the scabs are healing, and my ribs aren't so sore."

"And how's this?" he asked, tapping his head.

"What do you mean? The concussion?"

"How are you *feeling in here?* Come on, Rox, you can tell me. Are you sleeping? Are you taking your meds? Are you still depressed?"

"I have a lot to be depressed about, wouldn't you agree? A woman's dead, for Christ's sake."

Michael put his hand on my arm. "I know, I know. It's horrible about Cathy, it is. But I'm concerned about you, Roxanne. I don't know if your mom explained it to you or not, but you weren't in good shape before the accident."

"Actually, Betty hasn't explained much to me at all. I was hoping, Michael, that you'd do me a favor."

"Yes. Sure. What do you need?"

"Will you tell me about Roxanne as she existed before July 9? Tell me what was going on in her life."

"You mean between *us*?"

The man had a very healthy ego. "That, too. But I want to know about everyone in my life then. Tell me whatever you know."

"Is it okay? I mean, the doctors in the hospital said no one should hit you with too much. Overwhelm you. That's why I've been keeping my distance. Giving you space until you could remember something."

"I can take it." I met his eyes. "Please."

"Okay," he said after a few seconds. "But can I kiss you first? I miss you so much, Roxanne. And I thought you were dead. It's been horrible for me."

I felt a pang of empathy for him, but before I could answer, Michael pulled me to him and kissed me. I wasn't that surprised. I think I expected him to do this from the moment I saw him outside the door. Maybe I wanted him to.

When I didn't protest, he deepened the kiss, pushing his tongue into my mouth, demanding unspoken things my body responded to independently from my brain.

For a few seconds I was a spectator, watching as two bodies that knew each other very well got reacquainted. Then, despite the fog that filled my brain in the place of sweet remembrances, I became a willing participant.

Michael Cimino was skilled. Very, very skilled. He removed my clothes and his own without me noticing either while his hands, fingers, mouth and energy were all enveloping, leading, demanding, showing me what to do and when to do it.

Naked above me, he was gorgeous. Broad chest covered with silky black hair. Round, firm butt, muscular legs and arms. His penis was thick and he knew how to move and thrust and inside of ten minutes I was panting and moaning and begging him to move faster. Hearing that, he withdrew and put his mouth to work on me.

Oh my God, what he did with his tongue, and his lips, with the stubble on his chin. I climaxed and screamed softly, then came harder a second time, for what seemed like five minutes. I had the fleeting thought someone might hear me and call the cops for help.

Immediately, an image of another time having sex with Michael flooded my senses. I could see him in my mind's eye; we were on a beach in the dark. I felt the sand grinding into my naked skin and the hot hardness of his dick probing for the moist center between my legs. "I knew you wanted this," he said in the memory.

I'm remembering!

My brain recoiled from that revelation and whipped back to the present. I wanted him at that moment more than I wanted to breathe. Sex freed me from myself and my blank past in a way sleep, or drugs or therapy had not been able to.

I was free of the past, the future, and all speculation. I was only flesh, a bundle of nerve endings begging to be sated. Michael pulled me to the floor and rolled me over onto my hands and knees and entered me from behind like he owned me.

He cupped my breasts and pinched my nipples between his smooth fingers and did me for more thought-numbing minutes. I came again, then again explosively with him a final time.

When he was done, he collapsed over me. I was vaguely aware of rug burns on my knees and hands, but I was liquid flesh without a voice and didn't care and could not have moved if I did.

Minutes later, I took my first non-gasping breath and looked at my watch. It said 10:29.

"Jesus," I said.

He lifted his head. "Welcome home, Roxanne. I've missed you, babe."

"Is it always like this between us?"

"It's always good. But *that* was something. You've never been so willing."

"What, I'm usually a tease?" I didn't like saying that about myself and bit my lip.

"No, no. But sometimes, I don't feel like you want to let go. Like maybe you don't enjoy sex as much as I do."

"Wow." How anyone could not enjoy what he had just done to me, with me, was beyond me.

Unless of course, there were issues between us. Issues that came between your body's ability to enjoy because your heart and mind were distracted by other concerns. *Like fidelity.*

I touched his face. "You're very, very good at this. Thank you."

He kissed my hand and his smile was boyishly proud and unguarded. "Don't get me wrong. We've always been hot in the sack, but this, this was amazing." A shadow passed across his eyes and he squinted. "You seem different, somehow. Like you've changed, babe."

Which of course brought me right back to my question of an hour ago. "Yeah. Okay, so talk to me. Tell me about Roxanne."

Michael rolled onto his back. "Roxanne is a hundred percent prime cut. The most gorgeous girl in the room, any room. And Roxanne is smart. Maybe not book smart like Cathy Chance, but savvy."

Was I imagining it, or was there an edge to Michael's voice when he said Cathy's name?

"Cathy was book smart, huh?"

"Yeah. Phi krappa yahoo everything, so I always heard. Nose in a book all the time. And loved those snooty movies with foreign languages in them."

I thought of a foreign movie, something with Catherine Deneuve and black rain. I couldn't recall the title. "Were you friends with Cathy?"

"Me? Yeah, sure. I mean, we talked. Hung out. I like her husband. Nick's a good guy. Not as much fun since he stopped drinking, but that's cool." He stared off into the dark. "He's not doing so good, I hear."

My skin itched. I didn't want to talk about Nick with Michael. "Did you go to her memorial service?"

"Yeah. They had good food and wine at their place after. But I felt out of place."

"Why?"

He shrugged. "I don't know. You weren't with me, for one thing. And to tell the truth, I don't think your friend Cathy liked me much. I kept thinking about her. And you. I was thankful to God that you didn't die, too."

His words, while tender, chilled me. I grasped his arm. Michael misunderstood my touch and kissed my shoulder. "To tell the truth, I never could figure that chick out."

"What do you mean?"

"I don't know. She never seemed to know what she wanted, if you ask me. 'Co-flicted,' I think they call it. Like she had something to say, but had decided not to say it."

"Conflicted, you mean? Like she was unsure about something?"

He shrugged. "Yeah. I guess."

I didn't want to hear any more about Cathy or Nick from Michael, even though I had asked him to tell me. It felt disloyal, talking about her with someone who didn't like her much. "Okay. So I'm not smart?"

Hadn't Betty said I had helped Cathy get through school? I filed that discrepancy away.

"Hey, hey. I never said you're not smart. You did okay in school, but you didn't care much if you got good grades. You know people, know what they want. You should be in sales, instead of teaching. I always said you should come to work for me and my brother. With your looks, you'd make a fortune."

"What do you and your brother do?"

Michael frowned. "Right. The memory thing. My family owns three car dealerships. I manage Cimino Jaguar. Hey, and by the way, you're going need a new car now. Come in tomorrow and my brother Tommy and I will fix you up."

"With a Jag?" There was six hundred dollars in the checkbook I balanced yesterday. "I think that's a little rich for a second-grade teacher."

"You'll get a deal. A good deal." Michael flashed a smile. "I'll take care of you." His hand caressed my right nipple, sending a sweep of heat across my chest.

I covered his hand with mine. I was done and didn't want anything more from Michael in the physical sense. But I still wanted information.

"Look, I'm curious about the depression thing. Has that been going on the whole time you've known me? Do you know if this was a long-term problem?"

"I think it's a sickness you've dealt with since you were a kid. Brain chemistry, right? You don't like to talk about it, though. So, I can't help too much there. I think you take a couple of drugs."

"Paxil. And Xanax. Roxanne has bottles of them in the bedroom."

"Roxanne? I got to tell you, it's a little freaky how you talk like Roxanne is someone else."

I met Michael's stare. He was grinning, but his eyes were wary. I wondered what the doctors had said to him, or what Betty Haverty had told him, about my mental health issues.

"You're right. But I can't help thinking of Roxanne Ruiz in the third person. She's still separate from me. Another person. Does that bother you?"

"No. Not really." He ran his hand across my stomach. "It's like you're a new girl. Kind of exciting, in a kinky kind of way."

He moved closer and I felt him responding, developing a new need. I sat up quickly, now self-conscious about the naked body he was caressing. "Let me throw some clothes back on. It's cold in here."

"I can warm you up again." Michael's hand tightened on my arm. "Come on, baby, you know you want some more." He moved his hand between my legs.

A jolt of adrenaline coursed through me. The image I

had previously accepted as part of a memory of coupling with Michael filled my mind again.

It was a summer night. Were we hiding from someone?

I shook my head to rattle the memory into focus, not sure if it was sexual imagination or reality. "You better go now, Michael. I need to get some rest." I stood up.

He stayed put. After a moment he said, "You've got the sweetest tits in the world."

I covered them with my hands. "You better get dressed."

"Okay." He acted disappointed but didn't push the issue.

I threw my clothes back on and cleared the dishes off the table; snapped on more lights. It was almost eleven and I could barely keep my eyes open. I grasped the counter and took a breath.

"You okay?" Michael said from the kitchen doorway. "Roxanne?"

"Yeah, I'm just tired. Really. I'm fine. Thanks again for bringing the ice cream, and, and everything."

"Anytime, baby." Michael kissed my neck, his tongue leaving a cool trail on my skin. "I'll call you tomorrow. Remember what I said about getting you a car, okay?"

"Thanks." I walked him to the door, gave him a brief goodnight kiss and locked up.

"Would you buy a used car from this guy?" My question echoed in the empty apartment and it felt like I was tottering on the edge of hysteria. Something was happening in my brain. I needed to concentrate, but first I needed to sleep. I fell into the tangle of blankets and sheets and was out cold, probably before Michael reached the parking lot.

Chapter 10

Wednesday, July 27, 7 p.m.
Roxanne's Apartment

As I waited nervously for Bradley Chandler to take me to dinner, I thought about Nick Chance. I wanted to leave another message for him but after last night's encounter with Michael, I hesitated. My evening with Michael reinforced how tricky it was dealing with people when you did not know the dynamics of the relationship. All I could do was react and hope I wouldn't make a misstep, like an acrobat without a net.

I didn't want to damage things any further with Nick. Hopefully, Bradley would fill me in on what Cathy's husband thought of me, at least before the accident. I was counting on his memories of the three of us to help me make some real progress toward re-establishing my life.

I glanced again at the phone table. There were three messages on the answering machine from Betty. Her voice sounded strained in the last message. "The insurance settlement meeting with Nick was a disaster."

I didn't know what that meant, but figured it could wait until tomorrow. Living up to Betty's so far unstated, but obviously held opinion that Roxanne was selfish, could be taxing. The woman sounded needy, but in my current state of haziness I was certain I couldn't say anything to make her feel better. I prayed it would be easier with Bradley.

I reached for my right ear and put in silver hoops for tonight. At the last minute I added the dangling turquoise earring I had been given at the hospital. I hadn't found its match in Roxanne's strictly ordered jewelry box. It must have been lost in the accident. I shook my head and the delicate filigree work brushed against my hair, which I'd pulled off my neck into a bun.

My image in the mirror reflected back a print summer dress, strappy sandals and lovely face. Except for my chunky feet and hands, there wasn't much to complain about. I squinted, as if I could see some other detail that would help me understand more about this woman in the mirror.

I yearned to alter my appearance somehow that would make me more comfortable in my skin. It was difficult having everyone stare at me all the time. And I'd have liked to be taller.

Anyone have a rack they can stretch me on?

"Mirror, mirror on the wall, who's the most self-involved of all?" I frowned at the reflection and stuck out my tongue. Then the doorbell rang and freed me from dwelling on my least favorite subject—my looks—for the next few minutes.

Bradley Chandler was as funny and charming and as kind in person as he had sounded on the phone. He seemed genuinely glad to see me but declined my offer of wine and hustled me out to his car. We chatted and giggled during the short time it took to go the four blocks to Simone's, the café he had mentioned on the phone. At last, I relaxed. Bradley held the car door open for me after we parked, and winked as I stepped out into the warm summer night.

"Are you hungry?" he teased. "Wednesday is crepe night. I could kill for chicken and mushroom crepes."

"I'm famished."

"Yeah? Gee, that's good to hear. You never used to eat much. Which has always annoyed me since I enjoy three-course meals complete with two wines and at least one dessert."

"I like dessert." I thought of last night's ice cream. Which of course made me think of Michael. Which led me to think of that incredible round of sexual activity. I fanned my blushing cheeks. "In fact, I'm doing so much eating, I think I've gained weight since the accident. My clothes all seem tight."

Bradley looked at me, his eyes pointedly scanning my rear end. "I think you look the same, Rox. You always wear your clothes snug."

He saw my chagrin. "Hey, I like that in a girl. Got it, flaunt it. But all I meant is that you aren't one to hide your assets. You look fabulous in your little summer dress. But where'd you get the high heels? That's new for you."

Which explained why the shoe box was hidden in the back of the closet. "I've been feeling short."

"Yeah? You always said you hate wearing any kind of heels. But whatever, you look fabulous, and I always thought you could use a little weight, if you want to know the truth." He cocked his head sideways. "And I love your hair pulled off your face. I don't think I've ever seen you wear it that way."

"No? Well, you're getting Roxanne, 'version 2.0.' Who has no idea how to look like '1.0.'"

"Both versions are spectacular. Okay, let's go get you some dinner."

Simone's was in an old house at the corner of a residential community and Arroyo Boulevard, the main drag running through Sierra Monte. Three banks of beveled-glass windows looked out at the San Gabriel Mountains. Inside it smelled of fresh bread and roses. Intoxicating. My spirits lifted. "This is a wonderful place."

"Roxanne! Bradley! How are you both?" A gorgeous woman, somewhere around thirty, greeted us. Her closely-cropped hair followed the delicate shape of her head. The soft light gleamed off her diamond stud earrings.

"Jen, darling, how are you?" Bradley replied.

"Good. Good. And look who you've brought with you." Jen embraced me warmly, then looked me over head to foot. "Beautiful Roxanne. But how are you feeling, love? I called and spoke to you briefly in the hospital and you sounded pretty rough."

"I remember your call. Thank you for that. I'm doing better." My voice dropped as another couple came in the door behind me. "I still can't remember the accident, or anything else, though."

Jen squeezed my hand. "It will come. It will come. Don't worry. When you are strong enough, you will remember. God is taking care of you." She turned to Bradley. "But where have you been? I haven't seen you since, when?"

"Cathy and I were here a few weeks ago, but I haven't felt much like eating out since then. Until tonight, that is." He linked his arm through mine and pulled me next to him.

Jen nodded. "Of course. So, tonight we'll celebrate a little. Because my friends are here. It's only the two of you, right?"

"Yes, just us."

"I've got a great table for you." Jen gestured for us to follow her into the central dining area.

It was lovely, lit by candlelight alone. A fireplace crackled with a real fire, and despite it being the middle of summer, the temperature felt perfect in the thick-walled room. Jen seated us at a corner table near the windows where we had a view of the mountains.

"Crepes tonight, Jen?" Bradley asked.

"Of course. Chicken and mushroom, chicken and avocado with caramelized onions, or chicken and raspberries." Jen turned to me. "To refresh your memory, my chef, Bruno, has been with me forever, and he's very set in his ways. Monday, catch of the day with wild rice, Tuesday, roast sirloin with au gratin potatoes, Wednesday, three kinds of chicken crepes. And so on. If I suggest we vary things a little, he sulks." Jen shrugged her elegant shoulders. "It is not good having a sulking chef."

"But this is one of the things we love most about Simone's," Bradley said. "Nothing makes one feel more secure than constancy. Right, Roxanne?"

"I'm sure everything is great. It smells wonderful."

"Thank you," Jen said. "I'll send some wine right over, Bradley. Bogle? Or the Firestone? I also have some Australian Chardonnay that is very nice."

"Bite your tongue," Bradley replied. "Australia does golfers and sea captains, both very nicely, but with wine, they are still beginners. Send something from the Firestone vineyard, an '05, or '06 *sauvignon blanc*, maybe?"

"It will be right out." Jen smiled. "It is so good to have you back here, Roxanne."

My eyes burned as I took a sip of water. While I could not say I remembered Simone's, the dark wood and silver bowls of flowers, and wonderful still life above the mantle were so welcoming, I felt safe. As if I could be myself. I giggled.

"What's funny?"

"I was thinking that I felt like I could be myself here. Whoever that is."

"You're still you, kiddo. The accident didn't change that." Bradley leaned closer. "Do you remember it at all?"

"Everything seems *familiar*, but no, I don't remember being here before. Did we come here often?"

"Once a month, at least. And for everyone's birthday. Cathy insisted on that." He stared at me. "You're sure you can handle it when I bring Cathy up?"

"Of course." I patted his hand. "I just wish I could remember her."

"Be patient. You'll get her back. You called each other your 'secret sister,' did you know that? That's how close you were."

A pop of energy lit up in my brain, like a sparkler on a summer night. I looked away, recalling one of the photographs Betty had in her album, of Cathy and Roxanne, teenagers in short skirts. And sporting too much lipstick and matching gold necklaces with the initials "SS." I had wondered when I noticed the jewelry what club or rock group or boyfriend "SS" might signify, and now I knew.

Secret sisters. A club for two. Lupey loo.

Those strange words pinged around inside my head again. Did they also have something to do with Roxanne and Cathy? For the moment, I didn't trust my emotions enough to ask Bradley.

He busied himself with the wine steward. While the men chatted and went through a tasting ritual, I regained control of my tenuous emotions and took in the ambiance of the place. The floor was polished wood, worn in spots from years of footsteps. From my vantage point I saw a hallway leading back into what I surmised was a kitchen. A smaller, private dining room was across the foyer where Jen greeted more guests. A gleaming black piano sat the wall, and in my mind I heard it being played. I imagined the birthday parties Bradley mentioned.

"So, have you seen Michael yet?" Bradley asked.

I met my friend's blue eyes and took a gulp of wine. It was cool and smooth and did nothing to calm my fluttering nerves. "Yes, he came by the house last night. I saw him several times at the hospital, too."

"And?"

"He's nice. A little freaked, maybe. He's having trouble with the amnesia. You know, he's worried I don't remember him."

"I doubt that. If I were him, I'd worry more about what will happen when you *do* remember him."

I set the wineglass down carefully. "Why's that?"

"Why?" Bradley laced his fingers together. "How much do you want me to tell you about you and Michael?"

"How much do you know?"

"A lot. Most of it from you. Some from," he paused, as if weighing his words, "from others. Did your mom or anyone fill you in on where your current relationship was with Michael before the accident?"

"A little. I know we went out for a long time, but had recently broken up. Betty told me that, though she said she didn't have the specifics of why the break-up occurred, although she knew it wasn't the first time it had happened, and she didn't think it had been permanent."

"Interesting." Bradley's voice seemed shaded by a hundred unspoken opinions.

"So, Michael and Roxanne are a pretty volatile pair?"

"That's true."

"Did I love him?" I asked. I didn't ask if Michael loved me. After last night, I knew he didn't, not the Roxanne before the accident. Not the Roxanne he provided such skillful sexual services to last night.

While not exactly a mercy fuck, last night's fun and games weren't about love. They were, however, all about reassuring Michael Cimino about something. I just had no idea what that 'something' was.

My question had surprised Bradley. He took a long drink of wine. "Yes. I think you did love him. Do love him. To paraphrase the always less than chivalrous Prince Charles a couple of decades ago, 'love, whatever that is.' You stayed with Michael for several years, and seemed very content, the most content I'd ever seen you, when things were going well."

"Have you and I known each other for a long time, Bradley?"

"Forever. Since acne." Bradley grinned. "Not that you ever actually had it. Cathy claimed you had two zits during the entire run of puberty, while the rest of us looked like pizza ads."

We shared a laugh. My face felt tight. "So, back to me. I'm not usually 'content?'"

Bradley searched my face. "You do know about your battles with depression over the years? And about the . . ."

Several beats of time passed. "*The*? The what?"

Bradley blinked. "You tried to commit suicide once. With pills. In college."

A hum built up inside my head. "Oh? No one's mentioned that."

"God, I'm sorry. Maybe I shouldn't have."

"No, I'm glad you did. I'm glad to know about this." I would ask Betty. It certainly added to Dr. Patel's credibility about worrying about a suicide attempt. The fact I might still have to talk with the police came back to me. They hadn't shown up or called yet.

I hoped this meant they never would.

Bradley was staring at me. I reached across the table and gripped his hand, then nodded toward the wineglass. "Drink up. But I don't want you passing out. I'm not sure I can carry you out of here."

He laughed and followed orders.

Once another bottle of wine was delivered, I asked, "Bradley, is the depression a major thing? Did it keep me from working? Was I moody sometimes, maybe acted like a pain in the ass because of it?"

"Oh, no. You always went to work, no matter how you felt. You love the kids at school, the routine. The summers off." He grinned big. "You never let your illness interfere with that. You're always ready for adventure. Cathy said you're the fire in our engines, you're what will keep us all from becoming old fogies. Depression was one of the things you dealt with, and your friends dealt with, just like you dealt with all our foibles."

"You have foibles?" I asked with a smile. "What are they?"

"Besides having a big mouth, you mean?"

"Stop. Tell me something bad about yourself. Are you with anyone special now?"

"Me? I'm never with anyone long enough for them to be special. Not since Mitch died." He met my eyes. "He was my lover. He died of AIDS five years ago. But let's not get too serious tonight. Besides, we're not talking about me, cupcake. We don't have enough time tonight to tour that hellhole."

"Okay." Bradley's bravado was how he dealt with pain, I surmised. Even after several years, his love for his lost lover was clear. "Let's get back to Michael, then. It sounds like I'm the life of the party. Is that why Michael stays with me?"

"You want my opinion?"

"Yes."

"Michael loves to show you off. He stays with you because you make him look good to the other wolves in the pack."

I had formed the same opinion, but hearing it made me uncomfortable. After all, I had joined in the fun and games wholeheartedly last night. Did this mean I was basically shallow, too? I had sex with him willingly but not because of love. I did him and welcomed him doing me solely because Michael Cimino was handsome and available and, and . . . for some other reason I couldn't quite bring into focus. The words, "because I shouldn't," shot through my brain.

"I wonder what I thought was in it for me. With Michael. What do I get out of it?"

"Grief, mostly. Although rumor has it he's very good in the sack."

I clenched my right hand around my napkin. "But sex isn't everything, right?"

"Right. It's the only thing."

We laughed, but Bradley gave me a quick, inquiring look. I was sure he'd guessed what went on last night. My face grew hot and I took another drink.

"I don't know why you stayed with Michael," Bradley added. "The heart's a mysterious organ, Rox. Who knows why anyone loves anyone? There are very few well-matched couples in the world. I think it's dumb luck when two people who turn out to be good matches end up together."

Something buzzed in my brain. "It's fate, I think."

"Fate? Now you sound like Cathy. Or Nick. She finally convinced him there was such a thing as soul mates in this mean old world." He looked out the window, as if lost in a memory too tender to share.

I cleared my throat. "So, does Michael cheat on me?"

"Yes. Excessively."

"And I always found out?"

Bradley glanced at his hands. "Usually."

"But I forgave him and took him back every time."

"Yes."

"That's demeaning."

"Yeah. Michael's good at doing that."

"What an asshole." When the words came out, I heard an echo in my head. I'd said this before.

"Well, we all make allowances for people we're in a relationship with." Bradley sighed. "His dad was married like five or six times. I think Michael was mistreated by a couple of the stepmothers. He's got his reasons."

"Yeah, but what was mine for letting myself be treated like that?"

For the first time, Bradley looked as if he didn't know what to say.

"Let me change the subject." I braced myself. "Tell me about Cathy. What was she like?"

"You sure?"

"Yes."

His face softened. "She's wonderful. Cathy is, was, one of those people folks immediately take to. She was kind. Solid. Upbeat. Not in a Pollyanna, 'oh how wonderful life is' kind of way. Positive about things in general." He finished his wine, his eyes shining. "She told me when my mother was dying that you must always have *faith*. I got angry with her, and told her that was pretty naïve to run to religion when there was no hope for a cure, as in my mother's case. Cathy said I was missing the point."

"I don't understand," I said.

"I didn't, either. But then she said you had to have faith *in life.* That life always holds the possibility for a miracle. So we must never give up hope."

"She sounds too good to be true." There was an edge to my voice. Was I jealous of a dead woman? I put my hand to my neck and felt a guilty heat.

"Cathy had the biggest capacity for love of anyone I've ever known, Roxanne. And she was naturally happy. That's the best way I can explain her. She wasn't a saint, not by a long shot. She could be bossy. Very bossy. And arrogant if she thought you were uninformed or ignorant about something you were opining on. And she is, was, very extravagant. Loved parties. And presents. But overall, she was fabulous. Which was amazing, really, considering her awful upbringing."

"Betty said her mother and father both died young?"

"Yeah. Her dad, who she didn't remember much at all, when she was a three or four. And her mother when she was about ten. Her stepfather was a drunk, and I think even abused her. It was rough, but Cathy didn't let any of those experiences ruin her."

"What do you mean, he abused her?" I clenched my fingers so tight my nails cut into my palms.

"He didn't molest her. And he provided a home for her when her mom died. But when he drank, he broke things. Once, he broke everything in the house. A couple of times he hit her. He was a Jehovah's Witness or something. Kept trying to kick the alcohol thing but never could. He didn't believe in the holidays. But I think he was okay some of the time. She made allowances for him because he was the only family she had. A couple of times during high school, she had the opportunity to leave, but she didn't. I guess she felt responsible for him, or something."

"She sounds wonderful." My voice was almost a whisper.

"She was. Very maternal, too, even though she had no children yet. She'd keep after you, push you, when she thought you needed to do something to make your life or yourself better. But when she loved someone, she loved unconditionally. Way before it was fashionable. That was her gift to all of us." Bradley's voice cracked.

I killed this woman. My face felt numb.

The waiter placed salads in front of us. Bradley drained his glass. "Okay, let's eat. You'll love the dressing. Raspberry vinaigrette."

"Great." I looked past him, beyond the windows to outside, my eyes resting on Mt. Wilson.

"Are you up for a little more, Roxanne?" Bradley picked up the wine bottle. "Can you handle it?"

"Yes." I was probably legally drunk, but not drunk enough. I took another gulp. "When did Cathy meet Nick?"

"In high school. We were all at a party, Fourth of July, I think. A bunch of us, you and me and Cathy. Nick showed up with his friends, football players we'd invited because they always brought beer. He was cute and quiet, nerdy even, but with broad shoulders and the most delicious dimples. Cathy fell for him on the spot. I think you actually had your eye on him first, but Cathy connected with him, and the rest, as they say, is history."

I drew a sharp breath, remembering the image of Nick Chance in bed that had flickered in my brain. "Roxanne had a crush on Nick?"

"Yes, I think 'Roxanne' did. And to tell you the truth, I think Bradley did, too."

We laughed like drunken friends do, loudly and conspiratorially, and Bradley gestured to the waiter for another bottle.

"Wow," I said. "So we all loved Nick, but Cathy got him."

"Well, that may be going a little far. Let's just say we all appreciated the boy's charms. But hey, that was what, fifteen, eighteen years ago?" Bradley shrugged. "If you were interested in him, it was probably because he didn't pay attention to you. Which was unusual. When new guys came into a room, they *always* paid attention to you. But Nick only had eyes for Cathy from the get-go."

I thought of the pictures in the album Betty had shown me. The look of devotion in his eyes. "Sounds like I'm all about me. Was I envious of their relationship?"

"We all were, a little. But that was the great thing about Cathy. You always knew where you stood with her. She had the ability to make everyone around her feel secure. And she was never petty."

"Am I petty?" I made a face. "Sorry. I sound self-obsessed asking all these 'me, me, me' questions."

"Hey, if it helps you remember, ask away. As to you being petty? Sometimes. But never with Cathy that I saw." He gave me a smile. "Look, don't get stressed by what I said earlier. Your attraction to Nick never came between you and her. I'm not sure she ever knew about it, and if she had, it wouldn't have mattered."

Don't be so sure, Bradley.

Suddenly I was very nervous. Of what, I couldn't exactly say, but I was twitchy and anxious, like I needed to get up and run ten miles and exhaust myself.

As the waiter appeared with rolls, I stood. "I need to go to the powder room."

Truth be told, I had a dull ache in my head, and my vision was a little blurry. I hurried across the dining area and took a right at the dark hallway. The ladies' room was on the right, exactly where I expected it.

I pushed the door and entered the small room. On the wall directly opposite was a framed print. I gasped when

I realized what it was. Monet's *The Bridge at Bougival,* the painting I had thought of so many times since I left the hospital. It hung in all its splendor on the bathroom wall.

I suddenly recalled the first time I had seen the original painting: at the Los Angeles County Museum of Modern Art, during summer vacation. My mother took me with her friend, who was a member of the board, to see the magnificent Impressionist Paintings show called, "A Day in the Country." At eight years old, I had been very proud to be taken along to such a grown-up affair.

We had box suppers with exotic cheeses and tiny pastries and fruit. We ate outside in the leafy courtyard behind the museum, and spent hours inside looking at the Van Goghs, Pissaros, eighteen different versions of Monet's Haystacks. And then we came into the room with *The Bridge at Bougival*.

I had stood transfixed, my mother silent by my side. "Do you like it?" she asked.

I couldn't take my eyes off it. The play of light and dark on the picture was magical. I could not believe a person could create with paint and pigment the real glow of sunshine and the movement of water you swore would be wet if you touched the canvas. I yearned to step into the landscape, my mother beside me, and have us both disappear from our current life and become part of the scene before us.

With my child's naiveté, I thought she wouldn't be sick if we lived in the painting. "What's down there?" I asked her, pointing to the sun-drenched pathway curving along the hillside.

My mother smiled. "We can't know, baby. It's life. The unknown."

All these years later I was still moved by the magic of the scene, even in this poor quality print.

My knees went wobbly and I collapsed onto the wooden chair by the door. My pulse pounded in my ears as *I remembered* that my mother had died three months after our trip to the exhibition.

My mother?

I clutched my hands to my head and moaned. Across from me, the restroom mirror beamed back the image of a dark-haired woman who appeared in the grip of madness. I touched the dangling orb of turquoise in my left ear and in a rising flood of new memory saw a cloudless blue sky above a desert landscape.

A tall, smiling man with wide shoulders stood in front of me, holding a tiny jewel box. "Merry Christmas, sweetheart," he said, flashing a dimple.

It was Nick Chance.

More sparklers burst in my brain as the room began to spin. "Nick," I said aloud. "Nick."

Inside my head I heard the squeal of car brakes and the crash of glass breaking. My body crumpled and I fell from the chair to the cold tile floor of the bathroom as a scene of carnage and destruction replayed inside my mind.

I was screaming and hurt and bleeding. I was lying on asphalt.

I was dying.

Then, floating. A dark-haired woman hovered nearby. "It's all right, Cathy," she whispered. "Come with me."

"I'm not going!" I screamed.

With those words echoing inside my skull, the vision faded. I struggled to stand but could not, so I took some deep breaths and sat where I was.

A woman in a blue dress came in and stared at me with alarm. "Are you okay? Shall I go get some help?"

"No, I'm all right," I said. "Too much wine."

She washed her hands quickly and then left me alone. I stared again at the painting. I had worn a white eyelet dress to the museum, a gift from my mother.

She wore red sandals, and her legs were long and tan. I could see her face. Her smile. I stretched my hand out into space, as if I could touch her.

She reached back to me, patting my blonde hair, stroking my freckled face. "You have the prettiest blue eyes, honey," she said. "Just like your grandma's."

And at that moment I knew.

I knew who I was.

My eyes stared down incredulously at the body I inhabited. Terror spread from my gut and clawed up my neck into my skull. I was either insane or a freak of nature, the inexplicable product of the tragedy that occurred when Roxanne and Cathy were in a car accident and one of them died.

Shaking badly, I limped to the sink and splashed water on my numb face and stared at the brown eyes in the mirror. A torrent of images rushed through my brain. Dozens, hundreds of memories flooded from every cell in a riot of color and sound and confusion. People's voices, pain and happiness, the touches of loved ones; movies I'd seen, kisses I'd given and received, the taste of dinners eaten years ago. The glances and words of those who had hurt me and loved me blotted out my consciousness.

I blinked and the river of history slowed. I stood straighter and smoothed back the dark hair. Despite what I was seeing on the outside, I knew the truth.

It was *me* in the mirror, Cathy Chance, alive inside Roxanne's body.

Tears welled up, but as shocked and frightened as I was, I also felt a surge of gratitude and giddiness. I knew who I was, who I had been, and that I was still here on earth with those I loved.

It was then the enormity of what I had to do crashed over me like a million tons of sand.

Who was going to believe it? Who *could* believe it?

I touched my earring, the turquoise stone cool in my trembling fingers. "Nick," I said aloud. "Nick."

I hurried to the exit. Nick would believe me. It would take some doing, but I would make him believe the truth.

And if I can't?

If I couldn't, I'd be better off dead.

Chapter 11

Wednesday, July 27, 7 p.m.
Nick's House

"Nick?"

I was dreaming that Cathy was outside the house, sweating in the garden, her hands dirty. I couldn't make out all she was saying, but she wanted my help with something.

"Nick," Cathy called. "Nick."

"Cathy," I whispered in my sleep.

"Nick, wake up. It's after seven!" Zoë's voice cut through my dream and I woke with my heart racing. Cathy's presence was so real I reached out for her, but clutched only rumpled sheets and blankets. I turned to the doorway and saw my sister watching me.

"Hey," I said.

"Hey, yourself. You okay?"

"Yeah." I looked at my watch, and then dropped my head back onto the pillow. "What do you want?"

"What?" She took a few steps into my bedroom. "Jeez, two hours ago you said I had to stay home tonight because you were going to take me out to dinner. So I didn't go out with Amy and now all you're doing is sleeping. Get up and throw some water on your face. I'm hungry."

How can she be hungry? Cathy is dead. I rubbed my eyes and tried to focus on the now. My sister needed me tonight. She was ready to go out.

I lifted my head and squinted. "Are you wearing a dress?" She hadn't even worn a dress to my wedding.

"Yes. Do you want me to change?" Zoë looked down. "Does it make me look fat?"

Shit. It's her birthday. "No, you look great. Very foxy."

"Foxy? Is that good or bad?"

"It's good. Are you saying 'foxy' is an outdated compliment?"

"Not if you're fifty."

I threw a pillow at her, which she gracefully sidestepped. "Okay. You look hot. Or cool. Or sick. Whatever you guys say now." I rested my head in my hands. "Where do you want to go tonight, birthday girl?"

"I don't care. Where do you want to go?"

I felt like a hundred-pound anvil was sitting on my chest, but I forced myself up out of bed. "You're legal eighteen, little sister. That calls for a celebration, right?"

Zoë smiled. "After that scene at the lawyer's on Monday, I didn't know if you would still feel like celebrating tonight."

"Monday's over. I'm fine, and I hope you are, too." I glanced at the dresser—where the check from the insurance was half-covered by my shirt—and took a step back, as if it were a rabid dog. "Really, Zoë. I'm good. Don't you want to go out?"

"Yeah, I do."

"Good. So we'll do it. Tonight is your night." I headed to the bathroom. "Just let me shower. Is Mom coming?"

Zoë followed a half step behind me. "No. She's got that literacy thing tonight in L.A. The mayor or something is going to be there or she said she would have bugged out. She's cooking dinner for us Friday night. She told me to remind you when she called me at work this morning. Can you believe she sang "Happy Birthday" over my cell?"

"Yes. She always sings "Happy Birthday" to people on their cells. Despite the fact that she can not sing."

We laughed.

"And she sent me balloons and cookies. With M&Ms in them, no less."

"In the balloons?"

Zoë punched my arm. "No. In the cookies. Most of which I ate. But can you believe her? Fuck, I'm eighteen, for Christ's sake."

"Hey, watch your mouth." I gave her my fake stern look and pulled back the shower curtain. She was a woman, yet still that little bratty kid she'd always been. But for the first time in a long time she looked relaxed. Her eyes were shining, and she was excited about her birthday.

And about getting presents. In the back of my closet, wrapped in brown paper, was a framed poster of *Gone With The Wind*. She and Cathy loved that movie, and made a point of watching it together at least once a year.

Cathy had bought the poster for Zoë at an online auction a couple of months ago. Last week I doubted the wisdom of giving it to Zoë, and I still wasn't completely sure. I didn't know if she could take it. I didn't know if *I* could take it.

"Give me ten minutes, then we're off. Feed Pitty, okay?"

Zoë nodded but leaned against the bathroom door, keeping me from closing it, not cutting me much slack. When she was little she used to follow me around like this, like a duckling afraid to let its mom out of its sight.

"Ah, I'd like a little privacy, okay?"

She grinned. "Okay. Wear deodorant."

"Hey, you saying I smell?"

"No. You always smell nice. I'm just kidding with you, bro." She looked serious. "You sure you're okay? You were having a nightmare, I think. I came in your room because I heard you."

We stared at each other. "I'm okay."

"If you don't want to go to Simone's, I understand," Zoë said. "But I kind of want to go because I'll feel like Cathy is there, too."

A jolt of adrenaline coursed through my body. "No problem. Simone's it is." I pointed toward the kitchen. "The cat. I hear her wailing at the door. See if you can get her to actually come inside."

Zoë left and I took a deep, weary breath. I didn't want to go out. And I certainly didn't want to go to Simone's. But we always went there for birthdays. Zoë loved the place, ever since Cathy had insisted we take her there when she was thirteen. We'd gone every year since then.

I got in the shower and turned it on a full, icy blast. But I couldn't make it cold enough to freeze out the sound of my dead wife's voice saying my name inside my head.

A half hour later I held the front door of Simone's open for Zoë and followed her inside.

"Nick! And Zoë! How wonderful to see you both." Jen Landau, the pretty café owner, and youngest daughter of the original Simone, hurried toward us. As she walked, she glanced quickly over her shoulder into the main dining room, as if she were worried.

"Hi, Jen. How are you?" I kissed her cheek, which smelled of gardenia.

"Wonderful, Nick. Just wonderful." She turned to my sister. "You look more beautiful than ever tonight, Zoë. I adore your dress. Where did you get it?"

"The Rose Bowl swap meet. It's vintage. From the Sixties." Zoë blushed and answered a few questions while I glanced around.

Simone's looked the same as it had the twenty years I'd been coming here. Well cared for and elegant, but casual enough that I didn't feel out of place without a tie. It was busy tonight. Good thing Jen had made standing reservations for my family for all our birthdays. Mine in December. Zoë's tonight.

Cathy's on March 4th.

"Let me show you to your table, and I'll send the waiter in with some drinks." Jen took my arm and Zoë followed us to one of the two vacant tables in the dining alcove off the main room.

I sat and Jen leaned close to me and smiled. "You're looking well, Nick. I am so glad to see you out and about."

"Thanks. It's good to be here."

She knew I was lying. It was horrible being here. Dental work horrible. My body ached as memories flooded through my veins like warm wine. Cathy loved Simone's. She had discovered it when she was looking for her first job, a million years ago.

Jen had given Cathy a job as hostess the first summer Cathy had moved out on her own. In a flash like a knife cut, I recalled the first time I came here.

I'd promised Cathy I would come 'incognito' and pretend I didn't know her. When I walked in, I felt like the teenage geek I was, until I saw Cathy. She was prim and proper in a black skirt and white shirt, her blonde hair tamed into a bun on top of her head. She had on sparkling silver earrings and high heels and pink lipstick. She'd looked like an angel.

"It is just the two of you tonight, yes?"

"Yes. Mom was going to come, but she has a thing in L.A.," Zoë said. "So it's just us. Can I order the chocolate soufflé for dessert?" She grinned. "I know you need extra time for that."

"Yes, of course. And how about for you, Nick? Chocolate soufflé for two?" Jen looked as if she realized her gentle question drew too much attention to those missing tonight, missing forever.

"Sure. My little sister only turns eighteen once. We'll go nuts."

"Eighteen! I thought this was the milestone. Congratulations, Zoë. Eduardo will be your waiter. Nick,

watch him carefully. He has quite an eye for the ladies."
Again, Jen looked over her shoulder at the main dining room.

I followed her glance. "Is something wrong, Jen?"

"No. We're just unusually busy tonight. Enjoy. I'll see you both later."

She hurried away and I focused my attention on Zoë. "So, what did Mom get you for your birthday? Aside from the balloons and cookies, which I've not had any of, by the way."

"The balloons?" she replied with a giggle.

"The cookies. You didn't eat them all, did you?"

"No, I ate two giant ones. The rest are at home. You can have them for a midnight snack. Pitty still cries at the back door at midnight, right?"

"Yes, but tonight I'm not getting up. I've decided I'm forcing that damned creature to come inside during the day and sleep. I'm tired of her avoiding me."

Zoë picked up her menu and perused it as the waiter appeared at my shoulder. He was a new kid, very handsome, with a dark tan and a ponytail. This must be the Eduardo Jen had warned me about.

"Good evening," the young man said. "I am Eduardo, and I will be your waiter tonight. Would you like to see a wine list, sir?"

"No. I'll have a club soda with lime. Zoë?" My mouth felt dry and for the first time in many years I wanted, *really wanted*, a drink.

"I'll have diet cola. With a cherry." She blushed.

"Very good." Eduardo rattled off the specials for the night. I guzzled my water and realized I was sweating.

After Zoë ordered, Eduardo turned to me. Without looking at the menu I said, "I'll have the chicken and mushroom crepes, the Caesar salad, and we'll both take the chocolate souffle. Jen may have already told the chef." I gestured to my glass. "And could I get some more water?"

"Certainly." Eduardo gave Zoë a little bow and hurried off.

I finished my water and drank Zoë's. She was cutting her eyes toward Eduardo, who was introducing himself to the only other patrons in the room, a trio of women in their forties.

I smiled at my sister, preparing myself for a push to leave the handsome young man a more than generous tip. "So, eighteen big ones? How's it feel, kiddo?"

She shrugged. "The same, I guess. Twenty-one will be a much bigger deal."

"Why? You can vote now." I clutched my throat. "God help us."

"I'm not interested in voting. Who is there to vote for, anyway? Mostly rich old white men? Assholes."

"Hey. Stop swearing. Ever heard of a man named Barack? And there are lots of women to vote for. Your senators are women."

"Whatever." She took her water glass and glared at me, wiping the rim with her napkin.

"I don't have cooties," I said.

"Right." She drank a big gulp.

"So, what do you think will be so great about twenty-one?"

"I can buy a car on my own. And liquor."

I frowned. I'm an alcoholic. My dad was, too. My mom has never had a drink that I know of, and she and I have given Zoë plenty of stern lecture-rants about the evil of booze. "You can buy a car now. If you save enough money."

"I'm saving. I've got enough. But the car I want isn't safe, according to Mom. And she won't sign for a loan to get a good car because she says, 'No one in high school should have a car loan hanging over her head.' Jeez, I bring home over five hundred a month. I can afford a car payment."

"Five hundred whole dollars? Well, there's car insurance. And repairs, gas, registration and inspections."

"Don't." She held up her hand. "It's bad enough I'll end up the oldest one in my senior class. Do you know how embarrassing it will be to not have a car?"

I thought of the huge check lying on the dresser at home. I couldn't conceive of it being real money. Cathy and I had daydreamed about winning the lottery—who hasn't?—but our plans usually centered on moving to Paris so she could study art, or to a little farm in Ireland, places we'd never been and had no idea if we'd like. Of course, now Zoë's college education would be no strain for anyone.

"I'll loan you some money to buy a good car," I said. "You can pay me back a little, until next summer. Then you can work two jobs and pay off your brother."

"Really?" Zoë brightened. "Okay. All I need is about two thousand dollars. Then I'll have three thousand, two hundred. That'll be enough for a really safe car."

"Your idea of safe and mine might differ there, kid."

"Let's argue about that later. We can talk to Mom on Sunday about you loaning me some money, okay?"

"Yeah. On one condition."

"What?"

"No drinking."

"Ever?" Zoë's eyes widened. "Look, I know you have a problem with it, but that doesn't mean I will. I'm adopted, remember?"

I crossed my arms. "Dad had a problem, too, don't forget. There's a lot of evidence of a genetic predisposition toward alcoholism, but also socially acceptable alcoholism, which rubs off on adopted kids."

"I'll be good, I promise."

"Here's your drinks, folks." Eduardo sat the club soda in front of me and gave Zoë her diet cola, adorned with half a dozen cherries impaled on a stirrer shaped like a sword. "Your salads will be right out."

Zoë picked up her coke and took a sip, then removed the cherries and popped them all in her mouth. She chewed, looking for all the world like a ten-year-old instead of young lady of eighteen. She grinned. Somehow she'd managed to stick two of the cherries onto her front teeth.

I laughed aloud, which must have been what she was going for. "I knew I could make you laugh. Isn't this fun?" She wiped a trace of cherry juice off her chin. "A little bit like before, right?" There was a plea in those words.

"It is fun." I held up my glass. "To you, Zoë. Have a wonderful year!"

With that, despite my earlier restlessness, the evening became a party. We dropped the alcohol talk and moved onto sports. Zoë and I were both rabid baseball fans, she of the Angels, me Dodger Blue.

Cathy had never cared much for baseball, but she encouraged this sibling rivalry, said it was a good thing to share with your sister. My wife was big on sharing things with family members. That was why she had instituted movie night with Zoë when she began showing interest in love stories.

"We're bonding," Cathy announced not long ago to explain why she was so late getting home. "I'm going to make her watch Shakespeare. Olivier, and crazy Mel Gibson and the old coots. And DeCaprio as Romeo. And that *Hamlet* with Uma Thurman's ex who doesn't wash his hair, Ethan Hawke. They are so dramatic about romance. Zoë will love it and ace all the honors English classes her school can throw at her."

With a pang, I thought again of the poster in the closet at home. *I'll give it to Zoë later*. She'd treasure anything from Cathy.

The waiter cleared the salad plates, reassuring us our entrees would be right out. Zoë launched into a little history of how long she'd been coming to Simone's, and I realized this was a politic time to leave her with the dashing waiter for a moment.

"I'll be back in a sec, Zoë. And I'll take another club soda when you have a chance," I added, subtly reminding Eduardo that he did have real work to do.

When I crossed the foyer, I spotted Jen in the main dining hall, bent over in discussion with a man whose face I couldn't see, but something about him was familiar. Not wanting to have to make small talk with any acquaintance, I hurried to the men's room.

As I was washing up, I began sweating again, and loosened my tie. Despite getting into the party spirit for Zoë, my heart ached at being in this place where I'd shared so many happy times with Cathy. I turned off the water and dried my hands. Stood at the door for a moment. And imagined Cathy's voice again.

"Nick," she called. "Nick."

Breathing fast, I pushed at the door and walked into the narrow hallway. A few feet away, the door to the ladies' room opened and a woman appeared. She wore a silky summer dress and high heels, her dark hair pulled into a bun with a ribbon.

Like Cathy wore it.

The woman turned toward me, and in a voice too much like my wife's to bear, said, "Nick?"

I stepped back and banged my elbow against the wall. "Roxanne." My voice ricocheted around the small space.

She came closer. Her eyes were full of tears, and I felt her trembling when she laid her hand on my arm. "Nick, I don't know how to tell you this, but . . ."

"What are you doing here?"

At my harsh question, she looked sadder than any person I'd ever seen. She dropped her hand. "I'm, I'm having dinner with Bradley." A dangling earring glimmered in the light. "I didn't know you'd be here."

I stretched my hand toward her face and touched the single turquoise earring in her left ear. She grasped my fingers as I did this, sending a shock of emotion through me that threatened to overcome all restraint.

"That belongs to my wife." I pulled my hand away. "What the hell, Roxanne. What are you doing wearing it?"

For a moment she stared at me, tears running down her perfect face. Carefully she took off the earring and held it out. "I was keeping it until I could return it to you personally. Here."

I turned and hurried into the dining room. Zoë was sitting with a man.

"Nick!"

It was Bradley. He smiled. "Jen just said you and Zoë were here, so I came by to say hello."

"Let's go, Zoë. Now." I put my hands on the back of her chair.

"Nick, hold on." Bradley struggled to his feet, his voice unsteady.

He'd had a lot to drink, I realized with envy. "Bradley, this has nothing to do with you. But we're going. I'm not ready for any of this shit."

"Wait. I didn't know you two would be here. If I did, I never would have brought Roxanne."

"Roxanne is here?" Zoë pushed away from the table and stood next to me. "Where?"

"I just saw her in the hallway and I have no intention of chatting with her. Or with you, Bradley," I shot back. "Jesus Christ, how could you bring her to Simone's?"

"Nick, I told you, I had no idea you guys would be here."

"Don't yell at Bradley, Nick." Zoë's eyes darted around the restaurant.

I took my sister's hand. "Come on, Zoë, we'll go someplace else."

"Let's just go home." Her voice was mournful. She

grabbed her purse and then looked as if she saw a ghost over my shoulder.

"Bradley," Roxanne said behind me. "We should leave. It's Zoë's birthday and I'm sure they want to celebrate."

"Don't bother. We're going." I glared at Roxanne and threw money on the table, knocking over the club soda. The glass shattered when it hit the wood floor and the women at the corner table looked up.

I was hyperventilating. I felt the way I used to when I would get drunk, right before I blacked out, enveloped by twin sensations of anger and relief. I grasped Zoë's hand tighter and without looking again at Roxanne, we headed for the exit.

A few minutes later, sitting in the car with Zoë silent beside me, I didn't even try to apologize to her. Instead, I kept thinking about what happened after Cathy's memorial service.

She was cremated. There were carpets of flowers and child singers and everyone who mattered to her was there and they cried and mourned, *except her very, very best friend who'd killed her.* Despite the sunny skies above, I shivered like I had the flu during the entire service.

At the end, when everyone but my family had gone, the minister handed me the golden urn with Cathy's ashes. But I wouldn't let them scatter them off the cliff and out over the ocean, as they planned. I took the urn and ran with it down the slope from the chapel in Palos Verdes, sliding on the damp grass, oblivious to the cries of Mom and Zoë and the relatives from New Hampshire who'd trekked out to the land of fruit and nuts to lend support.

When I got to the limo, I yelled at the chauffeur to drive away quick, like we were leaving the scene of a crime. He took me home without asking a single question. I sat in the front seat beside him, clutching the cold, smooth repository.

When he pulled up to the house I fumbled for my wallet, as if he were a taxi driver. He wouldn't take any money, just hugged me and said, "Take it easy, man."

I hid the urn under my bed.

That night I told my mother and Zoë I took care of the ashes privately, but the truth was I couldn't part with them. Dust to dust, they were all I had left. Except for my love for her, which seemed to take a bigger part of my heart every day.

I prayed to a God I didn't believe in as we pulled out of the driveway of the restaurant; prayed that this cruel flame of devotion would consume me, and that I could be with Cathy, wherever she was.

I don't remember driving home, but I do know my sister didn't speak, just cried silently and stared into the darkening summer night.

Chapter 12

Wednesday, July 27, 9 p.m.
Cathy

"Bradley, we have to leave. Right now!"

He stared at me, his concern over Nick's reaction to my presence plain to see. "Okay. Yes, of course."

We hurried to our table and Bradley asked the waiter to bag our dinners. Five minutes later we were in his car, headed out of the parking lot. The air inside the car filled with the fragrance of roast chicken, but I felt sick. All I wanted to do was talk to Nick, and explain that it was all a nightmare, that I was alive.

And that I loved him.

"I'm assuming we're going back to your apartment?" Bradley asked softly.

"No. No. Get on the freeway. I want to go to Sierra Monte." I nearly blurted out, 'I want to go home,' but I swallowed those alarming words. "I want to see Nick."

Bradley braked at the corner and peered at me in the growing darkness. "Roxanne, I don't think that's a good idea. We can't just show up unannounced, especially after what just happened."

"It's because of what just happened that I need to see him," I said. "You saw how upset he was. And poor Zoë. I need to talk to them both."

"And I need you to slow down a minute and think. I mean, have you even spoken to Nick since the wreck?"

"No, this was the first time." My eyes filled with tears. "God, he looks terrible, doesn't he? Thin, and like he hasn't slept."

"He didn't call you in the hospital?"

"No."

"Well, don't you think we need to back off, then? I mean, I know it hurts, Roxanne. But it was clear Nick wasn't happy to see you. Or me." Bradley put the car in gear and crossed the intersection. "I can't believe I totally forgot about it being Zoë's birthday today."

"Me, too." I burst into tears.

"I'm taking you home right now, Roxanne." Bradley patted my arm. "I've never, ever seen you cry, much less come apart like you're doing now. I'm sure if you think about it you'll agree no one would benefit from you trying to talk to Nick and Zoë again tonight."

My heartbeat raced as the headlights on the passing cars glowed ominously. Outside I heard a loud bang.

Suddenly the car accident replayed again inside my brain. I shut my eyes and tried to stop the memory but it only got worse. I was lying in the street and could smell smoke and grease and hear sirens screaming. Nearby a tire spun round and around on its axle as the car it belonged to lay crushed on its side.

I opened my eyes and the memory dissolved, leaving me weak and breathless. I had only one thought. I wanted to be with Nick. I wanted him to hold me tight in his arms and tell me it was all going to be okay.

"Roxanne?" Bradley sounded frightened.

I must have been moaning aloud. "I'm okay, Bradley." I swallowed and steadied my voice. "And you're right. This isn't the time to talk to Nick. But could you just drive past the house?" I clutched his arm as if it were a life preserver. "Please."

Bradley kept his eyes on the traffic. "Okay. We can do that. It's not too far." He glanced at me. "But you won't try and jump out of the car and run to the door or anything crazy and dramatic, will you?"

"No." I folded my hands in my lap. "No, Bradley. I'll be good. I promise."

Forty minutes later Bradley parked his car at Roxanne's apartment and held the door for me. "Let's get you upstairs." He gave me his hand, and I stood unsteadily.

"Here's your purse. I'll carry dinner." He grabbed the bags and took my arm.

We walked up the stairs in silence. Bradley had humored me and driven past my house. There were lights on inside, and Nick's car was parked in the driveway.

Pitty the cat was sitting on the front porch, staring into the street. I had cried again, but Bradley had not stopped the car or commented on my reaction to being on my old street where Nick still lived.

But I could hear questions recycling inside his head as we walked through the summer night. I couldn't think of anything to say to him without telling him *everything*, which of course was impossible.

Almost as impossible as figuring out a logical way to announce to my husband that, despite my appearance, I was his wife. I was the dead woman whose memorial service he had attended two weeks ago.

When we arrived at Roxanne's front door, my mind was spinning like a pinwheel in a hurricane. Memories overflowed inside my head. An image of my dress from the high school prom was replaced by one of my mother in her coffin, followed by several from a Memorial Day weekend when Nick and I burned everyone's hamburgers and ordered pizza instead.

There were also millions of blank spots. I put my hand to my hair and realized I couldn't remember who cut it. Or where I went to elementary school. But then new images, faces, sounds carried me off into another gluttony of reliving the past. I made no attempt to stop them, just let them run through my brain like a TV set with no 'off' button.

"Let me have your keys," Bradley said.

I concentrated on this task, fishing them out and handing them over so we could go into my best friend's home and have coffee.

My *dead* best friend's home.

I moaned again, and Bradley's frown deepened. We went inside and he turned on lights and took the food to the kitchen. I sat on the sofa and tried to keep from exploding into a million pieces of grief. Front and center was the fact that Roxanne was gone, was dead. My friend, my dearest friend, was lost to me forever.

"Can I get you some water? Or make some tea?" Bradley called out.

"No. I think I'm going to go to bed, try to sleep."

He sat across from me, looking about ten years older than he had two hours ago. "Do you want me to stay tonight? Or call your mom to come over?"

"No. I'll be okay." I grasped his hand. "I'm sorry. It was just so sad, so terrible, to see Nick and Zoë."

"I know. I know, honey." Tears filled his eyes. "It brought the reality of Cathy's death to all of us, I think. It was shocking that she wasn't there with us, that she'd never be there with us again."

"Yes. And Nick hates Roxanne for that. He blames her for Cathy's death. I've never seen him so angry at anyone."

"He *is* angry." Bradley paused. "But Rox, you really need to work on not referring to yourself in the third person. People are going to think you're crazy."

"I am a little crazy now, Bradley." Right then, I thought of blurting out the truth, but I knew he wouldn't believe me. I let several moments pass while I got control of my emotions. "Give me some time. I'll pull myself together."

"I know you will." He got up. "Are you, are you remembering things, even a little now? I should have realized going to Simone's might bring too much back too quickly."

"It's not that, it's just that I'm beyond tired. Overwrought." I hugged him. "Thank you so much for dinner. We had an awful lot of wine, are you sure you're okay to drive? You've got what, ten miles to go?"

Bradley moved his lips into a caricature of a smile. "Aha. So you do remember where I live?"

"I know you live in Eagle Rock. But only because Betty told me." My face reddened as I added to this growing string of lies. "You're sure you're sober?"

"Stone sober. More's the pity. But again, I'm so sorry that all this happened tonight, Roxanne. I wanted this to be a special night for you."

"It was." I kissed his cheek, realizing I never used to have to get on my tiptoes to reach his neck. "I'll call you tomorrow, okay?"

"You sure you don't need to talk more tonight? I can stay. You could go to bed, but I would be here when you got up."

"No, Bradley. Just go home."

"Okay. But you go straight to bed, girlfriend. No trips to Sierra Monte, right?"

"Promise."

Bradley looked hard at me. "For the record, I think Nick has acted like a dick since the accident. There's no reason to ignore you, or treat you like he did tonight. We all miss Cathy. But we all accept what happened was a wicked twist of fate. Nick needs to understand that."

"I can't fault Nick. He's in a lot of pain. I'll think it through more, what I need to do to reach out to him."

"That's charitable of you." Bradley cocked his head. "You know, since the accident you seem really different."

"I am different."

"How?"

My heart seemed to stop. "No one can go through something like this and not be changed. Even if I can't remember everything, I understand what an enormous loss everyone has suffered." I thought of Roxanne and pinched the back of my hand to keep from crying. "Me included."

"Poor girl. She was your best friend."

"Yes." It didn't matter that Bradley was wrong on *who* I was mourning. He understood what I felt.

He left, and I locked the door behind him. In the silence, I leaned against it and closed my eyes. What now?

The phone in the kitchen rang. I let the answering machine handle the call. I prayed it wasn't Betty again. Her daughter, her only child, was dead and she didn't even know it. I was the only soul who knew it was Roxanne we should all be mourning.

As the phone rang for the third time, I walked toward it and thought about Roxanne.

She wasn't always easy for some people to like. Some were just jealous, and to others she could act the cold, aloof beauty. But to me she was always supportive. When we were teenagers, she was perfect and sought after, while I was gawky and lonely and insecure. Despite that, she chose me to be her best friend.

I remembered one day in particular. It was after school and we stood staring at our reflections in the mirror in her bedroom, looking at zits. Well, my zits. Her complexion was silky tan, not a blemish on her heart-shaped face. My plain, pale skin was marked with pimples and dark circles.

Suddenly Roxanne pointed out that we had an identical gold fleck in the iris of our left eyes. "My God. That does it, we're secret sisters!" she announced. "That gold fleck is a sign from God. Fate has brought us together. What do you think?" She stared at my eyes in the mirror, and I felt a bigger question in hers, but I was too overwhelmed to imagine what it was.

"I've always wanted a sister," I'd whispered.

"Well, you've got one now," she said. We hugged and danced around and I felt like I was golden, and no longer alone in the world.

As the answering machine clicked, I collapsed in the chair beside it and realized with the impact of a blow to the head that Betty was going to have to hear the truth someday.

God almighty, if I could only go back a couple of weeks. I would let Roxanne turn the car around and not go to Seth's. If I had, we'd both be in our rightful bodies, and none of this mess would be confronting me.

A male voice floated out of the speaker. "Roxanne. Pick up. It's me, Michael."

My mind lurched from the day of the accident to last night, roiling with the memory of Michael's touch.

How would I ever explain last night to Nick? Or that one other time . . .

Another incident in Cathy's life, *my life,* dissolved like time-speed photography inside my brain. This past spring, a few months ago on a beach, I was there. With Michael Cimino.

It was a chilly, damp night when Nick was away in New York on business, and Rox was asleep on the backseat of Michael's Jaguar, knocked out by the bottles of wine we'd shared at dinner. Michael and I sat on a blanket at Corona del Mar. We were drunk. Then naked. I saw his penis, pulsing and hard. I remembered wanting him to push it inside of me as we embraced on the dark beach.

Did he? Like several other memories that had bombarded

me, this one wasn't complete. I couldn't remember what happened next. I bit my thumb. What kind of person was I then? *What kind of person am I now?* My face burned with shame for what may have taken place on a night when I'd known exactly who I was.

". . . guess you're not home yet." Michael's voice continued, disembodied and pissed-off, as it billowed from the speaker. "Call me. I'll come by and tuck you in, like last night. Call me when you get this, Roxanne. You've got the number."

The answering machine clicked off. Outside I heard a police siren, and a car door slammed in the parking lot.

I couldn't move. For a painful few moments I confronted several less than flattering attributes of Cathy Chance. My failings loomed from all corners of my mind.

I was frivolous. I told white lies whenever they suited me. I was envious. *Bossy.* Arrogant with people I thought weren't as well-read as me on various topics. Music. Politics. Movies. I always ate a piece of the fruit I was buying before I paid at the grocery store.

And I might be a slut. And a cheat.

"Shit," I said. Maybe I should keep quiet and pretend to be Roxanne forever. *I'll cut Michael loose and make Nick fall in love with me, the new me.*

I shook my head at the ridiculousness of that thought. It wouldn't work, not on any level of karma I could come up with. Inside my head, I heard my mother's voice. "Oh what a dangerous web we weave when first we practice to deceive."

She had often warned me about lying when I was little. I should have listened to her.

I walked into Roxanne's bedroom and pulled off my clothes, kicked them away, then flopped onto the bed and buried my head in the pillows. What was I going to do first?

Convince Nick.

I'd need help with this. I thought of people I might turn to. Bradley? Betty? No, they both would take too much convincing.

Dr. Patel? I had an appointment with him next Monday. No, I couldn't wait that long and besides, Dr. Patel struck me as exceedingly logical. Not one to entertain my inexplicable, supernatural, logic-defying reality.

Althea? Jen? The tennis coach, who had called for the fourth time, Fred Apodaca? I didn't even know that Rox had been friends with him. And Nick thought he was a jerk, so Fred was out.

No, no, and no.

My thoughts flew to Zoë and my heart lurched. *That poor, sweet child, how she must be suffering.* Not only at what she thought was the loss of me, but for her brother. I loved Zoë more than a sister; more like a daughter. We had a deep, true connection. I could trust her. But the kid was clearly fragile right now. I would have to think hard about how I would ever explain this turn of events to her.

Maybe I could go to church, see a priest. "Excuse me, I've died and my soul, or something, was transported into my best friend's body, and I need to know how to convince my husband it's me inside this gorgeous human form. And by the way, my best friend is now dead, except for her body."

Hysterical giggles poured out of my mouth at this hypothetical conversation. I tried to imagine the reply. Since neither the mental ward nor an exorcist was what I had in mind, I kept thinking.

Dr. Ryan Seth. His name suddenly shimmered like a mirage. Roxanne and I had been going to see him the day of the accident. I'd met with him professionally before in my life. He could help me. He would know what to do.

I climbed out from under the blankets and picked up Roxanne's cell phone. I punched in Seth's number and left a long message, begging for his earliest appointment. He would see Roxanne's name, but I never lied and said I was her.

I shut off the cell and took two pain pills, craving blackout sleep.

Dr. Seth. I said his name over and over, like a mantra. Tomorrow would be the first full day in part two of the life of Cathy Chance. He could help me.

He must.

Chapter 13

Thursday, July 28, 10 a.m.
Dr. Seth's Office

"Roxanne! Come in!"
No, it's me, Cathy.
"Hi, Dr. Seth. How are you?" I paused for a moment and regarded him. He stood across the room, leaning against his desk.

Ryan Seth was over six feet tall and lanky. His shaved head accentuated his well-shaped skull. He had a manicured salt-and-pepper beard and generous mouth. Like his personality, Dr. Seth was equal parts inquisitive and comforting.

He held his arms wide open. "Come over here, Roxanne. Let me give you a hug."

"Thanks so much for getting me in here this morning." I walked to him.

Seth, as all his clients called him, took a couple of steps. Though blind, he moved confidently in his serene, sparely furnished office. He'd lost his sight as a child, when a pot of soup he pulled off the stove scalded him.

"Of course, my dear. I was delighted you reached out to me." He hugged me without reservation and then held me at arms' length. "How are you feeling? You have been much on my mind."

No beating around the bush with Seth. I settled myself on the leather sofa across from his rattan chair.

Where to begin? "I was lost, but now I'm found," I blurted out.

He showed surprise at my quoting lyrics from Judas Priest, Nick's favorite British heavy metal band from the Eighties. Not as surprised as I was, however. Another lyric from the song flitted across my brain. *Staying on course, I'm still alive.* But I couldn't jump that far into my story.

Seth sat in his rattan chair, his sightless eyes turned toward the glass walls of his office. He worked in a space connected to the log cabin he lived in, out in the woods, two thousand feet up into the Verdugo hills. The view from where we sat was heavily treed and quiet, with blue skies. Mt. Baldy loomed in the distance.

"You've been through hell since we last met," Seth said. "I hear it in your voice. Despite what you say, I think you may still be lost in the wilderness."

I blew out my breath as if I were in labor. "The accident was terrible." Those words mentally transported me to the scene of the wreck as violently as if I'd been jerked by the neck. I felt the heat off the pavement and smelled the gunpowder from the airbags, heard tires burst, a fire igniting. *And my bones breaking.* And screaming. Roxanne, screaming.

"I was so frightened," I whispered.

Dr. Seth remained still. "You remember everything, then? The accident? Dr. Patel said you had amnesia."

"I did. Until last night." I began to shake, head to toe tremors. In the past any despair in my voice brought Dr. Seth to my side. He's a touchy-feely guy in a totally non-creepy way, all comfort and no seduction.

But today he remained in his papa-san chair, his hands folded in his lap, his face averted.

I cried and grabbed the tissue box beside me. "I've been having glimpses and pieces of memories since I woke up in the hospital. I couldn't understand how they fit together, but since moving to Roxanne's apartment, more things started to click into place. When my friend Bradley Chandler took me to dinner at Simone's last night, I saw something that triggered a key memory, and I remembered everything. I remembered *who* I am."

"What did you see that brought your identity back to you?" Dr. Seth asked.

"*The Bridge at Bougival,* a painting by Monet. There's a print of it in the restaurant ladies' room."

"Is this painting special to you in some way?"

"Yes. I saw the original when I was a child. At the museum with my mother, at a wonderful show called 'A Day in the Country.' It was the last time I remember my mother not suffering. She died of cancer a few weeks later."

Seth didn't move. "Your mother is alive, Roxanne. Why would you say she died when you were small?"

"I . . ." My voice cracked. I searched for a way to start this extraordinary conversation, to convince Seth of what had happened, but of course there was only one obvious first sentence. "I'm not Roxanne."

Seth got up, walked to my chair, and knelt in front of me. He took my hands in his. "Go slowly, now. What's happened? Tell me what you mean, that you are not Roxanne."

Blood rushed to my head and I saw spots in front of my eyes. I swayed and started to slip into a faint and felt myself transported to that stretch of road in the Verdugo Hills, Roxanne by my side. The accident memory enveloped every cell of me. I floated above a scene of disaster and recognized my body, sprawled, unmoving and terribly hurt. My arm lay in the middle of the street amidst a flood of red.

A dark-haired woman pulled me, urging me not to look down. I floated higher, airless sky and blue stars enveloping me. A siren screamed, and everything went black and I could no longer see the road or the poor blonde girl with the missing arm.

The woman hovered above me, murmuring, "*I wish I were you, Lupeyloo.*" The words were a chant, a lullaby, a dirge, and I realized the truth. The dark-haired woman was Roxanne. She was dying. And I was already dead.

But then my friend grasped my hand, sending energy from her into and through me like a million volt shock, and I was reborn.

Above that blood-soaked highway, I turned to plead with my dearest friend in the world not to leave me, but she pulled out of my grasp and I fell spinning through space back to earth and woke up in the hospital nine days later. *Alive.*

Inside Roxanne's body.

I opened my eyes, gripping Seth as if I was a frightened child. "Roxanne's dead," I whispered against his ear. "I'm Cathy Chance. Oh my God, please believe me, Seth. I don't know what to do."

"Shh. Breathe in and out slowly," he said. "Come fully into the present."

I realized I had been narrating my memories of July 9 aloud. I felt lighter then, relieved that another person now knew the truth of what had happened to me. And to Roxanne.

"I'm here," I said.

Seth released me and sat on the floor. He crossed his legs and arms and rocked back and forth. He didn't appear shocked, or horrified, or even disbelieving. He seemed to concentrate, his brow furrowed.

After a few moments, he turned to me. "May I ask you a few questions?"

"Yes."

For what seemed like hours, Seth queried me. I poured out descriptions of scenes of my life I could remember, from childhood to July 9, rehashing in particular details of experiences that Seth and I had discussed years ago when he had worked with me on anxiety issues.

Occasionally I wouldn't recall the complete memory, but the vat of facts I disgorged astounded us both. My brain felt like a runaway locomotive, gathering speed and energy as Seth asked about events from Cathy's life, from *my life*. I knew he was testing me, asking me to prove who I really was to him. And maybe to myself.

When at last Seth stopped asking and I stopped answering, he brought me a drink that tasted of lemon and warmth. I drank it to the bottom and leaned into his leather sofa and fell into a restful state, awake but disengaged, one blink from deep sleep.

Seth returned to his desk. "Can you hear me?"

"Yes." My eyes drifted closed. "I'm so tired though, I may fall asleep."

"Let go and relax now. I'm going to call a doctor I went to university with, Elias Fox. He practices in Boston. He's an expert neurologist known for his research with people who were pronounced clinically dead but were brought back to life with intervention. He authored a paper a few years ago dealing with amnesiacs, and how this condition is commonly exhibited by patients declared dead but then revived. So, just rest for a few minutes while I try and reach him."

Alarm spread through my exhausted nervous system. "Wait, please." I sat upright. "Why are you calling him? You don't believe me?"

Seth blinked. "I believe *you believe* what you are telling me is true, my dear. But I am not a psychiatrist or a neurologist. I want to ask Elias a few questions about the physical structure of the brain, and rule out a couple of other things before I can tell you I accept everything you've told me is the truth."

"What if Dr. Fox says I'm crazy?" That possibility washed over me. Could I be Roxanne? Was I hallucinating that I was Cathy Chance? I had considered this explanation several times since my epiphany in the restaurant.

"I don't think you're crazy," Seth replied. "And I'll keep your name confidential when I talk to my old friend. Please understand I'm seeking more information so I can help put *your mind* at ease, not mine."

I lay back down on the sofa and listened, but not too closely, as Seth talked to Dr. Fox. I allowed my bruised mind to wander. Surprisingly, I felt full of joy. Someone now knew what had happened to me; someone I trusted might be able to help me find a way to convince Nick.

I could hardly bear to think of the pain Nick must be suffering. It wasn't hubris, or arrogance, to think he was devastated at losing me. I understood this kind of agony, for I now felt it for Roxanne.

Nick had looked gaunt and pained last night. Yet dear and familiar and wonderful. Seeing him sent a thrill through me I could not put into words. While his disdain stung because he did not, could not, see me waiting inside the flesh and bones I inhabited, I knew I could find a way to reach him.

As I relaxed on the sofa, Seth's side of the phone conversation seeped into my brain.

"Confabulation?" Seth's voice rose. "Yes, of course. Many patients who have false memories of being abducted by aliens, or molested by their parents, or who think they are Jesus Christ, can be said to be in the grip of a fantasy. But my patient recalls in almost total detail, with provable facts, her own discreet life experiences. Based on what she told me today, I would vouch for the authenticity of her identity in a court of law, if I had to."

I trembled and hugged myself, acutely aware how insane my story sounded.

"No, I don't plan to bring her to anyone else right now," Seth said. "Especially not as a study subject. It is my patient's information, her story to share. Or not to share. Surely you see the validity of this position, Elias."

A pause, then Seth laughed gently. "Thank you. Of course I trust your discretion. But before I hang up, may I ask if your research has ever led you to anyone who has similarly claimed to have died and been transferred, for lack of another word, into another person's body?"

Silence.

"So there have been other cases like this, but you're not willing to totally accept that they were telling the factual truth?" He smiled gently. "Are you not religious, Elias? No more 'leap of faith' capability? I seem to remember your grandfather was an Episcopal priest."

He listened for several moments and nodded. "Yes, but there are millions who believe in a resurrection, in heaven and hell. In other words, *in miracles*. I'm agnostic, but I do believe things happen that man can't explain but must accept . . ."

I closed my eyes in gratitude. Dr. Seth believed me. He accepted this un-provable story I told as provable fact. And if he had, then Nick could, too.

I *was* a miracle. It was as complicated, and as simple, as that.

I spent the next couple of hours on Seth's sofa dozing and recouping my strength. Seth left to teach an afternoon class, and came back with sandwiches. We ate and chatted like dorm school chums, steering clear of the topic at hand.

Finally, about four p.m., Seth asked, "So, what's next, kiddo?"

"I want to talk to Nick."

Seth wiped his fingers on the napkin he'd stuck in his shirtfront. "And say what, exactly?"

"Hi, this is your wife. I'm coming home." I laughed. "Of course I'd never do that."

Seth didn't look fully convinced. "Maybe I should call Nick," he said.

"You?"

"Yes. I saw him at the memorial service. Your service," he added. "Wow, how weird is that to say to another person?"

"Very weird." I took a deep breath. "How did it go? One of the women at St. Anne's said she found it moving."

"It was." Seth frowned as if unsure about sharing certain details. "Anyway, I've been meaning to call Nick and see if we could have a private visit. We have a long history together. I think I can lay some groundwork for him to think about what's happened a little differently."

I sat up straight. "You mean you'll tell him what I told you today?"

"No. That's not information that can come from me. But I can gauge his temperament, feel out his ability to accept the unorthodox. Is Nick a spiritual man, in your opinion?"

"Yes. No. Let me think." I wasn't sure what Seth meant by spiritual. "He's not religious. But he's compassionate. He's brilliant and curious about life. Nonjudgmental. That's one of the first things I loved about him. He's always open to new things."

"So he'll be open to the possibility that something amazing happened? To you. And to him."

"I think so. Maybe you could pose a hypothetical, 'So Nick, if you could get your wife back from the dead, would you want her?' That would be a start."

This time we both laughed.

"Okay, one last question, Cathy. Is there any chance Nick wouldn't be overjoyed at your return?"

I grinned at being called by name, but thought again of the sexual betrayal I'd committed with Michael, and sobered up. "None. Nick loves me. There's zero possibility my husband wouldn't welcome me back."

As long as I don't tell him some things. I pushed this aside. Someday I would tell Nick about Michael. He would forgive me. If it had happened to Nick, I would forgive him.

Wouldn't I?

My heart pounded faster.

"Do you have any plan about how you'll convince him it's you standing in front of him?" Seth asked.

"I'll tell him the truth, just like I told you." I could picture it, could feel his arms around me and his mouth on mine. "I can't wait to tell him."

"You need to slow down a little, Cathy. Patience really is a virtue in this situation."

"I know. But I will convince him. I convinced you, right?"

"You did." Seth smiled. "But I believe you because you told me facts I could confirm. It's different with me than with your husband. I don't have the same vulnerabilities, or anywhere near the same emotional stakes as Nick does. As fond of you as I am, and as delighted as I am that you're not lost to us, I've not been mourning you as profoundly as he has. I think with Nick there will be issues of self-protection and suspicion about the motives of the bearer of this wonderful news."

"Motives? What do you mean?"

"Well, let's turn it around for a minute. Say you had lost Nick. And this miraculous thing happened to him. And several weeks after you buried Nick, Michael Cimino showed up at your doorstep claiming to be Nick and asking to be welcomed with open arms."

I leaned back, my mind swimming with this scenario. My faced burned and I wondered if Seth could read my heart with his blind, all-seeing eyes.

"What do you think your reaction would be?" Seth pressed.

"I'd think Michael had come up with a ploy to get laid. I would throw him out. Call the cops. Or the nuthouse." My earlier joy evaporated and I felt a hundred years old. "You think Nick will be suspicious of me?"

"He won't know it's *you*, Cathy dear. It's not you he'll be suspicious of. He'll see Roxanne. And quite logically react to her the same way you explained you would to Michael."

I considered this. My brain played out another possibility. Roxanne's body, which I now inhabited, was gorgeous and desirable. Maybe Nick would pretend to believe me only because he'd wanted to sleep with her all these years. First he would bed me, believing it was Rox, then he'd call the nuthouse.

I looked down with green-eyed jealousy at the body I inhabited. "So what do I do? What *can* I do?"

Seth patted my hand. "I'll call and ask him to come in. That's the first step. I'll get a feel for how much I think he can handle. Then I'll call you."

"Okay." I desperately wanted to see Nick, damn all this careful planning. I thought of my turquoise earring. I could take it to him and test the waters myself. I didn't share this plan with Seth, knowing he'd disagree.

"Okay." I got up, exhausted by the drama and adrenalin of the past two hours.

Seth took out his cell and let me punch in Nick's number. He showed surprise at hearing Cathy's voice, my voice, on the recording. Neither Nick nor Zoë picked up, so he left a message. He smiled at me, the light glinting off his dark glasses. "Go home and rest. I'll get in touch as soon as I see him." Seth gave me a ferocious hug. "And welcome back, Cathy."

Chapter 14

Thursday, July 28, 6 p.m.
Nick

"I'm sorry, Zoë. That wasn't a very good birthday party yesterday."

Last night we had come home after the disaster at Simone's and not said a word to one another, just went to bed. This morning she was gone before I awoke. When I got home from work I found her in her bedroom, sitting in the dark, staring into space.

My sister turned to me. "Don't worry about the birthday, Nick. But you better start concentrating on yourself and getting past this shit. You can't freak out every time someone mentions her, or when you see Roxanne."

I rolled over on my stomach. I was lying on Zoë's cluttered, unmade bed. Her pillow smelled like weed. "Are you smoking pot again?"

"No. Yes, a little. But don't change the subject," she replied. "Maybe you should go see Dr. Seth. He left a message a couple of hours ago, by the way. And I'd been thinking about calling him myself. You know he helped you deal with stuff once before."

I shook my head. "I don't need a shrink."

"He's not a shrink. Cathy said he's more like a priest. Without the religious stuff."

"No." There was no point in talking to anyone about healing something that couldn't be healed.

My little sister stared at me with four-hundred-year-old

eyes. "You're hurting, Nick. If you won't go see Seth, why don't you talk to Roxanne without freaking out? Get your feelings out in the open. Give her a chance to make amends."

"Make amends?" I pictured Roxanne, how shockingly sad her expression looked when we spoke. But her pain didn't engender any empathy in me, it just made me furious.

I slapped my hand against the mattress. "Jesus fuck, Zoë. Roxanne was wearing Cathy's earring."

"What? Which earrings?"

"Those turquoise earrings I got her last Christmas. Cathy was wearing them the day of the accident. The hospital must have given one of them to Roxanne by mistake."

"And she thought it was hers because she doesn't remember anything. Is that why you were so mad at Bradley? Because you thought Roxanne was being insensitive about Cathy's jewelry?"

"I guess." My face twitched.

"Did you get it back?"

"What?"

"Cathy's earring. Did you get it back?"

I pictured Roxanne, her hand outstretched. "No. No, I didn't get it back."

"That's pretty sad." Zoë chewed on her lip for a moment. "Did Roxanne mention anything about what happened at the insurance guy's office?"

"No."

"Her mom must not have told her. She seemed so spacey and, I don't know, lost at St. Anne's the other day. I wonder if she should still be in the hospital."

I don't give a fuck. "She must be okay enough to go out drinking with Bradley. He was pretty lit. They were obviously partying. Short mourning period for some people."

"We were partying, too," Zoë said. "Bradley told me Roxanne asked him for information about everyone. Right before you came back to the table, Bradley said how strange it was to be with her, and that she seemed really different. Like she wasn't the same person as before."

"She seemed the same to me." *Gorgeous. Self-centered. Dangerous.* I told my brain not to go there.

"You never liked her very much, did you?"

Answering that question would involve a discussion too complicated to have with Zoë. "I'm not interested in talking about Roxanne." I stood. "Wait here a minute. I've got something for you."

I went to the closet for the present Cathy had bought for her a lifetime ago and returned to Zoë's room. I handed her the thing. She watched me steadily as she ripped off the paper, and her eyes filled with tears as soon as she realized what it was. I didn't have to tell her Cathy had bought it.

"This is so cool." She sobbed, tears falling onto the glass frame. "Did she get it online?"

"Yeah, eBay. She fought with a couple of dealers for it. Which means she spent way the hell too much." I grinned. "I'm sorry you didn't get it yesterday. Happy Birthday, Sis."

Zoë leaped across the space and hugged me. "She told me she saw this. It's the poster they did for the twenty-fifth anniversary. Thirty-six inches by twenty-eight. It's a weird size. She had to get it custom framed."

I nodded. Zoë cried harder. I handed her some tissues.

"Hey, how about some food?" Now, I was famished.

Zoë blew her nose. "Okay. Did you bring the chocolate soufflé home last night?"

"No, I'm so sorry, Zoë. I should have had Jen wrap up the food. I'll make it up to you next year."

"I'm kidding," she said with a huge sniffle. "How about you make pancakes tonight? With peanut butter."

"Anything you want. I'll make some eggs, too. Dry your eyes. I'll see you in the kitchen."

Zoë hugged the poster to her chest. I left her, relieved to have something to do besides watch someone else miss Cathy.

I snapped on the light and got busy. Pitty was asleep outside on the patio. She still didn't want to come in the house. I glanced at the blinking message light on the phone but ignored it. Zoë must not have erased Seth's message. I flicked the ringer off and prayed Zoë wouldn't notice. I needed some more time away from conversations.

Then, despite trying to avoid it, I thought more about Roxanne.

She had seemed different last night. More fragile, but also more vibrant than usual. I'd often thought Roxanne might actually be too beautiful. Her looks sucked all the air out of the room when she walked in, turning most people into tourists, gawking and plotting how to get a piece of her.

Since I'd known her, she had dealt with this attention with frosty indifference. Unless, of course, you didn't stare.

As I cracked an egg into the pancake mix and put a pan on to heat, I remembered the first time I'd seen Roxanne.

That summer between sophomore and junior year in high school, my family had moved us from the east to Sierra Monte and I had made friends with the guys I would play football with. They were telling me about the girls I'd meet in school. Roxanne Ruiz was the prize they all coveted. Slivers of those long ago snickers and their descriptions of her: 'hot,' 'great tits,' 'lickable,' slid through my brain.

I was at the grocery store when my mom introduced me to her. I was pushing Zoë in the cart, helping with the shopping, and we ran into Betty Haverty. Mom knew her from the PTA events.

Betty was standing with this girl who looked like a model. Or a movie star. She was dark-haired and had perfect skin, along with an ass most guys would die to get their hands on.

"Nick, this is Roxanne Ruiz," my mom had said. "Isn't she a pretty girl? You're in the same grade. Maybe Roxanne can introduce you to some of the kids at school."

I could still feel my face burning as it had that day. "Hey," I'd stammered. I wanted to turn and run away with the shopping cart and not look back.

"Hi." Roxanne looked me over quickly. I heard indifference in her voice. I judged it to be only a tiny bit less than what she felt for herself. Despite the killer looks, she gave off fucked-up vibes.

While our moms chatted and Zoë stared at Roxanne as if she were a living Barbie doll, I watched her out of the corner of my eye. She was a perfect babe and held her head as if posing for unseen cameras. I remember flashing on the thought she might be suicidal or something, she was so tense. But I had no skills to ask if something was eating her, and I really didn't care. My concern for Roxanne's psyche was squashed by my fifteen-year-old male fantasy of wishing I could see her naked, which wasn't going to happen.

She was completely out of my league and I knew I couldn't handle any kind of relationship with Roxanne Ruiz, even if one were possible. And I wouldn't have had one. Except that Cathy was devoted to her. And once I fell for Cathy, Roxanne became part of my life, too.

As I stood cooking Zoë's dinner, a more recent memory of Roxanne ricocheted inside my head. She sat behind me at the table in this same kitchen, eating waffles, crying. It was the middle of the night and Cathy was asleep.

Roxanne had begged for help. *And begged me not to ever tell Cathy.*

"How's it coming?" Zoë asked behind me.

Startled, I dropped the spatula on the stove. Grabbing hold of it again, I banished Roxanne from my mind.

"Good, good," I lied. "How many pancakes do you want?"

"A lot." She'd washed her face and put on baggy PJs. She went to the back door and called Pitty. Shockingly, the cat jumped off the chair and came inside, meowing. Zoë picked her up and nuzzled her. "Look, Nick. She's in and she's letting me hold her."

I glanced over. "You're going to get cat hair in your pancakes. And I can't believe she's letting you pick her up."

"I don't care about the hair. Are you making bacon, too?"

I smiled. Zoë was grinning and the cat was purring. Pitty only tolerated being held. She'd never lay next to you, or beg to get up and sit on your lap. Except for Cathy, she wouldn't let anyone hug her. She'd scratched Zoë numerous times over the years because the kid always wanted to kiss her.

"Be careful she doesn't scratch you. And no, I'm not frying bacon. We're out of it." I flipped the pancakes.

"Ouch," Zoë said. I heard a thump as Pitty hit the floor. A thin line of blood oozed on Zoë's cheek where the cat had scratched her.

I sighed and handed her a wet paper towel. "You better put something on that. You know how dirty they say a cat's claws are."

Zoë took the paper towel and dabbed her face. "Nick, look. She's limping."

I looked. Pitty limped around in the middle of the foyer. I took the pancakes off the griddle and my sister and I herded her into a corner of the living room. I picked her up and we examined her for damage but couldn't see much through the thick fur. The cat stared at us with intense suspicion and meowed as if in pain when I felt her right hip.

"We'll take her to the vet tomorrow," I said. "You can drive my car to work because I'm going to stay home and fix up the yard. After your job you can come get me and we'll both go to the vet."

This would be a new experience. Cathy always took the cat to the vet. The couple of times I had gone with her had ended in disaster. Cathy said my presence, along with our vet, was too much testosterone in one room for the hairball. The cat had an aversion to men after her treatment by Cathy's stepfather. It was a reaction I'd been unable to change despite being good to the goddamned thing over the years.

Zoë nodded. "You don't think it's serious, do you?"

"No. Pitty's tough. She probably sprained something." I put her down and she skulked quickly to the back door and meowed. "Don't let her outside, Zoë. She understands the word 'vet.' She'll disappear and we'll never find her."

I washed my hands in the kitchen sink and started serving dinner.

"I couldn't stand it if we lost Pitty, too," Zoë whispered.

"We're not losing Pitty. Come on, eat before the pancakes get cold."

We ate in silence. I had planned to sing a belated happy birthday to her, and put a candle on the pancakes, but the night had lost its sparkle. Now *I* was worried about the cat.

Zoë went off to bed with a small hug goodnight. I stayed in the kitchen and cleaned up. Then I settled in a chair and stared out the window, trying not to think of the golden urn under my bed, but thinking of nothing else.

I wanted a drink. Bad. I pulled out my cell to call my AA sponsor, a gruff old guy who taught American history at Pasadena City College, but my cell was dead.

I plugged the phone in the charger and returned to the chair, closing my eyes, willing myself to sleep. Hours later I woke up, my neck aching in pain. I rubbed it, imagining my wife's hands on me.

The house was dark, and outside the night was blacker still. I knew I wouldn't sleep if I crawled into my own bed. I thought of Simone's, of how Roxanne had looked walking toward me in the hallway, of the shock of seeing her wearing Cathy's jewelry.

I replayed the scene at the insurance company, the catastrophic dinner party, and my conversations with Zoë about Roxanne. I was haunted by thoughts of two women who were best friends, one whom I loved with my whole heart, the other whom I had ever only tolerated.

And I thought again of what had happened last November, how I'd lied to my wife. Somewhere in the house, a clock struck three.

My mouth was so dry I could hardly swallow.

I need to go to the grocery store. We're out of milk and bacon and cat food. I got up and grabbed my keys and quietly went out to the car. I drove past the Albertsons and pulled into the parking lot of the only liquor store in the area that was open all night.

I was five miles away from where my sister lay, sleeping and worrying about a sick old cat. I bought a fifth of scotch, twelve-year-old McClellan's, good stuff.

I went back to my car as if I were dream-walking, then drove a couple of blocks away and parked. My mind went on automatic as I pushed the seat back and opened the bottle, my hands shaking with anticipation.

Nothing chases ghosts away like booze. As the flames of scent reached my nose, my stomach tightened and acid spurted up my throat in protest.

I took several deep breaths and looked out to the street. A donut shop killed its lights. The hair raised on my neck as I watched a group of kids walk around the shop, talking loud, drunk or high, their body language saying they were looking for trouble.

The amber smell and hum of liquor lingered even as I screwed the cap back on. I thought about surrendering to Fear and undoing years of sobriety without a backward glance.

I opened the car window. It was quiet then, and I felt all alone in the world. I unscrewed the bottle cap and threw it out the window as far as I could.

This would be a very bad decision. Not the first or the last. *Well, maybe the last.*

Chapter 15

Friday, July 29, Noon
Cathy Watches Her House

I closed my compact and ducked low in the front seat of the rental car when a beat-up Volkswagen Beetle with a 'For Sale' sign stuck in the back window pulled into the driveway at my house. Zoë got out of the car and headed for the front door without looking across the street and seeing me. She had the cat carrier and her backpack with her. I could see Pitty's face smashed up against the door of the carrier, and heard her plaintive yowling.

The Beetle drove off, a young man I had never seen before at the wheel. His head was shaved and he wore a button-down shirt and tie. Maybe a boyfriend? I had to wonder, feeling a rush of hope. Zoë had never had a real boyfriend, and this might be a sign she was warming up to people her age.

I sighed and continued waiting for Nick to show. I had to see him, just for a few minutes. I had not heard from Seth yet, but even if he persuaded Nick to come in, I still needed to get my husband to look at me with something other than the contempt he had on his face at Simone's.

My excuse for coming to the house was going to be that I wanted to give him the turquoise earring. I hoped he still had the other one. I loved those earrings. They were my most favorite items of jewelry, next to my wedding band, which I also hoped he still had.

I wanted it back, and prayed he hadn't chucked it into the Pacific Ocean, or something crazy like that.

Zoë stood at the front door struggling with a key. She must have had to bring the cat to the vet. *What's wrong with Pittypat?* I tried not to fret. Zoë disappeared inside and I glanced at the watch I'd bought myself earlier today.

Feeling spooked about wearing Roxanne's things, I'd spent an hour this morning buying underwear, clothes, a purse and a couple of outfits. At least now I wore stuff that didn't have someone else's history imprinted on them, clothes that looked like me, *Cathy*, even if the body inside them looked like anything but me.

I tightened the leather watchstrap and glanced again at the time. Twelve thirty-six. Bradley mentioned Zoë told him Nick was going to be off today. Where was he? Could he be inside?

If he was inside the house, where was our car? I'd been sitting here for over an hour, calling, but no one had answered. Of course, Nick didn't always answer the house phone, I knew from experience. Maybe he was sick.

As my pulse rate climbed, I pawed through the stuff in my purse and pulled out the cell again. I punched in the number to our house and waited. Twice. Three times. Four times. The call went to the answering machine, which still featured my voice, cheerfully instructing callers to leave a message at the tone.

Why didn't Zoë pick up? I glanced at the house again. Nick probably shut off the ringer and Zoë didn't know someone was calling. I couldn't contain a nervous chuckle. That crazy husband of mine; we'd fought about his aversion to phones a million times. *Soon as I'm gone, he reverts to his old ways.*

I wasn't known for being patient, as Seth had told me to be. Not only impatient, but right now I actually felt akin to a stalker, so urgent was my need to spend a few moments in Nick's physical presence. I only wanted to see him again, and will him to look me in the eye.

And hope he wouldn't think I was trying to con him, the way I would think if Michael Cimino was pitching this tale to me.

I pinched the skin on the top of my hand and struggled to relax. I closed my eyes and felt myself drifting off.

"Hey!" someone yelled outside, and then rapped on the window. My eyes flew open and my heart thudded in my chest. Zoë stood next to the car, arms crossed, a scowl on her face.

I hit the button on the window, which of course did not respond because the car was off. "Hi!" I motioned for her to move back so I could open the door.

Zoë took a couple of steps back and I joined her. In the heat, the scent of honeysuckle from the walkway by my house wafted to us.

"Hey, Zoë. How are you?" I was unable to suppress a grin.

"What are you doing here, Roxanne?" Her eyes looked anxious.

I stopped smiling. "I, I wanted to try and catch up with Nick. I have an earring he asked me about at Simone's the other night that I wanted to give back. And maybe talk a little. I didn't get the chance to say anything I really wanted to him. Or to you the other day at school."

"Are you saying you remember stuff now? Like where Nick lives?"

"Yes, I do. I remember a lot of things. I remember it was your eighteenth birthday the other night, and my showing up probably ruined it. I'm sorry. And Happy Birthday, Zoë." I thought of the poster hidden in my bedroom closet and hoped Nick remembered to give it to her. I squeezed her arm.

She flinched. "I'll give Nick the earring. I don't think it's a good idea for you to talk to him right now." She held out her hand.

I dug into the pocket of my jeans and then hesitated. "Can I talk to you for a few minutes? Inside?"

"What do you want to talk about?"

"Nick. And the accident."

She blinked. To my ears, my tone sounded way too much like the pushy, 'big sister' attitude I always took with her. I told myself not to scare the wits out of the kid, but I couldn't play it cool. I was in front of my house, and I ached to go inside. "Please. I'll leave before Nick gets home, if you think that's best."

"I don't know when he's getting home," she replied. "I don't even know where he is."

"What?"

Zoë chewed her bottom lip and glanced around the tree-lined street. "He was gone this morning, early. I didn't go to work because I was worried about the cat, so I took it to the vet. He was supposed to be home. He said he was taking off to work in the yard. But he's not answering his cell."

"Has your mom talked to him?" Panic hummed through my veins. "Did you call work and make sure he didn't go in?"

"Yeah, I called work. He's not there. And my mom hasn't heard from him."

We both knew this wasn't like Nick. Since our marriage, he was very responsible about letting me know where he was and when he'd be home. "He didn't leave his cell home, did he?"

"I checked his room. It's not there."

"You didn't worry that he wasn't home when you got up this morning?" My voice rose.

"No."

"And you don't know when he left?"

"No." Zoë's eyes teared up. "And I need to talk to him about the cat. The vet said she's real sick." Her voice broke.

I pulled the child to me. "Hey, don't cry. What's wrong with Pittypat?"

"She's got some kind of growth on her hip. It might be a tumor."

"God, what's Dr. Erlich going to do about it? Can they operate?"

"I don't know. He said I have to talk to Nick because the x-rays and stuff would cost about five hundred bucks. I told him I would pay it, but he said I'd better clear it with Nick. Erlich said Pitty is so old, she might not even make it if they operated on her."

Now I felt like crying. "I'm sure when you tell Nick, he'll pay whatever it takes, Zoë. He'll probably want to get a second opinion, though. Preferably from a vet who is more up to date on things than Dr. Erlich. I think he went to vet school in the 1940s. Come on, don't worry. Pitty's a tough old cat, she'll come out of this."

Zoë took a rattling breath and started back across the street. "Come on in, if you want. I need to check the phone messages, anyway. Maybe Nick called."

I grabbed my purse out of the car and followed Zoë. She held the front door of my house open for me, as if I was a guest, and I stepped inside. For several moments, I stood silently and looked around at my home. It felt like years—and yet, only minutes—since I'd stood here.

It was almost too dear and familiar to bear. As I exhaled, my eyes stung with tears, but I blinked them away and took inventory of the living room.

The nice, big comfy sofa covered in the blue and tan batik print Nick hadn't liked at first but had finally agreed to use. My desk, the only furniture I owned that was my mom's. Next to it, Nick's stereo cabinet, full of his music, heavy on Stevie Ray Vaughan and Seventies and Eighties rock and roll. Most he bought when he worked as a disc jockey, his favorite of all his jobs.

The faded oriental carpet we'd bought at a garage sale in Alta Dena covered the wood floor and looked freshly vacuumed. On the wall above the fireplace were movie posters Nick had framed for me from some of my favorite movies: *The French Lieutenant's Woman*, *Ryan's Daughter*, and *Double Indemnity*, the one with Stanwyck and MacMurray.

I pictured the poster from *Casablanca* in the powder room, and the set of lobby cards from the Steve McQueen version of *The Thomas Crown Affair* in our bedroom. I loved old movies. After my mom died, I spent every Saturday at the dollar movie theatre that showed stuff from thirty years ago. With two screens, I snuck from one theatre to the next, losing myself in the triumphs and tragedies that seemed so much more bearable than my own.

I inhaled the scents of the cinnamon potpourri in the hallway, the lemon trees outside the open windows, the rose bushes we planted along the side of the house last summer. If happy was a scent, it would smell like this.

"You okay, Roxanne?" Zoë shut the door and walked a few paces into the room, her arms hugging herself as she studied me.

"Yes, fine." I sat by my desk, my knees shaking. "Go ahead into the kitchen and check the messages. I'll wait here, if that's okay."

Zoë looked like she was worried I might steal something. "I'll be right back."

Alone in the room, I ran my hand over the top of my beloved desk, an antique, walnut burl secretary, glossy with wax. It held framed pictures of Nick and me, taken over the years, now on display inside the glass doors above the writing surface. I picked up a framed print of us from high school, our arms wrapped around each other and huge grins on our faces. The summer we'd become lovers, right after junior year.

"Yeow." A gravelly voice from the floor announced the very pissed-off presence of the cat. I tapped the door of the cat carrier. "Hey, Miss Pitty, what's going on? You want to get out of there?"

The cat let out a yowl that would have been right at home in a horror movie. She butted her head against the door and purred. My eyes filled again. I missed that furry body against me. I undid the broken lock Nick had jury-rigged with a piece of bungee cord, and freed my old buddy.

Pitty rubbed my legs and yammered away. I picked her up and squeezed her gently, my tears falling on her fur. She licked my hand. "Hey there, baby, did you go to the vet? Did you bite the old bastard like usual?"

We snuggled and I felt gently along her flanks and found the swollen area over her right leg.

Pitty struggled but settled in my lap. She smelled a bit, as if she'd wet in her cage, but I was so overcome with the fuzzy, warm reality of my cat, my house and my amazement at being alive and restored to *my life,* that I didn't care. I cooed and cuddled and kissed her again.

I looked up and found Zoë staring at me. She stood frozen in the doorway, her skin paler than usual and her dark eyes full of anger.

"I can't believe Pitty let you pick her up. She doesn't let anyone pick her up, except Cathy." Zoë walked slowly into the room.

"Oh, she lets me hug her now and then." My voice was tight. "Did Nick leave a message?"

"How'd you know it was my eighteenth birthday on Wednesday?" Zoë asked.

"I remember when your birthday is. I told you I got some of my memory back. I've known you since you were a little kid, remember?"

"And you *remembered* I was eighteen this year?"

"Cathy told me."

"And she told you the vet's name? Why? You don't have any pets. Cathy said you hate cats."

I blinked. "I don't hate cats. Especially your cat." Pitty jumped down and I brushed off my jeans. "Did you hear from Nick? Did you try calling his cell or texting him?"

"He's still not answering. And I thought you were allergic to animals, Roxanne." Zoë's eyes moved over my face like a laser. She focused on my hair, which I'd pulled back into a braid. "Since when do you wear your hair like that?"

"Like what?"

"Like Cathy does," Zoë replied forcefully. "Why are you wearing your hair like Cathy? And what's with your clothes? I've never seen you wear jeans and smocked peasant blouses. That one looks exactly like a blouse hanging in Cathy's closet!" Zoë moved away from me. "What the hell are you, some kind of freak? Are you trying to remind people of Cathy? Are you trying to torture Nick?"

Her accusations stunned me. She was right, and so wrong, all at once. "Look Zoë, I wouldn't do anything to hurt Nick or you or anyone."

"Yeah, right," she said. "'*I wish I were you, Lupeyloo.*' Isn't that what this little routine is all about? You were always jealous of Cathy, and the fact she had so many people who loved her. But this impersonation shit is sick."

"What?" I was desperate to calm her down, but I couldn't just whack her with the truth. "Now, wait. I need you to listen to me—"

"I think I've listened enough," Zoë interrupted. "I've heard all about that 'Secret Sister' pact you and Cathy had when you were kids. But this is mean, Roxanne. Evil! Cathy's gone. You can't replace her. You're nothing like her at all."

The ironic misdirection of my sister-in-law's reasoning knocked me mute. Before any logical explanation came to my mind, the doorbell rang, followed immediately by two loud knocks. Zoë continued to glare at me as she crossed the foyer.

She opened the door and I heard the rumble of a male voice.

"Yes, this is Nick Chance's residence," she said.

The man spoke again but I couldn't make out the words.

"What? What hospital?" Zoë demanded.

I hurried to the door and caught the man's next words. "He's at St. Gregory's, in East Los Angeles. Get your stuff, we'll drive you over."

I stepped behind Zoë. Two cops, uniformed L.A. county police, stood on the front porch, their faces watchful.

"What happened?" I asked.

"Who are you?" The cop who'd been speaking, an older, African-American man, stared at me. A skinny red-haired woman, a wad of bubble gum in her mouth, stood beside him, her hand on her truncheon.

Zoë sent me a look that shouted, 'back off.' "She's no one. She's leaving. Thanks for coming to tell me about my brother, Officers. You said you've got his car?"

"Right. It's in an impound lot. You'll need cash to get it out. They don't take checks."

"I'm sure my brother has his cash card with him. Or I'll call our mom. Let me get my stuff." Zoë brushed past me.

I stared at the cops, who gave me professional, 'you are under suspicion of something' stares. I thought suddenly of Dr. Patel's insistence that the police wanted to talk to me about the car accident.

Should I ask these two about any of that? *No.*

"What's wrong with Nick? Is he okay?" I asked instead, my voice wavering.

"Are you family?" The woman shifted her chewing gum to the other side of her mouth.

"Not exactly."

"Not exactly?" echoed the other cop. "Who *exactly* are you?"

"A friend. I've known Nick forever."

"But you're not family?"

"Is he okay?"

Neither answered and they started to look cranky. If they asked for my ID, would Roxanne's name ring a bell? Maybe they'd want me to come in and talk to the detectives.

"Never mind," I said. "Thanks." I walked across the room and grabbed for my purse. It fell off the couch and spilled out crap all over. Hurrying, I stuffed everything inside and marched past the cops without another word. I jumped in the car and as soon as I turned off my street, I hit the gas. I made it to St. Gregory's Hospital in fifteen minutes, a couple of minutes ahead of the cops and Zoë.

The information desk was in the main corridor. The kind nurse helper, Carin, star of my *Hogan's Heroes* hallucinations, was standing with an older woman in a nurse's uniform.

"Hi, Roxanne!" Carin exclaimed. "How are you feeling? Did you get your memory back?"

I frowned and Carin reddened, aware that she'd blurted out top-secret patient info for all to hear. "Yes, I did. Thanks for asking." I looked at the other woman, who was probably in charge. "Hi. I'm here to see a patient named Nick Chance. I understand he was brought in this morning."

"Oh, I'm so sorry to hear that, Roxanne," Carin said.

I gave her a look and she shut her mouth with a clink of her teeth. I didn't mean to scare her, but I didn't want to get off-topic before the cops and Zoë walked in.

"What is your relationship to the patient?" the older woman asked.

"I'm his wife." Saying the words aloud gave me a shock, and Carin too, but she blessedly remained silent.

The receptionist punched some letters into her keyboard and finally told me Nick was on the third floor, room 314.

"The police weren't real clear about what had happened," I said. "He isn't badly hurt, is he?"

The woman glanced at the computer screen and lowered her voice. "Oh, no, he's okay. They told you he was admitted for drunk and disorderly conduct, right? And he's suffered a mild concussion and some facial wounds, probably from falling. They pumped his stomach, so he's going to be weak for a day or two. The doctors are ready to discharge him so I'm sure he'll be glad you're here, Mrs. Chance."

Carin's eyes were shining, no doubt with the fear that something not to regulations was going on in front of her.

I smiled. "Thank you. Take care of yourself, Carin." I made a show of hurrying toward the elevators.

But I didn't go upstairs. Instead, I ducked out the back exit and walked around to the parking lot. My hands were shaking and my pulse raced. It was all I could do to keep from screaming my head off.

Alcohol. Drunk and disorderly. My God, Nick had been sober for seven years. For him to take a drink was a huge disaster, a heartbreaker. He must have been feeling like hell. When he had given up booze for good, all those years ago, he told me he couldn't imagine ever drinking again. He said if he did ever take another drink, it would be because he was dying, or that he was without hope that life would ever be worth living again.

Tears burned my eyes and I realized again how the accident, which had killed Roxanne and thrown me into the 'Twilight Zone,' had many other collateral victims. It wasn't going to be so easy to heal any of them.

Not Nick, or Zoë. Not me.

Just because I knew the truth, just because I knew something miraculous had happened, didn't mean I could share this information and magically make everyone's suffering disappear. I couldn't even tell people, like Betty Haverty, that a loved one had been forever lost.

Out of my peripheral I saw the police car, with Zoë in the back seat, roll into the parking lot. I ducked behind a bench and waited for them to go inside, then hurried back to the car and hunkered in the front seat.

About twenty minutes later the cops left.

An hour later Nick and Zoë walked outside. They stood at the curb and looked like they were arguing about what to do next.

Over the past hour I had not formed a clear plan of how to get through to Nick, but maybe just being his friend was a good place to start. I pulled into the circular driveway the wrong way, stopping two feet away from Nick and Zoë. They stepped back and peered through the driver's side window. When they recognized me, Zoë's expression blackened. Nick looked confused.

"Can I give you guys a lift?" I asked. "I heard the cop say your car got impounded, Nick. Can I drive you over there? Or home if you need to get paperwork or anything?"

"Have you been waiting here this whole time?" Zoë's voice was harsh. "Jesus, you're stalking us."

"I just thought you guys might need a ride." I focused on my husband's face. Pale, huge circles under his eyes; lips stained black from the carbon they'd used to pump his stomach. More of the carbon gunk stained the front of his shirt. He had stitches above his left eye and his right cheek was purple and bluish with bruising. My whole body ached at the thought of what he'd been through.

He stared at me as if he didn't exactly know who I was. Which, of course, he didn't.

"Are you guys waiting here for your mom, Nick?" I asked.

"None of your business." Zoë stepped off the curb and leaned into the window. "And by the way, did you tell the woman at the front desk that you were Nick's wife? Honestly, Roxanne, that is so fucked up. You better back off or I'm calling the cops on *you*."

"Hang on, Zoë." Nick touched his sister's shoulder. His eyes were vacant of emotion when he looked at me. "My mother is out of town. I can't get hold of Bradley, or anyone else. And since my sister has no money on her, and I've lost my wallet, yeah, you can take us home."

"Nick, I don't think this is a good idea," Zoë argued.

"It's fine, Zoë. Get in. I need to call work." Nick opened the door and held it for Zoë, who slid in without another word. Nick shut the rear door, came around to the front passenger door, and sat beside me.

I gasped. I think Zoë did, too.

"Put your seatbelt on, Zoë," he ordered.

My neck burned at Nick's not-so-thinly veiled reference to the accident. Little did he realize he was making a crack about seatbelts to the person *solely* responsible for his wife's not wearing hers that fatal day. I would have to tell him he shouldn't blame Roxanne for the accident. A giggle of hysteria bubbled in my throat and I swallowed several times, glad he was staring out the windshield and not at my face.

Talk about strained, this moment was the definition of it. Here I sat, close enough to whisper into Nick's ear that I loved him, that I was with him and not dead, but I couldn't say a thing. Not a thing he would believe, anyway.

Carefully I put the car into gear and we drove off the hospital grounds, into the summer afternoon.

Chapter 16

Friday, July 29, 3 p.m.
Nick and Zoë in Roxanne's Rental Car

"So how are you feeling, Roxanne? Any progress with your memory?" I asked. I didn't really care, but the tension was pressing down on all three of us and I was worried Zoë might attack Roxanne from the back seat.

"Yes, as a matter of fact. I've got a lot of it back." Roxanne glanced in the rear-view mirror. "I was telling your sister that earlier when I stopped by the house."

"She has Cathy's earring," Zoë said. "You might want to get it from her before she forgets to give it to you *again*."

My sister's voice buzzed in my ears like a wet bee. I crossed my arms. In the hospital, after she stopped screeching at me for falling off the wagon long enough to find out what really had happened last night, she immediately launched into a weird rant. The gist seemed to be Zoë thinking Roxanne was being freaky and scary, and was trying to impersonate Cathy or something.

"Thanks, Zoë. I'll be sure to get it from Roxanne *when we stop.*"

Roxanne looked at me. "Those earrings are Cathy's favorites, I know."

"Were," I said.

"Of course. Sorry." Her face flushed. "Well, to finish answering your question, I still have a lot of holes in my memory but I'm starting to feel a little more normal."

"Lucky you," Zoë hissed.

"Knock it off, Zoë." I shifted in my seat. My stomach felt as if it had been stretched over a barrel and beaten with a stick, and then shoved back down my throat. I smelled my own body odor after too long in the same shirt.

"Sorry, that was tactless," Roxanne murmured.

"Don't worry about it." I stared straight ahead, wishing it were dark outside because the sunlight hurt my eyes. "I hear you're going to be teaching next month."

"Yeah. Summer's almost over. I stopped at St. Anne's again today. Things are starting to bustle. Lots of teachers in, and staff, so we're getting reacquainted."

"How's your new classroom?" Zoë asked. "All moved in?"

Roxanne pursed her lips. "It's very nice, a great space for the kids. Cathy was right, it is the best room in the school."

Zoë made no reply.

After one minute of silence, I flicked on the radio to take the anxiety down a degree. Percy Sledge was wailing about a man loving a woman, and I wondered if a person's head could literally explode.

I snapped it off. I'd worked at a radio station, in college and right after graduation. I loved music, all kinds, especially the old stuff from the Sixties and Seventies, but had lately gotten spooked about the radio. Some days I felt as if certain songs were playing to specifically harass me. Thinking these kinds of things could probably fit the definition of 'clinical paranoia.'

I leaned back and stared at the road. Roxanne cut her eyes to me but she didn't say anything else, thankfully. We drove the rest of the way to my house without anyone venturing another comment, each in our own emotional foxhole.

Roxanne pulled up to the house and killed the ignition. Zoë jumped out. Before I could yell at her to say 'thanks,' my sister ran across the lawn and disappeared inside.

I sighed and reached for the handle. For a moment, I

wondered if I had enough strength to get out. "Thanks, Roxanne. I appreciate it."

"I'm glad I could help." She touched my thigh with her hand but withdrew it when I tensed. "Don't be too angry with Zoë. She's upset, and seeing me got her stirred up. But she's a great kid. You know that."

I stared at Roxanne, in profile and backlit by sunshine. With her hair drawn into a braid and dressed college-casual in jeans and a filmy blouse, she looked like Miss America on spring break.

Cathy wore blouses like that.

I cleared my throat. "I don't know if your mom passed on what a dick I was a few days ago at the insurance company. When you see her, please give her my apologies."

She nodded. "I will. But don't worry about Betty. She understands about grieving, from her practice." Roxanne fidgeted with her watch. "Nick, I wanted to say I'm sorry, too, about the other night at Simone's. I should have realized, when I saw you in the hall, that you'd be upset to see me."

"Don't." I held up my hand. "I was an asshole then, too. I'm just not so good with anyone right now." I met her eyes but quickly looked away.

I opened the car door and for a second, I couldn't remember where I was, then I saw the house, the lemon trees, smelled the honeysuckle growing along the walk Cathy had planted several weeks ago. I felt worse at that moment than I had since I'd lost my wife.

Zoë peeked out from the front window. When she saw me, she moved back and dissolved into the shadowed interior.

Like a dead man walking, I got out and went around to the driver's window. "Thanks again, Roxanne."

Her face was contorted and her nose was red. She didn't look perfect as usual, but her eyes seemed more animated than I'd ever seen them. As if she could reach out and touch me with a glance. I stepped backward.

"Are you going to be okay?" she asked.

"Sure. Take care." I turned and headed for the house.

"Nick!"

A chill of recognition shivered through my body. I whirled around, but the woman who had called my name wasn't the woman my mind had heard calling me.

Roxanne was out of the car, her hand outstretched. "Don't forget the earring."

Just like at the restaurant the other night, I didn't take it.

She blinked and seemed to understand, even before I did, that I couldn't bear to touch her. She lifted her chin and squared her shoulders and stuffed the earring into her pocket.

We stood there for a moment like boxers waiting for the bell to start the last round.

"How much did you drink?" she asked.

Anger crested inside of me. Roxanne had often thought the worst of me. I didn't feel like telling her this time she had it wrong. "Not enough. Not that it's any of your fucking business."

"Are you going to an AA meeting tonight?"

"What?" My mouth went dry, then filled with a sour fluid. "What did you just ask me?"

"I'm not prying, Nick, but if you're drinking again, you need to go to a meeting as soon as possible. If you need a ride, I'll take you. We can go right now." She waved at the car. "Please do it. You can use my cell to find one."

"You've got a hell of a nerve, Roxanne."

"So do you." Her eyes blazed. "You think your mom and Zoë are up to this? How much are they supposed to handle? You're better than this, Nick."

"Don't talk to me like that. We go way back, but nothing we've been through gives you the right to criticize me about anything, Roxanne."

She stood her ground. "I care about you and your family. And I know what happened in that terrible accident has caused this relapse, or whatever it is, but I'm not going to stand around like a house plant and say nothing."

"You don't know anything. You don't even know what you don't know."

"If Cathy was standing here, she'd tell you to do the same thing. She'd tell you to suck it up and not let one misstep ruin your life."

I took a step toward her. "You don't know a goddamned word Cathy would say to me. Losing her changed everything, every goddamned everything that made my life any good."

"You're half of what made your life good, Nick. Your life can be good again."

This woman is insane.

I pointed at her. "Don't say another thing. And stay away from this house and my sister!" I stumbled toward the front door.

"Nick, I want to help you. Just take the car and drive yourself. Just go," she yelled behind me.

I slammed into the house.

Twenty minutes later, while I was lying face-down on my bed, I heard Roxanne's car start. The sound of the engine vibrated in my room like a fighter plane in a war sky. I stretched and felt underneath the bed for the urn.

It was there. I squeezed my eyes closed and passed out.

Hours later, in the dark of night, I awoke with a start when the hallway floorboards squeaked. Zoë walked into my bedroom. With her pale skin, she shimmered like a ghost.

"Are you awake, Nick?"

"Yeah."

She came over to the bed and leaned against the end of the mattress. "Do you need anything? The doctor said I was supposed to check on you every four hours and make sure you weren't dead."

She tried to make that sound funny but I heard the anguish in her voice.

"I'm not dead. That asshole who knocked me over the head hit me good, but my skull is pretty hard. It's only a mild concussion, honey. I'm going to be fine."

She started to cry then, and I sat up and pulled her into a hug. "Hey. It's okay. I shouldn't have been such a sitting duck, totally unaware of anyone around in a parking lot while I stood there pouring out good booze in the dark. I was asking to get robbed. Those punks probably thought I was retarded."

She nestled against me and cried harder. "They could have killed you, Nick. And why did you even have that liquor? Were you going to drink? After all your hard work?"

I wiped her face with my tee shirt. "I thought about it, Zoë. I won't lie to you. But I didn't take a single drink. I didn't because I know it isn't the answer to anything."

"Are you going to do it again?"

"What? Get rolled by some jerks and let them steal my wallet? Or get found by the cops smelling of booze and have my stomach pumped for no good reason?"

She shook her head. "No. Are you going to buy booze?"

"I'm going to try not to ever do that. And that's all an alcoholic can do, right? Try every day."

She sighed from deep inside her body. "Okay."

"Okay."

She stood up. "Go back to sleep. But don't die."

"I won't. Promise."

She walked toward the door, but turned around. "And you know, Nick, I'm still worried about Roxanne. I think you should avoid her. Don't let her remind you too much of the past. I think she makes you feel sad."

"I can handle Roxanne."

"I don't know about that. She's pretty manipulative about getting her own way with people."

I shook my head. Zoë, as usual, had zeroed in on a sore

point, sorer than she realized. "Don't worry. Neither of us needs to see her or talk to her for a while, right?"

"Right."

"Okay, now go to bed and stop worrying."

She disappeared into the dark hallway. I heard the shower running. Zoë was probably feeling as battered as I was, sitting here in my rank clothes. She'd been hurt by my poor judgment last night, and terrified by what could have happened.

I'd have to work hard to get her past this. I tried to think of what I could say to Zoë to ally her fears, and my mother's. Tried to think of some reason I could give everyone to explain why they shouldn't worry, that this was a one-time thing. But I couldn't come up with much.

I knew people lost loved ones every day. My mother had been a young widow. Cathy had lost both her parents when she was just a little kid. Bradley lost his mom, then his lover, all in the same year, and he had gone on with life without destroying himself.

Roxanne's words, '*Your life can be good again*,' wound through my brain like black smoke. Someday I might believe that, but right now I didn't. I needed to get a grip and bear down and get through the next days, weeks, months, years of my life.

Why? That damned voice in my brain wouldn't shut up. *So you'd feel, what? Better than you do now?* Shit, dead people probably felt better than I did.

Angry and edgy all over again, I got up and ambled into the kitchen and poured myself a huge glass of orange juice. It tasted terrible and the urge to hurl the glass against the wall was strong, so I did.

It bounced off the stucco and flew back at me, unbroken, whapping against my shoulder before it fell to the tile floor and shattered into a million pieces.

With a sigh, I retrieved the broom and dust bin, swept it up and dumped it in the trash can. I wondered what stage of grieving Betty Haverty's books would say I'd now entered. The '*self-destructive-dickhead*' phase?

I put food down for the cat, which I'd not seen, locked the house and sat on the floor in my room.

Zoë had shut the shower off. The hair dryer started up as the cat wandered in the hall and yowled at me from the door. I patted the carpet beside me, but she didn't come.

In the kitchen the phone rang, alerting me to the fact my sister had turned the thing back on. After five rings it went to the answering machine. The volume was set high enough to hear the caller's message.

It was probably Roxanne. I held my breath.

"This is Seth Ryan for Nick again. Hey man, give me a call back when you get this message. I would like to speak with you. It's important." He left his number. The machine clicked off.

Zoë opened the door of the bathroom and walked to her room. She shut the door but started playing music loud enough for me to hear. She chose one of our mom's old albums, *The Police*.

Oh God, not that song. My little sister upped the volume and the house thumped around me, like a big, cold heart, while Sting pleaded with *"Rox-anne"* not to wear that dress. When it ended, she played it again.

Three times.

I considered pounding on the wall but just laid there and ground my teeth until my jaw throbbed. It was clear Zoë wasn't going to drop her worries about Cathy's best friend, nor was she going to let up on warning me about her.

A half hour later she stopped and all was quiet.

For five minutes.

Then outside, above the house, a helicopter circled, the blades agitating a lazy, menacing rhythm, a second wave in the conspiracy of sound to keep me awake. At that moment, I decided I would go into the office on Monday and quit my job. I would travel. I could be a bum. A bigger bum. I could lock myself in the house and watch movies all day. I had money.

Cathy's blood money.

Something rustled in the corner of my room but I didn't open my eyes. It was probably Fear, ready to mix it up again, maybe remove my spleen and lungs this time around, see if I could survive the loss of a few other organs.

Go ahead, Jack. You've already hit me with your best shot.

Hours passed and the voice inside my brain quieted, and I was able to think more clearly. I had to do something. Talk to someone about why I bought that bottle.

I remembered the phone message from hours ago. *Of course.* I'd go see Ryan Seth. He'd helped me before.

But before, I'd had a reason to look forward to life. Her name was Cathy. Now, now I had nothing.

"How are you, Nick?" Ryan Seth clasped his strong hand on my shoulder.

"Good, good. Yourself?"

"I'm very well, thanks." Seth continued to hold onto me. I smiled a fake smile, unnerved at my reflection in the lenses of his dark glasses.

"I'm glad you came in, Nick. Sit."

I sat on the leather sofa and watched as the big man settled himself into his rattan chair. I noted, as I had all those years ago, the effortless way he moved around his office as if he could see. He never took a misstep.

Dressed in a white Mexican wedding shirt, loose white pants, and white socks on his shoeless feet, he looked like a sugar cane baron. This was my first visit to him in years.

I'd worked with Seth for a long time when I first stopped drinking. I'd steadily increased my consumption from high school weekend drinking, to binges in college, to every night inebriation when Cathy and I were first married.

He had helped me commit to a lifetime of sobriety and uncover a lot of the reasons why I drank. His sessions were mostly spent moderating while I argued aloud with myself about what I wanted from life, and if I thought I was up to getting it.

When I stopped seeing Seth, I left feeling he was the only one besides Cathy who believed I was capable of beating my addictions, even when I wasn't so sure. When I called him back this morning, Seth said he'd promised a friend he would check in and see how I was doing. I didn't ask who the friend was, and he didn't volunteer the information.

Bradley knew him. Zoë had seen him professionally, too. As had Roxanne.

While Zoë was driving me over, I'd come to the conclusion Roxanne was the one who had asked him to call me. My mind was still gnawing on the issue of Roxanne's newfound zeal to interfere in my life, and Zoë's strange take on that, when Seth asked his first question.

"So, did you make it to a meeting today, Nick?"

When we talked earlier this morning, I'd told him what happened. He hadn't sounded surprised.

"Yeah. At noon, before I came here." I ran my hands down my jeans to wipe off the sweat. "AA meetings run morning, noon, and all night. Even on Saturday and Sunday. I'm part of a big consumer group, I guess." I laughed nervously.

Seth sat completely still, his head turned toward the glass wall and the view of the wilderness behind his house that he could not see.

"How serious were you about drinking the other night?"

"Medium serious."

"What happened?"

"Well, after I bought a bottle, I sat and thought about downing the whole thing but I managed to get a grip. When

I got out of the car to pour it out, some kids jumped me, knocked me out and stole my wallet." I touched the stitches on my forehead. "The cops rolled up and found me in the bushes smelling like good Scotch, so they hauled me to the hospital and pumped my stomach, thinking I was drunk."

"That doesn't sound like fun."

"None at all. But at least the punks left my car. Shows you what a piece of crap I'm driving." I laughed again.

"Were you arrested?"

"Ah, no. Once my blood alcohol came back zero, they warned me about hanging out in parking lots in the middle of the night and said they could cite me for an open container, but they didn't."

"So you won't lose your license?"

"No. But I have a concussion, so the doctor says I shouldn't drive for a couple of weeks. Zoë drove me around today." I crossed my eyes. "Being chauffeured by a teenager will put the fear of God into you."

"You're lucky," Seth said.

"Right." I packed a lot of disgust into that one word, thinking he would approve.

Seth smiled, which wasn't a good thing when you were in a session with him, I remembered too late.

"You don't think you're blessed with luck, Nick? Are you feeling particularly picked on, in the cosmic sense?"

"I understand that despite all that's happened in the last month, that I'm responsible for not drinking, Seth."

"Is that all you're responsible for?"

I'd been in Seth's office for less than ten minutes but already my heart was pounding and my ego was on red alert. I'd forgotten how confrontational, on issues of personal ethics in particular, that Seth could be.

"I'm responsible for my whole life, Seth. I get that. It's those things outside my life that are causing problems for me right now."

"The accident. Cathy's death. Those are things outside your control, is that what you're talking about?"

My eyes stung. "Yeah. Cathy's death. I'm trying to come to terms with it, but I'm having some trouble."

"So you decided it was okay to get drunk?"

If I wasn't mistaken, Seth had contempt in his voice. "I didn't decide to drink because I just lost my wife. I can't really explain why I did what I did last night. Except it just seemed like the thing to do. To ease the pain, I guess."

"Your first thought was that drinking was a way to make yourself feel better?"

"I wasn't trying to feel better. I was trying to feel nothing."

"Wow."

I waited several moments for him to say more, but he didn't. "I'm not suicidal, Seth. I was just stupid. I wasn't thinking."

"Well, I'd say you were thinking. Just not about anyone else. How's your family taking this near-tumble?"

"Zoë and my mom are pretty shook up. They want me to be strong. I get that."

"But you didn't get that the other night?"

"I didn't think about them the other night."

Seth nodded and tented his hands together. "What does Gotye say in that great song, a person 'can get addicted to a certain kind of sadness?' That's always a risk after a loss, to return to ways to punish ourselves. Then the sadness gets comfortable and it's gets easier to feel worse every day."

"No one wants to feel worse," I said.

"Sure they do."

"That's bullshit, in my opinion."

"Well in my opinion, it's not. Because when a person feels bad, really bad, they feel entitled to misbehave, to let people down, kill themselves with booze, even get murdered by thugs. Hey, people know how to alibi bad behavior. It's one of the first tricks we learn when we're weak. It's a way to bail out from a tight spot."

"I think you're misunderstanding what's going on with me." A knot twisted in my empty stomach. "I know I acted stupid buying that liquor, but it's not what I intend to do with the rest of my life. I plan to work on it."

"How? How are you planning on working on feeling better?"

I cleared my throat. "I'll keep going to daily meetings for awhile. I'll spend more time with my family. I know they're worried about me, so I'm going to try and show Zoë and my mom I'm okay. That I'll be completely okay. Someday."

"Hmm, someday." Seth didn't act like he believed it. He rocked back and forth very slowly in his chair. "How is Zoë? You said she's living with you?" I forgot he did that. He reminded me of Stevie Wonder, except Seth was bald. And not a black guy. And he didn't sing. I blinked and tried to stay focused. Mostly I thought about leaving. And drinking. I licked my dry lips. "Zoë's okay. She's torn up about Cathy. She and my mom thought it would be good if she moved in with me for a while. It's been nice having her there. Most of the time."

"Yeah? Sounds like Zoë drew the short karma straw in your family. First she thinks she killed your dad, now she's worried you might self-destruct."

Our dad had dropped dead at Zoë's little league baseball game when she was ten. She had felt responsible, like kids do. "Zoë and I have a good relationship and we take care of each other. We always have. It's been going pretty good, too, considering all the grief and pain. Until Wednesday night." I caught myself. I shouldn't have mentioned it.

"What happened Wednesday night?"

Tersely, I told him we'd run into Roxanne. That she was with Bradley. That I'd lost it and ruined Zoë's birthday.

"Seeing Roxanne was a shock?" Seth pressed.

"Yeah."

"You've been friends with her for years, right?"

"Cathy was friends with her."

"You weren't?"

I thought a moment. "Yeah. We've been friends for almost as long as I've known Cathy."

"So how did you feel when you saw her?"

"Pissed off."

He cocked his head. "Because she was alive and Cathy was dead."

"That about sums it up."

"That was a reasonable reaction, Nick. Being surprised by Roxanne and Bradley, even blowing Zoë's dinner party. But did seeing her have anything to do with making you want to get drunk?"

"No, I don't blame her for living. But seeing her alive and beautiful and all dressed up made me furious. I was numb for a day, then I got to thinking about the accident. I got to thinking Roxanne was probably driving while her attention was elsewhere. She was evidently having some problems with the ape she's been with for years. Cathy told me that's why she had to go with Roxanne that day. So when I saw Roxanne, I felt enraged. I felt like she was a *selfish bitch* who my wife gave up her life for."

"So because Roxanne's a selfish bitch, you get to drink and hurt everyone who cares about you?"

I put my head in my hands. "I said I wasn't blaming Roxanne for my drinking. And I'm not. I'm trying to explain how I felt."

"Okay. As long as you know you're in charge, Nick." Seth inhaled deeply. "So what's the plan to get over the fact that Roxanne's still breathing? Do you have one, or should I alert the police that they need to put a restraining order on you?"

"Jesus, Seth! I'm not going to do anything to Roxanne."

"Good. So you've got a plan to get past your anger at her for driving that car."

"Yeah." *No.* "Shit." I looked over at him. "Cathy died in an accident. I accept that. But it's not fair. I just need some time to get a grip on that."

"Time. It's not on our side, no it's not." Seth smiled.

"Are you quoting song lyrics to me?"

"I always connect you with music when I see you. You were a great DJ from what I hear. And when the Santa Ana winds blow, I give into my own thwarted dreams of being a rock singer." He grinned wider. "My wife says the winds are weeks early this summer and crazy things happen when they come early. You're lucky I'm not singing the lyrics to you."

I didn't know what to say, so I said nothing.

"Let's change the subject." Seth leaned back and folded his arms over his barrel chest. "It sounds like Zoë has reacted sensibly to your lapse with drinking, don't you think?"

"Yes. She's disappointed."

"How do you know? Did Zoë complain?"

"Yeah." I cracked my knuckles. "We talked a lot about it last night, and then she and Mom gave me an earful this morning."

We sat in silence for a full minute or two. I felt like ants were crawling on me.

"Okay, Nick, I think the smart move for you is to certainly keep going to AA, but also you should emulate the people around you. You have some incredibly gifted women in your life."

"Gifted?"

"You don't think Zoë is gifted?" Seth's tone was prickly.

"Yeah. She's intelligent, if that's what you mean."

"No, Nick. That's not what I mean. I mean your sister is *gifted*. She has gifts, talents, and strengths that help her better herself in life. As your mom does. As Cathy did. As you do."

I stared at my shoes. I felt that rushing in my ears, telling me not to look up, that disaster was lurking, that I was going to get slapped with a tough question and I wouldn't have a clue what to answer.

I looked up. "Zoë thinks Roxanne is acting like Cathy. That she's stalking me, and trying to be like Cathy for some weird reason. She thinks Roxanne is trying to get to me some way. My sister's 'gifted,' all right. With an out-of-control imagination."

"That's a wild thing for Zoë to say. Has she spent a lot of time with Roxanne?"

"No. Just enough to make her run her mouth."

"Or maybe she feels something she can't identify and is just trying to protect you. I'd give your sister the benefit of the doubt, Nick."

I felt like a shit then, trying to shift the focus off my miserable butt by holding Zoë up to ridicule. "I hear you. I'm just not very good with anyone right now. I feel rotten from the time I open my eyes until I go to bed, but anyone who loses their wife suddenly feels like that, right?"

"Are you asking me if you're entitled to feel like you do?"

"No. I'm *telling* you I'm entitled to feel like I do."

Seth sat back. "It's good to hear you say that, Nick. It's healthy. Do you believe you'll eventually be able to move on from this great loss?"

"Yeah. I'm not addicted to any kind of sadness." I tried to grin but couldn't quite pull it off. "I want to have a life again. I just can't imagine it without her."

"I'm glad to hear that." Seth took another sip of tea. "By the way, do you believe in magic, Nick?"

"Magic?" I rolled my shoulders to get the kinks out. "You mean tricks, disappearing tigers, bunnies in hats?"

"No. Magic as in something that occurs in an ordinary person's life which has no logical or scientific basis in fact to explain it."

A memory from long ago washed through my brain. "Cathy did a paper in college on love and magic. She did tons of research, had hundreds of references, most from some pretty non-traditional sources, trying to prove that falling in love had a logical, scientific component."

Seth smiled. "That sounds like her. Did she go for the pheromones, that we smell each other and fall into sexual obsession theory, or was there another scientific explanation out there she hooked up with?"

"She cited that scent thing, that men smell women and are attracted to them. At different times in their cycle, or something. But she rested most of her case on some guy's essay claiming nothing in life was random. It said everyone crossed the path of everyone they met in life for a purpose, and that the energy propelling people toward one another had a logical biological pattern that one day would be proven by a mathematical construct." I laughed.

"This guy also thought the patterns of lightning strikes and snowflakes could be predicated on certain rules, but mankind wasn't advanced enough to understand or explain the formulas yet. So instead we label phenomenon like lightning, snowflakes or love, '*magic*.'"

"Wow. What did you think about all that?"

"I told her I believed in her, but that her man was smoking too much hash. I told her that even if it was true, I preferred not to know the logical design of snowflakes, or love. I told her I believed in magic. The kind the Lovin' Spoonful sang about."

"What grade did she get on her paper?"

"An F. She had to retake the class to graduate. But she said she was sure one day she'd be vindicated and someone would prove she was right."

We laughed at that together.

Seth put his empty teacup on the desk at the same moment a chime sounded somewhere inside the house. He stood and reached out to shake hands. "Stubborn, that Cathy. Not willing to give in if she believed in something. Well, you take care of yourself, Nick. And give my best to Zoë."

I struggled to my feet, offended at the lack of grief in his voice when he said Cathy's name. "Okay. I will."

Seth walked toward the door. Obviously our time together today was over.

"So, should I call in and make another appointment for next week?"

"Why?" He sounded surprised.

"I thought we'd maybe need to work together for a while."

"You're going to AA and you're not going to drink. And you believe that if you keep to that path, that your life will be good again someday, right?"

"Yeah." I cracked my knuckles, waiting for him to take another shot at me.

"You can call me if you want to schedule another appointment, Nick. But I think you know everything I would say already. The only thing I can add is to remind you that life changes every day. You need to be ready for the next painful or wonderful thing that walks in the door. Because something will."

"But what if I need help?"

"With what?"

He wasn't making it easy for me. "With grief," I blurted out. "And my anger."

"At Roxanne?"

"At life. It's not fair, what happened. I don't understand why Cathy had to die." It was a lame thing to say. Everyone knew life wasn't fair. I hung my head.

"Sane people eventually make peace with the past, whatever happened there. And you are totally sane, Nick. If I were you, I would focus on the fact that the future can be what you want it to be. It's the present we all struggle with, because we don't always see it for what it is."

"And what is it?" I stared at him.

"You're the only one who can decide that, Nick. But trust yourself. You've made some great decisions in the past. There's no reason to think you won't in the future. And don't ever give up believing in magic." He patted my shoulder. "Goodbye."

He opened the door. A young Asian woman sat in the waiting room. She wore a black tee shirt and jeans, and had white bandages wrapped around both wrists.

I left the office without a clue as to what the fuck Seth was talking about. Though I was exhausted and confused by most of what he'd said, I did feel a sense of relief when I got into my car.

And I had the sudden thought that Seth had told me something important, something I didn't completely understand right now, but that later I might see the significance of.

Chapter 17

Saturday, July 30, 12:30 p.m.
Cathy Visits Betty Haverty

As I knocked on the door, I glanced at my watch for about the tenth time. Twelve-thirty. Seth called the apartment earlier to say he'd spoken to Nick on the phone and that Nick was going in to see him this afternoon.

I considered driving over and trying to talk to my husband afterward, but didn't as it was obvious he needed some time before we met again.

Waiting for Betty to answer the door, I thought again how he'd looked at me when I tried to give him my earring. He hated me.

Well, he hated Roxanne. The *me* he thought I was.

Nick's animosity hurt my heart for Roxanne. She didn't deserve it.

"Roxanne!" Betty cut off my musings. "Why didn't you just come in? Did you forget you have my key on your key ring? It's the green-tinted one."

I never knew that. Roxanne and I were close, but we didn't share every detail of our lives.

"How are you?" I gave Betty a kiss on the cheek.

She hugged me hard. "I'm good. I'm so glad you're here." Her eyes roamed my face the way mothers do when their child is coming down sick. "How is everything? Come in and tell me what's happened with you this week."

I thought of Michael Cimino. Of Nick and Zoë. And the moment I realized I was Cathy, and that Roxanne was dead.

I couldn't tell her any of it.

I swallowed, cautioning myself to watch what I said. But I was giddy with nerves, the same way I'd felt in high school when Roxanne cooked up lies so we could stay out all night and live dangerously.

I followed Betty through her neatly kept living room into the kitchen at the back of the small Cape Cod she and Roxanne had moved into twenty years ago. On the table sat a pot of newly brewed coffee and a plate of cookies.

The cookies looked delicious. The yellow roses in the vase on the counter were fresh, as were the bowls of chicken salad and cut-up melon.

"This looks fabulous," I said. "But I thought we were going out to lunch? I would have brought something if I'd known we were staying in."

Betty reached into her cabinet for mugs. "Did I say that? You don't mind, do you? If you'd rather go out, I can change."

She wore jeans and a black sweater, and ratty blue slippers with faded pink nosegays. Her roots were growing out and showing a lot of gray. Overall, Betty wasn't as shiny and well-kept as usual. She looked older than I remembered.

Had Roxanne mentioned that her mother was seeing a doctor, a specialist of some kind? This was one of many fuzzy memories.

"You look fine," I said. "But let's stay here, this smells yummy."

Betty seemed relieved. She set the mugs on the table. "I've got buttered toast points in the oven. They're ready if you want to eat right away."

I pulled up a chair. "Sure."

We made small talk as we ate. The chicken salad was dry, but I didn't say anything because I remembered with certainty that Roxanne didn't like mayonnaise. My throat constricted as I contemplated again how much pain the truth of my situation was one day going to bring Betty.

As we chatted, I felt guilty that Roxanne badmouthed her mother so often. She really wasn't the harridan Rox always made her out to be. I had thought, more than once over the years, how Roxanne often set her mother up as the fall guy in some story she was telling. Mostly to win me to her side of the argument. She would relate something she had done, and how her mother had criticized her, depending on my knee-jerk loyalty.

Shame on me. Because it was clear Betty adored Roxanne. Her way of showing it may have rubbed Rox the wrong way, but Betty loved her daughter and always tried to help her out.

As I speared a piece of melon, I wondered if maybe that said more about Roxanne than it did her mother. And maybe my blind support of Rox said more about *me* than it did my friend.

I set my fork down.

"Do you want more toast?" Betty asked.

"No, no thank you, I'm full. I've gained ten pounds since I got out of the hospital. None of my clothes fit." I took a big gulp of coffee.

"Well, it looks good on you. Before I forget, let me give you something." Betty grabbed her purse off the counter and handed me a white envelope. "That's the insurance check to replace your car. It's a little over five thousand dollars. I endorsed it over to you. We can take the rental back after lunch if you don't have other plans."

"Do we have to do it today?"

"No. The contract is for an open-ended rental. But don't you want to look for a new car? I'm free if you'd like some company. And I'll be glad to kick in some more for a down payment if you need it."

Betty poured herself another cup of coffee. Her hand trembled as she stirred in sugar, and I again wondered if she was ill.

"Ah, let me think about it," I said. "I'd rather just pay another week on the loaner, and look around."

I stuck the money in my purse, feeling a total imposter. Wearing Roxanne's clothes and sleeping in her bed was one thing. Now I'd have to go to the bank and deposit the money, signing her name. I wondered what my legal status was.

Panic itched inside me as I pictured explaining to the bankers why my signature no longer looked like Roxanne Ruiz's. I massaged my temples and tried to listen with my whole brain to what Betty was saying.

". . . you can get the insurance again. That won't be a problem." Betty stared at me. "Headache?"

"No. No." There were three kinds of cookies on a plate; I chose the biggest one. "These are good. Macadamia nuts?"

"Yes. Why did you take that one, Roxanne? You don't like nuts."

"I like nuts now. I've changed." I kept eating, though I felt like I would choke.

"Really? Well, enough small talk. How's your memory? Anything coming back to you, now that you're in your own home?"

"Yes. I've got a lot to tell you there." I gripped the cup tighter, reminding myself to stick as close to the truth as possible. Wasn't that what the guys in the police shows on TV always told the undercover cops?

"On Tuesday night I went out to dinner with Bradley, and started to remember a few things. A lot of things. From the past. Places. Things that happened to me." I put my hand on Betty's. "I'm happy to report I remember who I am now. Not everything about my life," I added quickly. "But some major things, the big picture of people I know, my job at St.

Anne's. Some details are lacking, like who cuts my hair and what I got for my birthday this year, but I'm almost there."

I hoped she wouldn't ask as Seth had about details from Roxanne's childhood. I knew very little about her before we met.

"This happened *last* Tuesday, and you're just telling me now?" Betty sounded upset.

"*This* Tuesday, yes. A couple of days ago. I needed some time to digest all that. Please don't be hurt I didn't call you right away," I said. "I wasn't trying to keep you out of the loop. I just needed some space. It's all been so unreal."

Betty got up and surprised me with another hug. "I'm not hurt, Roxanne. I understand completely. But this is such wonderful news, sweetheart. I can't believe it!" She had tears in her eyes as she placed both hands gently on my face. "Did you call Dr. Patel? What did he say? I'm sure he's thrilled you've had a breakthrough like this."

"No. No, I haven't called him."

She dropped her hands. "Oh? Well, I think you should. Soon. You need to bring your doctor up to speed since it will certainly change the course of his therapy. If you don't remember everything yet, it's obvious you need more help. And if you tell him before your next appointment, it will give him time to plan."

"I don't think I need to see him anymore," I inserted quickly.

"Roxanne! Don't be ridiculous. Of course you need to continue your treatment. My God, you were in a coma for days, you had a major head trauma. You may not know this, but the EMTs at the scene said y*ou died!* There are many health repercussions you may not even be aware of. And if you have holes in your memory, you have to at least keep up with therapy until you get the whole thing back."

Betty had worked herself up in a way I'd never seen. My take on her up to now was that she kept a lid on her emotions, very self-controlled. But seeing her this overwrought, I felt her fear, and understood the hell it must have been for her as a mother.

A chill of revulsion crept down my neck at the realization she'd have to go through that again.

"Can you listen to me for a moment?" I urged. "I am still going to get some help with these issues. I'm just taking my time."

"Promise me, Roxanne. Promise me you'll call Dr. Patel and at least tell him what's happened." She laid her hands over mine. "He needs to know so he can help you."

A terrible pun, *'Caught between Rox and a hard place,'* flitted through my brain. "I don't feel comfortable with Dr. Patel. I might work with someone else. Or take a break from all psychiatrists for a while, especially since I haven't taken the antidepressants for almost a month now, and I feel fine."

"You stopped them all, cold turkey?"

"Yes. The days I was off them in the hospital kind of jump-started all that. And now I'm good, sleeping pretty well, and everything."

I could almost see the wheels spinning behind Betty's eyes.

"Who?" she finally asked. "Who are you going to work with? Eve Madison, the doctor treating your depression?"

"No. Dr. Ryan Seth. He's a good guy."

"Ryan Seth? He isn't a psychiatrist, Roxanne. He isn't even a medical doctor, for heaven's sake. What is his doctorate in, Eastern philosophy, or something?"

No, it's a little weirder than that.

His master's degree, from the long defunct Elysian University in Taos, was in the field of Human Spirituality, a fact that made even Seth cringe now. He once had the diploma on the wall of his office. Right next to a Beatles poster, the one from *Sergeant Pepper's Lonely Hearts Club Band.*

"Ryan Seth is very gifted. He gets to the heart of a problem faster than anyone I've ever met," I said.

"But, but, isn't he blind?"

"Yes. He is blind. But I'm not going to him for driving lessons. How is that relevant?"

Betty frowned. "It's not. Of course it's not. Forgive me for saying such an idiotic thing. But I'm concerned someone like that might not be equipped to help you with all the residual problems you may experience."

"Like?"

"Guilt, grief. My God, you've lost your best friend. Anxiety. A relapse into the depression you've suffered on and off your whole adult life. The stress you're sure to feel going back to work with people who were primarily Cathy's friends. That takes a psychiatrist, surely."

This was a surprising thing for her to say. Was that what Roxanne had told her? "They're my friends too, Betty. I think you're worrying ahead of the curve. Don't be so negative."

She inhaled sharply. "Roxanne, I'd appreciate if you would stop calling me Betty. I'm your mother. You never called me Betty before the accident, and I don't particularly care for it."

"Sorry." I pinched the skin on the back of my left hand, reminding myself to be more careful. "Look, this is the bottom line. I don't know what is going to happen with my psyche in the immediate future. But it's *my* psyche."

"I can accept that."

"Good. And for many reasons, I want you to understand I don't feel like the same person I was before the accident. I'm not the same person." My face warmed but I pushed on. "It's frightening, and stressful, but it's a fact. Experience changes a person. I need to learn to deal with that fact now. We *all* need to deal with that fact. Nothing is as it was before July 9."

Betty blinked several times. "I'm impressed, Roxanne. You sound strong and sure of yourself. All I want to do is caution you to not let yourself slide back into old problems without reaching out for help. You've done that a few times in the past, if I may remind you."

It felt as if she'd slapped me. This was the mother that Roxanne had always portrayed to me. The mother who thought she knew best. The woman who always seemed more than ready for Roxanne to fail or make the wrong choice.

"You don't need to remind me," I said. "I do remember many of the bad times I went through. But I need you to pull for me now, okay? Not bring up past mistakes, or expect me to fail."

Betty's eyes filled with tears. She started to speak, but hesitated and swallowed before promising, "I will. I always try to expect success, I hope you believe that. And try not to worry about feeling so different. Just remember, it's only been a few weeks. You'll be well some day, a brand new self. I understand that."

"Thanks." I took her hand. Her fingers were cold and stiff. "Are you okay? You look a little tired today."

Betty frowned. "I told you before the accident that I had what I thought were some pre-menopause problems. It's turned out to be more serious. I found out this week I have to have surgery. A hysterectomy."

"Oh, wow. I'm sorry. Are you sure? Did you get a second opinion?"

"Yes. I got three opinions, actually. I have had two suspicious Pap tests in the last year. My doctor thinks it best if we do this. Now, before there's any real problem."

"Well, let me know what I can do. I'll drive you. And I can come and stay." I felt awkward. This woman needed her daughter's compassion and support. And all she got was my offering to be a chauffeur or maid.

"Thank you, my dear. But Gran will come stay. You can visit and be the bright spot in our day. You know how I need that when Ruth's here more than a week."

Betty laughed. I joined in, thinking of the kind old gal who had visited in the hospital. I didn't remember ever spending any time with her before the accident. This was going to be tricky.

Betty leaned back in her chair. She seemed more at ease. "You look more gorgeous than ever, by the way. Have you seen Michael?"

"Ah, yes. He came by the apartment with some food."

"And?" Betty's voice was cool. I knew from Roxanne, and from personal observation over the years, that Betty never approved of Michael Cimino.

Which of course was a big plus to Rox, my newly critical brain realized. Roxanne liked to *not* follow her mother's advice.

"We had a talk." My cheeks grew pink. "It was no big deal."

"So he's backing off and leaving you alone?"

"Yes. Well, he plays it cool. He calls and leaves messages a lot. I told you I had dinner with Bradley, didn't I? He's doing well." We talked about him for a couple of minutes. And then I told her I had run into Zoë and Nick at Simone's. As I spoke, Betty's eyes widened and she crossed her arms over her chest.

I compacted the details of the conversations I'd had with Nick into one meeting. "Oh, and he said he owed you an apology over how he behaved at the insurance company. You mentioned on the phone that he acted crappy. If it's any consolation, he seems truly sorry."

"Does he?" Betty poured herself more coffee. "He's wound pretty tight, that guy. Always has been. I remember when you three were in college and his dad died that you and Cathy were pretty worried about him. How's he managing? Is he doing okay? Going to work? Staying off the booze?"

"What do you mean?" I'd told Roxanne a lot of personal information about Nick, but I would have been shocked to find out she'd passed on to Betty that he was a recovering alcoholic. This was one more thing I was wrong about.

"We both know he's an alcoholic, Roxanne. While he's grieving, he's very vulnerable to relapse. Didn't you tell me a few months ago you were worried he might be on the verge of drinking again?"

Her words hit me like a blow to the back of the skull. "What are you talking about? When did I say that?"

"You don't remember telling me that?"

"No." I rubbed my hand over my forehead and tried to think of what Roxanne could have been thinking, telling her mother something like that. "When was it, exactly? I told you there are a lot of blanks in my memory."

"Six, seven months ago. After you and Michael broke up. Before Christmas, I think." Betty's lips stretched taut. "I'm sorry, Roxanne, I didn't realize you couldn't remember anything about you and Nick."

This time her words pierced like a knife. I stood, knocking my mug over on the table. I started sopping up the spilled coffee with napkins.

"Roxanne." Betty grabbed my hand. "What's wrong?"

"I don't understand what you just said. What did you mean 'you and Nick?' There was no 'Roxanne and Nick.' It's Nick and Cathy, for God's sake."

She shook her head. "I'm sorry I even brought this up. But this is exactly why you need to continue to work with Dr. Patel, honey. Why don't we call his office right now and make an appointment? I'm sure he can shed a lot of light on why this particular memory is being blocked."

"No!" I shouted. "What particular memory are you talking about? What am I not remembering about six or seven months ago?"

"Sit down," Betty said.

I sat. "Please, this is very important to me." I could not imagine what she was going to say.

Betty threw the coffee soaked napkins in the trash. "Do you want some orange juice or something? You're white as a ghost."

I am a ghost. I bit my tongue to keep from spitting out those words. "No. Thanks. Please explain what you just said."

"Do you remember seeing Dr. Susan Haven last October?"

I had never heard this name before. "No. Is she *another* shrink?"

"No. Dr. Haven is an ob-gyn. My gynecologist." Betty sat and folded her hands.

I frowned. That was crazy. For years, Rox and I both went to Dr. Mary Brier for our yearly check-ups and birth control. I take the pill. Roxanne relied on condoms. Dr. Brier was our gynecologist. "Why did I see her?"

Betty sighed. "Last November you had an abortion, Roxanne. After you and Michael broke up."

My mouth went completely dry. I had to force my tongue off my teeth. This could *not* be true. Roxanne would have told me this. She told me everything!

Didn't she?

"Michael didn't want the baby?" I rasped. "That selfish son of a bitch!"

"You said it wasn't Michael's child." Betty's voice was emotionless. "You told me you had a brief affair with someone else. And it was impossible to keep the baby."

I met her eyes. My throat constricted and the room began to spin around me. I took a huge, sucking breath. "You're not saying . . ."

"You never came right out and told me it was Nick Chance's baby, Roxanne, and I never asked. But since you never told Cathy about it, and you ordered me to never, ever breathe a word to her, I don't know what else to think."

Nick. And Roxanne.

Nick and Roxanne? "I don't believe this. Why would you tell me this? You're lying!"

"Roxanne, calm down. You really don't remember any of this? I'm so sorry. You must be blocking it because you felt terrible about the abortion."

"Stop it! You don't have a clue how I feel about anything." I pushed the chair back from the table, grabbed my purse and headed for the door.

"Roxanne," Betty called after me.

But I didn't stop. I ran to the car and drove to Roxanne's apartment, my brain flashing through memories one by one. I went over everything I could remember about last fall, every lunch and dinner and telephone conversation I had with Roxanne.

She couldn't have kept a secret like this from me. It was impossible. I shook my head violently, trying to make sense of it. Surely Betty had everything wrong.

Was she fabricating the entire story, to make Roxanne think she was sick and force her back into therapy?

I took a deep breath as I pulled into the parking lot at Roxanne's apartment. *I wish I were you, lupeyloo* . . . the idiotic phrase from our childhood mocked me, playing over and over in my mind.

Slamming the front door, I rushed into the bedroom. "This can't be true," I cried in disbelief as I curled up on the bed. The inside of my mouth tasted bitter, like poison.

Could it be? Could my best friend have done this?

Could my husband have cheated on me?

No.

Why not? a voice hissed in my ear. *You cheated on him, didn't you?*

Did I? I couldn't count the incident a few days ago. That was not me. But what about before, that partial memory I had of Michael and me on the beach, months before fate had turned everything on its head? I pulled up the memory of that night and tried again to recall every detail. I could smell the sea air, hear the waves against the sand. Michael pushed me backward, his hands cupping my breasts.

"You know you want me, baby," he said.

I concentrated. But I could not remember what else had happened. My sob echoed off Roxanne's walls.

"Nick," I whispered. "I'm sorry."

The phone rang in the kitchen. *Seth.* I jumped out of bed and hurried toward the sound of Seth's voice. ". . . and Nick seems good. He's still shaken over the accident and his latest backsliding, but I think he's on the right road. Call me and we'll make plans to meet again. I have some ideas about how to break the ice with him."

My hand reached for the phone but I pulled it back. I didn't dare call Seth right now. He'd hear my voice and know I'd found out something terrible. I flung myself on Roxanne's hard bed.

Had Nick slept with Roxanne here?

This question made me moan and pull on my hair. I shut my eyes and tried as hard as I could to remember that night on the beach with Michael.

Was my memory of our married life together a lie, either due to my actions or Nick's? While love was never completely equal, with every action on the part of one person counterbalanced perfectly by the other, there had to be parity of commitment, mutual moral truths and an honest understanding of what was actually going on. For love to survive, both partners had to trust their commonly held vision of what they were as a couple.

Nick and I both always said, to anyone who would listen, that we were soul mates, meant for each other, and totally and happily committed to only one another.

Had we both been deceitful?

I stared at the ceiling. For the first time since waking in the hospital, I wondered if everyone involved wouldn't be better off if I had not survived the accident.

Because if I did find out that Nick and I had both cheated and lied, what then? Would Nick be better off if he never knew I *wasn't* really dead?

Would I be better off pretending I *was* dead, and try to make a new life for myself?

Who could answer these questions? I closed my eyes.

Not me.

Chapter 18

Monday, August 1, 1 p.m.
Cathy in Roxanne's Apartment

I pulled my hair back into a ponytail and stared at the face in Roxanne's gilded mirror. It looked ravaged, bags under the brown eyes, the tiny golden sparkle in the left iris cloudy with fatigue. There were dry patches on the tan cheeks where tears and sleeplessness had left their mark.

I brushed my teeth and rubbed on some lotion; looked in the mirror again. *A little better*. I considered putting on lipstick, maybe a brush of mascara, but 'more attractive' wasn't what I was going for.

The doorbell rang. I glanced at the clock. Michael was right on time.

I had called and asked him to come by as soon as he had the time. He had interpreted the invitation as I knew he would; no doubt thinking he was going to get an afternoon of sex.

He said he'd bring lunch. And dessert, 'for later.' The man was a complete egomaniac. It was a good thing Roxanne didn't own a gun, because if she had, Michael Cimino might not have a 'later.'

I pulled the door open. To my surprise, I didn't find Michael Cimino standing there, expecting to get lucky. Two men in suits filled the space.

"Miss Ruiz?" A good-looking stranger met my startled glance. "I'm Detective Henry Morales. And this is Detective

Strain." He gestured to the man with a bushy gray mustache standing a half-step behind him. Both men flashed their badges.

"May we come in for a few minutes? We'd like to ask you some questions about the car accident on July 9."

"I, ah. I'm expecting a friend. But yes, of course, come in for a moment." I stepped back and the two cops walked into Roxanne's apartment.

In a sudden panic I realized I was going to have to pass myself off as Roxanne, the driver of the car that was involved in a fatal accident that killed a woman. Who was actually alive and living camouflaged inside a body not her own. It was complicated to keep straight, even for me.

To heighten my anxiety, I was really bad at lying to cops. The three times in my life I'd been stopped for tickets, I got them. Unlike Roxanne, who never paid a fine in her life, despite being pulled over regularly.

"Please sit down." My voice shook. I folded my hands together as a tremble skittered up and down my arms. What if they arrested me? What if they gave me a lie detector test?

Wasn't the first question always, 'Please state your name?'

Oh, my God.

The cops took the sofa, two sets of eyes calmly appraising the surroundings and then me. Well, they appraised Roxanne. It was obvious they liked her looks.

"How are you feeling, Miss Ruiz?" Detective Morales asked with a flash of very white teeth. "I understand you were released from the hospital a week ago. You don't look any the worse for wear, if you don't mind me saying."

I folded my arms over Roxanne's breasts. "Thanks. So what is it you've stopped by to ask, Detective?"

Strain's eyes twitched but Morales kept an easy smile on his face. He pulled out a well-worn leather notebook and flipped it open. "We would like to know what you remember from the accident."

"Nothing." That was true, if I was Roxanne.

"Do you remember that morning at all, before the accident? What you were discussing in the car? Or where you were going?"

I pursed my lips. "No to all three questions. Sorry."

"So it goes without saying that you don't remember seeing the truck before it hit you?"

A flash of black and white, the image of a truck with a bent front fender, blipped through my brain like a heartbeat. "No."

Morales nodded. "Do you recall that Mrs. Cathy Chance was in the car with you?"

This was absurd. I just told the man I didn't remember anything from the whole goddamned day. He obviously didn't believe me. I was going to have to try harder.

"The past is blank, Detective Morales. All of it." Which was another lie, as I was at that moment remembering dying on the asphalt, and floating toward bright lights.

Maybe Morales saw something in my face, because he made a note, then put his pen and pad down and sat forward, lacing his long fingers together. "I assume your family has filled you in on the details of what occurred. Did their report sound plausible, or familiar, when they told you where you were going that day? And with whom?"

I shrugged. "I'm starting to remember some things in a very hazy way. I've been told I was going to a doctor's office and out to lunch with Cathy Chance, whom I was told is my best friend. Everything else is blank."

"Was your best friend."

"Excuse me?"

"Mrs. Chance was your best friend. You do accept that she's dead now."

My face burned. "Yes. Of course I know that."

Morales smiled gently. "Do you know that you were

taking prescription drugs for depression in the months before the accident?"

Though Dr. Patel had prepared me, the inference whacked me in the gut. "I've been told that. Yes."

"But you didn't have any significant levels of the drugs in your system, according to the medical reports, on July 9. Can you shed any light on why that was?"

"No."

"None?" His smile stopped at his eyes.

Morales was very handsome. The vibes he put out seemed professional, but had an undercurrent of personal availability. This made me feel completely out of my depth.

How the hell had Roxanne walked around every day, fending off unspoken come-ons and double meanings from every social and professional exchange she had with a man? No wonder she was depressed.

"My best guess would be that I had stopped taking them a while before the wreck. I understand that this was common for me."

"Who told you that?"

"Roxanne's mother." I froze as soon as I said it, then quickly added, "*My* mother. Sorry. As you've noticed, I'm still remembering who all the players are in my life."

Strain frowned suspiciously but Morales appeared unfazed. "Amnesia is a difficult thing to navigate through, I'm sure. I never actually believed in it, until I got your case. It must be hard to know who to trust."

I let the sentence hang in the air for a moment. "I think most of us have trouble with that one, even if we don't have amnesia, Detective."

"Touché, Miss Ruiz." His smile broadened and despite his disciplined eye contact, his gaze swept across my chest.

I stood. "Well then, if that's all you needed, I'm glad I could help."

The two detectives seemed surprised I was dismissing them, and then the doorbell rang.

"That'll be my friend. Can I show you out?" I took a step toward the entry, catching my reflection in the mirror. Roxanne's face was smooth and beautiful, displaying none of the anxiety I felt inside.

"Why don't you answer the door? I do have a couple of more quick questions. It won't take long," Morales replied.

I turned my back on them, aware of both men's eyes on my ass. On Roxanne's ass. *God, what a freak show.*

I pulled the door open.

"Hey, babe." Michael Cimino wore a huge grin. He leaned toward me for a kiss.

I offered my cheek. "Michael, there are two policemen inside. I have to answer a couple of more questions. But come in."

"Cops?" He blinked and walked slowly into the apartment. "Hey," he said to the two men. "How's it going?"

"This is Detective Henry Morales and Detective Strain," I said with a wave. "This is my friend, Michael Cimino."

"Whoa. Boyfriend. Miss Ruiz meant to say *boyfriend.*" Michael hugged me and smiled but I heard a warning in his voice.

"Mr. Cimino," Morales nodded. "We met at the hospital."

"Right, right." Michael turned to me. "He was waiting to talk to you one day when you were with that Indian shrink. I told him you didn't remember nothing about the accident." Michael held two bags of Chinese food and the smell of hot garlic wafted through the room.

I met Morales's eyes. They were intense. "You said you had two more questions, Detective?"

"I'll just put this stuff in the kitchen, Rox. Okay?" Michael said behind me. "If I had extra, I'd offer you boys some. But there's just enough for me and my lady."

"Thanks, anyway," Detective Morales said.

I flinched when Michael said 'my lady,' and Morales noticed.

"Okay. Shoot, Detective." I giggled suddenly, and put my hand over my mouth.

Morales didn't smile. Evidently he'd heard the joke too many times. "Why don't you sit down for a moment, Miss Ruiz."

I didn't want to sit down. I wanted the detectives to leave. My nerves weren't holding together very well and I was worried I might start laughing inappropriately at everything, as I had in the hospital.

"Okay."

"I'll make this short so you can get to your dinner," Detective Strain said and pulled out a similar notebook to the one Morales carried. He opened it and frowned at what was written there. "Do you know if the seat belts in your car were in good working order?"

The room was silent except for the clock ticking in the bedroom. A spark of memory exploded, like a flare a mile away. I remembered a wide belt pinching my chest and sunshine hot on my arm. I licked my lips. "No. I don't remember there being any problem with the seatbelts."

"Hey, it was an old piece of crap Chevy," Michael said. He'd returned to the living room, silently as a cat.

We all turned toward him.

He was trying to protect Roxanne, I realized. *From what?*

"Why are you asking, Detective?" Michael added.

"Because the seatbelt on the passenger's side was disconnected from the car at the floor. The bolts were sheared off. The insurance report stated it probably failed during the accident and came loose. But we needed to be sure it hadn't happened before," Strain said.

Michael shrugged. "What the fuck difference does it make when it happened? Her passenger wasn't wearing it from what the cops on the scene told the wreckers. I talked to those guys. I'm sure when the Chevy rolled, the thing busted loose. Roxanne didn't have anything to do with that."

"Are you her mechanic?" Morales asked.

Michael's eyes flashed. Before he could answer, I drew the men's eyes back to Roxanne. "Detective Strain, I don't recall there ever being a problem with the seat belts. But it was an old car, a 1999, as I'm sure you can see on your report. The seatbelts worked as far as I can remember."

"Okay. And, I guess you won't know the answer to this, but do you remember why you didn't brake before the accident?"

"What do you mean?" I said. The sound of women's screams and glass breaking echoed inside my skull. I clutched the side of the sofa and spoke too loud. "I don't think there was time to hit the brakes, from what the accident report said."

"But you don't remember?" Morales asked sharply.

"No."

"We found it surprising that there were no skid marks at all from your car, Miss Ruiz. Even in a head-on collision, there is a fraction of a section when instinct kicks in, no matter how shocked a person is about what's about to happen."

"I guess I don't have very good instincts."

"Hey, she said she doesn't remember. I think you need to leave it alone," Michael broke in.

"Right." Morales got up and Strain closed his book and stood next to him.

"Okay," Morales said. "Thanks, Miss Ruiz. We needed to at least ask. No one likes loose ends."

"Of course." The cops followed me to the door, which I opened for the third time in fifteen minutes. I wouldn't have been surprised to find a hanging judge waiting on the landing.

"Goodbye," I said.

Detective Morales inclined his head. "Thank you. I think

we can close this out in a day or two. The only other thing we have left to do is talk to Nick Chance."

"Why?" I blurted out before I could think not to.

"It's a courtesy. He lost his wife. We want to be sure he has the opportunity to be heard. That's standard in a fatal accident."

"What would he want to say?" Michael stepped between Morales and me like a bodyguard. "You know Rox and Cathy were best friends, don't you? Since they were kids. My girl is all torn up about her friend getting killed. What's Nick Chance got to beef about?"

"Who said he had a beef?" Strain's face was red.

"Do you know if he has hard feelings about Miss Ruiz?" Morales asked. "Does he blame her for the accident?"

"Whoa, slow down, buddy." Michael could probably tell he was being double-teamed and I figured he didn't like it. "Look, Nick's got no reason to hold anything against Rox. It was an accident. No one caused it intentionally, right? You guys aren't suggesting that, are you?"

I squeezed my fingers into fists.

"No. Of course not," Morales said after a long moment.

"Good. 'Cause like I said, his girl and mine were tight. He needs to get over what happened. A drunk killed Cathy Chance. But I understand how he's grieving. I would be, too, if I lost my girl."

Dizziness swamped me for a second. I wanted to slap Michael for calling me a 'girl' ten times. And I wanted to order the cops out because they were probably going to quiz Nick to see if he knew Roxanne wasn't taking her medication and why she had faulty seatbelts.

Jesus. Nick hated Roxanne already. How would he feel after he had that conversation with these two?

"Thanks again for stopping by, Detectives." I stuck my hand out and forced Morales to take it.

"Goodbye, Miss Ruiz." He pulled a business card out of his pocket and handed it to me. "If you think of something else or if there's anything I can do, give me a call. I'm available 24/7 on my cell."

I grabbed the card. "Thanks."

The detectives left and I shut the door. I wanted to lock it. But Michael was still inside, and I didn't want to give him the wrong idea.

I frowned at him. "What the hell? God, I don't need you acting like a pit bull."

"Pricks." Michael grabbed Morales' card from my hand, tore it in half, and stuck it in his jeans. "He's looking for trouble, that asshole. And more."

"Stop it, Michael. They were just doing their jobs."

"Bullshit. They're looking to get their names in the newspaper or something. And that Mexican was checking you out the whole time."

"He wasn't checking me out." But of course he was. I sighed and walked to the dining table. "So you brought food? Thank you. Can we eat some of it now?"

"Sure, we could do that." He walked toward me. "Or we could work up our appetites a little bit more. I told my brother I wouldn't be back to work until after five, so we've got time for a three or four course meal, if you get my drift." He pulled me against him.

I averted my face and reached around him for a carton of food. "Would you grab a couple of plates and forks from the kitchen?"

He let go of me. "Okay. I got your favorite at Jade Garden, egg foo young. You sure you want to eat now, or would you rather have a little 'me lick you?'"

"Not funny." I inhaled the fragrance of the food. Despite my frayed nerves, it smelled good.

"Ah, come on, you know that was funny."

"Just get the plates, okay?" I tried to push away the new worries I had about the detectives enflaming Nick's feelings about Roxanne, but they hovered.

I concentrated on the questions I wanted Michael to answer, the reason I'd invited him in the first place. I'd spent the better part of the last day and night going over what I wanted to learn from him before I could talk to Nick about what Betty had revealed. I envisioned sitting Michael down and having a serious discussion with him, mining some important information.

I hadn't counted on him being as frisky and completely self-absorbed as he was. Jeez, what had Roxanne ever seen in him? I flashed on the image of having sex with him on the floor a few days ago.

Okay, he was great at that. But he was all technique and no feeling. You would never be *making love* with Michael. It would always be screwing.

I felt a rush of pity for Roxanne, replaced by anger so strong I felt my skin flush; suddenly furious at her for all her bad choices. Her secrets. The possibility she'd slept with my husband. But most of all, right then I was overwhelmed with missing her, and mournful I would never have her to talk to again.

I moaned softly and blinked back tears. *Stay in the present.* I couldn't let my sorrow ruin this chance to talk to Michael.

He brought in plates, utensils, and a bottle of soda and sat down. "Talking about your piece of crap car reminds me." He spooned a huge helping onto his plate. "What about a new ride? Are you ready to come pick one out? What are you going to get for the payoff on the Camry? About six thou?" He broke the chopsticks apart and rubbed them furiously together, then attacked the food on his plate.

"I'm not ready to pick out a car." I put a spoonful of steamed rice on my plate, my stomach in a knot. I couldn't remember when I last ate. "And the insurance company hasn't settled everything yet." A lie.

"Really?" Michael slurped in a mouthful of noodles and frowned. "Before the detectives showed up, I figured the accident claim was settled. I guess when someone dies, it complicates the paperwork."

"That's probably it." I opened the soda. "How's it going, Michael? I haven't heard from you much since you dropped in a few days ago."

"Hey, I called you a hundred times, babe. But I have been busy. How you feeling?" He reached out and caressed my arm. "You still look a little ragged."

"Thanks."

"Oh come on, Roxanne. Even with a hangover and your hair needing some work, you're the best-looking chick in the state." Despite this backhanded compliment, he looked guilty.

I wondered suddenly how many other women he was currently bedding. Michael Cimino wasn't good at hiding the truth. Not too handy for a salesman. Or a cheating boyfriend. But it made for a good bet he'd reveal some hard facts.

"I appreciate you making time to come over today. I need to ask you some things."

"Sure. Anything, babe." He grabbed the dumplings and plopped them beside the noodles.

I stared at them. They looked like fetuses. "What happened with us late last year? Before Christmas? I know we broke up, but can you tell me why?"

He squinted at my face, and then at my plate. "How come you're not eating?"

"I'm not hungry," I said. "Are you stalling? Don't you want to tell me what went on between us?"

He speared a dumpling. "Try some egg foo. That'll get you into it."

"Come on, Michael. Talk to me."

"You're as bad as those fucking cops." He put down his fork. "Okay, you and I had a disagreement about where our relationship was headed, so we took a break. I started seeing Sheila Baker, that hot blonde in the Pasadena store." He lifted his eyebrows to see if I remembered her, then shrugged. "Anyway, that was pretty much it. I didn't hear from you until February. Around Valentine's Day. You sent me a giant chocolate chip cookie that said 'Eat Me' and I came right over. And we worked things out. Five or six times." He grinned.

I frowned. None of this sounded the least bit familiar. I remembered Rox telling me she and Michael were taking a break from one another. Then she got her apartment painted, and came to stay with Nick and me for a week. She said she and Michael were on the outs, but I didn't remember anything else.

Valentine's Day was a complete blank. "So you broke up in November?"

"What do you mean 'you broke up?'" Michael asked. "*We* broke up. Yeah. Before Thanksgiving. I remember, because Sheila came to my mom's for the holiday with me." He shook his head. "Boy, they didn't get along at all."

"Sorry to hear that." I rolled my eyes.

"No problem." Michael picked up a spoon and shoveled more food onto his plate. "So you're saying you don't remember any of this? Even the cookie?"

"No, I don't."

"Humph. It was good. Soft and sweet, just like you."

"Michael." I touched his arm. "This is going to sound weird, but I need to ask you about something Betty said."

"Who?" he interrupted.

"Betty. Betty Haverty. My mother."

"Yeah, okay. Why are you calling her Betty?"

"I just am. Look, she said I implied that I was seeing

someone else last year. After you and I broke up. Do you know if that's true?"

Michael stopped eating. A shadow passed across his dark eyes. He licked the tips of his fingers. "What are you asking me, Rox? What the fuck exactly are you asking me?"

A tickle of fear skittered through my stomach. "I know it's a weird question. But was I dating someone else last year?"

"Goddammit!" He slapped the box of dumplings with the back of his hand and the food flew off the table and smashed against the wall, leaving several greasy drips running toward the floor. He glowered at me.

I was stunned. I had no idea, ever, from Roxanne that Michael had a physical side to his temper.

"I don't *believe* you." He pushed away from the table. "Are you asking me if I knew you were fucking someone else? How the hell do you think that makes me feel?" He grabbed my arm. "I told you when we got back together that you were never, ever to bring up your little action on the side. I don't need you rubbing my nose in the fact you sucked some other guy's dick! So don't be asking me questions, pretending not to remember. That's bullshit. *You remember*. And you better remember I would have killed the cocksucker that knocked you up if I knew who it was."

There it was. It was true. Roxanne *had been* pregnant.

My heart pounded so loud I could hardly hear my thoughts. "Let go of my arm."

Michael's eyes bulged and he squeezed tighter for a second, but let go of me.

He got up and stared at his plate and then pushed it off onto the floor. He pointed at me. "Pretty convenient to forget that shit. Just so you can see me get jealous again. You like to make me mad, don't you?"

"No."

"Bullshit. You saying you don't remember your

boyfriend? Or that you had an abortion, all without telling me anything about it for months?"

"I don't remember that." I wrapped my arms around myself protectively. "Any of it."

"You don't remember? Or you still don't want to tell me who it was?" Michael's head nodded up and down, faster with each move, like a teakettle getting up a head of steam. "Well, I tell you, babe, I think I know who it was. And believe me, if I ever find out for sure, that married son of a bitch is going to be sorry."

I swallowed the lump in my throat. "The guy was *married*?"

"Yeah. And that's not the only fucking thing you told me about him." With his face pinched and angry, Michael no longer looked the least bit handsome. "You were a real cunt bragging about how big his cock was, and how his muscles turned you on, and that he left bruises on your sweet ass where he squeezed you when he fucked you."

I stared at Michael, speechless with shock and this crude verbal battering. How could Roxanne have put up with this? How could she have shut me out of so much of her life? I was also stunned Roxanne had behaved so ruthlessly with Michael. But I had no doubt what he said was the truth.

He'd hurt her, and she'd given the same treatment right back to him.

"I'm not trying to piss you off, Michael. But just so I understand, you think it's okay you had a fling with a girl in your office, but Roxanne couldn't see anyone else?"

"Oh, you're referring to yourself in the third person again? Yeah, it was wrong for 'Roxanne' to see anyone else because she always said she loved 'Michael.' But when 'Roxanne' decided to act like a slut, 'Michael' decided to give her a taste of her own medicine. So I went out with Sheila to show you I could. That bitch didn't mean anything to me. You know you and I were meant to be together, Roxanne.

We broke up a lot, but we always end up back together. It's in the cards." He reached out and poked me hard in the arm.

I flinched and Michael looked embarrassed. He picked the plate off the floor. "When I heard you were in the accident, I thought I would die. Did you know that? I told my brother I'd blow my brains out if you didn't make it."

I stared at him. Sitting here this close to a man I thought I had known for years, I realized I hadn't known him at all.

The greater shock was that it appeared I hadn't known Roxanne very well, either.

"Did you sleep with Cathy?" I blurted out.

Michael jerked like I'd slapped him. "What? When?"

"When? Ever! Like at the beach. A few months before the accident."

He shook his head slowly. "Shit. Did she tell you that? I can't believe she told you."

"Did you?" I was afraid. More afraid than any time I could ever remember. Not of Michael. For all his bluster and badass attitude, he was not a threat to me. I was afraid of myself, *me*, Cathy. What had I been capable of? What had I done?

"Did you?" I repeated.

"Did I what? Fuck Miss Goody two shoes?" Michael yelled. "Maybe I did. But whatever, if I did it wouldn't matter now any more to me than jerking off. You're the one I want, Roxanne. Don't you know that yet? Cathy Chance, and the rest of those girls, none of them could ever mean anything to me."

I wanted to scream. "Get out. For good this time, Michael. I don't ever want to see you here again."

"Oh, Christ." He rolled his eyes and then threw the dinner plate against the tile floor again, followed by mine. They banged and bounced and rolled off into separate corners of the kitchen, food splattering everywhere.

"Stop it!" I covered my ears with my hands. "Stop it and get out!"

"I'll go, but you better get some more help, because you're a fucking nut case. I'm through dealing with you. Call me if and when you can handle things like a real woman."

With that endearment, he stalked out of the room. A few moments later the front door slammed. I ran to lock it and then stood hyperventilating, my face pressed against the cold surface. And suddenly, I remembered it all . . . the beach, the night, the sand grinding into my skin.

I felt Michael's half-hard penis pushing against my naked inner thigh. "Stop," I had said, pressing against his chest with my fists. "Don't. We can't do this. Stop it, Michael."

"You're nothing but a goddamned prick teaser, Cathy Chance," he'd mumbled. "I should do you anyway just to show you what you're missing."

"Rape, Michael? Really? I'm saying no, and I mean it. I'll call the police if you don't get the hell off me now!"

"Bitch." He rolled off me then, and I scrambled up and into my clothes.

"Take me home," I had called out over my shoulder.

He followed me to the car. We rode without saying a word to one another, the smell of liquor and disappointment and fear all around us, punctuated by Rox snoring in the backseat. I didn't understand at that moment why I had weakened and given in to my longtime lustful urge to see what Michael was all about sexually.

But now, all these months later, I did understand. Because as I stood leaning against the door for dear life, I remembered what had happened the same morning of that beach encounter.

Nick and I had a vicious fight, something unusual for us. He was packing to leave on business and had made a surprising remark. "I think it's time we thought hard about having a baby."

I'd replied, "I don't. I think it's time you quit your job at the insurance company and took a stab at the career you've always wanted."

"What are you talking about?"

"Music. Being a DJ. Come on, Nick, you haven't mentioned it in a while, but I thought we were on the same page, that you were going to give this a real try before it's too late. You know how unhappy you are with your job."

He looked away from me. "That's out of the question. I'd make next to nothing, and if we're going to have a baby, we need stuff like my insurance and benefits. And some discipline."

"I never agreed to have a baby now," I'd shot back at him. "What's your hurry?"

"You never know what's going to happen tomorrow, Cathy. One of us could drop dead. I think we need to get started on being grown-ups."

"What's that mean?"

"You need to watch our money better. Stop spending so much on junk for the house, and on going out to eat all the time. Be more responsible and stop partying and shopping every chance you get with Roxanne. Just because she's irresponsible, you don't have to follow her around like a groupie."

When he said that I immediately thought of my mother, dying in the hospital when I was nine. When I was ushered in to kiss her goodbye, I saw agony in her eyes. She was in physical pain, but more than that, she was horrified to be leaving me alone in the world.

Remembering that helpless look on my mother's face made me realize now that what I had feared most that day, six months ago, was becoming a mother. I feared risking the loss of a child. How could I take the chance and love another person that much, and lose them, or leave them, like my mother had left me?

But that day I had not understood that. I had screamed at Nick. "I'm not ready to be a mother. And it's not your decision to make for me, Nick. To tell you the truth, at this point in my life I don't know for sure if I ever want children with you."

Nick snapped his suitcase shut. "Great. When the hell were you going to tell me that? I thought we were ready, Cathy. And what time of life is this, anyway? The 'flirt around, think about leaving your husband' time? Is that what you're saying to me? You don't want to be married anymore?"

I threw the magazine I was holding across the room at him. My face heated, my mouth drying with anger . . . but Nick was wrong. I wouldn't willingly leave him until I died.

"Yeah. That's it. I want to sleep with another ten or twelve guys I know. Have a nice trip, asshole. And don't bother to call me when you're gone because I won't be home. I'll be out partying with Roxanne. And having a lot more fun than I ever do with you!" I'd stormed out.

Nick left by cab for the airport. And that night I'd gone out drinking with Rox and Michael and flirted with ruining my life because I was feeling cornered. Thankfully I'd come to my senses on that beach and not succumbed to my impulse for self-destruction.

Across Roxanne's living room, the phone jangled as the memories of the fight with Nick all those months ago dissipated into the air like smoke, leaving just one question in my head. *Had Nick betrayed me?*

I walked to the answering machine and listened as it recorded the message. It was Betty.

"Roxanne? Are you there?"

No. Roxanne is not here.

I grabbed my purse and left the apartment. I had to see Nick. I could go to him now without feeling guilty that I'd betrayed him, but I had to know the facts about what had happened between him and Roxanne.

The only way I could build a future with him would be to know the whole truth about the past.

Chapter 19

Monday, August 1, 4 p.m.
Cathy & Nick

I pulled up in front of Nick's twenty minutes later. I had planned to sit and think and watch for my husband to come home, but his car was already parked in the driveway.

Why was he home at four in the afternoon? Was he inside, drunk again?

Maybe he was drinking because of guilt, not grief. On the way over, I had vacillated between believing Nick incapable of adultery and then being certain he and Roxanne had betrayed me.

Furiously I kicked open the car door and hurried up to the house. I tried the doorknob, but the house was locked up. I hit the bell, over and over.

"Nick!" I yelled. "Nick, open the door!"

I knew I should probably call Seth and talk out my feelings, but I was near to bursting with the need to confront my husband. I pounded on the door. "Nick! Nick! Let me in!" I felt crazed. Let Zoë or the neighbors call the police, for all I cared. I was going to stand here until someone opened the door.

After five minutes, my elderly neighbor, Mrs. West, glanced at me when she came out to get the mail. I waved, but realized too late she didn't see Cathy Chance. She saw Roxanne.

As soon as she went back into her house, I walked around to the rear yard and tried to think where we had hidden an extra key. I couldn't remember. I looked under the cushion on the patio chairs, under the lemon tree planter. Damn, where would I hide the key? I sat in the chaise and tried to think, but nothing came.

I got up and peered into the kitchen, which was a mess. Dishes piled everywhere, pans on the stove. Pitty was lying on the kitchen chair. She stared at me through the window. "Hey Aunt Pittypatt," I whispered, tapping the window. The cat blinked and rested her head on her paws, her ears perked.

I decided Nick must not be in the house. I'd go back and sit in the car. And when he returned, we were going to talk. I headed back to my rental.

A few minutes later, Zoë Chance drove into the driveway.

"Nick . . ."

I heard my name being called as if I stood at one end of a tunnel and the person yelling "Nick" was at the other end. I looked over at the clock; it read four thirty-five.

In the morning?

I rolled onto my back and tried to focus. I felt as groggy as if I'd taken sleeping pills. My bedroom was warm with sunlight drizzling in the edges of the windows, which meant it was four in the afternoon. What day was it?

Monday.

I had called in sick and gone back to bed, filthy sore from the beating I'd taken a couple of days ago. I got up and stumbled toward the front door, opening it to find Zoë halfway back across the lawn headed toward the driveway.

She turned at the sound of the squeaking hinge. "Why didn't you answer the doorbell?" she asked, hand on her hip.

"Why didn't you use your key?" I countered.

"I left it at Mom's." She nodded at the sedan in the driveway. "I borrowed her car and her keys to drive over so

I could take Pitty to the vet. I didn't know you'd be *passed out* in the middle of the day."

I sighed. "I wasn't passed out, Zoë. I was sleeping."

We stared at each other for a full minute. We used to do this when she was a little kid. I always turned away first.

I turned away. "If you're coming in, do it now."

My sister brushed by me and stomped across the living room. I shut the door with a little too much force and followed her to the kitchen. She called for the cat, which was nowhere to be seen.

"Why are you looking for the cat?" I asked.

"I just told you I'm taking her to another vet. The lady over by Mom's house, Dr. Nelson. I want to get a second opinion about that thing on Pitty's leg."

I rubbed my eyes. My mouth tasted like something had died in it. "Let me throw some clothes on and I'll go with you."

She frowned at my ripped UCLA tee shirt and baggy boxers, topped by three days of bruises, stitches and an unshaven face. "Why not go like that? We'll get *you* a rabies shot. In case someone hits you on the head again with a whiskey bottle."

I counted to three. "Look, I told you and Mom on Friday that I'm still firmly on the wagon. Buying that bottle the other night was a mistake. A bad mistake. I'm not going to do that again."

"I've heard it before. When I was a kid and believed most of the BS you told me."

I remembered Seth's words, about how my welfare was a heavy burden for my sister. It kept me from saying some pointed things about eating disorders and pot smoking.

"I know I've let you down, Zoë. I've let myself down. But give it a rest. I'm going to be okay."

"You think?"

"Yes, I do 'think.' Occasionally, anyway. And for your

information, it's a *tetanus* shot I'd need for broken glass. Rabies is if I get bit by a vampire bat."

"That could happen."

I grinned and was rewarded, finally, with a small smile in return.

"Okay, go get ready," Zoë said. "I'll keep looking for the cat."

"What time is the appointment?"

"Five. It's the last one of the day." Zoë opened the French door to the patio and called Pitty. The cat darted from where she'd been hiding under the kitchen table, scooted past her through the back door and ran under the gardenia bush.

Zoë called her, but the cat halted, then ran for the side of the house when she saw me.

"Go away, Nick. I'll try and coax her in."

"Leave the door open. Put some fresh food out and she'll come. I'll go get cleaned up."

Zoë nodded and reached out to pinch my arm. "Why are you home already, by the way?"

"I'm stiff and sore as an old man today, thanks to the beat down, so I took a couple of days off."

"Oh, God, you didn't get fired?" Zoë was very good at imagining the worst in any given situation.

"No, I didn't get fired. We can still buy groceries and pay for the freaking cat." I thought about telling her I was quitting my job, but if me taking sick leave rattled her, that would be too much.

I gave her a quick hug. "How's it going with you, kiddo?" I felt her ribs through her shirt. "Are you still looking for a car?"

"Yeah. My friend Ramon has a cool VW I might be able to get for three grand. Did you mean it the other night when you said you would loan me the money?"

"Yeah. What year is the car?"

"1990-something. It's way cool. Ramon and his brother put in a new engine. It has fabulous speakers."

Ramon, huh? "It's a *1990-something* and it's *three thousand*?"

"Yeah, isn't that a good deal?"

I smiled. "I'll run it past Mom."

"Okay." Zoë crammed her hands into the pockets of her jeans. "I'm going to stay with her at the house for a couple of days. While you're recovering. Unless you want me to come back?"

"That's cool. Whatever you want to do. I'm going to go get cleaned up. Oh, and I think I saw the cat carrier in the living room. By Cathy's desk."

I hurried through a shower and shave, tossed on the jeans and shirt I'd worn to see Seth, and found Zoë in the living room. While Pitty meowed inside the carrier, my sister sat beside her, staring at a folded piece of paper.

"I'm ready. You want to drive or you want me to?"

"Nick, look at this," Zoë replied.

I made calming noises at the yowling cat, and perched on the sofa next to Zoë. "What is it?"

She handed me a yellow sheet that looked like a bill of some kind. I looked it over; it was a car rental agreement, made out to Roxanne Ruiz several days ago. "Where did this come from?"

"I found it sticking out from under the ottoman."

"What's it doing here?" I turned it over and saw a list of items written in pen on the back of the contract. 'Underwear. Jeans. Tops. Watch. Purse. Deodorant.'

'Nightie' was crossed out and 'Men's undershirts' was written next to it. "Where'd this come from?"

"Roxanne must have left it the other day. I told you she was here when the police came. She was sitting at the desk." Zoë looked flushed, as if she had a fever.

"Okay, well, send it back to her, or throw it out." I tossed the paper on the sofa and it missed and hit the floor. It was obvious Zoë was ready to freak out again about Roxanne acting weird, and I didn't want to get into that whole line of discussion right now. "Come on. Let's go." I stood up.

Zoë grabbed the paper and held it up to my face. "Nick. Look at the writing. *The handwriting.* Look at the signature and the phone number!"

The skin on the back of my arm suddenly crawled, like there was a bug on me. I slapped at it with one hand and took the paper with the other. I scanned the list again, and then flipped it over to the rental contract side.

"Honestly Zoë, I want you to let go of this whole thing about Roxanne. I know you were upset about how she was acting, but . . ."

Then I stopped talking. Inside my head, a low, dull buzz of recognition morphed into understanding as I blinked at the signature. It said 'Roxanne Ruiz,' but it was in very familiar handwriting. The phone number listed under 'home phone' was mine.

"What the hell?" I mumbled. The list was in the same loopy, messy writing as the signature. Big letters, quickly written, a little childish in their form.

Cathy's writing.

"Jesus Christ, you're right." I looked at my sister who was staring into space like an alien child in a movie, listening for the mother ship.

She turned her blue eyes back to me. "I told you she was trying to be Cathy."

"But this is crazy. Do you know if Roxanne's writing looks this much like Cathy's?"

Zoë slowly moved to the desk. She pulled out a stack of greeting cards and sorted through them, then handed one to me. On the front of the card were two little girls in bathing suits, big floppy hats partially covering their faces. Their arms were around each other's chubby shoulders. 'Happy birthday, Sister,' it read.

I opened the card. Inside, written in a neat, almost anally perfect penmanship, were the words, 'Cathy—Happy 30 from your Secret Sister. Simone's at 8 p.m. Champagne for everyone! XXOOX Roxanne.'

Then I remembered that Cathy depended on Roxanne's help to print names on the student folders for her classes. Cathy's printing was so sloppy she was embarrassed, so she always had Roxanne do them. "Roxanne prints like a calligrapher. It takes forever but it looks perfect," Cathy had said more than once.

"I told you Roxanne's crazy," Zoë said. "I think she thinks she *is* Cathy."

My chest tightened as my head filled with static, like a radio slightly off channel. Pitty started howling inside the crate. "Zoë, get Pitty to the vet. I'm going to take care of this."

"How? What do you mean? Don't do anything dumb. I think maybe Roxanne should go back to the hospital." Her voice sounded hollow.

I took out my checkbook. "I don't know yet what I'm going to do, but I have to talk to her. Here's a check for the doctor to examine the cat. Don't let her operate or anything. And bring Pitty back when you're through, okay? If I'm not here, I'll call you at Mom's later."

"Why wouldn't you be here? What are you going to do, Nick?"

I picked up the cat's cage and gestured for Zoë to move toward the front door. "Come on. Don't worry. You don't want to miss this appointment."

I walked her out to Mom's car and put the carrier on the front seat, then watched Zoë drive away. I had a pang that maybe I shouldn't have let her drive, but she looked okay and was already back to worrying over the cat.

My fuzziness had worn off, replaced with a throbbing anxiety. *Something's happening here, and it isn't fucking clear.* Rewriting the classic line from Buffalo Springfield didn't help anything.

As I headed across my lawn, I glanced up the street. Three houses away, under the drooping branches of my neighbor's weeping willow, a compact black sedan was parked at the curb. I had seen the car before; last Friday when Roxanne showed up at the hospital. My pulse pounded in my ears and I took a couple of steps up the sidewalk.

The car door opened; Roxanne got out. Slowly she pulled off her sunglasses. Despite the distance between us, I saw she was a wreck, with a blotchy face and red-rimmed eyes. Even her hair was messy, and in all the years I'd known Roxanne, I'd never seen her go out with her hair half stuck in a ponytail and the rest falling around her face.

"Nick, I need to talk to you." She sounded desperate. "Please, it's very important."

"Are you stalking me, Roxanne? Do I need to call the police?"

"Just give me a few minutes, please." She crossed her arms over her chest, as if waiting for a blow.

A wise man would have run. But as my recent behavior suggested, wisdom is something I have often aspired to and seldom achieved. "Come inside. You've got five minutes to explain what the fuck you're up to."

I walked into my house, and couldn't say what I wished for more at that moment, for Roxanne to follow me so I could tell her off, or for her to disappear forever.

Roxanne sat at the table in the kitchen. Despite her appearance, she seemed in control. I felt her eyes on me as I poured myself a glass of water.

The kitchen was a mess. For a second I was embarrassed by the dirty dishes, the soured milk on the counter. Then I got a grip. This wasn't a social call and Roxanne wasn't someone I was trying to impress. Every time she walked into the room, she did so with an agenda.

I turned around. "Do you want something to drink?"

She shook her head.

I sat across from her. She was pinching the back of her hand, like Cathy used to do.

"What's going on? What do you want from me?" I sounded angrier than I thought I was.

"What do you mean?"

"You're fooling around with your hands exactly like Cathy always did. You never had that habit. Why are you doing stuff like that?"

"What else am I doing?"

"You're wearing your hair pulled back in a ribbon, and clothes like my wife wore." I pointed at her blouse. "And you're acting weird with the cat, like she's *your* cat, among other things. It's freaking Zoë out."

Roxanne fidgeted. "That's ridiculous," she said, but her face revealed I'd hit a nerve. "Look, Nick, those things are nothing. I know it's going to sound weird, but—"

I held up my hand. "Stop. Let me show you something." I got the car rental agreement from the other room and tossed it on the table. "Let's talk about this first." I sat back down. "Is this *nothing*?"

She looked at it uncomprehendingly. "What is this?"

"It's your car rental agreement."

Roxanne unfolded it. "I don't understand. What's your point?"

"What's your home phone number?" I challenged.

Roxanne rattled off a number and then put her hand over her mouth.

She had just recited *my* phone number. The same number she'd written on the form. "I don't understand why you're doing this. Where's it leading?"

She looked down. "Can I ask you a couple of things first, before I explain this stuff?"

"Shoot."

Roxanne leaned forward, her breasts pressing against the tabletop. Despite the drama around us, her ripe good looks were, as always, distracting as hell; the silky, tanned skin, her lush body. Staring into her eyes, my anxiety ratcheted up a notch.

"What are you doing home today? Are you sick?" she asked.

She was something. A real ball breaker. I had never figured her for this kind of pushiness. It was more Cathy's style.

Shit, now I'm doing it.

"That's none of your business," I retorted. "And if that's the kind of thing you came here to ask about, when you know it's none of your business, you can just get the hell out now. I'm not gonna play games with you."

"Okay." She cleared her throat. "Last year, in November, I came and stayed for a few days. I can't remember everything that happened during that visit. Will you tell me what went on?"

"What went on?" My heart beat an irregular rhythm. I put my hand on my chest and rubbed it. "What exactly is it you don't remember?"

"I remember you cooked waffles." She looked outside, staring at the sky as if it were a television screen. "I don't know what I don't remember, Nick. That's the problem. I know I was upset because of problems with Michael. With the relationship. The rest is sketchy."

"Why are you asking me this? Can't you talk to someone more in the know? Michael, for instance? How about Bradley, or your mom?"

"I did ask Michael. And Betty told me a few things I don't completely trust." She paused. "I was hoping you could tell me what you remember. I know you'll tell me the truth."

We stared at each other. I felt like I was treading water.

I knew she really didn't remember the week she spent here, for if she did, she wouldn't be this calm.

"What's so important about those few days, Roxanne? Do you remember everything else in your past except that hunk of time?"

"No, I don't. I've got a lot of gaps. But I remember most things I think are important, and something tells me this is a very significant point in time for me. But I can't bring the details into focus."

I looked up at the ceiling. What could I say? What *should* I say that would help anything now? What had happened last November couldn't be undone. I looked at the table and thought about how I had reacted when Roxanne, sitting in the same chair she now occupied, had announced, *"I'm pregnant, Nick..."*

My face tingled as the echo of her words bounced around inside my head. This must be how it felt to be a defendant, guilty as charged, sitting in a courtroom hearing a jury verdict of 'Not Guilty.'

I was being given the chance to escape reliving my betrayal of my wife. If I didn't tell Roxanne the truth, and she didn't remember the past, then would the damning details disappear forever?

A tree falling in the forest, and all that.

I stared at the woman across the table. What good would it do her to know the truth? I couldn't imagine.

"You told us you needed to get out of your apartment because it was being painted," I finally said. "Cathy invited you to stay here. You and Michael were on the outs, and you were pretty broken up. Cathy took you to see Ryan Seth, to get some help. You stayed a couple of days, life went on and you went home. End of story."

Before she could say a word, the shriek of the telephone nearly knocked me off the chair. The second ring seemed louder. Roxanne watched me with a wounded look in her eyes.

I answered the phone. It was Zoë, sobbing that the new vet wanted to do surgery right away on the cat.

"Hang on," I said, after listening to her shaking voice detail the cost, the risk, the fact that she had to sign a release acknowledging the cat might die from the anesthetic. "Tell me why exactly she wants to do surgery tonight."

"The mass is huge on her back leg," Zoë said. "I told her it was bigger than last week. And Pitty has a temperature. The vet says that probably means it's affecting her other organs." My sister cried harder and started gulping for air.

"Zoë, take a breath and calm down a little. Look, the cat's been eating and walking around okay. Tell the vet we want to wait. I can't believe if it's cancer that it would grow so fast."

"Did they check her for stingers?" Roxanne demanded.

I covered the mouthpiece of the phone and looked around. "What?"

"You're talking about Pitty, right? The thing on her left haunch?"

I must have looked at her like she was a witch because she said defensively, "Zoë told me about it Thursday, when I was here."

"Hang on a minute, Zoë." I frowned. "What are you talking about, Rox? A stinger where?"

"Remember a couple of years ago when Pitty got into the yellow jacket nest and they stung her right leg? She had a stinger buried in so deep the vet had to shave her to see the thing. Her leg swelled up and the vet said at first he thought she might be having 'kidney failure,' the pinhead. But we found the stinger."

She held out her hand for the phone. "Let me talk to the vet. I'll tell her to shave Pitty's haunch and see if anything is there."

"Sit down, it's my fucking cat." But she was right. This had happened, but it was Cathy who found the stinger.

Roxanne sat but kept talking. "We gave her a little Benadryl with an eye dropper, and the swelling got better, remember? If you won't let me talk to the doctor, make sure Zoë tells her exactly where to look."

I stared at her. Roxanne seemed agitated, charged up, ready to swoop in and save the day. She even acted maternal.

The Roxanne I'd known all these years was passive, cool and disconnected at times of crisis. A follower, not a leader. When she had told me she was pregnant, it was because she wanted me to tell her what to do.

Usually that task fell to my wife. But Roxanne had been adamant that neither of us could ever tell Cathy about the baby. My lack of judgment, among other things, had led me to go along with her, and lie a million times to Cathy over the next few weeks.

Who was this woman standing here? I wanted to scream aloud. *Who the hell does she think she is?*

I kept my eyes on her, as if she might morph into a monster, my gut as freaked-out as my churning brain.

"Zoë, listen to me." I related the yellow jacket story exactly as Roxanne had described. "Okay, then call me back. If you have to, leave Pitty there overnight, that's fine. But make sure they don't operate. The cat is too old to make it through anesthesia."

I hung up.

Roxanne had walked over to the corner of the kitchen and was leaning on the French door, looking out at the back yard. The air conditioning unit kicked on and she kept her face averted.

Suddenly she said, "So, tell me about the abortion."

"What?" The word exploded out of my throat.

She turned. Her eyes flashed and her voice was hard. "You lied to me just now, didn't you, Nick? You know what the little 'problem' was. Betty Haverty told me the whole pathetic story. How her daughter got pregnant and had an abortion last fall. Betty said she wasn't allowed to ever mention it to Cathy." She paused. "I asked Michael about it. He said the baby wasn't his. He said the father was a *married* man."

Salt tracks from recent tears glittered on her cheeks. "Tell me the truth about this, Nick. Tell me and break my heart."

I felt like I could not breathe. I had heard those words before.

The first time Cathy and I made love, she lay in my arms, warm and soft and naked, and asked me to swear I would never cheat on her. "If you ever want to be with someone else, just tell me and break my heart. But don't lie to me, ever, Nick. I would die if you lied to me. Promise?"

I had promised.

Roxanne could not have known about this conversation between Cathy and me. My wife shared many things with her friend, but I would bet my life she hadn't shared that.

A nerve under my left eye began to twitch. My vision clouded and suddenly she didn't look like the Roxanne I had known all these years. The way she held herself, the downward curve of her lip when she cried, the nervous pulling at the skin on the back of her hand, all these movements belonged to another woman.

"Who are you?" I asked as if I was dreaming.

"Was it your baby, Nick? Don't lie to me. Please."

I leaned against the counter because my knees nearly buckled. "Who . . .?"

She wiped her eyes and pointed at the chair. "Sit down. I've got something to tell you."

Chapter 20

Cathy's home, Monday, August 1
Nick & Cathy

Nick fell into his chair, tense as a hostage wired to a bomb. I had never seen my husband scared, but the light was gone from his eyes, replaced by a radiating anxiety I felt across the space between us.

"Something happened after the accident on July 9," I began. "Something that will be hard for you to accept. It has been for me. But it's something you're going to have to believe, because it's true."

Nick cracked his knuckles. His bruised face looked harder and leaner than I remembered and for a moment I was disoriented and felt as if I might be dreaming instead of awake.

With a deep breath and in a flood of words, I told him what happened to me, and to Roxanne. I factually recounted what I remembered about the sound, the smell, the frantic, horrible panic and nightmare of the wreck. I described the violence, the pain, and the blackness.

How I thought of him.

"And then I saw a woman with long, dark hair. She was trying to lead me somewhere, Nick. I was afraid of her and I didn't understand what was happening. Even when I think of those moments now, they're a blur of sound and fragmented images. I was dying and I didn't realize, until last week at Simone's, that when I was most in danger of leaving life behind forever, I was given a gift. That night, just before I saw you in the hallway of the restaurant, my past flooded back and I knew who I was. And the memory of the dark-haired woman made sense."

I wanted to cross the room and put my arms around Nick and melt into him, comfort him, make the horror in his face go away. But I stood as if bolted to the cool tile floor, pinching my hand so hard it felt like it would bleed.

I think he knew what I was going to say before I said it.

"It's me, Cathy. I'm here, Nick. I can't explain how or why it happened, but Roxanne died that day in the accident, and I did too, but then for some reason, by some power I don't understand, I moved into her body. It's me in here, Nick. Cathy."

I pressed my hands to my heart and whispered, "It's a miracle."

Nick gasped and pushed away from the table. His eyes were wild. "Get out." He pointed toward the front door. "Get the hell out of here."

"No." I braced myself against the chair. "No, I won't go, Nick. Not until you understand what I'm telling you. I know it will take some time to believe it, but tell me you understand." I took a step closer. "I've missed you so much. Please, tell me what you're thinking."

"What I'm thinking is that you're insane. Certifiable, Roxanne. And I'm not going to listen to this, this lie!"

"It's the truth!" My frustration bubbled out of control and I hit his arm with my closed fist. "You have to believe me."

"I don't have to do anything for you."

"Yes, you do. Starting with telling me what happened with you and Roxanne. You owe me that much!"

"I owe you?" he roared. "What do I owe you? I've known you for years and years, but I don't owe you anything. I think July 9 cancelled everything between us, Roxanne. You're nothing to me but heartbreak."

I wrapped my shaking arms around myself. "I'm not going to go away until I know the truth about everything."

"Everything?" His voice was ragged. "You want to know if you and I slept together and you got pregnant? Is that what someone told you? And since you can't conveniently remember, you want me to verify the sordid details because, by the way, you are not who you look like, *you're really Cathy Chance?*"

It sounded as crazy as it was. "I know it's shockingly weird. But you have to deal with it. *I'm not dead.*"

Nick pushed past the chairs and grabbed me by both arms, his eyes blazing. "You've always had a loose grip on reality, Roxanne. Why are you doing this? To get me to take you into the bedroom and fuck you in my bed, in *Cathy's bed?* Is that where this sick joke is going?" He shook me by the shoulders. "Are you this jealous of her, even though she's dead?"

I opened my mouth to yell at him for even thinking such a thing about Roxanne, but in that second I realized he was right.

She had been jealous, but not of me.

It was of him, and his love for me. It was something she'd never had. She'd never had a father in her life, and never trusted that any one had ever loved her for who she was inside. Except maybe for me. I looked into Nick's eyes and saw Roxanne's face reflected in his pupils and my heart broke again for my dead friend.

"You've got to believe me. I'm not Roxanne. I know it's bizarre and crazy, but for your own sake, please listen to me. I can prove this. I know things. I remember almost everything that ever happened between us."

My voice cracked but I kept talking. "I can tell you things that will convince you. Test me! I'll answer any question about anything you want me to."

"Who's your best friend?" His breath was hot on my face.

"You're my best friend, Nick Chance. And I'm yours."

He flinched. "You are such a liar."

I wrested myself out of his grasp. "I'm not lying. You're the only one who has been lying today. You said nothing happened in November, but it did. She was pregnant. Did you and Roxanne have an affair?"

His lips pulled over his teeth, as if he were going to bite me. "Are you done? Are you going to get out or am I going to have to bodily throw you out?"

"Nick, we can talk this out. If you were unfaithful, explain how it happened and I'll try to understand."

A strangled noise escaped him and he stomped out of the kitchen.

I followed, furious with him, but mostly with myself. I needed to stop bouncing around and stay focused on convincing him about the main issue at hand. Which was my true identity. I had to make him agree to at least try and understand what had happened.

He was in the bedroom, our bedroom, *my bedroom*, sitting on the mattress fumbling with his socks, trying to pull them on. His shoes lay beside him.

"Nick, forget about the past for a moment. We have to talk about me. Please just listen . . ."

"Get out of here! Get the hell out of my room and my house."

I came closer. He gave me a look that said if I moved, I would be in danger.

"Just because you can't accept the truth doesn't mean it isn't real. You can keep the past from me all you want, but you're going to have to deal with who I am. Please just say you'll think about everything I said."

"There's nothing to think about. My wife's dead. She's in an urn under the bed. And you are batshit crazy."

"I'm not lying."

"Well then, you're hallucinating. Or high." Nick's eyes made a quick journey of my body. "You're not my wife, lady. Not even close."

"Jesus, you're not listening. Can't you see past who I look like for a minute and see inside? Who else but me would keep at you like this?" I stomped over to the windows and pulled the shades, then slammed the door.

The room was now dark and dusky, warm and close. I walked back to where he sat and laid my hand on his arm.

I got a jolt from touching him. He was quiet, yet wound so tight I was afraid he might explode. But all I wanted to do was melt against him, so close that I would disappear into his body. I didn't even care if he had ever been unfaithful to me.

He was my whole world. I needed him and I wasn't going to ever give up and go away. I leaned over and whispered close to his ear. "It's me, Nick. Can't you see me inside?" And then I told him what I wanted him to do to me, a secret caress between us that he had to know I never would have shared with anyone.

Nick froze.

It seemed as if we both stopped breathing, and I felt as if I heard his thoughts, heard his heart beating. He met my eyes and I knew his mind had finally opened to the possibility it *was* me, and he might believe just a little.

Just enough for me to try.

"Do you remember the first time we made love in this room?" I asked.

He raised his left hand and put his fingers against my mouth. "Don't . . ."

I moved his hand from my lips. "It was the afternoon we had the house inspected, a week before we moved in. We threw our clothes on the floor and you lay down and pulled me on top of you. We were both so ready it took all of five minutes for both of us to come. You said huge debt must make us horny. Afterward we took a shower and shared that little motel bar of soap we found in the bathroom drawer. It smelled like pine trees. You dried me off with your ratty UCLA tee shirt and teased me that you'd tell our kids someday how Mom and Daddy celebrated in their new home."

Nick's face was a study in grief and yearning so naked I felt for a moment that neither of us could survive this conversation.

I slipped my arms around his neck and kissed his throat so I wouldn't have to look at him. "Remember, baby? I love you. Always have. Always will. I know you love me, too. Don't you, Nick? Don't you still love your wife?"

He moaned then, and pulled me against him so hard, he almost squeezed the breath out of me. He kissed my eyes and covered my mouth with his as if he would devour me and we fell backward onto the bed.

We tore at each other's clothes. When we were naked, I pressed into him and kissed him and it was the sweetest, most passionate skin-on-skin communion I have ever shared with another human being. He was crying now too, kissing me, touching me, running his hands flat against my skin, digging his fingers into my flesh like a drowning man would delve into a saving stretch of sand.

I cried out when he entered me and everything else disappeared. We made love like starving people eat when they at last find food. Too much, too fast, desperate to gorge on what had been missing for oh, so long.

For several minutes afterward we lay entangled in each other's limbs, like one creature, drowsy and sated in the room's warm silence.

The front doorbell rang.

I twitched and tried to sit up but Nick pulled me back down onto the mattress. "Shh. Zoë probably forgot her key. Stay here, I'll tell her to go to Mom's tonight."

Nick rolled out of bed and pulled on his jeans, staggered

out of the room. I burrowed into the covers, wanting to sleep, but knew if I closed my eyes I'd be gone for hours.

I listened for Zoë's voice, but instead a low rumble of male voices seeped into the bedroom.

There was a chilling tone in those voices that made me get out of bed. I slipped Nick's tee shirt over my head and crept to the door; peeked around the corner. Nick and two men were in the living room; the detectives, Morales and Strain.

"So, Mrs. Chance never expressed any concern about Miss Ruiz's mental state? She never confided to you that she was worried her friend might try to commit suicide?" Morales asked.

The cops were sitting on the sofa. Nick leaned against the hallway doorframe, his naked back partially blocking my view.

"No," Nick said.

"Would she have confided such a worry to you about her friend?"

"Yes."

"Are you aware Miss Ruiz had tried to commit suicide in the past?"

Nick hesitated. "Yes. When she was in college, I think. Look, where is this going? Are you guys saying you think Roxanne wrecked the car intentionally, trying to kill herself?"

Oh my God.

I covered my kiss-swollen mouth with my hand as panic coursed through me. I couldn't let Nick just stand there and listen to those men talk about cut seat belts and skid marks. Not after I had made progress getting him to trust me enough to begin to grapple with our impossible situation.

Morales looked down at his notebook. "No, sir, we're not saying that at all. We're just tying up loose ends. The evidence says it was an accident."

"Well, then, that's what it was, right? Sounds to me as if there's nothing left to say."

Morales stared at Nick. "There's always more to say if someone has doubts."

"I don't have doubts it was an accident."

"That's good to hear, Mr. Chance." Morales edged forward. "There's another issue I need to ask you about. Do you know a Mr. Michael Cimino?"

There was a moment of silence. "Yes." Nick crossed his arms. He sounded exhausted.

"Mr. Cimino contacted me with some information about you and Miss Ruiz."

"What kind of information?"

Detective Strain cleared his throat and took up the conversation. "Mr. Cimino stated that you and Miss Ruiz had an affair last fall and that Miss Ruiz wanted you to leave your wife for her. He said we should consider this before we accepted that the car accident was just an accident."

I nearly fainted at these words. I gripped the wall, ready to rush in and stop them from saying another word when, shockingly, Nick stopped me cold by bursting into laughter.

His tone was derisive. "That guy's a tool and he's blowing smoke, Detective. Cimino has always been paranoid that Roxanne is going to leave him for someone else."

"Like you, Mr. Chance?"

"No. She's not my type at all." As he spoke, Nick seemed to turn reflexively toward the hallway where I hid.

"Why do you think he would tell us such a thing?" Strain asked.

"I don't know. Maybe they're having trouble and he's trying to cause her grief. Which he's done since you two are out here now accusing her of this shit."

"No one is accusing Miss Ruiz of anything. We're just following up on questions he raised."

"Yeah? Well, Cimino is the guy you need to ask questions of. He cheats on Roxanne with anything with tits. He probably got caught going out on her while she was in the hospital, recovering. I wouldn't trust a goddamn thing he tells you."

"He cheats on a woman who looks like that?" The detective seemed incredulous.

"What can I tell you? Some men are never satisfied. Roxanne and Michael are known for fighting and breaking up every couple of weeks because Cimino is an asshole. He mistreats her. If he calls again, ask him about that."

"Physically mistreats her?" Strain's voice was sharp.

"I can't say I've ever heard that, but it wouldn't surprise me. I know he shows her no respect. Look, Roxanne was my wife's best friend. They cared about each other. They were tight and shared everything, maybe too much sometimes, if you want to know the truth, but the extent of my involvement with Roxanne is that she was my wife's friend. Other than socializing, I didn't have anything to do with her."

"Did you dislike Miss Ruiz?" Morales asked quickly.

Nick stuck his hands in his pants pockets. "Frankly, I don't know how I feel about Roxanne at this moment. Can you blame me?"

"Just one more thing, Mr. Chance." Morales said. "Our final report rules out any reason to believe the accident was anything but just that. Do you have any issue at all with that conclusion?"

"Was it ever in doubt that it was an accident?"

"There were no skid marks from Miss Ruiz's car."

"And the seat belts on the passenger side were cut," Detective Strain added. "But we think the EMTs did that at the scene when they were trying to get Miss Ruiz out of the car."

Nick's back twitched and he stared at the floor. I pressed myself against the hallway wall but kept my eyes glued to the men. I prayed Nick didn't know I was standing there.

Nick looked at Morales. "The guy driving the truck was drunk, right?"

"Blood alcohol was one-point-five."

"So bottom line, a drunk destroyed a couple of families and walked away alive. Unfair, but it happens every day of the year, right? Some of them do it more than once. Maybe the cops should start shooting the drunk sons of bitches at the scene. Save everyone a lot of heartache." Nick cracked his knuckles.

I inhaled sharply and the floor under me creaked.

For a moment the house was dead silent.

Finally, Morales said, "That's a pretty harsh suggestion."

"It's pretty harsh having your wife ripped to pieces by three tons of steel."

Morales nodded. "If I haven't said it before, you have our condolences on your loss, Mr. Chance. I don't think we'll need anything more." The detective snapped his notebook closed and stuck it in his jacket.

I dared to move my head a fraction so I could see more of the living room. Morales shook Nick's hand and the three men walked to the front door.

As soon as Nick opened the door I turned and hurried back into the bedroom and crawled under the covers. I wanted Nick to come back and lay beside me. I wanted him to hold me again, to come back to the cocoon of just 'us' that we'd shared a few minutes ago.

I heard Nick walk down the hallway and go into the bathroom. Water ran and then he walked toward the kitchen. The refrigerator door creaked. I hoped he was getting us something to drink. I was parched but couldn't make myself move. I felt like a boneless mass of flesh.

What is he thinking right now? Is he making peace with what we just shared? Is he trying hard to accept the reality that I'm really here?

Suddenly I thought of Michael Cimino. I would never forgive his lying rant to the police. But a new awareness rushed into my brain, a reality I had not focused on before.

Convincing Nick of my true identity was only part of the difficulties ahead. I was trapped inside a body everyone else we knew recognized as Roxanne's. There was no way to explain to the world in general, including that scum Michael, who I really was. When Michael, or anyone else, neighbors, co-workers, Nick's extended family, saw us together, it would surely lead to a gossip fest scandal that might never go away.

Everyone would be whispering and wondering how Nick and Roxanne could be so cozy after Cathy's tragic death. They would wonder, the way I did, if their relationship had started before the accident. And if today's visit from the cops was any indication, there would be many more conspiracy theories and vicious rumors to contend with.

I'd have to quit my job. We'd have to move.

I sighed and put the pillow over my head. This was too complicated to think about right now, but I would bet Nick had already started to wrestle with it.

Pushing the pillow off my head, I opened my mouth to call him when I heard the front door slam. A moment later, Nick's car started and screamed off down the street. I lay still, disbelieving.

On trembling legs I dragged myself out of the bedroom and into the kitchen. The same messy emptiness I had come into hours before greeted me.

But there was a piece of paper, the car rental agreement, lying in the middle of the kitchen table. I walked closer. Nick had scrawled something on it in black marker.

'I won't do this.'

After I stared at the words, I collapsed in a chair and put my head in my hands and cried harder than I ever had.

I'd found a way to say the unsayable, finally come home to my husband, to all my own things and our memories. But he wouldn't take the next step and stand with me against the world.

I was alive, but what good was that if I could not convince my husband? What good was this miracle life if I lost Nick?

I walked to the sink and drank some water out of the glass Nick had used, but it didn't soothe my constricted throat. I eyed the large carving knife lying in the sink, then dumped dish liquid over everything and washed all the dishes, furiously scouring away dried cereal, egg yolk, grease. I left it all to drain and scrubbed the counters and tables. Then I attacked the refrigerator, ridding it of old food and empty cartons. I carried the trash outside, my brain numbed.

As I walked back into the house, the phone rang. I stood still and listened. Was it Nick, calling to tell me to stay there, he was on his way home? I took a step as the machine clicked on, but the caller did not leave a message.

I put on my clothes. Washed my face. The image in the mirror now looked like no one I knew. Not Roxanne, not Cathy, just a desolate stranger.

I circled slowly through the house, staring at every wall and room, memorizing all the details. I didn't know when I'd be back.

In the bedroom I saw a vase on the dresser, filled with dead flowers; roses I'd picked weeks ago that Nick had not thrown away. There were also piles of clothes, and dust motes hovering in all the corners. I rubbed my cheek against the robe I'd given Nick for Christmas.

It felt familiar, but it seemed as if everything I remembered was from years, not weeks, ago. When I opened my closet I saw Nick had not given my clothes to the Salvation Army as I'd imagined. But as I looked through them, dragging the hangers across the closet rod, I realized they wouldn't fit this new, smaller body I now inhabited.

The accident had truly changed everything and nothing else would ever be the same again. Even if Nick someday accepted that the soul, spirit and memory inside this body

SECRET SISTER | 251

were mine, he might always look at the physical exterior and see only Roxanne.

I grabbed my favorite sweatshirt and wrapped it around my shoulders. I let myself out the patio door and went back to Roxanne's car. But I just sat there for a long time, hoping Nick would come home.

I knew he wouldn't. I prayed he wasn't drinking. I didn't know what to do.

As dusk settled around me, I finally started the car and headed back to the apartment, watching my house on Manderly Drive grow smaller in the rearview mirror. And I prayed to all the powers of the universe to please take care of Nick.

It was he who needed a guardian angel now, not me.

After one in the morning, the phone in Roxanne's apartment rang. "Hello," I said on the second ring, swimming up from a dark hole of sleep.

"Roxanne? It's Bradley. Did you call and leave a message earlier tonight? You didn't say your name, and your voice sounded so strange."

I had. I'd called Nick at home twice every hour until midnight, and then left a message for Bradley, hoping he could help. "Yes, I did. Where are you?" There was music in the background.

"I'm at a party. But I just checked my messages and got worried when I heard you say you needed me to do something right away. Is everything okay?"

No, nothing is okay. "Bradley, I need you to do me a big favor."

"What?"

"Call Nick. And if he doesn't pick up at home or on his cell, can you go by his place and see if his car is there?"

Silence.

"Bradley?"

"I'm here, Roxanne. What's going on?"

I took a deep breath. "Nick got picked up for being drunk a few days ago. I'm worried about him, and I don't think Zoë is staying at his house tonight. But I think he's having a really tough time, and I hoped—"

"He's drinking? You're kidding!"

"No, no, he had a relapse last week. He passed out in his car and the cops hauled him off to the hospital."

"How do you know this? Did you see Nick *after* the other night at Simone's?" Bradley was clearly shocked he hadn't heard this directly from Nick.

"Yes. I've seen him a couple of times since then."

A second round of silence. "You have? So what's up with that?"

I knew Bradley was trying hard to keep from asking me more direct questions. "It's hard to explain." I stopped, ambushed by a thought. Did Bradley know about Roxanne's affair? The abortion?

Would he know who her lover was?

"Rox? Are you still there?"

I focused. "Sorry. I'm zoning out. So, Bradley, can you go now if you can't get him on the cell?"

"Yes. Of course. Geez, I can't believe Nick's drinking. Is he going to meetings?"

"He said he was."

"Well, that's a good sign. I'm a few minutes away in Eagle Rock. Shall I come by and see you afterward, or in the morning? We can talk about everything that's going on. With you and Michael. And Nick."

I pinched my hand. "Sure, we can get together tomorrow. But could you call me when you get in tonight? I'd like to know what you found out. That Nick's okay."

"Yes, I will. But wait a minute, did you already try to call him at home?"

"I did. But I don't know if he's there and just not answering." I took a breath. "If he is there, he wouldn't pick up if he thought it was me. And I don't want to go over there. We had words earlier today."

"Words?"

"A fight. Please, Bradley, it's really complicated. I can't explain it all now."

"Okay, okay. I'm leaving as we speak. Talk to you as soon as I know anything." The line went dead. Wide awake now, I put the phone beside me on the pillow.

I covered my chilled body with blankets and wondered for the hundredth time if my husband and Roxanne had been lovers. I shuddered and blocked the images of them lying together in this bed.

Only one thing Nick had said today, his vicious, "Are you that jealous?" gave me a shred of hope that he had not betrayed me. And while he'd told the cops he only knew Roxanne through me, did that prove he hadn't slept with her and fathered her child?

The phone shrieked and I jumped and dragged myself back into a sitting position. The caller ID said private. "Hello?" No one answered. "Hello," I said again.

"Cathy," a male voice whispered softly. The hair on the back of my neck rose. Who would call me by my true name? "Who is this?"

"It's Ryan Seth, Cathy. My wife and I are at Simone's Restaurant. Nick is here, too. I think you should come."

I swallowed. "Did he ask you to call me?"

"No," Seth said. "But I think this is a good time to talk to him."

"I'll be right there."

This is it. Seth and I could convince Nick together. Nick would believe Seth. He would listen to him.

Wouldn't he?

The phone rang again. Bradley's voice, leaving me a message that Nick wasn't at home or picking up on his cell. I pulled on my shoes. I had to go.

My husband was waiting.

Chapter 21

Tuesday, August 2, 2 a.m.
Cathy at Simone's

Most of the lights at Simone's restaurant were off when I drove into the parking lot. I recognized Nick's car and Jen's Mercedes. The last, a sleek white BMW, must belong to Seth's wife.

I stood in the entry a moment, letting my eyes adjust to the candlelight. There was a fire going in the main dining room.

Jen waved and called out to me. "We're over here."

The café smelled of flowers and baked bread and some rich wine sauce that had been cooking all night. My stomach said I was famished, but I could not imagine taking a bite of food. I made my way through the chairs and empty tables to where Jen was sitting with a slender, silver-haired woman.

The woman rose halfway from her chair. "Hello. I'm Inga Olson, Seth's wife. Please, come sit. Would you like some wine? Jen recommended a wonderful chardonnay tonight."

"Yes, please, I'd love a glass," I said.

Jen pulled a glass from the cart behind her and held it for the woman to fill. I had seen pictures of Seth's wife, but in person she was far more beautiful, like an art deco hood ornament on a vintage Rolls Royce, elegant and unattainable.

Inga handed me the glass, her pale fingers tipped with scarlet polish. "Drink up, my dear."

"Thanks." Wondering what Seth had told these two women, I took a large gulp of wine and welcomed the buzz and warmth coursing through me. "Where is Seth?"

Jen looked toward the alcove off the hall. "He's in the private dining room. He said to tell you to relax for a few minutes while he talks to Nick."

I sat beside Inga, who wore a blue silk tunic that matched her eyes, and a lavender scarf around her long neck. Next to Jen, ever chic in a black satin dress, they looked like a Vogue cover for an issue on eternal beauty.

I glanced at my jeans and the baggy gray sweatshirt with 'Ohio State University' in faded letters. I'd taken it from my closet because it was one of the few things I'd kept that had belonged to my mom. My hair was a straggly mess and my makeup nonexistent. I drank more wine, thinking it ironic how quickly I'd transformed the gorgeous Roxanne Ruiz into a bag lady.

"How long has Nick been here?" I asked Jen.

"He came in about ten tonight."

"Is he okay?"

Jen raised her brows. "He was very low key. He ordered dinner which he didn't eat and then asked Eduardo, his waiter, to bring a bottle of champagne to the table."

Inga lit a cigarette. It was illegal to smoke on the grounds of a commercial establishment in California, but Jen ignored her.

Inga blew out a smoky cloud, which hung over us like a ghost. We sat in silence and drank, three chatty women without a word to say.

A moment later Seth walked up to our table. I'd never seen him with a cane before. He used it surely and discreetly, moving past chairs and tables without mishap. He looked more handsome than I had ever seen him in dark turtleneck, pants and jacket. The firelight glinted off his skull and the lenses of his sunglasses.

"Inga?" he said.

"Here, darling. With Jen and another lovely friend."

"Hello, Dr. Seth." I got up and gave him a hug. Inga stood beside me.

"Glad you could come by," he said gently. "Why don't you go in and talk with Nick."

"How is he?" I asked.

"He's about how you would expect him to be. I talked with him awhile, but he needs a friend now, not a therapist. He's miserable. But not lost."

My heart raced at these words. It seemed as if Seth spoke to me in code, one I didn't have the key to. I glanced at Jen. She stared at me, her black eyes betraying nothing of what she knew and little of what she thought.

"Does he know I'm here?"

"No." Seth settled beside his wife, his arm encircling her possessively. "I didn't tell him I called you. But since *you* were all he talked about, I made the decision to put you in front of him as a favor to the boy." He waved toward the small dining room. "Enough stalling. Go join him. Find out what's on our friend's mind."

I put the wineglass down. "How late are you staying tonight, Jen?"

"As late as you need. Inga and Ryan and I still have half a bottle of wine to drink before their soufflé is done. We're here for awhile."

I walked toward the hallway, my heart racing. Nick had probably spent the evening thinking about everything and wanted to ask me for a little time. He was probably going to tell me we had to go slow. That he knew there would be problems with people accepting this strange, unexplainable event. But he'd want us to be together in the end.

I smiled, so sure it was going to work out that I had to fight to keep myself from running. Candlelight flickered from the wall sconces and Nick's profile loomed in the shadows.

My breath caught at the sight of him, leaning back in his chair at a corner table, his arms crossed. His bruised face was gorgeous to me, full of our shared history. A wine bucket sat in the center of the small table, an opened bottle of champagne inside. There were two sparkling wine flutes beside him.

"Nick." The sight of the opened alcohol shocked me but I couldn't keep a smile from spreading across my face.

When he saw me, he sat upright and ran his left hand through his hair three times quickly, as if his fingers were a comb. The gesture was so familiar, tears welled in my eyes, but they dried before they fell.

Nick wore the same clothes, jeans and a blue dress shirt, that he'd had on earlier when he'd left the house. He looked more presentable than I did.

I stopped at the chair opposite his. "May I sit?"

Nick nodded. "Be my guest."

"Are you going to run out on me again?"

"I'll try not to." He narrowed his eyes.

I glanced at the bottle and saw the glasses were dry. "So, where did you go after you left the house?"

"I went to the vet, to help Zoë with the cat. The doc found two stingers in her flank. They dug them out and put her on an IV with some antibiotics. I'll bring her home tomorrow. The vet said we saved the cat's life, getting the stingers out today. They were abscessed."

I nodded.

"So you were right about that," he added.

"Good."

His left eyelid twitched. "After the vet, I took Zoë to my mom's. Then I took a drive up into the Verdugo hills. Then I went to an AA meeting before ending up here." Nick moved his eyes to the bottle.

"Are you going to drink tonight?" I whispered.

Nick chuckled without a trace of humor. "You're nothing if not consistent, I've got to hand that to you, Rox." He sighed. "No. I'm not going to drink. I'm going to pour a toast to my wife. It's the eighth anniversary of buying our house. A special day."

August 1. I'd forgotten that we'd closed on the house on this date. Before I could think how to reopen the conversation that had ended so dramatically this afternoon, Nick spoke softly.

"How did you find me here? Did Jen call you?"

"No. Seth did."

"Oh." He laughed. "Must be the *devil winds*."

"What?"

"It's a private joke."

"Oh." I knew I had to go slow. I pinched my left hand. "What now? Did you talk to Seth about me? Did he tell you he knows?"

"Knows what?" Nick asked. "That you think, or at least say you think, that you are Cathy?"

"I *am* Cathy." My voice rose. "Didn't today prove that to you?"

"All today proved was that I'm not the man I thought I was."

His words cut into my heart like jagged glass. "Seth believes me. Doesn't that mean anything to you? Did he tell you I came to see him? That he asked me a hundred questions about things only Cathy could know? Did he?"

"No, he didn't tell me that."

I slumped back in the chair and felt as if this afternoon had never happened.

"You look like you could use a drink," Nick said. "Shall I pour you one?"

"No, thanks. Not much for me to celebrate, is there?"

For an instant his face held compassion, but it quickly vanished. "I'm leaving," he said. "I told Seth I decided to quit my job and bum around a little. Maybe go to Europe."

"When?"

"As soon as I can. In the next couple of weeks for sure. I need to get away from all the memories. Get over Cathy's death. Well, not get over it, but learn how to live with it." He met my eyes. "I need to start over."

'Without you,' he didn't add, but those unspoken words crowded into the room with us. I wanted to grab him and shake him, but I couldn't move.

Nick leaned on the table. "When I was talking to Seth earlier, I told him about our conversation today. Everything you said and asked me about. I told him I lied to you when I said I didn't know about the abortion. He told me I should level with you, tell you the truth. He said that I owed it to Cathy."

My heartbeat slowed and I felt dizzy. Was he saying Seth didn't believe me, either?

"Okay," I said. "So tell me."

He didn't blink. "When you stayed with Cathy and me, last November, you told me, when we were alone in the kitchen in the middle of the night, that you were pregnant. I was shocked."

I thought I might stop breathing.

Nick looked beyond me into the shadows. "You said you'd been having an affair with Freddy Apodoca, Cathy's friend Vera's husband."

My mind hummed with this news, shaken at the extent of Roxanne's secret life, but my shock was overshadowed by elation. Roxanne hadn't won my husband to her bed. Nick was faithful; he had not cheated.

"Thank God it was Freddy . . ."

Nick's face was impassive. "You asked me to drive you to a clinic the next day, and not to tell Cathy. You said you couldn't go to your mother because you didn't trust her to help you and not throw it in your face for the rest of your life. And you said you couldn't ask for Cathy's help because she and Vera were very close." He stopped and fished out a mint and popped it in his mouth.

"I told you 'no' at first, Roxanne, but you begged me. You said things wouldn't ever be the same between you and Cathy if Cathy found out what you and Freddy had done. You spilled that Vera had been taking hormone treatments for years, trying to get pregnant. Had even tried in-vitro, but it had failed. Plus she's hardcore Catholic, and if Cathy told Vera about you and Freddy, Vera would probably try to get you to keep the baby so she could raise it."

"Roxanne would never do that," I blurted out.

Nick's eyes narrowed. "*You* said it was too complicated to resolve any other way but by ending the pregnancy and what you really cared about most was that Cathy not find out. You said she was the only real friend you ever had and you wouldn't be able to go on living if Cathy broke off being friends with you."

"I would never have abandoned her."

Nick shook his head at my words. "I knew you had tried to kill yourself before, Roxanne. So I believed what you said, that you didn't have anyone else to ask."

"But why not tell your wife?" I asked. I wasn't overjoyed he'd kept such a thing from me, but I was thrilled to find out that Nick was true to me. And now I expected to hear him say he hadn't told me because he didn't want me to be hurt about Roxanne feeling she couldn't trust me.

But instead, he said something very different.

"Why didn't I tell Cathy? I didn't admit the real reason to myself until today. When I left the house earlier, driving down the street, I had one of those self-awareness moments people write books about." His glance ran over my face and down my neck and chest, then back to my eyes. "Today I admitted to myself that I've been attracted to you since the first day I met you, Roxanne."

I couldn't speak.

Nick's eyes glistened. "I've thought about your body more often than you might believe over the years, and I betrayed my wife with you in my imagination more than once. So I think that night in my kitchen, it was my dick I was thinking about, not Cathy's feelings. I think I kept your secret, and helped you out, because my reptilian male brain thought someday I might get something from you in return. Something like I got today."

He looked like he hated Roxanne, but hated himself even more. Then he leaned back in the chair and waited for me to reply.

"That's a lie," I protested. I clutched the tablecloth in both hands. "And I know it's a lie because I know you. I'm your wife and it doesn't surprise or hurt me that you were attracted to Roxanne. Every man who ever met her, including our gay friend Bradley, is sexually attracted to her. A person can't control their mind from fantasizing about having sex with someone."

I crossed my arms over my chest. "I know *that* from experience. But the important fact is that you never betrayed me. You were honorable and empathetic when you helped Roxanne, and kind to try shielding me from the pain I would have felt if I knew about Freddy and the abortion. Everything you've said here tonight has only made me love you more, not less. You're being too hard on yourself."

I stretched my hand across the table to him, but Nick didn't move. Instead, he met my eyes. "For Christ's sake, Roxanne, this fantasy of yours is going to lead to more grief. I just told you the God's honest truth, and you can't accept it. I'm sorry, but that's the last thing I've got to say about the past. Get some psychiatric help, and leave me alone."

After he spoke those cruel things, relief seemed to flash across his face.

No matter what he said now, I wouldn't accept it. I knew Nick *did* believe I might be Cathy. I had seen it in his eyes when he held me earlier today. My husband had believed he was holding *Cathy* in his arms. He was with *me*, Cathy, movement for movement, caress for caress. He had let his guard down and given in to instinct and accepted the truth.

But when the passion was sated and the cops showed up full of Michael Cimino's gossip, he had reverted back to his logical, 'trust only what you see' self.

I took a deep breath. "You've always been such an honorable man, Nick—"

"Honor doesn't have anything to do with me, or *you*," he interrupted. "I lied to Cathy when I kept your secret. And I concealed things from her, like when I called you about how you were feeling, and when I stopped over to check on you a couple of times. And I continued to lie over the next few weeks, including when Cathy and I went away at Christmas, when she asked me if I thought you had been acting strange."

Nick twisted his napkin into a knot. "Do you know she was worried about you the whole time we were in New Mexico? I never told her what I knew. It's the only time I ever lied to Cathy. I betrayed the one promise I'd made to my wife, and now she's gone and I can't ever tell her I'm sorry. Thank God she'll never know about what happened today."

For the first time since I realized who I was, I confronted the reality that I might not win him back. My brain froze, for I was almost out of energy. Nick was ready to move on with his life, to fall back into his disbelief in my identity, and put his sins, real and imagined, behind him. And, imagined or not, in his heart I *was* one of those sins.

Nick stood and threw some money on the table. "I'm sorry for what happened earlier today, Roxanne. I never should have let it go that far." He touched my shoulder and said in a spent voice, "There's no reason for us to see each other again. Take care of yourself."

Then he walked away.

"You're *not* the man I thought you were, Nick." I got up and hurried after him.

He turned.

"The man I love wouldn't give up on me if there were the smallest, one in a million miracle chance that what I said was true. He would listen to his heart, and trust the truth when he heard it. He would believe *me*."

Nick's eyes glittered but he said nothing.

"If you won't take a risk and give me a little more time to convince you that, despite what your eyes tell you, it really is me, then you're going to lose me, Nick. You're going to lose us."

Nick shook his head. "Roxanne, what you're saying can't be true. You know that. I don't believe you, and frankly, who would?"

"Okay," I whispered. "You win. But just remember, your wife fought for you, Nick. Her love is real."

He turned and left without speaking again.

And what, really, was there left to say?

Only goodbye.

Chapter 22

Monday, August 15, 7 p.m.
Nick at Ryan Seth's Office

I'd been sitting in Seth's reception area about fifteen minutes, an unusually long time. He was good about not keeping his clients waiting, although I wasn't here for an appointment. I'd called to tell him I was leaving town and he'd asked me to stop by so he could say goodbye in person.

I stared at my watch. It was nine minutes after seven and my plane left at midnight. Just as I considered calling in to the answering service to check if Seth was behind the closed door, his wife, Inga, knocked on the window outside.

"Nick. Hi there." She walked in. "Seth phoned up to the house a minute ago and asked me to see if you were here. He's had an emergency with one of his patients, but he'll be here soon."

"Oh, nothing bad, I hope," I replied.

Inga pursed her lips. "Very bad, I'm afraid. A suicide. A sweet young woman he's been seeing only a few weeks. She'd tried several times before. I'll never understand how people can give up when there is so much to live for."

Her words shocked me. They seemed indiscreet from a therapist's wife. I thought of the young Asian woman with the bandaged wrists I'd seen a few weeks ago.

I wondered how much Seth told Inga about his clients. *Like me.* I couldn't guess what he might have told her about my story, or about Roxanne, or the other night at Simone's.

"Thanks for bringing the message," I said.

"No problem. It's nice to see you again." She draped herself over the only other chair in the tiny room and lit up a cigarette.

I rubbed my hands on my thighs, unsure of what to say. Inga was incredibly good looking; tall and curvy, with eyes as blue as the Pacific. Though her hair was silvery, it did nothing to make her seem past her prime. In every way she was sexy and alluring. I smiled nervously.

She returned it. "Seth told me you were going to Europe for a while."

Obviously he did talk about people he saw professionally. "Yeah. France."

"Oh, how wonderful. Where, exactly?"

"Outside Paris, Bougival. I've rented a place for a few months."

"Bougival? Umm, so you're interested in the French Impressionists, are you?"

"Well, only because of my wife. She minored in art history in college and loved Claude Monet. She said some of his paintings were of the area, so I thought I'd go look around. See if the bridge he painted in Cathy's favorite painting is still there."

"That's very romantic of you, Nick. Is that something you planned to do together, before the accident?"

I cringed. "No. We never discussed doing that. It's something I came up with myself."

"But what about your work?" Inga's blue gaze stayed on my face. "Aren't you a musician of some kind?"

"No, I used to want to be one, but I work for an insurance company, and they agreed to let me take a year's leave of absence."

"A year?" She raised her eyebrows. "Always fun to think of what a year can bring, isn't it? Maybe enough time to become a musician."

"Now there's an idea." I didn't want to talk about my plans for the future. I didn't have any. Only to get away and not think about Cathy, or deal with Roxanne. My mind flashed on that afternoon in bed with her and my hands began to sweat. "I love music, but I have no real talent. I'm tone deaf, I think."

"The deaf can learn other ways to hear." Inga blew a smoke ring and rubbed a spot on her neck. "I'm sure Seth said you were a rock and roll kind of guy."

My pulse percolated. I had no clue what Inga was thinking. I seldom got the implications of what women meant versus what they said. Cathy always laughed about that. She said it was an endearing male quality, but lately it seemed a critical deficiency.

"No," I said. "No rock and roll here. Seth might have been referring to one of my jobs in the past. I was a disc jockey at KRLA, in Pasadena, a long time ago. Before I got a real job."

"I remember that station! When I was a med student at USC, that was a good one. Crazy, sexy DJs playing all the classic stuff. The Beatles. The Doors. Bob Dylan! *Real music.* Not like my daughter listens to today. All those whiny girl singers talking about revenge, or rappers boasting about fancy cars and getting shot. I do love Adele, though. She sings about those things that never change. Men and women, and how they love and *hurt* each other."

My uneasiness increased. "A lot of critics say popular music reflects the times in a society more than any other art form."

"Maybe. But how does anyone make love with one of those songs playing in the background? I heard a Jay Z song this morning. He said, 'I've got 99 problems but a bitch ain't one.' That's not at all seductive, is it?"

"Ah, no. I guess not." But it was sure applicable to me,

which I thought was what Inga might be reaching for. "So, ah, you're a doctor, too?"

Inga snubbed out the cigarette on the bottom of her shoe and tossed the butt into the trashcan. "Yes. I'm a plastic surgeon."

"That must be interesting."

"Oh, it's like working at an auto body shop, patching over problems. People are what's interesting in life. Their stories, their personalities. My profession requires me to interact with them during stressful periods, if they've been injured, or ill. So yes, I guess it is *interesting*. But not fun." She got to her feet. "Surely not as *fun* as being a DJ."

The office door opened and Seth stepped out. "Nick, are you here?"

"Hello, darling." Inga walked to him and planted a kiss on his head as she pressed the length of her body against his. "Nick Chance has been keeping me company, telling me about his plans for France. You didn't tell me he was such a romantic young man."

Seth put his hand on Inga's pale face as if he were seeing her with his fingers. He kissed her fully on the mouth. For a moment they seemed lost in each other and oblivious of me.

Finally, Seth nodded in my direction. "I didn't know he was a romantic young man. Come in, Nick."

I got up, tense from the vibes of sexual communication between Inga and Seth. It made me sick with longing. I followed Seth into his office, remembering how it felt to pull Cathy's body next to me, knowing I could have her, do anything to her I wanted to, when we were alone.

I shut the door and walked into the middle of the room. Outside the glass walls of Seth's office, the late August sky was darkening. Seth snapped on a light on his desk and the bulb dimmed and sizzled and then went out. Seth couldn't see it was nearly dark, and he evidently didn't understand the significance of the sound, as he made no attempt to put in a new bulb.

He seemed preoccupied. "Make yourself comfortable, Nick. I'm glad you could come to say goodbye. What time is your flight?"

I told him and we talked for a couple of minutes in the darkness about the security at the airport, the food, the length of the flight. We fell into an awkward silence, at least on my part. I glanced at Seth and he was leaning back in his rattan chair, very still.

"Inga mentioned you lost one of your patients today. That must suck," I said.

Seth frowned, his brow wrinkling. "Inga talks too much sometimes. But you are correct. Anytime someone gives up on life, it is very difficult to accept. You question yourself, feel like you could have or should have done more. Especially in this case. A beautiful girl. She'd recently suffered a severe disappointment in her personal life, but still . . ."

Something in his voice, some undercurrent of criticism, increased my discomfort. I shifted in my chair. "Everyone can't be saved. I think you told me that once."

Seth didn't reply.

I took a breath. "Well, as I told you on the phone, I'm heading to Europe for a few months. I got a lease on a flat and a lead on a job at a small radio station. They play American rock standards. I'm hoping they'll let me lend a hand, maybe even do some on-air stuff."

"Can you find AA meetings there?"

"Yes. I called the embassy in Paris and they told me AA is everywhere. There may be a bit of a language barrier, but the feelings should come through loud and clear." I laughed and the noise I made sounded more like a yelp.

"See, you are gifted, too, like your sister. It's a great asset to be able to understand emotion without benefit of the words that explain it. Bravo."

I wasn't sure about that, but I didn't argue. Instead, I asked the question I suddenly knew was the real reason I'd come to see Seth tonight. "Have you spoken to Roxanne since that night at Simone's?"

"Yes."

I waited. "How's she doing?"

I waited some more.

"Is the light on?" Seth asked suddenly. He got out of the chair and put his hand against the side of the lampshade. "Why didn't you tell me the bulb was out?" He opened a desk drawer and pulled out a new one. He took the shade off and tried to unscrew the bulb. It appeared to be stuck.

"Can I help with that?" I asked.

"No, no, I can get it. But I don't like my clients to be in the dark. You should have said something." Skillfully he screwed the new bulb in and flicked it on. He raised his hand as if feeling the heat from a campfire, and sat. Seth seemed weary tonight, and I noticed a few gray hairs in his bushy eyebrows.

"Now, what was that you asked?" Seth said.

"How's Roxanne?" I repeated.

"What do you mean?"

Great, Seth is in that mood. "I just wondered how she was doing."

"In what way?"

"Has she stopped saying crap about how she's not Roxanne, and all that bullshit?" My hands shook. I ran them through my hair and realized my emotions were pretty goddamned out of control. I wanted to get to the airport. I pictured the cart on the plane that held all those little bottles of scotch, and swallowed.

"So you don't believe her?" Seth asked.

"No. Of course not. It's absurd, like something out of a horror movie. Which is where Roxanne belongs, if you ask me. She was always jealous of Cathy. I think she's taking advantage of this situation, and trying to ditch her own past and latch onto Cathy's."

Seth sat very still, his hands grasping the sides of his chair. "Have you always felt Roxanne was unstable enough to try and pull something like that off?"

"I don't know. No, I guess not. I'm not saying she's nuts or anything." I put my head in my hands. All I could think of was lying in bed, my arms around the only woman who had ever made me feel whole. Tears stung my eyes and I squeezed them away, glad Seth couldn't see me.

"She was very upset after you left Simone's that night." Seth spoke softly, as if relating a bedtime story. "I talked to her for a bit that evening, and a couple of times over the next few days. But I haven't talked to her for about a week. She's been at the hospital day and night."

I jerked my head up quickly. "The hospital?"

"Yes, she's at the hospital caring for Betty Haverty, who is very ill. Ovarian cancer. Terminal, from what I understand."

"Jesus." I was shocked. Beyond shocked.

Seth fell into another distracted silence. A chime struck in the distance, measuring the half-hour.

"Well, I wish you well on your journey, Nick. Let me hear from you. Send a card." Seth stood.

I struggled out of the chair. "Thanks. And hey, tell Roxanne, if you see her, I'm sorry about her mom."

He grasped my hand. "I'm no good at passing messages, Nick. If you want to say something, you should say it yourself."

"You don't really believe any of what she says, do you, Seth?"

We stood gripping each other's hands. I felt like I couldn't breathe, as if something important was about to be revealed.

But it wasn't. Seth squeezed my hand and walked with me to the door. The light glinted off the sleek, silver frames of his sunglasses. "Are you asking me if I believe what she says happened to her is the *truth as she knows it?* I'm blind, not deaf, you know. And in my line of work, it's very easy to *hear* honesty and sincerity. And that's what I hear."

"But it's crazy! It's science fiction, for fuck's sake. You can't think that, that during the accident . . ." I couldn't form more words for a moment. "You don't believe she really *could be* Cathy, do you?"

Seth crossed his arms. "Do you find my wife desirable, Nick?"

"What?"

"Do you think Inga is beautiful? Sexy? Do you think most men would want her, want to go to bed with her if they had the opportunity?"

"I, uh, yes. I guess. Yes. Yes, of course."

"So you would agree with me if I said she could probably have her pick of men?"

"Yes."

He nodded and then reached up and took off his sunglasses. I gasped. His eyes, what should have been his eyes, were a mass of reddish-purple scar tissue, a smear of flesh grown over one eye socket, an empty hole where the left eyeball should have been.

"Sorry for the shock." Seth slipped his glasses back on. "Inga never knew me before the accident that did this. She didn't fall in love with me first, and then have that reservoir of love to overcome this horror. Instead, like people with great spirit and loving souls, Inga listened to me with her heart, and looked past my outer self.

"Despite what her sight, and logic, told her, she trusted I wasn't what I looked like, which was a damaged and unlovable mate. She trusted instead what she felt. Inga's loving me taught me to believe in the inexplicable, Nick. To trust that sometimes, what can't be explained is still true. So yes, to answer your question, I do believe Cathy's story."

I couldn't speak, or argue.

He walked the rest of the way to the door. "Betty Haverty is at Sierra Monte Hospice, the Spanish style building behind St. Anne's church on Alpha Drive. If you want to stop there before your plane leaves, I'm sure they'd let you in. The people that run the place are lenient with visiting hours for the dying."

"Dying?" I pictured the red-headed woman I'd seen at the Schribner Insurance office. "I saw her a few weeks ago and she looked fine."

"Life is a gift, no guarantees from moment to moment. You know that." Seth opened the door. "Let me know when you get back to the U.S. of A." He patted my back as I walked by, and then closed the door of his office, leaving me in the waiting room, which still smelled faintly of smoke.

Thirty minutes before when I'd stood on this spot, I'd known exactly what the immediate future was going to bring. I was headed to the airport. I would have dinner, buy a magazine. Fly to New York, then on to Paris. Tomorrow I would be thousands of miles away from my past, from Roxanne, safe with my memories of Cathy.

Now as I walked out of the waiting room and into that dark summer night, I was sure of nothing.

The nurse at the desk at the hospice said Betty Haverty was in room nine.

"Is her daughter with her?" I asked.

"Yes, I think she is still here. She was reading to her earlier tonight. Are you a friend of Roxanne's?"

"Thank you." I headed down the corridor and found Betty alone in the room.

I was stunned at her appearance, and had I not been told who she was, I would not have recognized her. Her hair was gray at the roots and grown out an inch or so where it faded into a pale red. Her sallow skin stretched gauntly over the bones of her face.

She squinted at the door when I knocked. "Who's there?" Her voice was sticky with drugs.

"It's Nick Chance, Mrs. Haverty. May I come in?"

"Nick?" She didn't say anything else for a few moments and I wondered if she'd fallen asleep. "Please come in, Nick," she whispered.

I sat in the wooden chair beside her bed. She was hooked to an IV, but there were no other pieces of medical equipment in the room. There were two bouquets of flowers, and a stack of books and magazines. There were also several prints of paintings taped to the wall by the window.

I recognized many of them, by Monet, Pissaro, and Van Gogh. *The Old Bridge at Bougival* was pasted onto a piece of purple construction paper, eye level across from her bed. Cathy's favorite painting. I had taken her to see it twice, when visiting my relatives in the east. She sat and cried when she looked at it, but always seemed happier for having done so.

My heart beat faster. "How are you feeling, Mrs. Haverty?" I took her hand, which was dry and hot.

"Not too good, Nick. They discovered that I have the most virulent type of ovarian cancer there is. I don't have too long."

"I'm sorry," I said, overwhelmed.

"Me too."

Silence filled the room. There were low voices in the hallway, and I listened for a familiar one.

"Thanks for coming to see me," Betty said.

"I'm glad to. I've wanted to call you for a few weeks now and tell you I was sorry for my behavior at the insurance office. I acted like a jerk and what I said was unfair. I hope you can forgive me."

"I understand. You were suffering. It's a part of the

grieving process, lashing out." Her eyes closed, then opened wide. She seemed to be trying to focus.

"Is Roxanne around?" I asked.

"She'll be back. She's gone to get me some soda. Orange Crush. I told her I kept thinking of when she was little and we would buy a six-pack of Orange Crush, the kind that came in the tall glass bottles, for a summer treat. She went to get me some, but I don't know if I'll be able to drink it."

I leaned toward her, sorrow swelling in me like an ocean wave. "I have to get going, Mrs. Haverty. I'm catching a plane later. And I don't want to tire you out."

Betty's eyes were watery. "I have good days and bad days, and except for falling asleep every few minutes, this is a good day, actually. So I'm glad to see you. I asked Roxanne to call you a few days ago. She said she left a message but she never heard back from you. I think she was lying. She never did ask you to come, did she?"

"I'm here now."

She laid her hand, light and insubstantial as a bird, on my arm. "You're being tactful. That's good of you. Can you stay a few minutes? There are a couple of things I want to tell you that you don't know. That you should know."

"Of course." Had Roxanne told this woman the same story she'd told me and Seth? I hoped with all my heart she hadn't hurt Betty by trying to convince her that her daughter was actually dead.

"I was married only once, when I was very young. To a Mexican guy, Francisco Ruiz," Betty said. "He was handsome and smart, but wild. Not a good match for me at all. He wanted us to move to Texas because he had family there, and he wanted to get a job in the oil industry. I didn't want to quit college, and told him frankly I didn't plan on being married to a man who worked on an oil rig." Betty shook her head. "I've been a snob my whole life."

I didn't know what to say so I just patted her hand.

"So he left me, and like a lot of people who are jilted, I looked immediately for someone to make me feel good about myself again." Betty's eyes stared off toward the window. "I met another man very quickly after Francisco left me, one night in a bar. A good-looking white-collar type. His name was Padrig Sullivan." Betty's voice caught.

My brain whirred as it processed the information. The name Padrig Sullivan was vaguely familiar, but I couldn't place it. I worked in the insurance industry, which was full of guys with Irish and Italian surnames. I'd known plenty of Sullivans.

Betty swallowed, and I heard her teeth scrape against each other. I asked her if she wanted a drink, but she shook her head.

"Padrig was married, happily he told me the last time I saw him, but he was a drinker and when he drank, he overlooked that fact. I had an affair with him, if you could call a week of sleeping with someone an affair, and I got pregnant with Roxanne. When I told him, he broke off seeing me, and told me he had a wife, who was also pregnant. They moved away to Arizona, I understand, and I had Roxanne with only my mother to help me. It was hard, but I always fantasized he'd come back to me. And to Roxanne. Be a father to her. A girl needs a father to love her, or she'll have many problems with men when she's an adult. That's a pretty well established fact."

Betty ran out of steam then, and closed her eyes. I didn't understand why she was telling me this. Roxanne's father wasn't some guy named Ruiz, and Roxanne had been raised without her real father.

Is she trying to get me to feel sorry for Roxanne?

Betty opened her eyes. "Can you bring me a few of those ice chips in the pitcher?"

I took a spoon and clumsily fed her some.

"Padrig and his wife and their daughter came back to Sierra Monte a couple of years later, when Roxanne was only three. Padrig called when he got back to town, but I wouldn't have anything to do with him if he wasn't going to leave his wife. He died of a heart attack shortly after that. But I met his wife several years later, by accident. She and I were on a PTA committee together. She had remarried but it wasn't working out. She knew I was a professional woman, and asked if I knew a lawyer."

"Did you?"

"Yes. I gave her the name of someone good. But she never got divorced. She died shortly after that. Like Padrig, she was shockingly young. Cancer, I think." She chuckled mirthlessly as if she found this ironic. "I don't think she ever knew about my affair with her husband. And she didn't live to see her daughter grow up, like I got to."

I nodded as if I understood. But I didn't. My throat was tight. I glanced at the pictures taped to the wall and thought about where the closest AA meeting was. I wondered if I had enough time to get there before I had to leave for the airport.

"When Roxanne was about thirteen, I told her the truth about who she was," Betty said softly. "Maybe I shouldn't have." A tear dripped down her cheek.

"No, no I think you did the right thing," I said. "She should know who her father was."

"And who her sister was."

"Sister?" My voice didn't sound normal to my own ears. "I didn't know Roxanne had a sister. Oh, you mean half-sister? Padrig Sullivan's other child?"

"Yes. Catherine. Catherine Lorraine Sullivan." Betty stared directly into my face. "Cathy. Your wife."

Chapter 23

Nick at Sierra Monte Hospice

I gasped and stared at Betty.

"Your Cathy," Betty repeated. "It was a shock to me, when Roxanne met Cathy and took a shine to her. She always referred to Cathy as her 'secret sister' when they became best friends, even before she knew the whole sordid truth about me and Cathy's father. I thought Roxanne would have revealed all this to Cathy at some point, but Rox said a few months ago she never told Cathy this story. She couldn't think of any way to explain the truth without Cathy hating her." Betty's eyes welled with tears.

"But that's insane," I protested. "Cathy would never have blamed Roxanne for something *you* did."

"I agree. But Roxanne said that Cathy's life was a horror after Padrig died, and then Cathy's mother got sick and she was stuck with a stepfather who was a drunk. Roxanne felt Cathy would hate both of us on her mother's behalf, maybe even blame my infidelity with her father for her mother's illness."

"Cathy didn't have it in her to hate anyone."

"You may be right," Betty replied. "But Roxanne has always been so insecure. She never believes anyone will love her unless she's perfect. She's incapable of trusting anyone. Even Cathy. Roxanne loved her, and would have done anything for her, but I don't think my daughter even trusted her. Roxanne told me once that someday she would get the opportunity to do something special for Cathy, to make it up to her about our family's indiscretions. And then the accident happened . . ." Betty's voice collapsed and she closed her eyes.

I sat mute and numb while these facts roiled around my brain. Cathy, *my Cathy*, was Roxanne's half-sister. Cathy's father, who she always referred to as Patrick Sullivan, was Roxanne's father, too.

Happenstance, coincidence, 'twist of fate.' Call it what you will, the story was stunning. A hundred comments over the years from my wife and her friend, about how close they were, how they thought alike, even the funny golden spot in the iris that they both had, suddenly took on a new significance.

"Nick!"

I jumped as Betty opened her eyes, her voice loud and firm. I leaned toward her. "Yes?"

"I told you this because I think it might explain why Roxanne has tried so hard to connect with you lately. I don't know what went on between the two of you last November, with the abortion. She didn't tell me everything. But since the car accident, Roxanne has changed so much. She's different from the daughter she was before. More loving, and more giving. More open and ready for life than I ever dared dream she would be. I don't understand it, Nick, but maybe this change is the gift she hoped to give Cathy."

My thoughts were spinning so fast trying to keep up, I heard humming in my ears. "How do you mean?"

"I think Roxanne is trying to be like Cathy in the hopes that you'll rekindle your affair with her, and she can take care of you *for Cathy*."

Betty stopped talking. Her eyes closed and her breathing, though ragged, fell into a steady rhythm as she fell asleep.

I stood and buried my fingers in my hair, thinking if I pulled on it hard enough, my brain would quiet down and let me think clearly.

Betty had seen changes in her daughter's temperament, demeanor and personality. Everyone who met the 'new' Roxanne commented on these differences.

She wasn't the woman everyone knew before the accident. *But what did it mean?*

Betty thought Roxanne was emulating Cathy because she had a plan to rekindle a love affair with me. Betty didn't know there had *never* been a love affair.

Which proves what? I felt like banging my head against a wall, but I knew it wouldn't help. It wouldn't drown out the only conclusion that bubbled up through the muck inside my head.

Could what Roxanne said be true? Could she really be my wife?

No. It's absurd.

I knew I had to get the hell out of there. I turned to the door and took a step but stopped.

Roxanne stood at the entrance clutching a carton of soda. Her face was pinched and tears flowed in two silent rivulets down her tan cheeks. She had obviously been there long enough to hear what Betty said.

But why would Roxanne be upset at hearing her mother recount that story? That she and Cathy were half-sisters *wasn't* news to her. Roxanne had known the truth for years.

But the shock on her face was real. Roxanne was undone, her body trembling, her nose red and running.

"Are you okay?" I asked.

"No." She stared beyond me at Betty, the tiny gold glint in her eye bright as a lit match against a night sky. "I had a sister? My God, I never, ever guessed. Why didn't Roxanne ever tell me?"

This woman standing in the doorway with her hair pulled back, her gauzy blouse and faded jeans and dangling earrings, should have been the picture of a free spirited California girl. Instead, she was a study in grief.

It can't be.

I told myself Roxanne was pretending, playing this to the hilt. But her shock and grief was too compelling to be faked. Unless she just didn't remember, because of the accident.

I crossed my arms across my chest as the air in the room thinned. If this woman standing here wasn't Roxanne, was it really Cathy, holding vigil at the deathbed of her best friend's mother?

"What are you doing here, Nick?" She set the soda on the floor beside her and leaned against the wall, dashing her tears away with the back of her hand. "I thought you left town."

"I'm leaving soon."

"When?"

"Tonight." I checked my watch. "I should head out now, I guess."

She stuck out her chin as if bracing for a blow. I couldn't begin to imagine what she was thinking.

I didn't know what the fuck *I* was thinking.

"Have a safe trip, Nick," she whispered.

I opened my mouth to say something that was half-forming in my mind, but a gasp from Betty silenced me. Roxanne hurried across the room.

"I'm here, shhhhh." Roxanne's voice was soft as a balm. "What can I get you?"

Betty opened her eyes, but looked past Roxanne and focused on my face. "Nick? Nick Chance, is that you?" She turned to Roxanne and her smile faded. "Oh, hi Cathy. You brought your hubby to see me?" Her voice was hoarse. "He was mad at me before, but he's not now. Can you find Roxanne for me, dear? She said she'd be back soon. She's going to sleep here tonight again. I'm going home tomorrow, but I don't think I can drive."

Roxanne sat and took Betty's hand and curled her own around it. "It's me, Mom. *Roxanne*. Things are a little confusing for you right now. Just go to sleep. Rest, okay?"

Betty squinted and then a rattling sigh escaped. "I'm losing it, Roxanne. It must be the medicine. I'll be a drug addict when I get out of this place. But I *can* see you now. Such a pretty girl. Prettiest girl I ever saw."

"Just close your eyes and rest. I'll be here when you wake up."

Betty closed her eyes. She was snoring in seconds. Roxanne straightened the blankets, ignoring me.

"So you are Roxanne. At least you've finally admitted it," I said. I wasn't ashamed at sounding angry.

She stood up and motioned for me to follow her. Outside in the corridor she glared at me. "The woman is dying, Nick. I told her that to comfort her. It's a kindness I'm doing for her, and for my best friend, for my sister." Her voice roughened. "Can't you understand that?"

"How generous of you. To change identities out of the goodness of your heart."

She looked like she might hit me. For a long moment, she searched my face. "I do have a good heart, Nick. And if Roxanne is who *you* need me to be so you can get on with your life, well, okay. I'm not going to argue with you anymore."

"Good."

"So go. Leave," she said. "Goodbye."

Say what you will about Roxanne, she sure knew my wife well. Because she'd figured out that if this exquisite woman standing so near *had* been my Cathy, this is what she would say and do. Cathy would be empathetic enough to humor a dying friend, would pretend to be Queen Elizabeth if it took away a little pain.

A lump formed in my throat. Around me, everything felt as if it was moving, like a slow motion earthquake. The racket in my head started up again and I wondered if this was how it felt to lose your mind.

I needed a drink. *A hundred drinks*. Anything to get away from this impossible situation.

"Bon voyage, Nick." Roxanne sighed. "Say hello to Bougival for me." She brushed her lips against my cheek and walked down the hallway.

I couldn't think about this anymore.

I looked through the doorway at Betty. How could this woman be so near to dying? A few weeks ago, she was the picture of health.

It was the same as when my dad died. One morning, while I was lying in bed pretending to sleep to get out of doing my chores, he was outside washing the car, mowing the lawn. By late that same afternoon, he was in a morgue, cold and dead, and none of us even got to tell him, 'You were a great dad, thank you, we'll miss you forever.'

A few weeks ago, my wife was bursting with life and good will with a hundred years of future, our future, ahead of her. I never got to tell her she was the best part of my life, the best part of me. I never got to kiss her goodbye.

My hands shook. I balled them into fists and clenched my teeth together. I was a grown man. I lived in the post 9/11 world. I knew life wasn't fair, and that tragedy struck out of nowhere even on a sunny, sky-blue summer day. But I was furious that it was my world that had crumbled.

I looked at the spot where Roxanne had stood a few moments before, but there was no sign of her. I couldn't leave things like I had with her, though I had no idea what else I could say. I knew I should go after her and tell her . . .

Tell her what?

I didn't know. But I had to see her one more time.

I rushed down the hallway, trying to rehearse an articulate, conclusive argument to make it clear to Roxanne that I would never believe her claims about Cathy, but I didn't resent her and wasn't angry with her anymore.

Cathy would want me to do this. She would want me to help her friend. *Her sister!*

My heart raced. I trotted around the corner to the left, following the signs for the lounge. For the first time since Cathy's death, I was doing something positive. I just had to find Roxanne and tell her to let the past go, let the crazy thoughts about what had happened to her dissolve and to believe she would be happy again someday.

The lounge was empty. I retraced my steps, but ended up near the emergency exit. I turned on my heel and a minute later found myself back at the receptionist's desk.

"Did Roxanne Ruiz go by here?" I asked the woman.

She hadn't seen her. She'd just come on duty.

I hurried out to the parking lot, the sunlight fading into shadows around me. The visitor parking lot was empty, except for my car.

Roxanne was gone.

The scream of an ambulance siren blasted out on the street, but I didn't bother to look at it. I walked over to my car, accepting it really was too late for me to try and make peace with Roxanne.

I had a plane to catch. All I had to do now was drive to the airport, crawl inside that wide body, and fly through the night, forevermore to live a day ahead of my old life, thousands of miles away from my loss.

'The Green Parrot' is a gay bar in Silver Lake where Cathy and I used to meet Bradley for drinks. It's in a block of buildings just past the reservoir on Lemon Avenue, a quiet road on the residential edge. The bar stands discreetly between Rosa's, a small Mexican take-out, and a commercial nursery that had been closed for a couple of years.

I'd been sitting in my car in the nursery parking lot since 11:45 p.m., waiting for Bradley. It was now one-thirty in the morning. I looked back at the bright red entry door of the Green Parrot, wishing Bradley could read minds and hear me calling him. He always hung out at this place on Saturday night. When I first spotted his car, I decided not to go inside and look for him. Not that gay bars freaked me out; I just wasn't up to dealing with anyone except Bradley.

But I needed to talk to him about Cathy, about how much I missed her, how I was feeling insane. Bradley would understand. He'd stayed home for six months after Mitch died. And he'd almost overdosed himself—accidentally, he still swears—after his mom passed. I could talk to him about how I was feeling, without him judging me or blaming me, the way Seth seemed to.

I looked at my watch again. One thirty-three. I leaned back and closed my eyes. When I left the hospice clinic a few hours ago, I had driven to LAX, and gone into the terminal, though I never made it to the Air France boarding area. Instead, I sat for a couple of hours at Coco's Bar, a little joint tucked in the International concourse, across from a Bed, Bath and Beyond.

A Scotch was ordered, straight up. It sat on the bar in front of me while I smoked half of the pack of cigarettes I had paid eight bucks for.

The noise inside my head had subsided but I was definitely lightheaded from the cigarettes. I hadn't smoked since high school and I wondered what they were filling them with these days.

Finally I'd folded a ten for the waiter under the untouched booze, and called Zoë from a pay phone. I left a message telling her and her friend Ramon not to come get my car at the airport as we'd planned, because I had changed my mind about flying to France tonight. I told her I loved her and that I was going home instead and would call her tomorrow.

I didn't tell her I was considering driving up to Mt. Wilson and jumping off one of the power station towers later tonight, but if she listened closely, she might have heard the stress in my voice. For about two seconds I had also considered saying, "*I found out tonight that Roxanne and Cathy were actually half-sisters, and Betty Haverty is dying of cancer, and, oh by the way, Roxanne says she isn't Roxanne. She's says she's Cathy.*"

But I didn't. Even in the screwed up state of mind I was in, I wouldn't do that to Zoë. Despite what Seth had said about me being a dick to my family, I always tried to be the brother and son Zoë and my mom deserved.

I opened my eyes and turned toward the bar at the moment Bradley walked out. I fumbled with the car door and nearly fell onto the sidewalk. "Bradley. Hey, wait up!"

He stopped, body language on guard, and then he recognized me and jogged across the street. "Nick. What the hell, dude? I thought you were on a plane."

We shook hands, then hugged and slugged each other on the back. I smelled the hot, sweet scent of whiskey on his breath. It made my mouth ache and I forced myself to swallow. My spit tasted like an ashtray.

"Yeah," I said. "I had a change in plans, buddy. So what's up with you? You're leaving alone? No hotties in there tonight?"

"No one that interests me." He grinned. "And nothing about me interests any of them," he added. We both laughed.

"So, you want to go get some coffee?" I asked. "I'm sure the pancake joint is still open."

"Sure." Bradley regarded me, his glassy eyes still sharp. "But tell me first, did something happen tonight, Nick? Something to make you change your mind about leaving?"

"Yeah. I went to see Roxanne's mother. She's dying, Bradley. Cancer. She's at Hospice."

"Oh my God." A shudder went through him. "Wow, Roxanne didn't say anything about her mom being sick when I talked to her last."

"When was that? When did you last talk to Roxanne?"

He blinked. "I saw her a couple of weeks ago. I've left her some phone messages since then, but she hasn't called me back. I thought she was avoiding me because I pissed her off."

"You? What would Roxanne get pissed at you about?"

"Same thing she'd get pissed at you, or any other guy, about. Not paying enough attention to her." Bradley looked down at his pristine running shoes. "Although since the accident, Roxanne hasn't been so much all about herself, has she? She's changed a lot, don't you think?"

"Why ask me?" I could hear the edge in my voice.

"Why not you?"

"I don't know her that well."

"You've known her for more than fifteen fucking years, Nick."

Several moments passed. "Okay," I finally mumbled.

"What's up with you and Roxanne, anyway? Last time I talked to her, she spent most of the conversation asking me to check up on you."

"On me?"

"Yeah, *you*," Bradley retorted. "She told me you'd been drinking. That you and she had a fight. Now you're telling me you've been over to see her sick mama." His eyebrows rose. "Sounds like a lot is going on there, friend. What gives with you and Cathy's best friend?"

The noise in my head started up again, at low level, insistent. I hovered for a moment between laughing and throwing a punch at him for what he was implying. A fight could clear the air. Or maybe I'd get a handle on what to do with the rest of my life if I spilled my guts to Bradley.

But I could no more share the story of the last few weeks, and what had happened between Roxanne and me, with him than I could have with Zoë.

Jesus, what would he think if I told him I'd slept with her?

Despite what I'd seen in the movies, I realized there were some things too impossible to say out loud, even to a good friend.

"Nothing gives, Bradley. If there were something more to say, I'd say it. Look," I glanced up at the stars for guidance, but they glittered silently. "The reason I didn't go to France tonight is that I didn't feel up to all the shit with security and everything right now. I'm tired. But I may change my ticket and go on a flight in a couple of days. If they let me. Do you think there will be a hundred red flags up on my name if I try to rebook now?"

Bradley nodded. "Probably. And with that institutional haircut of yours, they're sure to think you're a terrorist."

"Hey, Zoë cut it for me."

"Great. Okay, so you don't look like a terrorist. More like a cheap-ass nutcase. And were you really going to wear that piece of shit old jacket to Paris?"

I looked at my coat, a bruised leather bomber with a broken zipper that my Dad had worn a million years ago. "Hell, yeah. Ugly American. That's me." I laughed and Bradley joined in.

My joke seemed to dilute the tension between us. We drove my car to the pancake joint on Grand that stayed open all night. On the way over, I told him the truth about what had happened a few weeks ago, that I'd considered getting drunk but got mugged instead and ended up in the hospital. That earned me some kudos from Bradley, and he was relieved I'd gone back to AA.

We went inside and ordered, talked about sports, cars and his latest techno gadget with a price tag of two grand. I relaxed as we managed to eat enough for four people. When the waitress brought the check, and the last cup of coffee, I felt drowsy and less panicked than I had for several weeks.

"Mitch and I used to come here," Bradley said suddenly.

"He always wanted hot fudge sundaes, and they have good ones. Well, they used to, anyway."

"You mean when he was sick?"

"No. Back in the day. When we were young, studly men around town." Bradley shoved his change into his jeans, and slumped against the booth. His eyes had lost their liquor luster, and he looked older than his thirty-five years.

"How long has Mitch been gone?" I asked quietly.

"Six years. You know, sometimes I miss him so much I think I could die."

"Still?"

"Forever. Tonight, I miss him as bad as if he died this morning. He was at Sierra Monte Hospice, where you were earlier with Betty Haverty. They're very good. Decent."

Mitch was there the last three weeks before he died at twenty-five of AIDS. All the new drug regimes in the world hadn't helped him. I'd only gone to see him once, at Cathy's insistence.

"I'm sorry, I forgot about that when I mentioned the clinic."

"No problem. And I'm sorry to be such a downer, Nick. But sometimes you can't fight it. How are you doing with it?"

I fumbled for my remaining cigarettes, took one out, then remembered you couldn't smoke anywhere inside a building in Southern California. I stuck the thing behind my ear and folded my hands together. "'It?' You mean Cathy?"

"I mean *losing* Cathy. The grief. You lose a love like that, a real love, it leaves a wound that in my experience does not heal over. You can run from it, like to Paris," he added. "But you can't hide."

"I'm not trying to hide."

"No? I thought that might be why you decided to stay in town a little longer. I thought, when I saw you tonight, that you needed to grieve a little more, give yourself some extra time before you set off on the next great adventure."

"How much is enough time? You've had six years. And tonight you're no better than when it happened." I replied. I thought of the young man Bradley had been seeing a lot of last year. "This surprises me, man. What about that guy, Stephen? Weren't you happy with him?"

"Yeah. I was 'happy' with Stephen. But Stephen isn't Mitch. And happy doesn't mean content. With Mitch, I felt like I had everything I needed. He was my other half. When you get involved with someone new, you'll know what I mean. No one will ever replace Mitch for me, Nick. No one."

I felt jittery again. "I'm not interested in getting 'involved' with anyone. Jesus, Cathy's only been gone for a few weeks. Besides, who could replace her?"

"No one," Bradley said. "But here's the thing. People do go on. They build new lives. The trick is letting go of your yearning for the old one. As long as the new life feels like second place, it ain't going to cut it."

"That's what your problem was with Stephen? He felt like second place?"

"My problem with Stephen was that he wasn't Mitch." He shook his head. "Poor guy. I called him 'Mitch' one night. He said it didn't bother him. I told him it should have. Because I would have given my life—or his—if I could have Mitch back for five minutes."

With his words, a searing, vivid memory flooded through me. I was holding a woman in my arms, kissing her, smelling the sweetness of her hair where it curled lushly at the nape of her neck. In the memory I was filled with joy that she loved me, that she was mine, that she was safe in my arms.

I swallowed. The memory was of the day Roxanne followed me into my bedroom, when she shut the blinds and told me to trust my heart. No matter what my brain had told me, my heart said something different. It had told me Cathy was back in my arms.

What kind of madman trusts his heart over his brain?

Fear tapped on my shoulder then, leaned over and whispered in my ear, his breath foul. He told me what I could do to end my pain. He suggested I do it quick, put myself out of my misery, *suck down a bottle of Jameson's and drive off a cliff.*

"Nick?"

My head jerked up. "What? What's wrong?"

"Nothing," Bradley said. "I just asked you a couple of times if you were ready to go. But you kind of zoned out on me."

"Sorry." I needed to get out of this restaurant. I needed to go, right now. "I'll drive you back to your car."

"You going to be okay?" Bradley asked. "You want to come by my place? I can make you some coffee. Or you can crash there, if you don't want to go back to your house tonight."

"I'm fine. But thanks. Thanks for everything, buddy."

We knocked fists and slapped each other's back one last time.

After I dropped him at his car, I concentrated on the road. The buzzing inside my skull got louder. On the radio, the DJ spun an ancient Randy Newman tune, about love, about how love makes your heart pump and your blood pound.

And how they don't know what love is. But Randy knows.

And I knew. And I knew what I had to do.

Fear chuckled, along for the ride. He was happy. He figured he'd won.

When I got to Roxanne's apartment, she wasn't asleep. Somehow I'd known she wouldn't be. She answered the doorbell on the first ring, almost as if she'd been waiting for me.

"Hello, Nick," she said. "Do you want to come in?"

"Yeah."

I walked past her into the dark living room. On the coffee table a single, squat candle burned, smelling of vanilla bean. I perched on the couch and folded my hands, like I was in church.

She shut the door. "You didn't go to Paris." She sat down a few inches away from me.

I looked at her face, tanned and smooth, washed clean of makeup. She had dark circles under her eyes, and the tiny spark of gold glinted at me.

"I couldn't go without you," I said. My brain sizzled as I forced the next words. "I couldn't go to France without my wife."

Tears spilled down her face. "What?" she whispered. "What did you say?"

I took her in my arms and crushed her to me. I did not think in words, only in sensations, like an animal. I cried and kissed her and buried my hands in her hair. "Cathy. Oh my God, Cathy. I love you. I am so grateful you're still here. And that you fought so hard to make me see the truth."

"You believe me, then?" Cathy cupped my face. "Please, Nick, don't lie to me. You really believe me?"

"I believe you, baby. I do."

And I did.

Cathy collapsed into me and I dragged her onto the floor and undressed us both in what felt like one motion. If flesh could devour flesh, there would have been nothing left of the two of us. Those hours passed in a blur of motion and sensation, not of explanation, and I reclaimed my wife.

We finally stilled and lay quiet as the sun peeked through the curtains at six a.m. In the faint light I saw only Cathy, her sweet face, her familiar, thrilling body curled against me now.

My Cathy, in my arms.

Epilogue

July 9, One Year Later
Bougival, France

I watch Nick leave for work in the evening, then have a bath and read in bed. Around me the sounds of the quaint little village we live in seem magical, and it is a rare night I don't close my eyes and pray, thanking the universe for my blessings.

Nick and I left Roxanne's apartment the day after he came to me and told me he believed me. Determined to be together from then on, we secretly fell back into the rhythm of our early-married life, cooking, making love, and talking about everything and anything.

We spent a lot of time rehashing Betty's story about how Roxanne and I were sisters. I am still shocked when I think of it, and I mourn Roxanne's loss from my life every day.

Knowing we were blood kin didn't increase my pain, for I don't think I could have loved her more than I did. But I so wish Rox had told me the truth before she died, and I wish that I'd been a better friend to her, so that she would have trusted me and told me the truth about *everything*.

But of course, I don't know, even now, what I could have done to reach Roxanne, to make her believe she could tell me anything. I loved her, she loved me, but I've learned there are limits to how much love can chase away the demons for some of us.

During those first two weeks after Nick and I got back together, I spent several hours every day at the hospice, and Nick was very kind, bringing flowers and sitting with us, reading while Betty slept. She died twenty days after entering the hospice, not peacefully, but stoically, her papery dry hands in mine, her eyes fixed somewhere I could not see, and I comforted her as a daughter would have, as I never had the chance to comfort my own mother.

It was another gift from Roxanne, that chance.

After the funeral, I gave notice at school that I was leaving at the end of the fall term. Nick and I stayed in California through the end of December, and then we closed Roxanne's apartment, sold Betty's house, and moved to Europe.

We were seen together on occasion before we left Sierra Monte; a late dinner at Simone's, a Christmas cocktail party Bradley had, but we didn't tell anyone we were leaving together, or try explaining my true identity.

But I think Zoë knows. She caught me at the house a couple of times early in the morning. She'd stared at me with a faraway look in her eyes. One night she and I baked brownies and watched *Gone with the Wind* together. When I started crying over little Bonnie's death, she put her arm around me and said, "That scene always made you cry."

She was right.

I kept waiting for her to bring 'it' up, who I was. But she didn't. If she ever does, I'll tell her everything. Nick agrees with me on this. Of all the people in our lives, we want Zoë to know the truth.

But for now, she's concentrating on being in love with a boy named Ramon. Nick and I bought her a used car before we left California, and in her letters and phone calls she seems content with school, her job, and Ramon.

Zoë and Nick's mother are living in our house, and taking care of Pitty while we're away. It was hard to leave my old fur ball friend behind, but I'm sure she'll live long enough to greet us on our return.

Althea Cordell acted as though she sensed something strange was going on with me, though she is too God-fearing a churchwoman to consider it possible that an illogical karmic wrinkle in the universe enveloped my life as it did.

Vera Apodoca was relieved to see me go. In light of what Nick revealed about Roxanne and Freddy, it's no wonder. I avoided talking to Freddy, mostly because I can't pretend to be Roxanne very well anymore, and I thought I might punch him out.

I never saw Michael Cimino again after that night with the Chinese food. I'd be lying if I said I never thought of him or the surreal night of sex we shared before I knew who I was.

I haven't gotten around to telling Nick about that. Frankly, I'm not sure if there's a confession in the cards. My husband is the best, but even the best husband has his limits.

Bradley wondered about this new, 'changed' Rox, but his imagination, or his rational, 'all things can be explained' math brain hasn't carried him to the truth. He knows Nick and I are together, and he wishes us well, though I am not sure if he completely approves. He loved the 'Cathy and Nick perfect couple story.' I wish I could tell him the real ending is a million times better than his fantasy.

I'll work on my friendship with Bradley someday. And hopefully he'll love me as this new Roxanne he knows, not as his old friend Cathy.

As with Betty Haverty, I realized I have to accept that to the rest of the world I will always be only who they think I am. And that's okay. Love is love, no matter who the person behind the smile really is. Betty felt my caring, so did it matter that it was Cathy Chance calling her 'Mom' as she died?

Neither Nick nor I called Seth to say goodbye, but Jen told Bradley, who told me, that the good doctor and Inga came in to Simone's a few weeks ago and got the scoop from

Jen. Seth told Jen not to worry about Nick, that he would find his way home.

We have a small inheritance that came to me as Betty's heir, and the life insurance money from the accident. Nick feels queasy about all this money falling to us as it has, but I don't. I enjoy the freedom, but let him handle the day-to-day allocation of it, as it will take a whole lot longer for us to spend our windfall if Nick is the designated budget guy.

I don't know when we'll go back to live in the States. We are content for now in Bougival. Our flat is very small but charming. It's in a stone building that's a couple of centuries old, and the floor is uneven in the kitchen, which is modern by 1940s American standards, but the view out the bedroom window is glorious.

Below the front windows is a wooden box Nick keeps planted with flowers that burst with color and fragrance. We have furniture we bought at the street fairs, and good books and ancient, charming dishes.

We spend a lot of time in bed, and sometimes make love with the lights on, but mostly not. I look in the mirror and, with my now-dyed blonde hair and extra pounds I managed to gain, I think I look a lot like my old self. In a kind of 'Benicio del Toro looks like Brad Pitt' way, I mean. When I told Nick I thought those two actors looked like brothers, he cracked up and said I was nuts. But when I told him to look at their eyes, the way they squint, the way they are quiet and watchful, he said he could see it.

I think, as usual, he was humoring me. But you get the picture. I see 'me' in the mirror now. Sure, I've got a way, way nicer body, but I don't see a stranger like I did when I woke up in the hospital after the accident. The expression in the eyes is mine, the movements; and the new skin growing on this form I inhabit is imprinted daily with my experiences, *my life.*

I still don't recall all of my past. Sometimes things are a jumble. One night I awoke and remembered a dream I was having, one that even today feels almost like a memory of something that actually happened. In my dream I was sixteen and meeting Nick for the first time, but not like I had, on the Fourth of July. In this vision I was standing with Betty in the grocery store, and Nick and his mom and Zoë introduced themselves to us, and Nick looked at me hungrily, and I wanted to kill myself, I felt so alone.

I woke Nick up and told him about this dream because it upset me so. He was very quiet for a long moment, but he kissed me and hugged me so tight I couldn't move, then told me to go back to sleep.

"Don't worry," he said. "We're fine, don't worry about the past. It's over."

So I don't. If Nick can accept this weird, hybrid me, then I certainly can.

Nick goes to AA meetings a couple of times a week. He's doing well, though he says he can feel his mouth sweat whenever he smells a particularly good bottle of red wine at the Café Roget, where we eat most nights. He's working at a little radio station for a few Euros and loving it. He's the on-air man on the midnight-to-six a.m. shift on the weekends.

He lets me tag along and help him pick out songs to play from their collection of oldies, which they only spin at night. They don't have much, mostly rock standards from the sixties and seventies, but that's the stuff Nick grew up with, listening to his folks' collection, and it's stuff he loves. I choose the Doors and the Stones and the Beatles and all the others, though Randy Newman's "You Can Keep Your Hat On" is Nick's favorite. I like that song, too, although it seems a little desperate to me.

I worry Nick has a bigger melancholy streak than he admits to. I'm planning a strip tease to that tune for his next birthday, though, so maybe that will take away the chill I always feel when Newman growls that he "knows what love is."

Nick knows damn well what love is, too. It's hard and painful. It's wonderful and complicated, just like him and me. Which is why I always choose Etta James and that "At Last" chestnut for him to play when I'm in the studio visiting him. Nick's taken to playing it for me as the last song every Saturday night.

I'm studying painting and French and plan to get another degree to teach art someday. God, there are literally hundreds of museums in this part of the world. And people go to them in droves. I love it.

The public schools are ridiculously difficult, but I've made inquiries at several private American schools and have already had a couple of offers. I miss my kids from Sierra Monte, but am not ready yet to spend time or effort on anything but Nick.

He took me to see my old bridge at Bougival, the one in my favorite painting. It's still there, surrounded by modern buildings as well as vestiges of the nineteenth century world Monet lived in. The sunlight on the path is the same, seductive and pure, begging you to leave the road and slip down the banks to the cool blue water below. We walked up the hill to a tiny café and sat outside, oblivious to the traffic sounds.

Nick asked me why this painting was my very favorite, of all the ones we've seen at home or here in Paris. I had tried to explain this once to Seth, but am not totally sure I've ever made anyone understand what it does for me.

"I don't know if I can put it all into words," I told Nick. "Everything wonderful is in this picture. Trees and flowers, sun and water. The charming little town, people walking, a gorgeous sky, a mother holding her child's hand." I cried when I remembered this, and Nick wiped my tears.

"When I saw it at the museum with my mother," I added, "she read to me from the exhibit notes about the strict geometric structure of the painting, the traditional notions of scale and style, blah, blah. But one thing she said that I remember most is that Monet took great pains not to showcase the one recognizable landmark in the picture. He hides the spire of the church in Bougival behind the leaves of the trees."

Nick grinned and pulled me close and kissed my lips, still frothed with latte. "So Monet hides the identity of the church. Why?"

I smiled. "Maybe it was just for him. Maybe he didn't want to make religion or faith the point of that beautiful location, but wanted those who stared at it to see and then realize the spiritual was always there, influencing your life." My grin got bigger. "See, I can't explain why I love it, but I do."

Nick crinkled his forehead and I saw he couldn't completely understand either, but it didn't matter. He was happy that I loved it, for whatever reason.

Words fail, but the heart understands.

"Let's go home," Nick said. I nodded and he took my hand and together we were, indeed, *home*.

I can't explain our love, or understand the significance, if any, of Roxanne and the secret sister bond we shared, or the generous gift of a second chance at life that she gave me.

I don't know if I am still here by accident, or selflessness, or if it was God with a capital 'G' that chose which one of us survived and which would perish. But I accept my good fortune, and celebrate it for the near perfection it is.

Sometimes, when he is sleeping, I look at Nick's face and wonder, for I cannot ever really know, if he truly believes *that I am me* or if he is going along and pretending, *hoping.* Nick's always been an optimist. It's one of the things I love about him.

But I don't let this small doubt poison my happiness. I put it aside and inhale the delicious breath of each new day, so thankful for him. *For love.*

Also check out another book

from **Emelle Gamble**:

Dating Cary Grant,

available now from

Soul Mate Publishing!

of scale and style, blah, blah. But one thing she said that I remember most is that Monet took great pains not to showcase the one recognizable landmark in the picture. He hides the spire of the church in Bougival behind the leaves of the trees."

Nick grinned and pulled me close and kissed my lips, still frothed with latte. "So Monet hides the identity of the church. Why?"

I smiled. "Maybe it was just for him. Maybe he didn't want to make religion or faith the point of that beautiful location, but wanted those who stared at it to see and then realize the spiritual was always there, influencing your life." My grin got bigger. "See, I can't explain why I love it, but I do."

Nick crinkled his forehead and I saw he couldn't completely understand either, but it didn't matter. He was happy that I loved it, for whatever reason.

Words fail, but the heart understands.

"Let's go home," Nick said. I nodded and he took my hand and together we were, indeed, *home*.

I can't explain our love, or understand the significance, if any, of Roxanne and the secret sister bond we shared, or the generous gift of a second chance at life that she gave me.

I don't know if I am still here by accident, or selflessness, or if it was God with a capital 'G' that chose which one of us survived and which would perish. But I accept my good fortune, and celebrate it for the near perfection it is.

Sometimes, when he is sleeping, I look at Nick's face and wonder, for I cannot ever really know, if he truly believes *that I am me* or if he is going along and pretending, *hoping.* Nick's always been an optimist. It's one of the things I love about him.

But I don't let this small doubt poison my happiness. I put it aside and inhale the delicious breath of each new day, so thankful for him. *For love.*

Also check out another book from **Emelle Gamble**:

Dating Cary Grant,

available now from

Soul Mate Publishing!

CPSIA information can be obtained
at www.ICGtesting.com
Printed in the USA
BVOW10s2237240417
482158BV00016B/332/P

9 781619 354555